Only One Winner

Part 4
of
The Ambition & Destiny Series

By
VL McBeath

Only One Winner
By VL McBeath

Valyn Publishing is a trading company of Valyn Ltd.
For more about this author please visit
https://valmcbeath.com

Editing services provided by Wendy Janes at WendyProof and Susan Buchanan at Perfect Prose Services.
Cover design by Michelle Abrahall

ISBN: 978-16978271-0-1 (Large Print Edition)

Main category – FICTION / Historical
Other category – FICTION / Literary Collections

Legal Notices

This story was inspired by real-life events but as it took place nearly two hundred years ago, parts of the storyline and all characterisation are fictitious. Names have been changed and any resemblance to real persons, living or dead, is purely coincidental. Although the story took place in and around the Summer Lane area of Birmingham, and Handsworth, exact locations have been changed.

Explanatory Notes

Meal Times

In the United Kingdom, as in many parts of the world, meal times are referred to by a variety of names. Based on traditional working-class practices in northern England in the nineteenth century, the following terms have been used in this book:

Breakfast: The meal eaten upon rising each morning.

Dinner: The meal eaten around midday. This may be a hot or cold meal depending on the day of the week and a person's occupation.

Tea: Not to be confused with the high tea of the aristocracy or the beverage of the same name, tea was the meal eaten at the end of the working day, typically around five or six o'clock. This could either be a hot or cold meal.

Money

In the nineteenth century, the currency in the United Kingdom was Pounds, Shillings and Pence.

- There were twenty shillings to each pound and twelve pence to a shilling.
- A crown and half crown were five shillings and two shillings and sixpence, respectively.
- A gold sovereign was equivalent to one pound.
- A guinea was one pound, one shilling (i.e. twenty-one shillings).

It can be assumed that £1 at the time of the story is equivalent to approximately £100 in 2018

Politics

During the second half of the nineteenth century,

two parties dominated politics in the United Kingdom: The Conservatives and The Liberals.

Conservatives:

Originally derived from the Tory party, during the time of the story they were lead by Benjamin Disraeli and latterly by Lord Salisbury (otherwise known as the Marquis of Salisbury).

Their main aims were to support the monarchy and the British constitution, the British Empire and the Established Church of England.

They also believed that the landowning aristocracy were the given rulers of the country.

Liberals:

Initially a party called The Whigs, they evolved into the Liberal Party in 1859.

They saw themselves as a party of reformers and called for the supremacy of parliament over the monarch.

They offered the opportunity for non-conformists (ie those whose religions were outside the Church of England) to have greater status in society and supported the abolition of slavery and the expansion of votes for men.

In 1886, owing to deep divisions in the Liberal Party over the granting of a limited self-government for Ireland (which was part of the United Kingdom at the time), a separate **Liberal Unionist** party was formed. They forged an alliance with the Conservative Party to oppose Irish Home Rule although they remained as separate parties.

MP stands for Member of Parliament

For further information on Victorian England visit:
https://valmcbeath.com/victorian-era

Please note: This book is written in UK English

It is recommended that *Only One Winner* is read after Parts 1-3 of The *Ambition & Destiny* Series

Previous books in
The *Ambition & Destiny* Series:

Short Story Prequel: *Condemned by Fate*
Part 1: *Hooks & Eyes*
Part 2: *Less Than Equals*
Part 3: *When Time Runs Out*

Join my mailing list for further information and exclusive content about The *Ambition & Destiny* Series.

Details can be found at **www.vlmcbeath.com**

The Family Tree shown on the next page represents the family at the start of this story.

For larger versions please visit:
https://valmcbeath.com/one-winner-family-tree/

To Mum, Dad, Keith and Yvonne
Had it not been for their story, we wouldn't have ours...

The Jackson and Wetherby Family Tree

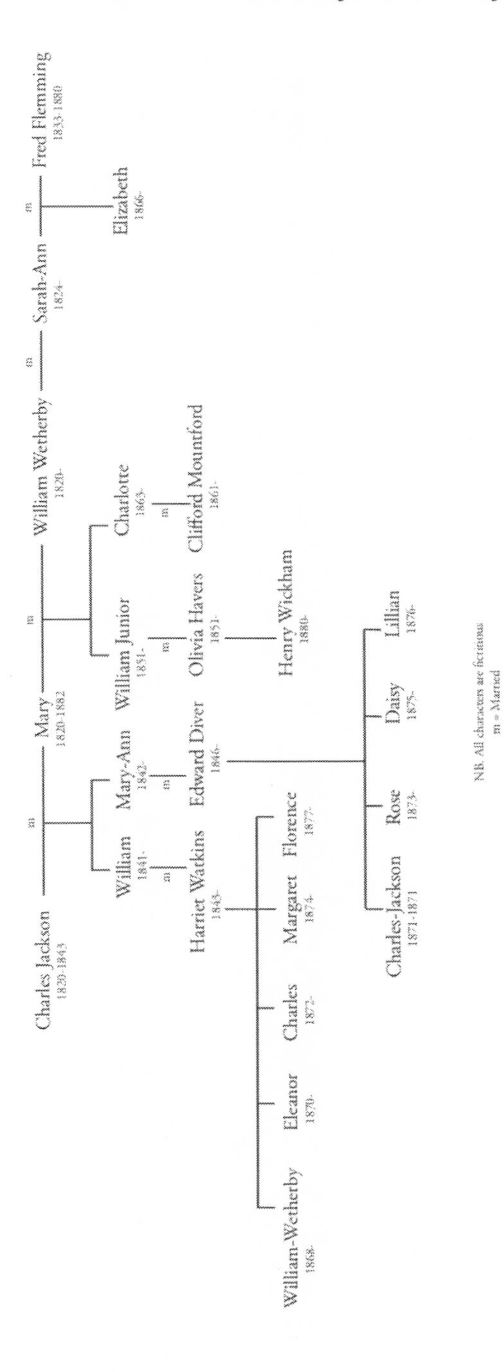

CHAPTER ONE

Handsworth, Staffordshire, England. September 1885

The Old Crown Inn was a cold and dreary place, particularly after dark, but William-Wetherby didn't notice. He sat alone in a corner of the bar, a blanket pulled tightly around his shoulders and his head resting against the wall. His attention was focussed on a cobweb hanging from the ceiling and he couldn't look away. To do that would let the images of his mother flood back into his mind.

He was roused from his trance by a police constable shaking his arm. "Your father's here." He nodded towards the door and William-Wetherby followed his gaze to see a man he barely recognised. His dark beard appeared too big for his sunken face and the once proud, upstanding stature seemed inches shorter as he shuffled forward with his shoulders hunched. William-Wetherby struggled from his seat and limped to help his father into a chair. Once they were both settled, he averted his gaze from the dark watery eyes staring at him.

"She's gone," his father said.

"I know. I'm sorry, I did everything I could."

"You saw her in the water?"

William-Wetherby pulled the still wet fabric of his trousers. "I jumped in to try and save her, but ..." His sobs echoed around the empty room. "There she was ... floating in the water ... I heard her splashing before I saw her." He wiped his eyes on his jacket sleeve. "If only I hadn't twisted my ankle, I might have been able to save her ..." He covered his face with his hands. "It's all my fault."

The police constable put two brandies on the table in front of them.

"The doctor asked me to give you these."

William waited for the constable to leave them. "Of course it wasn't your fault. You can't blame yourself. What was she doing at Tower Hill?"

William-Wetherby shook his head. "What was Mr Wetherby doing at Tower Hill?"

"Mr Wetherby was there?"

"He was ... but then he wasn't. I'm certain of it, but once I'd pulled Mother to the side of the canal, he'd gone." William-Wetherby picked up his drink and took a large mouthful but as the liquid hit the back of his throat, the burn choked him, forcing him to put the glass down.

"You have to drink it slowly." William reached for his own glass and took a sip.

William-Wetherby stared at the glass. "Have you seen the body?"

William nodded. "It wasn't your mother though."

William-Wetherby sat up straight, his dark eyes shining for the first time that day. "Not Mother? You mean she might still be alive?"

William shook his head. "I mean your mother wasn't in that lifeless body, with its stiff limbs and no colour in its cheeks. Her soul's gone. I saw nothing more than an empty corpse. The only way to keep her alive is with our memories."

William-Wetherby's shoulders slumped. "Why did she leave home? Why did she think we'd send her back to the asylum?"

William didn't give him an answer but focussed on the brandy as he swirled it around the glass. As he took another mouthful the police constable approached.

"There's a carriage waiting to take you home ... when you're ready of course."

William glanced at William-Wetherby. "When we're ready. Will we ever be ready to return to a house that's lost its soul?"

"She'd be angry with us if we didn't."

A smile flitted across William's lips. "She would. She'd be furious if we didn't carry on. I can hear her now. 'We should have our own house; you should be running your own business; I'll do the bookkeeping for you.' She was so happy once we had all those things ..." He took a deep breath and wiped the corner of his right eye. "As long as we can make a success of things, I suppose her spirit will always be with us."

William-Wetherby grimaced as he finished his brandy and put his glass back on the table. "I suppose we'd better go then. We have to make her proud."

CHAPTER TWO

If it was possible, the Old Crown Inn appeared shabbier in daylight than it had by gaslight two nights earlier, but William-Wetherby didn't notice. He hadn't expected to be invited to the inquest, but as he had found the body he needed to say his piece. Climbing down from the carriage, he followed his father inside. The inn wasn't open for business and they were shown straight upstairs to a room that had been set aside for the morning. It had been laid out with about thirty chairs arranged in rows of eight, facing a table and chair at the far end of the room. The witness stand, nothing more than a tatty-looking lectern, stood to the right.

William and William-Wetherby took their seats

on the front row, which had been reserved for witnesses.

"Who are the other witnesses?" William-Wetherby asked as he gestured to the empty chairs beside them.

"I don't know. Maybe the police."

William-Wetherby's brow creased. "There were only two of them. How do they decide who to ask?"

"I've no idea. Perhaps it's other people who knew your mother."

"Do you think they'll ask Mr Wetherby?"

It was William's turn to look puzzled. "Why would they?"

"I told you, he was standing at the top of the steps when I found Mother."

"Are you sure? You were very upset. Maybe you imagined it."

"I didn't." The image of Mr Wetherby standing on the bridge, his eyes peering down from his angular face, sprang to the front of William-Wetherby's mind. "I told the police and they said they'd speak to him."

"Well he didn't say anything to me," William said. "Besides, he wouldn't have stood by and done nothing."

"I know it doesn't make sense, but I saw him

seconds before I jumped into the water. By the time I got back to the bank, he'd gone."

William shook his head. "Now you're talking nonsense. Why would he do that?"

Before William-Wetherby could answer, Mr Watkins, his mother's uncle, arrived and took the seat next to William.

"Have you been called as a witness?" William asked.

Mr Watkins winced as he took a seat. "What can I tell them? It was over a week since I'd seen her. Happy as you like, she was."

"Perhaps that's what you need to say. Did you see the paper this morning?"

"The speculation about suicide, you mean?"

William nodded. "I don't know where they get this stuff from, but she didn't take her own life. I'm certain of it. If you tell them she was happy, at least we'll be able to bury her at the church."

As the start of the inquest drew closer, William-Wetherby gazed around the room. It was almost full but there was no sign of Mr Wetherby. It would be most unlike him not to attend. Finally, as the coroner entered the room, he arrived with his son

William Junior and took the seat next to Mr Watkins.

Once the coroner had taken his seat, the court sat in silence while he summarised the events of the previous week: Mrs Jackson's mysterious disappearance from her home in Handsworth; the five-day manhunt, that led to the events of two days ago, which saw her pulled from the canal. When the coroner had finished, he called Mr Wetherby to the witness stand. William-Wetherby straightened his back. *Why is he the first witness?*

"Mr Wetherby," the coroner started. "You said in your statement that your stepdaughter-in-law had been of unsound mind for several months and that in your opinion she should have been in Winson Green at the time of the incident. Is that correct?"

Mr Wetherby stood upright, his shoulders pulled back, and greying hair and beard neatly trimmed. "Yes, sir."

"No, that's not true." William-Wetherby jumped from his chair, but a withering glare from the coroner forced him to sit down.

"Mr Wetherby, please continue," the coroner said. "When was the last time you saw Mrs Jackson?"

"I went to the house of my stepson on the

afternoon she disappeared. She was in the back room when I arrived."

"And how did you find her on that occasion?"

"I'd gone to see Mr Jackson on a private matter and so we went into the front room."

"And therefore you can't comment on her state of mind?"

"It was her state of mind I'd gone to see Mr Jackson about. I'd received some information to suggest she was mentally incapacitated and I wondered if she should be sent back to Winson Green asylum."

William-Wetherby glared at his father. "You didn't tell me that."

William said nothing while the coroner continued.

"And what gave you these concerns?"

Mr Wetherby gave a slight cough. "It had been brought to my attention that she was attending meetings on women's suffrage, something I imagine every man in this room opposes."

William-Wetherby's gasp was drowned out by the noise erupting around him. He pulled on William's arm, forcing him to look him in the eye. "You knew about this, didn't you? Why didn't you stand up for her?"

"I did." William's voice barely carried over the commotion.

"Well if you did, why ...?"

"Silence!" The coroner banged his hand on the desk. "I will not have such behaviour during this inquest. If I hear any more, I'll clear the room." The coroner let his eyes rest on each man before he returned his attention to Mr Wetherby.

"Please continue, Mr Wetherby. Do I understand correctly that you believe supporting the women's suffrage campaign is grounds to be sent to Winson Green?"

"I thought that sending Mrs Jackson to an asylum would act as a deterrent to other women and make them realise that this sort of behaviour won't be tolerated."

"Was she aware of your position on this?"

Mr Wetherby shook his head. "No. I was talking to Mr Jackson and as far as I'm aware, she didn't know."

The coroner peered at his notes. "You said in your statement that you thought she may have committed suicide. If she was unaware of your position on Winson Green, why do you think she would have done such a thing?"

"I believe you are aware that she had recently been released from Winson Green Lunatic Asylum following an attack of insanity. The doctors had described her as being depressed, which could be reason enough for her to have taken her own life."

"Did you see her again once you'd spoken to Mr Jackson?"

"No, sir, I didn't."

"That's a lie!" William-Wetherby jumped from his seat again. "You were on the bridge when she was in the water. You watched her struggling but did nothing to help."

The coroner was on his feet. "Silence or you'll be ejected from the proceedings. Officer, will you stand by this individual and make sure he causes no more trouble."

William-Wetherby glared at the coroner and was about to continue when a policeman pushed him into his chair and put a hand on his shoulder.

"You can't say that without proof," William whispered.

"I saw him and he's blatantly lied under oath. We can't let him get away with it."

"One more word and you'll be out," the officer said.

The coroner inspected his notes. "So, Mr Wetherby, you believe the deceased may have been in such a state of mind as to commit the unlawful act of suicide."

"Yes, sir, I do."

The coroner dismissed Mr Wetherby from the witness stand and called William Jackson, husband of the deceased. "Mr Jackson, can you tell me what your wife did to pass the time."

"All sorts of things. We have five children, the youngest of whom is only eight, and they took up a lot of her time, as well as managing the house. Most recently, she was excited because I've set up my own business and she was helping out."

"You let her help you? What line of work are you in?"

"I manufacture eyelets and rivets, but she was good with numbers and so she did the bookkeeping."

The coroner raised an eyebrow as murmuring started in the room. "And who checked her work?"

"Nobody, I trusted her."

"You trusted her? A brave man. Could her position have put her on bad terms with anyone?"

"Not at all. There weren't many people she didn't get on with; she was a happy, sociable person."

"And so what do you think of Mr Wetherby's assessment that she may have committed suicide?"

William-Wetherby saw a trickle of sweat running down William's temple as his father held on to the lectern. "With all due respect to Mr Wetherby, he hadn't seen her since she'd returned home. She was as happy as I'd seen her and certainly wouldn't have taken her own life."

"So what about these claims of her attendance at the suffrage meetings? Were you aware she'd been attending?"

William reached for his handkerchief and wiped his forehead. "I knew she'd attended a couple ... months ago, but I'd asked her to stop."

The coroner again raised his eyebrows. "And had she?"

"I-I don't know. I thought she had, but she'd been so excited about the prospect of women getting the vote, perhaps she carried on going."

"Perhaps she felt despondent at the lack of enthusiasm in parliament?"

"No." William shook his head. "She was someone who would fight for what she thought was right. She wouldn't give up that easily."

"And so in your opinion, taking her own life would have been out of character?"

"It most certainly would."

Once William had been dismissed, the coroner called Mr Watkins. "Mr Watkins, when did you last see your niece?"

Mr Watkins's shoulders slumped. "Five days

before she disappeared. We always visited on a Thursday and she went missing on the Tuesday."

"Was this after she came out of Winson Green?"

"Yes, that's right."

"And how would you describe her mood?"

"I'd agree with Mr Jackson. She was in high spirits when my wife and I saw her, although she wouldn't tell us why."

"Could it have had anything to do with the suffrage movement?"

A brief smile flitted across Mr Watkins's lips. "It wouldn't surprise me. If ever there was a woman who wanted to have her say it was Harriet. It took me a long time to accept her as she was but she was always forthright and wanted to be treated as an equal."

"Do you think the futility of the 'movement' may have caused her to despair and take her own life?"

Mr Watkins shrugged. "I can't say for sure, but I wouldn't think so. By the sound of things this was a new hobby and she wouldn't give up that easily."

Following Mr Watkins, a string of Harriet's friends, including Aunt Mary-Ann and several ladies from the suffrage group confirmed William's view that Harriet was in high spirits at the time of her disappearance. They also emphasised, most eloquently, that many of those supporting the suffrage movement were intellectual middle-class women and that attending weekly meetings was no grounds for anyone to be sent to an asylum.

Eventually, the coroner reviewed his notes and called William-Wetherby. "So, Master Jackson, you're here I believe because you found the body."

"Yes, sir."

"You said in your statement that the body was in the canal when you found it. Did you see her entering the water?"

"No, sir, but I believe Mr Wetherby did."

The coroner paused and took a deep breath. "Answer the question, please. Was Mrs Jackson dead at the time you found her?"

"I can't say for certain, sir. I thought she was alive and one of the police constables gave her the kiss of life when she was out of the water, but we were too late."

"Ah yes, the police constables. Did they come to your assistance quickly?"

"Yes, sir, within a minute."

"And other than the police, was anyone else assisting you?"

"No, sir."

The coroner picked up his papers and placed

them to the side of his desk. "Thank you; that will be all."

"But what about Mr Wetherby? You haven't asked me about him. He was there, he saw everything."

"That will be all." The coroner waved over the police constable. "Please escort Master Jackson from the building."

"No, you can't ignore me." William-Wetherby struggled as he was manhandled out of the room. "He's lying. Why will nobody listen? How much did he pay you?"

"If I hear another word from you, I'll have you locked up," the coroner said. "Now be off with you."

Before William-Wetherby could reply, the policeman dragged him to the door and pushed him down the steps, closing the door behind him.

William remained motionless as William-Wetherby was removed from the room. He should have supported him, but he couldn't. What was the point? It wouldn't bring Harriet back. He stared down at his hands and took a deep breath to ease the flutters in his chest. Would they never end?

Once silence returned to the room, the coroner called the police constables who had aided William-Wetherby. They confirmed his statement about finding Harriet and trying to revive her, but neither of them had seen Mr Wetherby. William wiped a tear from the corner of his eye. *He's going to get away with it again.*

As it approached one o'clock, the coroner called for silence. "Despite the evidence that's been presented this morning, it would appear to me that the reason the deceased left home will never be fully known. She went without a word, and no one has come forward who spoke to her after she disappeared. That she left of her own accord seems to be in little doubt and the fact she managed to survive for five days before the tragic events of Sunday suggests she deserves some admiration.

"So what of her death? As we have no witnesses who saw her enter the water, we'll have to make a judgement based on what we do know."

William glanced at Mr Wetherby, who sat with a neutral expression giving no hint of the lie.

"A verdict of suicide has serious implications both for the deceased and for the remaining family and therefore in order to pass such a verdict I would have to be satisfied beyond reasonable doubt that this was indeed what happened. Based on what I've heard this morning, I don't believe we can make such a decision. The only thing we can be certain of is that the body was found in the canal and that in all probability it was deceased by the time it was removed from the water. As a result, the cause of death will be recorded as '*Found drowned in the water of a canal*'. I'll send a copy of my report to the registrar by the end of the day."

As the coroner left the room, William leaned forward and put his head in his hands. They had the verdict they wanted, so why did he feel no better?

"At least we can have her buried," Mr Watkins said from beside him. "Nothing we said today would bring her back."

"You're right, and thank you for standing up for her."

"What else was I going to do? We may have had our disagreements but she was like a daughter to me. I wouldn't have wished her any harm."

"No, of course you wouldn't." William pushed himself up from his chair. "Come on, we'd better be going. William-Wetherby will be waiting for us."

Mr Watkins pushed himself up to follow him. "What do you make of his claim about Mr Wetherby?"

William glanced around the room and let out a

sigh when he saw Mr Wetherby disappear through the door. "I don't know."

"You're going to have to have a word with the boy. Mr Wetherby won't take kindly to his name being sullied."

William's eyes grew wide. "If William-Wetherby's waiting outside for me and sees Mr Wetherby first ..." William didn't finish his sentence before he rushed to the door.

As he stood on the steps outside the inn, William studied the scene before him. His stepbrother William Junior had his young son pressed against the wall of the building. His large frame and rounded waistline dwarfed William-Wetherby's slim features and William winced as Mr Wetherby prodded his son with his walking cane.

"What's going on?" William hurried towards them.

"We need to teach your son a lesson." The sun highlighted the green flecks in Mr Wetherby's hazel eyes. "I will not have my reputation ruined by slanderous talk."

"Well why didn't you admit you were at the canal?" William-Wetherby freed himself from William Junior's grasp and stepped towards his father. "All you needed to say was that you saw what happened."

"But I wasn't there. You didn't see me any more than you saw your own father. Have you got that into your head? I expect you in work first thing tomorrow morning, and if you speak about this again, not only will you be out of a job, you won't find another one anywhere else in Birmingham. Is that clear?" Mr Wetherby checked his pocket watch and signalled to William Junior that it was time to leave, before he faced William. "I'll see you at the funeral."

William and William-Wetherby waited in silence until Mr Wetherby's carriage pulled away.

"Who started that?" William asked.

"They came over to me ... I didn't say anything, honestly."

"Both police constables told the coroner they hadn't seen him at the canal, so he has a perfect alibi."

"I'm not surprised." William-Wetherby's shoulders slumped. "The first thing they did was pull Mother out of the water and while one was trying to revive her, the other was helping me. By the time I mentioned Mr Wetherby to them, he'd gone. I didn't imagine it though; he was there. It wouldn't surprise me if he bribed the coroner to ignore the fact."

William sighed as he settled himself into the back of his own carriage. "That's a serious accusation. You remember what he was like when he found his brother Thomas thieving? If he had no sympathy for him, he won't hesitate in firing you. In fact, if you're not careful, I could imagine him prosecuting you for slander."

"It's not fair though. Why do some people have so much power and people like us have to put up with it? We'd be better off without him."

William closed his eyes and rested his head on the back of the carriage. "You sound like your mother; she wanted nothing more to do with him either."

"Poor Mother. She must have heard him say she should go back to Winson Green and panicked. Why didn't you tell him she wasn't going anywhere?"

"I did. I persuaded him to allow her to attend the suffrage meetings so she would tell us what was going on. I'd promised I'd never send her back to Winson Green, but she mustn't have stayed long enough to hear me say that."

"Why, oh why ...?" William-Wetherby turned

to face the window as a fresh wave of tears welled up in his eyes.

William said nothing for several minutes until he realised his son wasn't aware of the verdict. "The coroner said he couldn't say for sure she had committed suicide and recorded her death as found drowned in the canal. At least we can hold our heads up and give her a proper burial."

William-Wetherby sighed. "I suppose that's something. Have you spoken to the reverend about it yet?"

"Not as such. He paid me a visit yesterday and we discussed giving her a Church of England burial, but we had to wait for the verdict today before we could make any firm plans."

"But she'd hate that. She hadn't set foot in St Mary's, other than for deaths and marriages, for years."

"I know, but I was never comfortable about it and I'd be happier if she was given a proper burial. I'm going to go back to services at St Mary's from now on. I can't go to the Congregational Church without her."

CHAPTER THREE

Two days later, William shuddered as he opened the front door and took his first glimpse of the hearse waiting outside. It was magnificent with its six jet-black horses and polished, glass-bodied carriage, but it was wrong. Harriet shouldn't be lying inside. He took a deep breath and with his two sons and close family behind him made his way down the drive to the waiting carriage. Letting William-Wetherby and Charles climb into the first carriage, he followed them and settled into the seat opposite.

They travelled the short distance to the church in silence and as soon as the carriage stopped William stepped out onto the gravel. The sun was bright as he waited for the other mourners and as he followed the coffin into the gloom of the church he paused to allow his eyes to adjust. The pews were full. Full of women he didn't know and hadn't invited. As he hesitated, his sister Mary-Ann whispered over his shoulder.

"They're Harriet's friends from the suffrage meetings. A couple of them came to the house earlier in the week to pay their respects, and I invited them. I hope you don't mind."

William nodded and took another deep breath before he walked down the aisle to the pew at the front. By the time he arrived, his heart was pounding and he clung to the rail in front of him.

Half an hour later, with his heart still pounding, William followed the coffin outside but as the breeze blew across the burial ground, he caught hold of William-Wetherby to stop himself swaying.

"Are you all right?" his son asked. "You're white."

"I'll be fine. I just need to catch my breath. You go on ahead."

"Don't be ridiculous. We can't go to the burial without you. I'll ask them to stop. They're going the wrong way, anyway."

William's gaze rested on the pallbearers. "No, they're not."

"What do you mean?" William-Wetherby said. "They're heading towards the pauper graves."

William fought to keep his voice under control. "It was the only plot the rector would let us have ... given the doubt about the suicide."

"There isn't any doubt. The coroner said there was no evidence she took her own life, and either we can bury her in the church grounds or we can't. You're not given a plot based on how good you've been."

As William stared towards the grave, the trees on the horizon drifted in and out of focus. "Please, we can't talk here. We'll buy a headstone and make it special, but let's get this over with."

Noticing the deathly pallor of William's face, William-Wetherby sighed. "As long as you don't forget."

With the rest of the mourners becoming impatient, they made their way to the lower level of the churchyard and the plot that would take the remains of his dear wife. *It shouldn't be like this. Why didn't I buy a family plot when I had the chance?* William wiped his eyes with his handkerchief before he bowed his head over the grave.

"Those born of a woman hath but a short time

to live ..." the rector started but William couldn't listen.

Why God? Why did you take her? Just when everything was perfect.

He was brought back to the service by William-Wetherby handing him a piece of earth.

"We therefore commit this body to the ground," the rector continued. "Earth to earth, ashes to ashes, dust to dust ..."

William tossed the soil onto the coffin before he squeezed his eyes shut to hold in his tears. *Who'll help me now?*

"Come on, let's take you home." William-Wetherby took William's arm and led him from the grave.

Once he arrived home, William sank into a chair in the front room and accepted the glass of brandy Eleanor handed to him.

"You look like you could do with this. Will you be all right?"

William smiled at his daughter but the lump in his throat wouldn't let him speak. She had such a strong resemblance to the Harriet he had met all those years ago, although her blue- grey eyes didn't have the same mischievous twinkle as her mother's. He nodded and took a large mouthful of brandy.

"Give me a couple of minutes."

He hadn't finished his drink when the first of the guests arrived at the house. Almost immediately, Mr Wetherby was shown into the front room, closely followed by his Aunt Sarah-Ann.

William stood up as a maid offered them a drink. "Thank you for coming. I wasn't sure if you would. Not after the other day."

Sarah-Ann stared at William. "Of course we were coming. We're family. William Junior, Olivia and Charlotte are here too. They went into the other room."

"William-Wetherby needed to be taught a lesson the other day," Mr Wetherby said. "You need to stop bad behaviour before it starts."

William gripped his brandy glass. "Why didn't you admit you'd been at the canal and seen everything?"

Sarah-Ann's eyes were wide as she watched Mr Wetherby step closer to William.

"I didn't think you'd want a verdict of suicide."

William's face stiffened. "She didn't commit suicide. She wouldn't have done such a thing."

"You've no idea what went on in her head. She'd been behaving erratically all year. Did you want me to tell the coroner I watched her jump?"

William felt the blood rush to his face as he

glared at Mr Wetherby. "You did not because she wouldn't have done that. She was happy. Happy about being out of hospital, happy about being part of the business, happy with her hobbies and yes, happy about being part of the suffrage group. She had no reason to jump ... unless ..." A flicker of realisation crossed William's face. "You'd have been the last person she saw before she went into the canal. You'd have frightened the life out of her if she thought you were going to take her back to Winson Green."

"Don't be ridiculous ..."

William paced the floor in front of Mr Wetherby. "If you admitted being at the top of the steps, it would have raised some awkward questions ... like why didn't you try to save her?" William stopped and glared at his stepfather. "How would you have explained that to the coroner?"

Mr Wetherby slammed his glass onto the tray of a passing maid, almost causing her to drop it. "I did no such thing." Mr Wetherby grabbed Sarah-Ann's arm. "Come on, my dear, we're going. I will not be spoken to like that."

Moments later the front door slammed and William watched through the window as Mr Wetherby and Sarah-Ann left, taking his daughter Charlotte, William Junior and his wife Olivia with them. William didn't wait for their carriage to pull away before he went into the back room to find Mr and Mrs Watkins.

"Thank you for coming. I hope the service wasn't too traumatic for you, Mrs Watkins."

Mrs Watkins wiped the back of her chubby fingers across her eyes. "You've no idea. I don't think I'll ever get over losing her. We'd been getting along so well ..."

Mr Watkins put his arm around his wife as she sobbed. "This is the first day she's been out of bed since it happened. Her breathing's been so bad I thought I was going to lose her as well."

"Please don't say that. We'll need you for the children."

"She can't take care of them." Mr Watkins glanced up at William.

"No, I don't mean that, but they need to keep seeing you. You're like grandparents to them. We can't have anything happening to you as well."

Mrs Watkins held her handkerchief to her face as her sobbing increased. "You must watch out for Florence. She's only eight. She needs her mother ..."

Mr Watkins guided his wife to a seat and William turned to those on his right.

It was almost three hours later before he found

himself alone with only Mary-Ann and Mr Diver for company.

"You know I'll help with the children, don't you?" Mary-Ann's face was pale against the harshness of her black mourning clothes.

William showed his sister and her husband into the front room. "You've got enough on your plate. I was going to take Eleanor out of school."

"You'll do no such thing." Mary-Ann pulled herself to her full height and glared up at her brother. "Can you imagine what Harriet would say if she knew you'd even considered it? She was so proud of her."

William shrugged. "What else can I do?"

Mary-Ann's features softened as she studied the lines on her brother's face. "You only need to worry about Margaret and Florence. I'll advertise for a cook-cum-housekeeper for you, but in the meantime, assuming they can both get themselves to school in the mornings, they can come home with me for some tea. You and William-Wetherby are welcome too, which means you'll only need to put them to bed."

"What would I do without you? I hope you don't mind, Mr Diver."

"Not at all, it's the least we can do. I have to say,

though, I'm concerned about how you'll manage with the business."

William's smile disappeared. "Do you think I haven't thought of that? The only reason I started the business was for Harriet and now I wonder if there's any point carrying on."

"You must keep going," Mary-Ann said. "You can't walk away from it; that would be the last thing she wanted."

"But I can't do it on my own ..."

Mr Diver held up his hand. "Would it help if I suggested you took on a partner?"

William stared at him blankly. "To do what?"

"To do the bookkeeping. When you worked with Mr Wetherby, someone ran the office while you were in the workshop. If you had a partner, you could split the work the same way."

William nodded. "Do you have anyone in mind?"

"Not at the moment, but if you like the idea I'll make some enquiries."

William shrugged. "I don't suppose it will do any harm."

"It can only help. You've a lot of money invested in that business; you can't afford to lose it."

CHAPTER FOUR

Birmingham, Warwickshire

Litter swirled around Mr Wetherby's feet as he strode down Summer Lane, his coat pulled tightly across his chest. At last he could focus on the general election, instead of wasting time looking for that damn woman. He'd lost two weeks while they'd searched for her and got her buried, and he didn't have two weeks to lose. They'd have to double their efforts to attract voters. When he arrived at the Conservative Association, William Junior was waiting for him.

"Father, where've you been? I was expecting you half an hour ago."

"Don't you start, I've just about had enough of

today. William-Wetherby should thank his lucky stars there's an election on. If I had time, I'd be finding someone else to do his job."

"What's he said now?" William Junior asked.

"Nothing new, but he'd better watch his mouth. I've told him he's on his last warning. Now, enough of him. What's going on here?"

"We're working with the Central Ward on the meeting they're arranging. They're expecting Lord Churchill to attend and we need to invite our supporters."

"We need to run this like a military operation." Mr Wetherby went over to a table near the wall. "We need a list of all the streets in the ward up on the wall and everyone needs to do their fair share of canvassing. Put a list of all the members next to it and add William's name too. The best way to get over Harriet is to throw himself into a campaign like this. We can't mess things up again."

William Junior raised an eyebrow but changed the subject. "Have you heard the news from the Central Ward? The dames from the Primrose League are going to do some of their canvassing."

"Don't be ridiculous. Where've you heard that from?"

"I was talking to Mr Barton last night. It's all Lord Churchill's idea, but it won't be any women, the Duchess of Marlborough's leading them with Lady Churchill and all their sort."

"He's getting his mother and his wife to do his canvassing for him?" Mr Wetherby's eyes were like saucers.

"It'll be the talk of the town. The Churchills are due to visit Birmingham at the end of the month to establish a dames' habitation and once that's done, they'll be out on the streets."

"Unbelievable. Are they covering our streets as well?"

"I've no idea, but there's bound to be an effect, we're not far away. The meeting for the dames will be at the Grand Hotel next week; I imagine we'll receive an invitation."

Mr Wetherby gave a deep sigh. "I know Lord Churchill's a competent politician, but what's he thinking of? It's bad enough that the rural workers are allowed to vote in this election, never mind bringing women into it as well. It makes it all the more important to get Lord Salisbury elected so we can stop this nonsense."

~

Handsworth, Staffordshire.

William sighed as he lowered his aching body into his usual seat at the dining table in Mary-Ann's back room. With three of his children at home and the support of his sister and her husband, it still wasn't enough to fill the hole left by Harriet. *How can I feel lonely when I'm surrounded by people?*

"Have you had a bad day?" Mary-Ann placed the teapot on the table and fastened a piece of loose hair back into the knot at the nape of her neck.

"Compared to yesterday, it was no worse, but compared with six months ago, yes, it's been terrible."

"I may have some good news for you." Mr Diver folded up his newspaper and joined him at the table. "I think I've found you a partner."

A flash of interest crossed William's face. "Who? Anyone I know?"

"Probably not. His name's Ball and he's based in Birmingham. I know him through my father."

"Can he do accounts?" William said. "If he can, he can start straight away. The paperwork's building up and I can't do it."

"That's not how things work. He'll need to review the books before he signs anything to make sure he's buying into a viable business. Can you get them to a reasonable state?"

William sighed again. "I'll have to ask William-Wetherby to sort them out."

"He's a good lad; I'm sure he'll help."

"Have you any idea how much Mr Ball's prepared to put into the business?"

"You're going to have to discuss that between the two of you. If you tell me when the books are ready, I'll set up a meeting for you."

"Thank you, Mr Diver. I do appreciate your help."

William helped himself to a slice of bread, but looked up when the door flew open and William-Wetherby rushed in.

"I'm sorry I'm late, I didn't realise the time."

William raised his eyebrows at him. "You left work late because you didn't realise the time? That's not like you."

"I wasn't working. I was thinking."

"They must have been deep thoughts."

"They were. I had words with Mr Wetherby again this afternoon and I've decided I can't carry on working for him. The more I think about him, the more I'm sure he's hiding something ... something major about Mother's death. I reckon not only does he know how she died, but he might have been responsible. Nobody ever questioned whether she'd been murdered, but why else would he take so much trouble to hide what went on?"

Mr Diver put down his knife and fork and smoothed his impressive moustache. "You can't go accusing him of murder."

"I don't necessarily mean he pushed her into the water, although I wouldn't rule it out, but I think he's the reason she's not with us today. For one, she ran away because she heard him say he was sending her back to Winson Green. What if she saw him at the canal? She'd have been terrified. Whether it was an accident or not, I can't be sure; but I think the fact he was by the canal is the reason she drowned."

"We can't be sure that's why she ran away," William said.

"What else would have made her disappear for five days? You said yourself you heard the front door slam shut after you mentioned Winson Green."

"I've challenged Mr Wetherby about it and he won't admit to being at the canal," William said.

"Whether he admits it or not, I'm certain he was there and this makes the most sense. I only wish I could make him talk."

"You won't ever do that, even if you were in the police force. I've seen him avoid police questioning before; it's one of the privileges of being in his position."

William-Wetherby stopped buttering his bread. "When else was he questioned by the police? You've not mentioned it before."

William pushed his food around the plate. "I'll tell you one day, but not now. Let's just say there was more evidence then to suggest he was guilty than there is now and he wasn't even reprimanded. You're going to have to drop it. He's never going to admit he was at the canal and whether you like it or not, you still have to work for him."

William-Wetherby pointed his knife at his father. "That's what I was saying, I can't. Can I come and work for you instead?"

William shook his head. "I wish you could, but we need a regular income that doesn't depend on my business. If our orders dry up, neither of us would be earning any money. I'm afraid we're going to have to take a deep breath and rely on Mr Wetherby for a little longer. With the general election coming up, at least he's not at the workshop much at the moment."

"No, but heaven help us if the Liberals win again, which is most likely. I don't expect the new voters to support the Conservatives."

CHAPTER FIVE

Birmingham, Warwickshire

Mr Wetherby marched into the Conservative Association, his face crimson. No more than an hour earlier he had received a letter saying Lord Churchill had withdrawn from their meeting.

"Just look at them." He pointed to a pile of leaflets on the table next to William Junior. "The meeting's next week and they're ready to go, but we can't give them out as they are. His name's all over them."

"I think we should send them as they are," William Junior said. "The meeting's going ahead and we can always say he withdrew at the last moment."

Mr Wetherby's face was red. "Don't be a fool, we can't lie."

"It's not much of a lie and they'll be none the wiser. If they'd gone out yesterday when they should have done, there'd be nothing we could do about it. Besides, voters shouldn't only be coming to see him."

"Whether they should or not, many will."

William Junior rolled his eyes. "If you want my opinion, the man's a liability. This is the fourth time he's failed to turn up. I heard somebody say he only stood as a candidate to make sure Mr Bright had to fight for his seat. He's more interested in his safe seat in South Paddington."

"But the fact is he's still a Conservative candidate for Birmingham and we need to support him."

"He's not making it easy though," William Junior said. "Did you read what he said last week? Even Conservative supporters have been writing to the paper saying they're embarrassed about him."

"You have to wonder if they really are supporters behaving like that. They should be ashamed of themselves, criticising their own candidate. Whether we like it or not we must support him. Now I don't want you talking like this to anyone else, is that clear?"

. . .

When Mr Wetherby and William Junior arrived at the Town Hall, two hours before the start of the meeting, Mr Diver was waiting for him.

"Here you are," he said. "I was beginning to wonder where you'd got to."

"Last-minute canvassing to make sure people turn out. Hopefully, they'll all come," Mr Wetherby said. "Did you bring William with you?"

Mr Diver shook his head. "He's not up to it at the moment. It's only a month since he buried Harriet."

"Damn woman. Is there no end to her meddling?"

Mr Diver's jaw dropped as he stared at Mr Wetherby.

"I don't mean it of course." Mr Wetherby glanced at William Junior. "How's William doing? Did he meet this Mr Ball you were telling me about?"

"He did, and they're going ahead. They should have all the paperwork signed this week. It will be a relief to have him sorted out."

"And about time, but enough of that. I need to find out what's going on here." Mr Wetherby inspected his pocket watch before he strode towards his colleagues from the Central Ward.

The chairman sighed when he saw him. "Where is everyone? The place was full last week for the Liberals but it's half empty tonight."

"Is there anything I can do?"

"Short of going outside and pulling people off the streets, I doubt it. The press are going to have a field day if it stays like this."

As half past seven approached, Mr Wetherby glanced around the room again. There were still too many empty seats, but what else could they do now? With a deep sigh he took his seat at the front of the room and leaned back to listen to the first speaker. He had barely started when shouting and jeering erupted from the middle of the room. The colour drained from Mr Wetherby's face when he spun around to see a bunch of about fifty men approaching him.

"They've only gone and let in a bunch of Liberals." He spoke to William Junior as he jumped to his feet. "We need to get them out."

"Not you." William Junior put an arm across his chest. "We have men twice your size to do that."

"But they're doing nothing, in fact, they're joining them. I'd say someone deliberately let them in. Why weren't you on the door supervising them?"

Most of the audience were on their feet as Mr Wetherby ran onto the street. "We need the police here. We can't get rid of them on our own."

It was over an hour later before they cleared the room and the Conservative Association chairmen gathered by the stage.

"What do we do now?" Mr Wetherby asked. "We lost most of our supporters in the commotion and nearly half of those left are press. They're not going to let us forget this."

"We'll have to abandon the meeting. The press will only focus on the trouble, and ridicule us if we try to carry on with the place almost empty."

Mr Wetherby's nostrils flared. "Damn newspapers, we'll need to double our efforts on the streets over the next few weeks. I will not be defeated by a bunch of thugs who have no respect for an orderly and democratic society."

CHAPTER SIX

Three weeks later, Mr Wetherby paced across the raised platform at the front of the main room in the Town Hall, staring down at the rows of men sorting and counting the votes. He took several deep breaths, but it didn't help; nothing would calm the churning in his stomach. He had spent the last two weeks walking the streets, talking to every potential voter he could find, but it would seem he'd wasted his time. Even Lord Churchill hadn't bothered turning up to hear the results.

"They're going to win all seven constituencies, aren't they?" he said to the Central Ward chairman standing next to him.

"How do they do it? The Liberals have been so unpopular, but they can still win. Once the news appears in the morning papers, we'll likely lose the whole country."

Mr Wetherby shook his head. "They're going to humiliate us despite all the effort we've put in. You can almost hear the Liberal catcalls now."

His colleague nodded. "Gladstone knew what he was doing when he enfranchised the working classes. Damn him."

Mr Wetherby closed his eyes and took a deep breath. "Don't expect me to be in Birmingham for the next few weeks. I'll be in Handsworth if you need me."

~

Handsworth, Staffordshire.

Mr Wetherby sat in the back room of Wetherby House, staring at the ceiling. *How did it all go so wrong?* He pushed himself up and ambled to the window, watching the rain as it streaked down the glass. It was as if the weather was shedding tears for the whole country. It would need to rain for a lot longer yet to wash away all the pain. He put his hands to his face and rubbed his eyes.

"You've moved," Sarah-Ann said as she walked

in. “I was beginning to think you’d become attached to the chair.”

Mr Wetherby glared at his wife, but she appeared not to notice.

“Are we going to go to the new hospital this afternoon to see the Prince of Wales?” she asked.

“You can go if you like, but I’m not.”

“You’re not going? You have a ticket for the dignitaries’ tent.”

“What’s the point?” Mr Wetherby returned to his chair. “The place will be so full of people I won’t see him.”

“You were full of excitement last week saying your ticket would give you a front-row view.”

“Sharing a small tent with over three hundred people isn’t going to give a decent view. Trust those damn Liberals to make a mess of the arrangements.”

“I thought it was the hospital who’d organised everything; the council haven’t done anything from what I can tell.”

“Exactly. When His Royal Highness comes to Birmingham, you’d expect the council to put some effort in, but no, everything’s been left to individuals, even decorating the streets. I bet Birmingham’s a mess.”

“I’d like to go, even if only to catch a glimpse of him.” Sarah-Ann ran her hands down the bodice of her dress. "I've got a new dress for the occasion. Do you like it? You always said lilac complemented my eyes." She moved towards him, the short train of her dress trailing on the floor behind her. "Please come with me."

"Why do you want to go?"

"Because he's the heir to the throne and we might never get the chance again. It would be good for you to go; it might stop you brooding about the election."

Mr Wetherby folded his arms. "I'm not brooding."

"Yes you are and it doesn't suit you. You shouldn't forget how well you did compared to previous years. Lord Churchill only lost by about seven hundred votes, which is quite an achievement considering the huge majority the Liberals had in the last election. Now fetch your hat and coat, the carriage is already waiting."

CHAPTER SEVEN

Travelling home for Christmas in the back of her father's carriage, Eleanor blinked to hold back the impending tears. It was a journey she'd dreading making and as they approached Havelock Road, the reality was every bit as bad as she'd been expecting. She glanced at Charles, who sat opposite her. He hadn't spoken since they left Birmingham.

As they turned into their father's driveway, the coachman stopped and opened the door to let them alight.

"There's no hurry with the bags," Eleanor said. "Settle the horses first."

The coachman nodded before he closed the door and got back in his seat.

Eleanor gazed at the house.

"What are you waiting for?" Charles asked. "Come on; I'm starving."

"It doesn't feel right, coming home from school and Mother not being here. She'd be out on the driveway by now, asking me all manner of questions."

Charles put his head down and marched to the front door. "You can't think like that, we have to forget about her. It's the only way."

Eleanor nodded at her younger brother. "You're right. I just hope Father's coping without her."

"He won't care ..."

"Of course he'll care, Mother's not been gone three months, now please behave when he's around. Don't deliberately try to annoy him."

Charles's shoulders slumped. "I won't."

"Father, are you home?" Eleanor called as she went into the house. When she got no reply, she continued. "Hopefully, that means he's at work."

"He'd better have left us something to eat," Charles said as he went straight to the morning room. Eleanor sighed as she watched him disappear before she hung her hat and coat on the stand. She was about to go into the back room when there was a knock on the door and her Aunt Mary-Ann walked in.

"You're early," Mary-Ann said. "I was hoping to be here waiting for you when you arrived."

Eleanor smiled. "You'd no need. We must get used to coming home to an empty house."

"Perhaps, but I didn't want it to be the first time you came home. I presume your father's not in yet?"

"No, I don't think so. He didn't answer when I called."

Mary-Ann glanced around the hallway before she took Eleanor's arm and escorted her into the room.

"I need to warn you that I'm worried about him," Mary-Ann said. "I don't know what he's up to; he's become rather secretive and has taken to going out more than usual of an evening. It's better than sitting in the chair staring into space, which is how he spends the rest of his time, but nobody has any idea what he's up to."

Eleanor sighed. "Not even William-Wetherby?"

Mary-Ann shook her head. "No, but if I'm being honest, he's making things worse. He's still angry with Mr Wetherby, and seems to think he was responsible for your mother's death. Can you tell him not to say anything to Charles? You know how he'd react if he suspected foul play."

Eleanor's eyes widened. "What does William-

Wetherby think happened? He hasn't said anything to me."

"I'll let him tell you, but I'm frightened he's making things up because he can't bear the thought that your mother took her own life."

Eleanor paled as her aunt spoke. "I thought the coroner said it wasn't suicide."

"There was no hard evidence ..."

Tears welled in Eleanor's eyes. "I'm not ready for this. Father needs to be my priority but it won't help if William-Wetherby's upsetting him."

"I'm only next door," Mary-Ann said as she squeezed Eleanor's hand. "Come round whenever you want."

The following day Eleanor walked to Wetherby House. As she arrived, Aunt Sarah-Ann and her daughter Elizabeth were busy packing a variety of home-made pickles and preserves into boxes.

"What's all this for?" Eleanor asked.

"The Christmas bazaar at the school tomorrow. Are you coming?" Elizabeth asked.

Eleanor shrugged. "I've not heard about it. Where is it?"

"At St Stephen's, the church needs money for repairs; your Aunt Olivia and I are hosting a stall.

We've had so many donations we're going to need to take the large carriage to transport everything."

"Will Aunt Charlotte be helping you?"

Elizabeth's blonde ringlets bounced around her face as she shook her head. "She can't. She has another engagement."

"She's been generous with her donations though," Sarah-Ann said. "I'll be going as well. Why don't you bring Margaret and Florence with you? I'm sure they'd enjoy it."

Eleanor smiled. "You're right; they would. I'm going to try and bring Father with me too. I think he's putting a brave face on for me, but Aunt Mary-Ann said he's still feeling sorry for himself. This might cheer him up. I'll tell him he has to get the carriage out in the morning."

William paced the back room, his heart pounding. He hadn't slept a wink last night, and now Eleanor expected him to go to a social event. He wasn't ready for this.

"You'll have to go without me," he said as Eleanor arrived downstairs.

"I promised Aunt Elizabeth we'd all be there and

I'm not letting her down. We're not disappointing Margaret and Florence either. They're looking forward to it. I bet you haven't thought of getting them Christmas presents, have you? This is your chance."

William winced. "Can't you do it?"

"No, I can't. Imagine what Mother would say if she saw you now. She wouldn't be happy. Christmas was always her favourite time of year and she'd expect you to make an effort. You'd better make sure you take plenty of money with you as well; this is for the church funds."

William sighed and pushed himself out of the chair. There was no point arguing. Once she'd made her mind up, Eleanor was as determined as her mother. With the carriage waiting, William helped his daughters into the back before he climbed in after them.

"Didn't Charles want to come?" he asked.

"No, he's gone off with some of his friends. I don't suppose we'll see him again until he's hungry."

"I like you being home from school," Florence said as she nestled into the side of Eleanor. "Do you have to go back?"

William glanced from Florence to Margaret, who clung to Eleanor's other arm. "Yes, she does,"

William said. "Mother wanted you all to go to school and we don't want to disappoint her."

Florence squeezed her eyes closed as she held on to Eleanor more tightly.

"I'll only be away for one more year," Eleanor said. "Then I'll be home for good. It will be something to look forward to."

The church hall wasn't big and by the time they arrived people were jostling for space. Eleanor headed straight for Elizabeth and Olivia's stall.

"We made it," Eleanor said, a grin spread across her face. "And we brought Father."

William smiled. "It was more than my life was worth to say no to my daughters."

"Well, I'm glad you're here," Olivia said. "I had no success with William Junior."

"It's not the sort of thing my brother would enjoy."

"Can we go and find some toys?" Florence said. "If we see something we like, will Father Christmas bring it for us?"

"You'll have to wait and see."

William excused himself and let his daughters lead the way around the stalls. He watched as they picked up a couple of dolls, and waited for them to continue walking before he moved in to buy them. Much to his surprise, a smile settled on his face as he watched, but as they approached a stand selling roasted chestnuts, he froze. Mr Wetherby and Aunt Sarah-Ann were heading straight for him. For a moment he considered changing direction, but before he moved they were upon him.

"Good afternoon, William," his aunt said. "Eleanor said she was going to bring you; I'm glad you could make it."

"I came for the girls ..." He watched the heads of his daughters as they chattered together beside a stall.

"How's that business of yours going?" Mr Wetherby asked.

"Fine." William spoke with as much confidence as he could muster.

"I met your new partner, Mr Ball, last week. He says things appear promising. You have a full order book at any rate."

William glared at Mr Wetherby. "That happens to be private business between me and Mr Ball. He had no right to show you the books."

"Someone's got to keep an eye on you. He's not seen much of you since he joined. I gave you a lot of money to start that business. I want to make sure you don't lose it."

"I've just lost my wife; I'm entitled to some time off."

"You're not entitled to be reckless. I still miss your mother, but I'd be in a sorry state if I ignored my businesses. If you want my advice, get yourself back to work and make a success of yourself."

William glared at his stepfather. "If I want your advice, I'll come and ask for it. Good day."

CHAPTER EIGHT

William lay in bed, staring at the ceiling. Christmas Day, the day he had been dreading, had arrived. If Harriet were still here, she'd have been up for hours, preparing the food and getting the girls dressed in their best clothes, but what could he do to fill her shoes? It sounded like the girls were up. Eleanor had been planning the day for weeks, but he couldn't hear Charles. That was always a worry. He hoped his wayward son hadn't opened all the presents he'd left downstairs.

William rolled out of bed and lifted a clean shirt out of the cupboard. Yesterday's wasn't dirty, but Eleanor would complain if he wasn't in his best clothes. He stood in front of the mirror and straightened his collar and tie. How had his hair and beard gone white so quickly? They had been brown when Harriet died. He shrugged and reached for his jacket; there was nothing he could do about it now.

The church service seemed to go on for an eternity, but as soon as it was over, William joined Mary-Ann and Mr Diver as they prepared to make their way home.

"Merry Christmas," Mr Wetherby said as he approached the group. "What are you doing today?"

"Mary-Ann's prepared dinner for us all," William said. "What about you?"

"We have all the family joining us. It should be an enjoyable day," Sarah-Ann said. "It's a shame you couldn't join us, but I'm afraid we don't have the space. We'll see you soon."

Mr Wetherby offered his arm to Sarah-Ann before they tilted back their heads and paraded towards the door. William and the Divers waited for them to leave before they followed them out.

"We're obviously no longer part of the family if they're all going to Wetherby House and we're not," William said.

"They didn't have the room. Who's she trying to fool?" Mary-Ann looked around for the children and beckoned them over. “It was never a problem for Mother to fit us all in at Mr Wetherby’s table.”

“I can’t say I’m surprised after the way William objected to their wedding,” Mr Diver said.

“Nothing’s been the same since Mother died. Mr Wetherby wouldn’t have dared behave like this if she was still here.”

Mary-Ann shook her head. “Looking back, you realise he only ever did things for us because of Mother. He never cared much for me.”

William nodded. “He didn’t have much time for girls in general.”

“Except Charlotte,” Mr Diver said.

William’s smile faded into a grimace. “You’re right. If ever anyone was born to have everything ...”

“Did you know she’s getting married next year? To someone called Mountford. He’s from a well-to-do family in Edgbaston.”

“No less than you’d expect. I imagine there’ll be no expense spared for the wedding. It’s as well she chose someone with money and a family business.”

“She was never going to choose a pauper. Whoever she married was going to need a lot of money to maintain her lifestyle, and by all accounts, Mr Mountford can do that. Having said that, I do like her. She’s generous and gives a lot of money to charity. Did you hear she’s persuaded Mr Wetherby to host a tea party and concert in Birmingham after Christmas for a group of old people?"

William laughed. "Mr Wetherby's nephew, Sid, told William-Wetherby. Sid's had to spend a few nights at William Junior's house, practising with him and Olivia."

Mary-Ann chuckled. "Poor him. Don't you feel left out?"

William pulled a face. "No, I don't. We should be thankful for our lack of musicality ... and that we can have our own family dinner without worrying about them."

CHAPTER NINE

As William entered the workshop, the sound of machines and the hammering of metal on metal brought a smile to his face. He stepped forward to see his eight workmen concentrating on the pieces of metal in their hands. It was good to be back. Mr Ball had been a godsend too and with the order book full, they had enough work to keep the men busy for the next couple of months. He returned to his workbench as Mr Ball walked towards him, his diminutive stature causing him to look up at William.

"Can I have a quick word?" he said. William nodded and followed him into the office. "I wanted to tell you I won't be in tomorrow. I didn't think you'd mind."

"Of course not. Is everything all right?"

"I've some business to attend to, but I wanted to warn you I'm expecting a visit from a commercial traveller tomorrow. I'm sorry to trouble you with him, but you can tell him to come back next week."

"Can I deal with him?"

"I wouldn't waste your time on him, to be honest. I'd rather not see him myself, but you know what they're like. Send him on his way and I'll deal with him next week."

With the workshop in full flow, William immersed himself in his work. He hummed quietly to himself as he leaned over a lathe, but was jolted to attention by a tap on his shoulder.

"Excuse me." A stranger stood before him with thickset shoulders and a rough beard and moustache. "I'm here to see Mr Ball, is he here?"

William gestured to the office. "What did you say?"

"I'm looking for Mr Ball, can you tell me where to find him?"

"Are you the traveller? I'm afraid he's not here. He asked if you could call again next week."

The traveller banged his hand on the desk.

"That really is inconvenient. I'm based in London and I'm only in Birmingham for a couple of days."

"I'm sorry you've had a wasted journey, Mr ..."

"Excuse me, Copeland the name is, Mr Copeland."

"I'm sorry, Mr Copeland, but there's nothing I can do. Mr Ball does all the ordering; I'd be in the doghouse if I ordered anything without him."

"You wouldn't be Mr Jackson by any chance, would you?"

"I am, and I apologise that my manners have left me. The best thing to do is write to him next time you plan to be in the area."

"I wrote to him last week to confirm today; is he avoiding me?"

"I'm sure he wouldn't do that."

"Am I right in thinking you're in charge of the workshop? It'd be more appropriate for me to show you the metal, rather than him."

William shook his head. "No, I don't think so. Mr Ball knows what we need."

Mr Copeland hesitated. "As you wish, but before I go, may I ask you a favour? I have my daughter with me and we've been travelling all day without a rest. Could I trouble you to provide her with a glass of water?"

"Where is she? You haven't left her on the street, have you?"

"She's by the door. May I bring her in for a minute?"

"I suppose so, although the water isn't particularly pleasant," William said.

"Please, just to wet her lips before we reach the tavern."

William sighed and gave a slight nod. "I'll fetch the water."

Mr Copeland disappeared but returned a minute later. "Mr Jackson, my daughter Miss Copeland; Lydia, this is Mr Jackson." William's heart skipped a beat as he glimpsed her blue-grey eyes. Was he imagining it or did she have a look of Harriet twenty years earlier?

"N-nice to meet you, Miss Copeland. Please come and sit down."

Lydia allowed him to take her arm and once she was in the office she accepted the water. William took a deep breath as he watched her take a sip. "I wouldn't drink too much; it's not the best."

"I've had worse." Lydia smiled up at him. "Thank you for caring."

William stood fixed to the spot until Mr Copeland took the glass from his daughter and pulled her to her feet. "That's enough, I've got work to do."

William flinched at the way he grabbed her arm. "There's no hurry. Let her stay here until she feels better."

"She can't stay here all day. I need to find another customer thanks to your Mr Ball."

"I'll tell you what." William looked from father to daughter. "If you're still in the area tomorrow, why don't you call in then? Mr Ball will be back."

Mr Copeland took a crumpled piece of paper from his pocket. "Let me see. Tomorrow, yes, I could call at about half past four."

William breathed a sigh of relief. "That should be fine. I'll tell Mr Ball you're calling."

The following morning, William was in work by ten past seven but Mr Ball was already at his desk.

"Good morning," he said as he went into the office. "Did you have a successful day yesterday?"

"Yes, thank you." Mr Ball spoke without looking up.

"Splendid." William shuffled from foot to foot and when he didn't speak, Mr Ball glanced up at him.

"Was there anything else?"

William coughed to clear the lump in his throat. "Yes, one more thing. Mr Copeland was disappointed to miss you and so we arranged for him to call today at half past four."

Mr Ball closed his eyes and took a deep breath. "I told you to arrange it for next week."

"He couldn't make it then."

"Yes, that's why I suggested it. I don't want to see him today."

William's forehead creased as he studied Mr Ball. "Well, why didn't you say so?"

"It's not that simple. He never takes no for an answer and resorts to all sorts of underhand tricks. He didn't have his daughter with him, did he?"

"She only came in for a moment to have a glass of water."

Mr Ball let out an exasperated sigh. "And you fell for her as most men of your age do."

"There was nothing to fall for."

"Then why are they calling today? I'll bet it's not because you wanted to see Mr Copeland again."

William's cheeks coloured. "I thought you wanted to see him. I'll deal with him if you don't want to."

"You will not." Mr Ball's face was red. "I don't trust him one bit and so I'll be the one to deal with him."

. . .

Despite the noise of the machines, William straightened up to listen to the voices filtering into the room. It was twenty-five to five. Mr Copeland must be here, but why the shouting? He walked to the hall to see Miss Copeland being pushed through the door before it slammed behind her.

"What on earth's going on?" William said. "Are you all right?"

"Mr Ball's angry we're here. Father wanted a word with him in private."

William raised his eyebrows. "Private? I should think the whole street can hear them."

A second later Mr Copeland stormed from the office and grabbed his daughter's arm causing her to bang into the door frame.

"Mr Copeland, what are you doing?" William said.

Mr Copeland stopped and glared at William. "I've just wasted two hours getting here only to be told Mr Ball never had any intention of seeing me."

"But your daughter's face ... You can't take her out like that. Let me find a cloth to wipe it."

Miss Copeland touched her cheek where a trickle of blood ran from a gash.

"That looks nasty," William said. "Come with me."

Prising Miss Copeland's arm from her father's grip, William rinsed a cloth in a bowl of water before guiding her to a chair near the entrance to the workshop. While Mr Copeland waited by the outside door, William pushed the ringlets from her face and held the cloth on the cut. She gazed at him with tears in her eyes.

"Does he often do things like this to you?" William asked.

Miss Copeland shook her head.

"Thankfully I don't think it's too bad." William took the cloth from her face and smoothed her hair back into place. "You really are very pretty. I expect you have men telling you that all the time."

Miss Copeland lowered her eyes and studied her fingers. "I don't spend much time with other men; I'm usually travelling with Father."

"That can't be much of a life for you. Don't you have a mother?"

"No, sir, she died when I was eleven. That was when I started travelling with Father."

William thought of his daughter Margaret who had been eleven when Harriet died. "That must have been hard. Have you ever thought of settling down?"

Lydia's ringlets shielded her face as she shook her head. "I don't know that I'll ever be able to. Father would have to stop working if I did."

"How old are you?"

"Twenty-one."

"Perhaps I can help." William's thoughts were forming as he spoke. "My wife died last year. I have five children, the youngest of whom is only eight years old. Florence her name is. My sister helps with them, but I'm looking for a housekeeper-cum-nanny. What would you say to taking the job and moving in with us? Naturally, I'd pay you and you'd have a room to yourself."

Miss Copeland's shoulders slumped. "I've never taken care of children before, sir. I don't have any brothers or sisters."

"I'm sure it would come naturally. If your father was agreeable, would you be interested?"

Lydia paused before she smiled at him. "Yes, sir, I would."

"Wait here a moment." William left Lydia alone while he went outside to find Mr Copeland.

"Mr Copeland, can I have a word with you?" William took his arm and steered him a little way from the door.

"You have a delightful daughter. I congratulate you on bringing her up so well by yourself. I hope I can do as well with my daughters."

"You've lost your wife?"

William nodded. "Less than six months ago. I've five children to take care of as well. The youngest is only eight."

"I'm sorry."

William glanced at Mr Copeland. "I've been trying to find a housekeeper-cum-nanny for the last few weeks, but haven't had any success. I wondered ... would you consider letting your daughter take on such a role?"

"Lydia? You mean leave her here with you?"

"I'm sure your life would be easier, only having yourself to take care of and you'd know where to find her."

"You can't expect me to give up my daughter. How can I be sure you'll take care of her?"

"You wouldn't be giving her up and you'd be able to visit whenever you wanted. I can guarantee she'll be well cared for. If she's not, she can leave at any time."

"What about money?"

"She'll receive a wage as well as food and lodgings."

"Not for her. For me. How much do I get for her?"

William hesitated. "I hadn't planned on giving you anything. The savings you'll make on food and accommodation should be enough."

"I can't possibly agree to that."

William's heart was pounding. "She's twenty-one now. Why don't you ask her?"

"I'll do nothing of the sort."

"I'll tell you what." William stopped to catch his breath. "What if I speak to Mr Ball about you becoming one of our suppliers?"

Mr Copeland studied William before he smiled. "If you can do that, you've got yourself a deal. If I can call in the morning to take an order, and a decent one at that, you can have Lydia as soon as the paperwork's signed."

CHAPTER TEN

William felt as if he was floating when he walked home from work; he even struggled to keep the smile from his face. He was getting a housekeeper, but not just anyone. One who would remind him of Harriet.

He was almost home when he saw Mr Watkins staggering down the street towards him.

"Mr Watkins, what's the matter?" William ran towards him and grabbed the old man's arm, bringing him to a halt.

Mr Watkins's shoulders sagged. "Mrs Watkins ... she's stopped breathing ... I need the doctor."

William turned him around. "You go home and stay with her. I'll fetch him for you."

Mr Watkins nodded. “He needs to be quick. She can’t breathe.”

“I’ll be as quick as I can.”

By the time William arrived with the doctor, Mr Watkins was sitting on the floor, rubbing the limp hand of his wife.

“She won’t wake up.” Tears welled in Mr Watkins’s eyes as William took him by the arm and helped him stand up.

“Come now, let the doctor see her.”

“She will be all right, won’t she? She needs to make tea.”

“Perhaps tea can wait for tonight. Come into the front room with me.”

Mr Watkins resisted. “I need to wake her up; she won’t sleep tonight otherwise.”

The doctor knelt by Mrs Watkins before he stood up and faced her husband. “I’m sorry, Mr Watkins, but she’s not going to wake up, not this time.”

Mr Watkins looked from the doctor to William and back again. “But she has to; she can’t leave me on my own. Who’ll take care of me?”

William thought of Miss Copeland. No, he couldn’t ask her to take on Mr Watkins as well.

“There were four of us when we moved in here,” Mr Watkins continued. “I’m the only one left. I can't stay here on my own, not with so many memories."

William cast his mind back to the time he had moved into this house with Harriet and Mr and Mrs Watkins. "Come now, don't think like that. We'll sort something out. Perhaps you could stay with us for a while."

Mr Watkins shook his head. "Harriet wouldn't have me."

"Harriet's not ..." William stopped before he finished his sentence. Had Mr Watkins forgotten about Harriet's death? Now wasn't the time to remind him. "Don't worry about Harriet. She's forgiven you."

Mr Watkins smiled. "She's forgiven me? I don't deserve her."

It was late by the time William arrived home, but he went into the back room and sat by the fire. He stared into the flames until all that remained were the fading embers in the grate. The image of Mrs Watkins's limp body, propped up in the chair, was still in his mind, but that wasn't what consumed him. He hadn't yet told Mr Ball about the deal with Mr Copeland. *He's going to be furious.* William's stomach churned at the thought. *I need to break it to him gently.*

. . .

William was out of bed and in the office early the next morning but as usual Mr Ball was in before him. He sat at his desk, surrounded by books and pieces of paper, studying them through the wire-rimmed spectacles he wore on the end of his nose.

William coughed to clear his throat. "Good morning."

At first, Mr Ball didn't look up, but when William remained by the desk, he took off his spectacles and stared up at him.

"What can I do for you?"

"I've something to tell you." William took a deep breath as a bead of perspiration trickled down the side of his face. "Last night, after you left, I ended up talking to Mr Copeland's daughter. She's had a difficult life. Her mother died when she was only eleven and ..."

"Get to the point, man. I don't need to know all this."

"No ... quite. The point is, she doesn't have an easy life travelling from place to place with her father and so I asked her to come and live with me and be a housekeeper and nanny for the children."

Mr Ball leaned back in his seat, his face lined with incomprehension. "What possessed you to do that? You'll never be free of Mr Copeland now."

"That's what I'm coming to."

Mr Ball was on his feet. "What have you done?"

"He wouldn't let her stay unless I promised ..."

"Promised what?"

William jumped at the volume of Mr Ball's voice.

"Promised to use him as one of our suppliers." William kicked at the bottom of the desk.

"You did what? You had no right to do that. I manage this business and I don't ever want to see that man again."

"I'm sorry, but this is my business and I'm still the majority shareholder. I thought it was a small price to pay to keep his daughter safe."

"Have you any idea what you've done? The man's a charlatan and a liar. That was precisely what he wanted to happen."

"I thought you'd never met him."

"I've not, but I know plenty who have. They say he's only out for what he can get and liable to overcharge at any opportunity."

"But if you know that, you can manage him. You're not going to pay over the odds for anything."

"I most certainly will not, but I don't want to have to deal with someone like him."

"I'm sorry, but I've agreed to it. He's bringing his daughter here this morning while he talks to you. Once the paperwork's signed, I'll take her over to Handsworth."

Mr Ball shook his head. "For your sake, I'll give him a trial run, but if I have any trouble with him, anything at all, either he goes, or I do."

CHAPTER ELEVEN

William listened to laughter coming from Eleanor's bedroom before he knocked on the door and waited to be let in.

"I'm sorry to spoil the fun," he said when Margaret opened the door. "Can I come in?"

"Look at me, Papa." Florence twirled around in front of him, her fair hair falling loose around her shoulders. "Isn't this the prettiest dress you've ever seen?"

William admired each of his daughters in their deep blue gowns and smiled. "It most certainly is, along with Eleanor's and Margaret's of course."

Lydia stepped to one side as Eleanor stood up from her dressing table.

"You're going to be so proud of them, Mr

Jackson. Let me put young Florence's hair up and they're all yours."

"Are the Divers here yet?" Eleanor said.

"No, not yet. I popped up to say the carriage will be here in about ten minutes. You carry on and I'll wait downstairs." He smiled at Lydia as he turned to leave. *What a godsend she's been. I couldn't hope to manage a day like this without her.*

William went downstairs to where William-Wetherby and Charles waited for him.

"I want you two on your best behaviour today. Are you listening?" He looked directly at Charles as he spoke. "There'll be a lot of important people at this marriage ceremony and I don't want you embarrassing me."

"Why do we have to go?" Charles said.

"Because Aunt Charlotte's getting married and Mr Wetherby wants the whole family there." *As if we're one big happy family.* "You can always go back to school, if you'd prefer."

Charles glared at his father but said nothing.

"It was probably Aunt Sarah-Ann who invited us," William-Wetherby said. "I don't suppose Mr Wetherby would miss us."

"Well, whatever it is, we're all going and there'll be trouble if you don't behave."

"Why wasn't Lydia invited?" William-Wetherby asked.

William glanced at his son. "She's our housekeeper, that's why."

"She's more than that though, isn't she, and she's really pretty. I wish she was coming."

William raised his eyebrows. "We'll have less of that. You're not eighteen yet."

William-Wetherby rolled his eyes as he stood up. "The girls are here now. Are you coming into the front room to see them?"

By the time William and his sons arrived at Wetherby House with Mr Diver, a crowd had started to congregate outside.

"He's sparing no expense." Mr Diver admired the row of carriages lined up outside the house.

"What did you expect?" William said. "Those dresses the girls are wearing must have cost him enough. He had them all made in London and had a tailor adjust each one for size once they got here. I hope the girls don't grow too quickly."

Mr Diver laughed. "At least the younger ones will be all right. They can grow into the larger sizes."

As soon as they reached the top of the drive a

butler opened the front door and showed them into the front room.

"Here you are," Mr Wetherby said. "I'm glad you could come. Your mother would have been upset if you weren't here."

"Of course we're here," William said. "Charlotte's my sister."

"Yes, of course she is. It's such a shame your mother isn't here. She'd be so proud of her. At least she has Sarah-Ann, Olivia and Mary-Ann to attend to her."

William studied his feet. *Who'll help my daughters when the time comes?*

"How about a drink?" Mr Wetherby continued. "I've got some champagne that I had delivered from London. Have you ever tried it?"

William shook his head.

"Not me," Mr Diver said.

"You're in for a treat then." Mr Wetherby summoned over a maid carrying a tray of glasses. "See what you think of this."

William took a mouthful of champagne and screwed his face up. "That's not what I expected."

Mr Diver laughed. "It's as well we only have small glasses."

William took a smaller sip. "That's better although I think I prefer sherry."

"Champagne is only for special occasions and so you're not likely to have it regularly."

"So you're happy with the marriage?" Mr Diver asked Mr Wetherby.

"Yes, of course; they wouldn't be getting married otherwise. If I'm honest, I couldn't have made a better match myself. Decent chap and when his father retires he'll take over the business. You should see the house they have in Edgbaston too. It makes Wetherby House appear small."

Mr Diver let out a low whistle. "It must be impressive. Where will they live once they're married?"

"I've bought them a house around the corner on St Peters Road. I expect they'll move to Edgbaston at some point, but not yet. Mr Mountford's going to be extremely wealthy one day."

As they were talking, William Junior joined them. "Not seen you for a while, William. How's the new business going?"

William puffed out his chest. "Very well. Our order book is full for the next few months. What about you? Are you still in Handsworth?"

"I am. Father leaves the day-to-day running to me, but we have a firm of accountants doing the bookkeeping now. It's a waste of time for us to do it."

"Are you in the workshop then?"

"Good Lord, no. I oversee everything. Bring in new business, that sort of thing."

William's eyes rested on his brother's waistline; he knew exactly what he meant. Going out for long dinners at the company's expense with people who had no intention of buying anything.

"We need to go." Mr Wetherby moved to the door to encourage people to leave.

William Junior turned to William and Mr Diver. "We're travelling to church in the same carriage. The rest of my family are part of the ceremony."

"I heard Olivia's a bridesmaid, but what about Henry? Is he here?" William glanced around the room.

"He's a pageboy." William Junior smiled. "You should see how smart he looks. He wasn't at all keen on being the only boy with all those girls though." He let out a loud laugh. "Here he comes. What do you think? I can't believe Charlotte's having nine bridesmaids. They need two carriages to transport them all."

Once the guests had filed from the house, Mr

Wetherby checked his pocket watch and walked to the bottom of the stairs. Sarah-Ann had taken a carriage with the younger bridesmaids, but as he glanced up, he saw Charlotte standing on the landing surrounded by her older attendants: Elizabeth, Olivia, Mary-Ann and Eleanor.

"You look wonderful." He took a deep breath as tears formed in his eyes. "That dress was worth every penny."

As Charlotte descended the stairs, the train of her white silk gown floated behind her. With her blonde hair taken up onto the top of her head and her blue eyes smiling at him, she had more than a hint of her mother about her.

As she approached him, Mr Wetherby coughed to clear the lump in his throat before lowering the veil over her face. "Mr Mountford's the most fortunate man in the world."

The scent of fresh flowers caused William to stop and survey the inside of the church. Vases of roses with carnations, fuchsias and dahlias filled the front of the church. What a shame Harriet isn't here, he thought before changing his mind. No, she'd be furious. She'd have compared everything to their wedding and ended up in a foul mood. Lydia wouldn't be so judgemental though. He smiled at the thought of his housekeeper. Lovely, sweet Lydia.

"We need to sit down." William-Wetherby nudged him. "Aunt Charlotte will be here any minute."

"Yes, of course." William led the way down the aisle and took a seat on the left-hand side of the church. Only a couple of feet in front of him Mr Mountford was talking to someone William presumed to be his brother. Both wore elegant morning dress, and had neatly trimmed black hair and moustaches. He studied the rest of the guests on the groom's side of the church and felt the hairs prickle on the back of his neck. Charlotte was going to want for nothing.

CHAPTER TWELVE

The following Sunday, while William read the newspaper in the back room, he was surprised to hear the front door being opened to Mr Wetherby. He stood up, waiting to receive him.

"Mr Wetherby, what brings you here? I thought you'd be having a well-deserved rest after the wedding."

"I wanted to speak to William-Wetherby. Is he in?"

"No, he's taken the girls to Sunday school with Miss Copeland. He won't be long. Can I help?"

"I wanted to tell him I won't be in the office much for the next few weeks. I presume you've heard the Liberal Party is in disarray over the issue of Irish Home Rule? Well, I have it on reliable authority that we'll have another election called this week."

"Not another one, it's no time at all since the last one."

"Nine months to be precise."

"And you're going to have to do all that canvassing again?"

Mr Wetherby shook his head. "To be honest I'm not sure we will. The exertions of the last election were too much for most of us and there's no appetite to repeat it. We've still to make a formal decision though."

"You mean you'll let the Liberals in unopposed?"

"That's what we need to work out. We're not going to have the likes of Lord Churchill this time and I believe the Liberals who oppose the Home Rule Bill will stand as Liberal Unionists. Not only that, I believe they may fight the election with the Conservatives. If so, the best option may be for us to have an unopposed Liberal Unionist candidate."

"That's a turn-up, so what will you do, work for the Liberal Unionists?"

Mr Wetherby puffed out his cheeks. "I hope it doesn't come to that, but I suppose it depends how many of the Gladstonian Liberals stand against them."

"That could mean you'd be supporting Chamberlain. He'll be a Unionist, I suppose."

"Don't think I don't know, but the Irish issue is too important to let a thing like that get in the way. The Lord moves in mysterious ways. Anyway, can you tell William-Wetherby this means I won't be in the office much?"

William's brow furrowed. "Do you want me to ask him to stay in Birmingham while you're busy? It might make things easier for you?"

"I hadn't thought about it to be honest; he probably doesn't need to."

"If he's going to be opening up each morning and locking up every night, it would make sense if he did."

Mr Wetherby shrugged. "I'll leave it up to him. He could stay with Betsy, he gets on well enough with her lad Sid."

"He does." William nodded. "When do you expect the election to be?"

"We're not sure yet, but I'd imagine we've got another couple of weeks. Across the country we expect the election will run throughout July, but I haven't heard when the Birmingham vote will be.

To be honest, if all the seats are uncontested, I might not be gone for long."

An hour later, hearing the front door close, William stood up and looked down at Lydia.

"Would you mind making a pot of tea? I'd like a quick word with William-Wetherby, alone."

"What's going on?" William-Wetherby stared at his father as Lydia hurried from the room.

"Mr Wetherby called and asked if you'd stay in Birmingham to open and close the workshop. There's going to be another election."

William-Wetherby flopped down into a chair. "I don't see why I have to. Birmingham's horrible."

William smiled. "You sound like your grandmother, God rest her soul, but it's only for a few weeks."

"What about Miss Copeland?"

"What about her? She's our housekeeper, not a house guest; besides I can keep her company."

"She needs someone her own age and you're out a lot lately. You can't leave her on her own."

"I have no intention of leaving her. She's travelled with her father for years and I'd say he's older than me and so I think I can manage. Now go and pack a bag, you won't be back here again until Saturday."

"I'm not packing a bag because I'm not staying; I'll speak to Mr Wetherby and tell him I'm not moving to Birmingham. If he wants to fire me, then he'll have to find someone else to do the job at pretty short notice."

"You can't do that, you still need a job."

"I don't care, who does he think he is ordering me around like that."

The following evening William couldn't keep the smile from his face as he walked home from work. With William-Wetherby staying in Birmingham, he'd be able to spend some time alone with Miss Copeland. *She's so much more than a housekeeper.* She brought a sense of normality to the house and having such an uncanny resemblance to Harriet sometimes made him forget he no longer had a wife. She was kind and gentle with the children, in many ways more so than Harriet, and William felt he had a family again.

Once he finished tea, William took his seat by the fire while he waited for Miss Copeland to join him. It was still a beautiful evening and he was going to ask her to take a walk with him while the sun was still bright. As she came into the back room, the front door burst open and a moment later William-Wetherby joined them.

"You lied to me," he shouted at William.

"I didn't. What's Mr Wetherby been saying?"

"You know damn well what he said, that there's no need for me to stay in Birmingham."

"I won't have language like that in front of Miss Copeland. You're not too old for me to take my belt to you."

William-Wetherby stopped and stared at Miss Copeland, who had slipped into the chair opposite William.

"That's what all this is about, isn't it? You wanted me out of the way so you could play happy families with Miss Copeland."

"Go to your room this minute and don't come down here until tomorrow. Miss Copeland was about to do some mending and it's more comfortable for her to do it here than in her room."

William-Wetherby glared at his father before turning to Miss Copeland. "He's old enough to be your father." He stormed from the room, slamming the door behind him.

"I'm sorry about that, my dear, I don't know what's got into him. He's not been the same since his mother died and I fear he sees you as a replacement for her."

Miss Copeland raised an eyebrow. "I like him though. It's not the same when he's not here."

"What do you like to do of an evening?" William changed the subject.

"I usually do some sewing or mending; there's always plenty to do. If not, I like to read."

"My wife used to like reading, but it got her into trouble in the early days. Her uncle didn't believe women should read."

"But that's terrible, of course we should. What was she like, your wife? A lot of people seem to miss her."

William smiled to himself. *How do I describe Harriet?*

"To tell you the truth, when I first met her she looked a lot like you, but she had an independent streak unlike any other woman I've known. She always wanted what she couldn't have. To me it made her exciting and fun to be with, but to her uncle and Mr Wetherby, she was a threat."

"Didn't Mr Wetherby like her?"

"Let's just say they didn't always see eye to eye. They were going through a particularly bad spell when she died."

"William-Wetherby doesn't think it was an accident."

William shot her a glance. "What's he been saying to you?"

Lydia's cheeks flushed. "Nothing, only that he thinks Mr Wetherby had something to do with it."

"Let me tell you he has no proof. I don't think we'll ever find out what happened."

"It must have been hard though, especially with Margaret and Florence being so small."

"It wasn't the best time of my life but I'm feeling more optimistic than I did ... in no small way, because of you."

Miss Copeland shifted in her seat. "All I'm doing is looking after the house and the children, nothing out of the ordinary."

"You're doing a lot more than that, believe me." William watched as she focussed on her sewing. "It's thanks to you that this family hasn't fallen apart. You're very special, did you know that?"

Miss Copeland blushed. "It's not something my father says to me."

"Ah yes, your father. Has he written to you since you've been here?"

"I wrote to tell him I'd settled in, but he hasn't replied. He's not much of a letter writer."

"He was in the office last week. Didn't he tell you he was in Birmingham?"

A frown settled on Miss Copeland's face. "He was in Birmingham? No, he didn't say."

"I'd have thought he'd miss you; after all, you

must have been close after travelling together for all those years."

Miss Copeland glanced up from her mending. "Just because you're constantly at a person's side doesn't mean you're close. We didn't talk, not like this. It was always him telling me what to do."

"I hope you don't mind me asking, but did he often hurt you ... like he did when I met you?"

Miss Copeland said nothing, but raised a hand to brush aside a tear.

"I'm sorry, I shouldn't have brought it up." William tapped his hands on the arm of the chair before he pushed himself up and walked to the window. *It's too late to ask her to go for a walk now and she's busy. Damn. I'll have to wait until tomorrow.*

"I've been meaning to ask you," he said when he tired of the silence. "Are you happy here? Is everything to your liking?"

"Yes, thank you, you've been most generous."

"I don't only mean the money, I mean with the arrangements; I want you to be happy."

Again Miss Copeland said nothing, but this time tears ran down her cheeks.

"Please don't cry, I didn't mean to upset you."

"You didn't make me cry, not in a bad way, but

you're so kind. I'm not used to it. My father would never ... well, I don't know what to say."

"Don't say anything." He moved forward and knelt by her side. "I'm here now. I won't let anything bad happen to you again."

CHAPTER THIRTEEN

Mr Wetherby gazed through the window at the rain and sighed. It had been bright and warm for the last two weeks but now election day had arrived, this downpour would keep the voters at home. Although they hadn't shown much excitement in another election; in fact they had made it perfectly clear they had had enough. The nomination of candidates had been one of the most subdued political events of recent years and with most of the seats in Birmingham being uncontested, there was little interest from voters. Not that it would stop him from enjoying the day. He didn't remember ever feeling so relaxed on election day.

"Aren't you going into Birmingham today?"

Sarah-Ann asked as she carried some plates into the morning room.

Mr Wetherby glanced at his pocket watch. "I am later, but I'm not needed and so I can go in my own time."

"Well, I for one am glad you're not doing so much this year." Sarah-Ann settled herself at the table. "It took you months to get over the last election. Now, come and eat these eggs before they go cold."

"Things have changed this time, you can sense it. People have had enough with the Liberals and they don't want the Irish to have Home Rule. I'm more optimistic about this one."

"I don't know how you do it, after everything you've been through over the years. I'm still not convinced we'll see another Conservative government."

"Of course you will," Mr Wetherby said. "In fact, I might go so far as to predict there'll be a Conservative government by the end of the month."

"You said that last year if you remember, when Lord Churchill gave you all false hope. That didn't work out so well."

"That doesn't mean we should give up. We need to guarantee as many votes as we can for Mr

Mathews. He's the only Conservative candidate standing in the area and we can't let him down."

As Saturday afternoon came to a close, William-Wetherby left work a few minutes early hoping to be home before his father. As he walked into the back room, he was delighted to find Miss Copeland alone.

"What's that you're reading?" he asked.

She looked at the cover. "A library book, another one by Charles Dickens."

William-Wetherby feigned interest before he took the book from her and placed it on the table.

"I was wondering if you'd like to go for a walk. It's a lovely evening, it seems a shame for you to waste it in here."

Miss Copeland cocked her head as she smiled at him. "Yes, I'd like that, let me go and get my bonnet."

Five minutes later, they left the house and headed in the direction of the woods. They hadn't gone far when they heard footsteps behind them.

"William-Wetherby, Miss Copeland," William shouted. "Where are you going?"

The pair stopped and turned to face him.

"We're going for a walk," William-Wetherby said. "It's such a lovely afternoon."

William's brow furrowed. "What about tea? Miss Copeland needs to prepare it."

William-Wetherby smiled at Miss Copeland. "We'll be back by then."

"I wanted a word with Miss Copeland," William said. "You go on ahead."

"I'm not walking on my own. We won't be long; you can speak to her once we're home, I'm sure it can't be urgent."

As they walked away, William-Wetherby and Miss Copeland's smiles widened and before long they were giggling like schoolchildren.

"I'm telling you, he's got a soft spot for you," William-Wetherby said.

"As if! He must be twenty years older than me. Why would I walk out with someone like him?"

"What about someone who's four years younger than you, tall for his age and extremely handsome? Could you handle that?"

"It would be easier." Miss Copeland spoke with a glint in her eye. "Do you have someone in mind?"

"I might." He returned her mischievous grin. "He's mature for his age, has a steady job and a father with his own successful business. A fine prospect for any woman, I would imagine."

"You'll have to introduce me; he sounds like the sort of man I'm looking for."

~

Birmingham, Warwickshire.

The following day, William-Wetherby sat at his desk staring out of the window. He was brought back to reality by the sound of the workshop door banging and Mr Wetherby striding to his desk.

"What's all this? Am I paying you to sit around and do nothing?"

William-Wetherby flushed. "No, sir, I'm sorry, I was just thinking."

"It had better have been about those ledgers. You can thank your lucky stars I'm in a good mood."

"Is that for any particular reason?"

Mr Wetherby stared at him. "Aren't you aware of what's been going on over the last month? We've had a general election! I found out earlier today that the Conservatives have been asked to form the next government."

"That's excellent news, congratulations. You must be delighted."

"I most certainly am, particularly as we have the first conservative Member of Parliament for Birmingham in nearly twenty years. With the support of the Liberal Unionists, Lord Salisbury will be able to form a government."

William-Wetherby smiled. "So the Irish debate ended up doing us a favour. At least they'll stay in the union now. Will you be here more often now?"

"I will, although not every day. I'll be down at Bennetts Hill for a couple of days a week as before."

"How's the slum clearance work going?"

"Very well, we're due for another round of demolitions any time now, once everyone's out."

"What about the rebuilding? You can't move anyone else out before you've finished some of the new houses."

"We're finishing some now, as it happens." Mr Wetherby smiled as he stood with his hands behind his back. "The Lisson Grove estate is almost ready and we've filled Noel Park, which is why we can start the demolitions."

"But you're still only renting them, aren't you? What about the people who want to buy their own house?"

"Nobody wants working men to own their own homes more than I do, but unfortunately it's not that simple. We sell the houses in good faith but for one reason or another they either end up with small landlords who overcrowd them again, or they're converted into public houses, neither of which we can let happen. We're thinking of ways to deal with it, but for now it's time you did some work."

CHAPTER FOURTEEN

Handsworth, Staffordshire

For what felt like the whole summer, the weather had been dull, but now, as the end of August approached, the temperatures had remembered how they should behave. As the curtains flapped in the breeze, William-Wetherby paced across the back room of Havelock Road waiting for Miss Copeland, unaware he was punching one fist into the other. He paused momentarily when his father walked in.

"What's wrong with you?" William said. "You look like you're about to pick a fight with someone."

William-Wetherby studied his hands. "Maybe I am. It depends."

"On what?" A frown settled on William's face.

"You. Why do you always stop me being alone with Miss Copeland?"

"Because you're only eighteen years old, which is no age to be spending time alone with a woman, especially not a woman like Miss Copeland."

"Why not? If I like her and she likes me, what's the problem? Boys I went to school with are married now."

"Maybe boys from the elementary school, not from the grammar school, and if that's what you're thinking it's all the more reason to keep you from her."

William-Wetherby glared at his father. "Now you're being ridiculous. As it happens, I've asked her to walk out with me, and she's agreed."

"Well, you'd better uninvite her. I am not having a son of mine walking out with someone older than him. Your grandmother would have been horrified if I'd started walking out with anyone at your age, not to mention Mr Wetherby."

"But that's the difference, you're over twenty-five years older than me and times have changed."

"I don't care. I will not have you two walking out together and that's the end of the matter. Until you come of age, and while you live under my roof, you'll do as you're told."

William-Wetherby smashed his right hand into the palm of his left. “You’ve not heard the end of this. I’m going out.”

~

The following day William arrived at the workshop at the usual time and was surprised to find the door to Mr Ball’s office closed. Hearing voices coming from inside, he shrugged, took off his hat and walked into the workshop. Several minutes later the sound of shouting caused him to put down what he was doing. He was about to enter the office when Mr Copeland charged out and headed straight for him.

“You.” He pointed at William as he stormed towards William. “I want a word. I made a deal with you, but your partner’s ended our agreement and refuses to give me any more orders. Tell him it’s not his decision to make.”

Beads of perspiration formed on William’s forehead. “What’s happened? Why has he stopped the orders?”

“Because, this man is a crook.” Mr Ball was now behind Mr Copeland in the workshop. “He’s trying to charge us twice as much as other suppliers and I won’t be blackmailed into paying over the odds.”

"Is that true, Mr Copeland?"

"Of course not. I may charge a premium compared to other suppliers, but only because I provide a premium product."

"That's utter nonsense," Mr Ball said. "Mr Jackson, have you noticed how much better the metal has been since Mr Copeland started supplying us? Because I haven't."

William looked from one man to the other, his eyes wide. "Mr Copeland, if you drop your prices a little, I'm sure we could work something out."

"I won't drop them as low as he wants to go; he'll have me bankrupt."

"That's a lie," Mr Ball said. "He's deliberately trying to exploit us and I want nothing more to do with him."

William breathed a heavy sigh. "Forgive me, Mr Copeland, but would you mind if I have a minute with Mr Ball? In private."

"Be my guest if you think you can talk some sense into him, but let me remind you my daughter's only staying with you as long as I have this contract. If I lose this I may as well move to another part of the country and she's coming with me."

William stared at Mr Copeland. *I can't lose*

Miss Copeland; not now. Seconds later he gestured for Mr Ball to join him in the office.

"What's going on?" William asked, once the office door was closed.

"He's going to bankrupt us. His prices were high when we started dealing with him, but they've crept up, month after month, until now. Enough's enough."

"But I can't let his daughter return to her old life, she's so happy with us."

"That's not my concern, you can't run a business based on such nonsense. I won't work with him any longer and if you insist we use his services, I'll have to consider my position here."

"But you can't do that, we're partners." William wiped his forehead again.

"I can and I will and so you need to make a decision. It's either me or him."

William stared at Mr Ball, his mouth gaping. He couldn't do without Mr Ball or Miss Copeland. *What do I do?* When Mr Ball sat back down at his desk, refusing to look up, William returned to the workshop.

"I'm sorry, Mr Copeland, I don't know what to say. He won't budge unless you drop your prices."

Mr Copeland shrugged. "In that case I'll have

to remove my daughter from your employment. You either have both of us or neither."

"But she's settled and so helpful with the children. Surely it makes life easier for you knowing she's being taken care of, rather than you having to pay for her upkeep."

"It's nothing to me if she sleeps in my room; besides, if I lose this order I need her help."

"How does she help?" William asked.

"Didn't you notice? She has a way with the customers, knows how to soften them up and prepares the way for me. You're not the first businessman to have fallen under her spell. If I need to find other customers, I need her with me."

William shook his head. Mr Ball had warned him about this, but he hadn't believed him.

"Will you give me until tomorrow?" William said. "Everyone's angry at the moment, let me sleep on it and I'll talk to Mr Ball again in the morning."

Mr Copeland's black eyes pierced through William. "You have one day, otherwise I'll be calling to collect my daughter."

The following morning as he arrived for work, William felt bile rising to his throat when he saw

Mr Copeland leaning against the wall to the workshop.

"What are you doing here so early?" William climbed down from his carriage. "I've not laid eyes on Mr Ball yet, let alone spoken to him."

Mr Copeland took his pipe from his mouth. "I'm here to make sure you don't forget."

"Well, you can wait there." William glared at him as he walked into the building. As he entered the office, Mr Ball was at his desk, his head bent over the order book.

"Is that fool still there?" Mr Ball asked.

William stared at him. "You mean he was here when you arrived?"

Mr Ball grunted. "He can stay there for as long as he likes, I'm not changing my mind. If you give that man any business, I'll be looking for an alternative partnership."

William took a seat. "Please, Mr Ball, can we just give him something? It doesn't have to be much."

"You heard what I said. If you give him anything, you won't get rid of him and he'll be back week after week until he gets what he wants."

"But I can't let his daughter go back to him ... she's so happy."

Mr Ball stood up from his desk. "That, Mr Jackson, is not my problem. I will not run a company based on the needs of a young woman who is of no concern to me." Mr Ball pulled open the front door and beckoned the traveller inside. "Let's get this done with." He glared at Mr Copeland. "I've told Mr Jackson that I won't buy any further stock from you. If he overrules me, I won't hesitate to look for another partnership."

"And you're just going to accept that?" William jumped up as Mr Copeland took a step towards him.

"Mr Ball is an integral part of this business. We have to work together."

"Well in that case I'll go and get my daughter."

Mr Copeland turned and headed for the door.

"Please, don't do that, I'm sorry, but you can't punish your daughter for something that's not her fault."

When Mr Copeland refused to stop William grabbed his hat and followed him. By the time he got outside Mr Copeland was halfway up the road and William ran to his carriage. *I should get home before him.*

When he arrived at Havelock Road he ran into the morning room and found Lydia polishing the cutlery. She looked up as he stumbled in.

"What's the matter?"

"Your father's coming. He wants to take you away."

Lydia's eyes were wide. "Why? What's happened?"

William paused for breath. "He's had an argument with Mr Ball and we won't be using him as a supplier any more."

Lydia's shoulders sagged as she put down the fork in her hand. "I suppose I should go and pack then."

William stared at her. "You mean you're just going to go ... without putting up a fight?"

Lydia shrugged. "What else can I do? He's my father and it's more than my life's worth to disobey him."

"But ... but, what about the girls?"

Lydia's smile betrayed the sadness in her eyes. "Say goodbye to them for me. I'll miss them of course, but I'm sure you'll find someone else."

William scratched his head. "I can't believe you're just going to walk out of here as if you were a casual visitor. What about ... the rest of us?"

Lydia's smile disappeared. "Please don't make this any harder than it is. I'd better go and pack."

She ran down the hall and William was about to chase her up the stairs when banging on the front door stopped him. He watched as the maid came out of the front room and opened the door to Mr Copeland, who pushed his way into the hall.

"What have you done with her?"

William glanced at the maid causing her to retreat to where she came from. "I've done nothing with her. She's upstairs packing."

"Lydia, get down here now."

William flinched. "There's no need to be nasty."

"You mind your own business."

Both men watched the top of the stairs, and a minute later Lydia appeared clutching a small bag with clothes protruding from the top. Her other hand held a screwed-up dress.

"It wouldn't fit in my bag." She nodded at the dress as she hurried down the stairs.

"You can carry it, we're not going far." Mr Copeland flung open the front door and stepped onto the drive. "Come on."

As Lydia made to follow him, William caught hold of her arm and saw the fear in her eyes. "Let me know where you are."

Lydia nodded. "I'll write to William-Wetherby and explain."

"No, write to me. If you need anything,

anything at all, I'm the one who'll be able to help. I'll tell William-Wetherby what happened."

Lydia's shoulders sagged as her head dropped, but a second later her father grabbed her by the arm and pulled her out of the house.

CHAPTER FIFTEEN

William lay in bed listening to Margaret and Florence getting ready for school. They had no idea today was the anniversary of their mother's death and he wasn't about to tell them. He would usually be in work by now, but he wasn't going in. Not today. He needed time to himself. Closing his eyes, he stayed where he was until he was sure he was alone.

Once up, he went downstairs and was helping himself to some breakfast when the maid brought in a delivery from the postman. Putting down his bread, he flicked through the selection of letters but stopped abruptly when he recognised the neat, childlike handwriting on one of the envelopes. He shut the door to the morning room and placed the remaining letters on the table before carefully opening the envelope. He smiled when he confirmed it was from Miss Copeland. Although he'd asked her to write, he hadn't believed she would.

He read the letter several times before he set it on the table in front of him. Was it wishful thinking or did she need his help? She hadn't asked for any, and the letter only spoke of the life she was now living, but she didn't sound happy. Should he go and see her? He had her address now; was that what she wanted?

Having reread the letter a dozen times over breakfast, William put on his hat and coat and stepped outside. The weather was mild for September, but he shuddered at the thought of finding their room. It wasn't an area of Birmingham he was familiar with, but what else could he do?

It was almost an hour later before he found the right address and looking at the number of children in the street he presumed several families occupied each house. *How could I have let her come to a place like this?* He took a deep breath and knocked on the door. A man who had clearly been drinking answered instantly, but it was several minutes before William was allowed in. He picked his way over the bottles that littered the floor and as soon as he reached the far corner, he hurried up the stairs until he stood on the top landing. He paused to catch his breath before knocking on the door.

"Miss Copeland, are you in there? It's Mr Jackson. I got your letter."

He waited a few seconds and was about to try the handle when the door opened and a red-eyed Miss Copeland appeared before him.

"My dear, whatever's the matter?" He stepped into the room, his mouth open as he took in the scene. It was barely big enough for the double bed, but squashed at the foot of it, alongside a wall black with damp, was a second single mattress. "Is that where he makes you sleep?"

Lydia nodded and turned her face from him.

"You shouldn't be living in a place like this, in fact nobody should be. And your face. What happened?" He reached out and turned her towards him to inspect the bruising on her right cheek. Slowly his eyes moved to hers, but she lowered her gaze as if to hide the unbidden tears. A moment later she shook her head and turned away.

"You shouldn't have come."

William put his hands on her shoulders. "Did your father do that?"

"Please, you need to go."

William coaxed her to face him and let his hand stroke the bruise above her right cheek.

"I can't leave you here if he's going to treat you like this." William leaned forward and let his lips brush across her cheek. "I should never have let you come here in the first place."

"What the hell do you think you're doing to my daughter?" Mr Copeland's voice boomed across the room as he stood in the doorway.

"I'm taking her away from this ... mess." William waved his hand around the room. "The whole place should be pulled down."

"We can't all live in fancy houses in Handsworth, some of us have to make our own way in life."

"Your daughter can live in a house in Handsworth. Any self-respecting father would be glad to give her the opportunity."

"So she can play happy families with you? What about me?"

"What about you? You're a commercial traveller. You should be able to make your own living without relying on your daughter to make up for your shortcomings. Is that why you hit her, because she didn't get you an order?"

Mr Copeland stormed into the room and

grabbed his daughter by the arm. "What have you been saying to him?"

William saw the fear in Miss Copeland's eyes and pushed Mr Copeland away from her. "She hasn't been saying anything, but it's obvious."

"Don't you touch me." Mr Copeland rushed forward, punching William firmly in the stomach.

"Father, stop," Miss Copeland screamed. "Leave him alone."

William staggered backwards towards the door, his eyes boring into Mr Copeland. "She's coming home with me. I'm not leaving her here with a brute like you."

"She's doing no such thing; and unless you get out of my room and leave us both alone, you won't be in a fit state to go anywhere either."

"If I walk out of this room alone, I'll be going straight to the police station."

Mr Copeland laughed. "And do you think they'd take any notice of you? She's my responsibility, not yours, and what goes on in this room is none of their business. Now get out before I have you arrested for trespass."

"You good-for-nothing ... scoundrel," William said. "Mr Ball was right about you. You've not heard the last of this; I won't have the woman I love being beaten up for no reason."

The room fell silent as Mr Copeland and his daughter stared at William.

"Love?" Mr Copeland said.

William glanced between the two of them. "Yes, love. Have you any idea what it is?"

"Well, you've got a funny way of showing it. From where I'm standing you think more of your business and Mr Ball than you think of Lydia."

"That's not true. You were the one who gave me such a dilemma. I had to think of my own children first, but it doesn't mean I don't care for your daughter." He glanced over to Miss Copeland who was staring at him, her eyes wide.

"I'm sorry for being so forward," he said as he walked towards her. "It wasn't meant to be like this, but you've no idea how much I've missed you over these last few weeks. Being without you has made me realise that I love you and want to share my life with you. Would you do me the honour of being my wife?"

"You want to marry her?" Mr Copeland spoke before his daughter could reply. "Why didn't you say so? That changes everything."

"So you wouldn't object?" William eyed him suspiciously.

"It depends on your price."

"My price?" A crease formed in William's forehead. "I'm sure there's no need for a dowry."

"I'm not paying you. I mean, what will you give me? You can't expect me to give up my daughter and receive nothing in return."

"Father!"

"Shall we say twenty pounds?"

"No, we shall not say twenty pounds. I'm not made of money."

"If you want to marry her, you'll have to give me something. Either that or you make Mr Ball change his mind about using my stock."

William stepped towards him. "You keep Mr Ball out of this. I don't want you going near him. I'll tell you what, if you promise not to go near the workshop I'll give you five pounds on the day of the marriage ceremony and two shillings a week for the next year. You can go back to London, or wherever you came from."

Mr Copeland's eyes were like slits as he stared at William. "It's a deal, but she stays here with me until the wedding. She's not working as a housekeeper if she's to be your wife, and she's not living with you if she's not working."

William nodded. "Only on the condition that you take care of her and agree to me visiting whenever I chose."

"What about my feelings?" Lydia glared at her father.

The lines on Mr Copeland's forehead deepened as his eyes questioned his daughter. "What?"

"Come on, my dear," William put his arm around her. "There's no need to be nervous, I'll take care of you."

By the time he stepped outside, William's heart was pounding and he leaned against the front wall of the house to catch his breath. That hadn't gone as planned. What had he been thinking proposing marriage to her? And today of all days. Not that he regretted it. He hadn't lied when he said he loved her. The girls loved her too. And William-Wetherby. As his son's name crossed his mind, William's heart skipped a beat. His son would be furious. *How on earth do I tell him?*

CHAPTER SIXTEEN

When William arrived home, his son was in the back room polishing his shoes.

"Where've you been?" William-Wetherby asked.

William picked up the newspaper from the table and took a seat by the fire. "Nowhere. Just out for a walk."

"You haven't time to read that. We're going next door for tea and Aunt Mary-Ann called to say we weren't to be late. Margaret and Florence have gone already."

William released a deep sigh and pushed himself back up. *I could do without this.*

By the time they arrived, tea was on the table

and Mary-Ann put her head out of the back door to shout for the girls to come inside.

"You were out for a long time this afternoon," she said to William as he took his customary place at the table.

"Yes. I had something to do. I'll tell you about it later."

As the meal came to an end, Mary-Ann watched William play with the potatoes on his plate.

"Aren't you hungry tonight?"

William put down his knife and fork and took a mouthful from his cup of tea. "No, I've no appetite."

"That's not like you. I hope you're not sickening for anything."

"No, I'm fine, just got something on my mind."

Mary-Ann glanced at the empty plates of her daughters and nieces. "Have you girls finished eating? If you have, off you go back outside. You've got half an hour before bedtime."

With only four of them left at the dining table, Mary-Ann turned to William. "So, what have you been doing? Does it have anything to do with your loss of appetite?"

William pushed his plate away before he spoke.

"I had a letter from Miss Copeland this morning. She sounded unhappy and so I decided to pay her a visit."

"She wrote to you?" William-Wetherby's voice was an octave higher than it should have been. "Why didn't she write to me?"

William shrugged. "I didn't ask, but when I arrived she was living in an appalling room and I would say her father had been beating her."

"Why didn't you tell me? I need to see her. I'll go straight after church tomorrow," William-Wetherby said.

"There's no need for that." William paused. "She's coming to live with us again."

"When? You should have brought her with you if things were so bad."

"I wanted to but her father wouldn't let her come straight away."

"Why not?" A puzzled expression settled on William-Wetherby's face.

"He said he wouldn't let her work for me if she was to be my wife." William glanced around the table to see three faces staring at him.

"You asked her to marry you?" Mary-Ann said eventually.

"I did."

William-Wetherby was on his feet. "She was

walking out with me before she left. You had no right to ask her. I bet she only said yes because she was desperate to leave her father. Once she's back, you can tell her it was a mistake."

"I'll do no such thing," William said.

"But you're far too old for her. She told me she doesn't like older men. You can't do this to me."

"May I remind you that you are eighteen years old and in no position to be walking out with anyone."

"William," Mary-Ann interrupted. "Have you thought this through? Harriet's only been gone a year and now you want to marry someone half your age. How could you? You should have been in mourning all this time, but instead you were looking for a new wife."

"I wasn't looking for a new wife, she happened to come along. What's wrong with me getting married again, anyway? You've been very generous, but a man needs a wife and I have five children who need a mother. She's perfect in every way, I can't see why her age is such an issue."

"Because you're forty-four years of age and she's twenty-two," Mary-Ann said.

"And I don't need looking after," William-Wetherby added. "Neither do Eleanor or Charles."

"And have you thought of what Mr Wetherby will say?"

William glared at his sister. "It's got nothing to do with him. He remarried, didn't he? And he didn't marry just anyone, did he? He married Mother's sister-in-law."

"Yes, but at least he waited another year and Aunt Sarah-Ann is almost the same age as him," Mary-Ann said. "Nobody's saying you shouldn't get married, we're only questioning the timing and whether she's the right person."

"Well, she is. Margaret and Florence adore her, and at least they should be happy for me."

"Only because they're twelve and eight years old and don't know any better." William-Wetherby spat his words out. "Margaret'll be off to school soon, so she won't need looking after any more."

"That's enough," William said. "We're getting married before the end of the year and we'll be married by licence. I'm not giving anyone the chance to object. Now if you'll excuse me, I'm going to my club."

William-Wetherby glanced at Mr Diver before he spoke. "Your club? Since when have you had a club to go to?"

"Since last month." William grabbed for the door handle.

"Where? Which club?" William-Wetherby called after him.

"It's none of your business. I'll see you tomorrow."

CHAPTER SEVENTEEN

On the first Thursday in December, William stared into the bedroom mirror before he ran the comb through his hair and beard. He sighed as he studied his white hair. He didn't look as young as he had even a year ago but at least it didn't seem to trouble Miss Copeland. She was happy with him as he was.

Hiding his best suit under his overcoat, he left the house as if he was going to work for the day. There was no point telling anyone what he was doing; they'd already objected to his plans and Mary-Ann wasn't speaking to him. No, he'd let Mr Ball open up the workshop while he was in Birmingham.

As he waited in the entrance hall of the registry office with its filthy windows and bare walls, his mind drifted to the last wedding he had attended. The marriage of Charlotte to Mr Mountford had been one of the grandest events he had been to. How different things would be today.

At five minutes to ten o'clock, Mr Copeland arrived with his daughter. William ran his eyes over Miss Copeland's outfit, a navy blue dress with an elaborate bustle at the back. He had seen her wear it for church but today she wore a matching hat, which he guessed was new.

"You look beautiful," William said as she approached. "You've had your hair arranged differently. I like it."

Lydia said nothing as she lowered her gaze to the floor.

"Enough of that," Mr Copeland said. "Have you got my money?"

William stared at him before he retrieved five pounds from his pocket. "The rest of the money will only come if you stay away from the workshop. Is that understood?"

"If the money doesn't come, I'll be at your workshop before the end of the day. Is that understood?"

Both men glared at each other as two acquaintances of William's arrived to act as witnesses. Moments later, the registrar invited them into his office and began the service. With no hymns or prayers it was completed in a little over fifteen minutes. Five minutes later William took his wife's arm and they walked to Mr Copeland's room to collect her belongings, before setting off for Handsworth.

Lydia stared out the window of the carriage as it entered the outskirts of Handsworth, butterflies dancing in her stomach at the thought of seeing William-Wetherby again. As they entered Havelock Road, she closed her eyes to control the wave of nausea that passed over her.

William patted her hand. "The house should be empty when we get home, so you'll have time to unpack and make yourself at home."

"What time will everyone else be home?" Lydia's voice squeaked as she spoke.

"Margaret and Florence go to Mary-Ann's house straight from school and so we can pick them up when we're ready. William-Wetherby gets in at about six o'clock."

"You did tell them we were getting married today, didn't you?"

William shook his head. "I wanted to surprise the girls; I'm sure they'll be thrilled. William-Wetherby may be less so."

Lydia squeezed her eyes together. *That's what I'm afraid of. It should have been him I married, not someone old enough to be my father. I won't be able to look him in the eye again.*

With her few items of personal property unpacked, Lydia sat in the back room by the fire. She had a magazine on her knee, but she couldn't read, not knowing what was coming. At ten past six she stiffened as the front door opened and a minute later William-Wetherby came in.

"What are you doing here?" His tone was abrupt. "And where's Father?"

"Good afternoon, William-Wetherby. Your father's popped upstairs. He'll be back in a minute."

"He's told me you're getting married. Are you actually going to go through with it?"

Lydia fixed her eyes on the fireplace and covered her wedding ring with her right hand.

"You are, aren't you? How could you? I thought we were friends; we were more than friends, we were walking out together. What possessed you to accept a proposal from someone like him?"

A lump stuck in Lydia's throat. "He'll take care of me."

"I'd take care of you if you'd give me the chance." He stepped forward and softened his voice. "It's not too late to change your mind."

Lydia felt a tear run down her cheek and moved her hand to brush it away. William-Wetherby was about to kneel beside her when he stopped.

"You've already married him, haven't you? That's why you're here."

Lydia fixed her eyes on her ring and nodded. "I'm sorry, really I am."

"Sorry! You think that's all you need to say and everything will be fine? You're only four years older than me but now you're my stepmother? Was he a better prospect than me and you imagined yourself as a rich widow?"

"That's a dreadful thing to say. Please don't be like this, I want us to stay friends."

"Friends, I don't think so. And don't try to take the place of Mother."

"I wouldn't dream of it ..." Lydia let her tears fall.

"Ah, here you are," William said as he joined them. "I'm glad you're getting along."

"We're not." William-Wetherby glared at his

father as he strode towards the door. "And don't think I'll forgive you for this, because I won't."

"Come on, we don't need to argue."

"Don't worry, we won't be arguing. I'm not staying here with the two of you. I'll find myself somewhere else to live."

CHAPTER EIGHTEEN

Birmingham, Warwickshire

A week later, as William sat in the back of his carriage, he wondered what had possessed him to pick Eleanor and Charles up from school. They were perfectly capable of making the journey themselves, but given Lydia's presence in the house, he'd wanted to tell them about the marriage before they arrived home. Now, as his heart pounded in time to the rhythm of the horse's hooves, he wondered if it was such a good idea. *Why didn't I tell them in a letter and give them time to get used to the idea? That would have been much easier.*

His first stop was at King Edwards School for

girls. The driveway was full of carriages as parents arrived to pick up their daughters, and he waited in the queue for the driver to pull to one side. As they approached the entrance, he saw Eleanor waiting for him. How she'd grown in this last year. She was now the same height Harriet had been and had her mother's fair hair and blue-grey eyes. The dark blue school dress did nothing to conceal she had developed into a young woman.

"Are you ready?" William said as he climbed down from the carriage.

"I am. My trunk's inside, but look at this." Eleanor waved a school certificate at him. "I passed my exams with a third-class honours. What do you think of that? There were only six of us who passed."

William allowed himself a smile. "I'd say you've done your mother proud. Well done."

Once Eleanor's trunk was on the carriage, they proceeded to the boys' school. Many of the boys had already left, but Charles was nowhere to be seen.

"Where's he got to?" William sighed. "I'll have to go inside."

William stepped through the elaborate arched doorway into the wood-panelled entrance hall. *Still no sign of him.* He was about to search elsewhere when the headmaster approached him.

"Mr Jackson. Here to collect Charles, I imagine."

"Y-Yes. Is he here?"

"I asked him to wait in my office. There was some trouble earlier with a couple of other boys and I didn't want him getting involved."

William breathed a sigh of relief. "So he's not in trouble?"

"Not this time."

William wondered if he detected the flicker of a smile across the headmaster's face, but decided he was imagining it. Charles was not the sort of child to smile about.

Once they were all in the carriage, the driver set off for Handsworth. William took out his handkerchief and wiped his forehead.

"You can't be warm on a day like today," Eleanor said. "It's freezing. I wouldn't be surprised if it snowed. Wouldn't that be splendid if it did?"

"Not especially," Charles said. "Nothing will make Christmas splendid again now Mother's gone."

William coughed to release the lump that had formed in his throat. "No ... you're right, but I have some news that might cheer you up."

Eleanor and Charles both stared at him but said nothing.

"Do you remember before you went back to school in the summer, Miss Copeland left us to return to her father?"

"Yes, that was a shame. Margaret and Florence loved her," Eleanor said.

"Well, she's back. I managed to talk her into it."

Eleanor smiled. "Excellent. You need a housekeeper. Will she be with us for Christmas?"

"Yes ... but the thing is; she isn't a housekeeper any longer."

Charles sniggered. "Is it because she's walking out with William-Wetherby?"

William's face flushed red. "No, no it isn't. She's now Mrs Jackson. I asked her to marry me and she said yes."

Eleanor and Charles stared at each other, their mouths open, before Charles spoke.

"You! How did that happen? What about William-Wetherby?"

"William-Wetherby's not nearly old enough to be walking out with anyone."

"She can't replace Mother," Eleanor said. "Nobody can."

"And she won't try, I promise, but I couldn't manage on my own and you said yourself

Margaret and Florence like her. Please give her a chance."

"You can forget that. I'm off." Charles leaned over to reach for the door handle before William pulled him back.

"Sit down this minute. You're not going anywhere."

"You just watch me." Charles glared at his father.

"I told you, she's not going to take Mother's place, but I need her to take care of you and your sisters."

"I don't need looking after."

"You're fourteen years old and you'll do as you're told. Now, if I have any more of this from you, you'll be locked in your bedroom."

"You just try." Charles slumped into the seat, his arms folded across his chest. "If I'd known about this, I wouldn't have bothered coming home in the first place."

"What do we call her?" Eleanor asked. "I'm not calling her Mother."

Charles nodded. "Me neither."

"You can call her Mrs Jackson."

Eleanor shook her head and stared out of the window. "She's more like a sister than a mother, I'm not calling her Mrs Jackson. I'll carry on calling her Miss Copeland and pretend this isn't happening."

"You'll do no such thing. She's my wife now, not the housekeeper. If she feels like a sister, I suggest you call her Lydia and put a smile on your face."

CHAPTER NINETEEN

Handsworth, Staffordshire

As Christmas approached, William arrived home with a Christmas tree tucked under his arm.

"Have you only got one?" Eleanor asked as she came down the stairs to meet him.

"One's enough, isn't it? Lydia thought we could have it in the hall."

"No! She can't come in here and change everything. We have one in the window in the front room and one in the back room, you know that."

"I thought we should do something different this year."

"Well, you needn't involve me. You're acting as

if Mother never existed, but I won't forget her and I won't let you change everything she loved."

"What's the matter?" Lydia asked as she came into the hall.

"You're not coming into this house and changing everything Mother did," Eleanor sobbed. "She loved Christmas and we had our routines and I won't let you change them."

"I think it's time you went to your room." William's voice was gruff as he spoke.

"No, wait please," Lydia said. "I didn't mean to change everything, but nobody's told me how things used to be. Will you help me to make this Christmas as special as they used to be?" She held out her hand to Eleanor who was halfway up the stairs.

"Can we have two trees, and all share in decorating them?"

Lydia smiled. "If you want two then of course we can. Come downstairs with me and tell me what we need to do."

William smiled as he watched Eleanor and Lydia walk into the back room. He was about to join them when he was stopped by a knock on the front door.

"Mr Wetherby, what are you doing here?"

William's brow creased as he gestured for Mr Wetherby to come in.

"I've come to talk to you about your son."

"William-Wetherby? Where is he?" William hadn't seen him since the day of the wedding.

"I've no idea, it's Charles I came to see you about. Are you wondering where he is too?"

"He's upstairs in his room. I locked the door myself when he refused to join us for breakfast. I was about to take him something to eat."

"Well, I'd suggest you save your energy. He's currently at Wetherby House."

"What?" William walked to the foot of the stairs and looked up. Charles's bedroom door was still closed.

"He arrived about half an hour ago with some enlightening information."

William didn't wait to listen to Mr Wetherby and raced up the stairs and rattled the door handle on Charles's room. "It's still locked," he called down to Mr Wetherby. "Charles, are you in there?" When he received no answer he reached in his pocket for a bunch of keys and opened the door. As he did, a gust of wind caught him unawares and he stopped where he was. Taking a cautious step into the room, he saw an unmade bed and the heavy navy curtains flapping in the wind.

"What did I tell you?" Mr Wetherby stood behind him and watched as William went to the window and slammed it shut.

"He must have climbed down the drainpipe." William peered through the window to study the roof of the outhouse directly below him. "I'll kill him."

"He was clearly upset when he arrived at Wetherby House," Mr Wetherby said. "He came with a tale about you being married again. Why didn't you tell us?"

"I thought you'd have heard by now."

"I shouldn't hear news like that by chance. It would have been common courtesy for you to tell me."

William glared at Mr Wetherby. "Charles shouldn't have said anything, it's none of his business."

"In the same way my marriage to your aunt was none of your business. It didn't stop you interfering though, did it?"

"That was different ..."

"Yes, it was different. At least I had the decency to wait for two years after your mother died and your aunt wasn't some young housekeeper I took a fancy to."

"And neither is Lydia. In case you've forgotten,

when Harriet died, not only did I lose my wife, I lost the mother of my five children. I needed someone to take care of them and Lydia is perfect. If Charles doesn't like it, he needn't bother coming home again. I'm sick to death of him and you can tell him from me, I don't want to see him unless he can be civil." William walked back onto the landing. "The only reason he ever behaved himself was to please Harriet, but we don't have her disappointment to threaten him with any more."

Mr Wetherby nodded. "All the more reason I suggest you ask this Lydia to pack a change of clothes for him. He can stay with us until he's ready to come home."

Several minutes later, with a bag prepared, William showed Mr Wetherby to the front door. "Thank you for calling. At least it's saved me worrying about him when I eventually realised he was missing."

"You're welcome. Oh, by the way, there's something else your aunt Sarah-Ann asked me to tell you. She had a letter from Mrs Richard yesterday. Your uncle's been admitted to an asylum."

William froze as he glared at Mr Wetherby. "Uncle Richard's in Winson Green and you nearly forgot to tell me?"

"I thought you'd be more concerned about your son than some wayward uncle; besides, he's not in Winson Green, he's at the asylum in Hatton."

"Hatton? What's he doing in there?"

Mr Wetherby waved his hand in the air. "Oh he's up to his old tricks again. Has ideas above his station, that sort of thing ..."

William's eyes narrowed. "What do you mean? When did you last see him?"

Mr Wetherby shrugged. "A few weeks ago. Your aunt invited him and his wife to Wetherby House, but I called home while they were there. Just like all the Jacksons he wanted money off me, apparently he's given up work."

"He's getting old. Carrying those bags of coal must have got too much for him. Did you turn him down?"

"Your aunt may have given him a couple of pounds." Mr Wetherby put on his hat. "I must go."

William stretched his foot across the back of the door. "Hold on a minute. You've not liked him for years, did you say something to upset him?"

Mr Wetherby pulled on the door handle. "Why is it always my fault? I told him my money wasn't his to help himself to and that his own family should support him. It's not my fault he had an attack of hysteria and started telling everyone he was the wealthiest man in the area. I made my money through sheer hard work and I won't have anyone telling me they're entitled to it." Mr Wetherby pushed past William and walked onto the driveway. "And that includes you."

At four o'clock on Christmas Eve, William closed the workshop and arrived home to find Lydia in the kitchen making some mulled wine.

"That smells nice," he said. "What's the occasion?"

Lydia put her finger to her lips and closed the door behind him. "William-Wetherby and Charles have both come home for Christmas. They're in the back room with the girls."

William's eyes widened. "Is that good news or bad? What sort of moods are they in?"

"Good I think. They seem to be as thick as thieves and when they arrived they both wished me a Merry Christmas."

William let out a deep sigh. "I hope you're right, I so much want us to be a family. Perhaps I'd better go and see them."

"Why don't you wait until the mulled wine is ready? We're expecting some more visitors."

Lines formed on William's forehead as he studied Lydia.

"Eleanor went next door earlier to invite your sister in. She's coming for a Christmas drink at five o'clock with Mr Diver and the girls. Eleanor said it was the sort of thing her mother would do and she doesn't like the fact you're not speaking to each other."

William smiled and put his arms around Lydia. "What would I do without you? Thank you."

CHAPTER TWENTY

With winter now a memory, the sun streamed through the window of the morning room as William finished his breakfast. He drained the last of the tea from his cup and was about to leave when Lydia joined him and handed him a letter. He gave it a cursory glance and tossed it onto the table before standing up.

"Aren't you going to open it?" Lydia asked as she sat down.

William shook his head. "I'll open it tonight."

"That won't change the contents and it might be good news."

"You don't believe that any more than I do. We know it's from the school and it's not the sort of thing I want at the start of a busy week."

"You may be surprised. Charles was on his best behaviour when he left here after Christmas. Pass me the letter and I'll read it."

William reluctantly handed her the letter and she read it slowly. "You were right, he's in trouble again. The headmaster wants to see you tomorrow."

William's shoulders sagged. "What's he done this time?"

"Run away."

"Where to? Have they found him?"

"I think so."

William's face was red. "What's he playing at? It's as if he's deliberately trying to get expelled."

Lydia took William's hands. "Calm down. It might not come to that."

"It will. He never wanted to go to school in the first place and the only way we managed to keep him there was by telling him his mother didn't want him home if he misbehaved. With her gone, we've no deterrent."

"But he's in his last year, and it's not long until his exams."

"I imagine that's why he's doing it. God, I could screw his neck."

William noticed Mr Ball in the office when he

arrived, but went straight to the workshop to switch on the machines. As he checked the last machine, Mr Ball joined him.

"Can I have a word with you in the office?" The tone of Mr Ball's voice left William in no doubt that the request was not optional.

"What can I do for you?" William remained standing and watched the top of Mr Ball's balding head as he sat down.

"I won't beat about the bush," Mr Ball said. "I'm giving you notice that I'm leaving the business."

William gasped and took a deep breath before he found his voice. "Why? What's happened?"

"I told you a year ago, almost to the day as it happens, that despite my reservations about Mr Copeland, I'd give him a trial run. I left you in no doubt about my feelings towards him and how he was abusing us. I thought you'd put a stop to it, but last month I found out you've married his daughter. What were you thinking of?"

"Who told you?"

"He did. He wrote trying to swindle more business out of me ... as a result of being part of the family."

William's nostrils flared. "He had no right to do that, he's in London now and I married his daughter with his blessing. There were no conditions attached, at least not as far as the business was concerned."

"I don't know where he's living, but I've told you before, you can't trust men like him. What you do in your private life is your own business, but frankly I've had enough. He's likely to be back and won't take no for an answer. I can't stay and watch my investment wasted on his order book."

William took a seat and wiped his hands on his trouser legs. "I made an agreement with him not to trouble you again. I'll talk to him."

"I would suggest you do that anyway, but whatever you do, it won't change my mind. I've spoken to my solicitor and based on the money I initially put into the business, we estimate you'll owe me one thousand two hundred pounds."

A cold chill ran through William's body. "How much? You only put four hundred pounds in."

"That was when it was a fledgling business struggling to survive. It's established now, which is in no small part down to me. Also, for that price I'd let you keep trading as Ball and Jackson."

"Of course I'd need to keep the name, but I'll need to get the figure verified. Where am I going to find that sort of money? As you're aware, we've invested everything in machinery, property and stock. I don't have it to give you."

"You'll have to find yourself a new partner. If they pay one thousand two hundred pounds into the business, you give it to me and you're back where you started."

"Where will I get another partner from?"

"You'll have to advertise … or you could ask among the brethren at the Masonic lodge."

William stared at his partner. "How did you know about that? I've told nobody outside the organisation."

"I make it my business to know about the people I work with; I also happen to have a close friend who's a member at your lodge."

"Who? That information's supposed to be confidential."

"Never you mind, but it might be worth asking around for a new partner. In the meantime, I appreciate you can't pay me until you have one and so I'll post an advertisement to help things along."

William stood up and stared down at his partner. "Can't we sort this out? I thought we were getting along well, the business is in profit and the order books are full …"

"I told you last year it was either him or me. Since I learned of your marriage I've found another position and I'd be foolish to turn it down."

"Where are you moving to?" William spoke to

make conversation while he thought of the implications.

"I've been offered a partnership in a brass foundry in Birmingham. It's a much bigger concern than here with potential for growth and so it feels like a better way to invest my money. The growth phase is over here and things will plateau over the next few years."

William closed his eyes and took a deep breath. *Can today get any worse?*

When he arrived home that evening, Eleanor was preparing the tea.

"Are you on your own? Where is everyone?"

"Margaret and Florence are next door and William-Wetherby isn't home yet."

"Where's Lydia?"

"She got a letter this morning to say her father isn't well and so she's gone to visit him."

"So he's in Birmingham?" William thought he was speaking to himself and was surprised when Eleanor answered him.

"No, she said she was going to London."

"London! On her own? Why didn't anyone come and tell me?"

Eleanor shrugged. "She left in a hurry; she said it was serious."

"But she had no right to go without asking me first. Even your mother wouldn't have done that." William stopped when he realised what he'd said. That was precisely what Harriet had done, and he hadn't seen her again.

"She told me to tell you not to worry and said she'd write when she's coming home."

"Do you know what's the matter with him?"

Eleanor shook her head. "She didn't say."

"Well, let's hope it's nothing trivial. That man is more trouble than he's worth."

CHAPTER TWENTY-ONE

As the dawn light found its way through the gap in the curtains the following morning, William struggled to open his eyes. Surely he had only just fallen asleep. Not that it was any excuse to stay where he was. He needed to have the machines running in the workshop before he left for Birmingham and his appointment with the headmaster at ten o'clock.

By the time he reached the school his stomach was in knots, but after spending thirty minutes with the headmaster and being publicly escorted from the building with his son, he could feel the blood pounding though his head.

"You wait until I get you home." He spoke to

Charles through clenched teeth. "I have never been so humiliated in my life."

"Don't blame me," Charles said. "I told you years ago I didn't want to go to school, but you took no notice of me. Don't worry though, once we're in Handsworth you won't see me again."

"Don't think you're walking the streets every day getting into trouble, because you're not. You'll go and find yourself a job tomorrow and start repaying some of the money Mr Wetherby's wasted on your education."

"I'm not getting a job, I'm going to sea."

William's face was crimson. "Don't be ridiculous, we live in Birmingham. You've never seen the sea. What's given you that stupid idea?"

"It's not stupid. Mr Wetherby's brother used to talk about it when he was here and it's what I want to do."

"You're not old enough to go to sea, whether you want to or not. If you disappear and I have to call the police, you'll be in serious trouble."

At six o'clock the following morning, William marched into Charles's bedroom and dragged him out of bed.

"Don't think you're staying in there. You're

coming with me to see Mr Wetherby before he leaves for work. I'm not explaining to him why you're not at school."

"What time is it?" Charles rubbed his eyes to open them.

"Time you were up. I want you downstairs in five minutes."

Ten minutes later they sat side by side in the carriage heading towards Wetherby House.

"I wouldn't blame Mr Wetherby if he took a stick to you the way you've abused his generosity," William said. "All you had to do was stay at school for another six months and you'd be finished and with some qualifications behind you. All you'll be fit for now is a labourer. Your mother would be furious."

Charles stared at the scars on his hands from previous canings but said nothing. Once the carriage pulled into the driveway of Wetherby House, William leaned forward to open the door.

"Mr Wetherby's about to climb into his carriage, he must have a busy day planned. You'll be the last person he wants to see. You'd better be on your best behaviour." William pulled Charles from the carriage and marched him up to Mr Wetherby.

"What's all this?" Mr Wetherby frowned.

"Charles has something to tell you, haven't you, boy?"

The lad stood with his hands clasped in front of him, staring at the ground.

"I told you to tell Mr Wetherby what you've been up to."

Charles's brown eyes were wide as he pleaded with the older man. "They were beating me at school and so I ran away."

Mr Wetherby addressed William. "Has he been expelled?"

"He has. The headmaster said his behaviour had become intolerable. He won't give him any more chances."

"What had you done to warrant the beatings?" Mr Wetherby's eyes were like slits as he stared at Charles.

"Nothing. I swear. They pick on me for no reason ..."

"Who? The teachers?"

Charles nodded.

"Did you speak to the headmaster?" Mr Wetherby asked William.

"I went to see him, but he did all the talking. It seems Charles has gone from one extreme to the other. Rather than fighting with half the school, he's become the class clown and enjoys nothing better than disturbing the rest of the class with his tomfoolery."

Mr Wetherby turned to Charles, the lines on his face softer than they had been. "And they've expelled you for being a little high-spirited? Let me go and talk to the headmaster."

"Please, Mr Wetherby, I don't want to go back. Please don't make me. I want to go to sea. Your brother told me all about it when he was last here and that's what I want to do."

"You're still too young to go to sea, but I'll tell you what." A small smile crossed Mr Wetherby's lips. "Why don't you go back to school and behave yourself for six months. If you can do that, I'll pay the indenture for you to become an apprentice as a ship's mate."

"You'll do that for him?" William stared at Mr Wetherby, his eyes wide.

"This is his last chance. If he doesn't make it to the end of school, there'll be no apprenticeship for him." He turned to Charles. "Is that understood?"

Charles nodded. "Thank you, Mr Wetherby."

CHAPTER TWENTY-TWO

William cupped his hands together and plunged them into the water before splashing it over his face. At least it was easier getting out of bed now the mornings were brighter. When he arrived downstairs the maid had taken in some mail and left it on the breakfast table. He flicked through the letters until he came to one that had been posted in London the day before. A smile crossed his face as he recognised Lydia's handwriting. How he hoped she was coming home; he'd missed her more than he would have imagined. He tore open the envelope but his smile dropped as he read. Lydia was coming home but only because Mr Copeland was dead. A part of him wished he could be sorry, but the truth was the man had caused him too much trouble to deserve sympathy.

As soon as he finished work, William took his carriage down to Birmingham to meet her from the train station. He saw her before she noticed him and he couldn't help staring. She seemed so young and vulnerable standing alone with her small case. After a few seconds, she saw him and walked over.

"Welcome home." William put his arm around her, but Lydia pulled away.

"Can we go home? It's been a long day and I'm tired."

"Of course we can, I've missed having you here. How are you feeling?"

Lydia shrugged. "How do you expect when I've just lost my father?"

"I'm sorry. It must be difficult, I know how hard it was when I lost Mother."

Lydia said nothing.

"When's the funeral?"

Lydia gazed up at William, her eyes moist. "I'm not going back."

"Not going back? Who's making the arrangements?"

"The doctor offered to speak to the undertaker. He'll have a pauper's funeral. No one will expect me to attend."

"So there'll be no mourners?"

"The doctor said he'll find some mutes. After the way he treated everyone, it's all he deserves."

William stopped, confusion clearly showing on his face.

"Don't look at me like that," Lydia said. "You didn't have to live with him all those years. I did what I had to, I won't do any more."

When William arrived in the office the following morning, Mr Ball's door was closed and it sounded as if he had someone in with him. William shrugged and continued into the workshop but an hour later, while he was engrossed in finishing a batch of rivets, Mr Ball called for him.

"Mr Jackson, can I introduce Mr White; potentially your new partner." William offered his hand to the tall, thin man with a dark pencil-thin moustache that matched his neatly trimmed hair. "Mr White is searching for a small business to invest in," Mr Ball continued. "I've taken him through everything to show him what an excellent company he'd be buying into."

"I hope you like what you've seen so far," William said. "Would you like me to show you the workshop?"

The tour was brief and within five minutes the three men were back in the office.

"I'm sure you have a promising business here," Mr White said. "My problem is that I'm not sure this is the type of business I'm looking for."

"Then what are you looking for?" Creases formed in William's brow.

"That's what I'm trying to determine."

Mr Ball walked around his desk to face Mr White. "You didn't express any concerns earlier. Has something changed?"

"Not at all, but I'd like some time to think things through. One thousand two hundred pounds is a lot of money."

"It is, but you were aware of the price before you joined us today. I'm sure the information I've shared must have reassured you about the business."

"I still need more time. I'll return by the end of the week with my decision." Mr White picked up his hat and bid them farewell.

"What was that all about?" William said after he left.

"I'm sure I've no idea. He was full of enthusiasm when he arrived and I expected to close the deal today. This process has dragged on for long enough, I need my money."

"Is there any way I can make you change your mind?" William asked. "I found out yesterday that Mr Copeland's died."

"I'm sorry, but it's too late. I've made a commitment to the brass foundry and I have to honour it. I need Mr White to sign the agreement. If he hasn't made up his mind by the end of the week, what would you say about reducing the amount he needs to pay?"

"How much were you thinking? I can't pay one thousand two hundred pounds to you if he won't give me that much."

Mr Ball nodded. "No, I realise that, but how about if I only ask you for one thousand one hundred pounds and we ask Mr White for one thousand pounds? That way we've both dropped our price by one hundred pounds."

The frown on William's face deepened. "Can I afford that? We've bought the properties in Duddeston, don't forget."

"I've not forgotten and I've gone through the books. You shouldn't have any trouble finding one hundred pounds."

"As long as you're sure, but I don't want to offer it unless we have to."

~

Birmingham, Warwickshire.

As soon as Mr White left the workshop, he turned left and walked towards a suburb of Birmingham. He wasn't a beer-drinking man but the public house in Nechells had become a convenient meeting point. Mr White hesitated in the doorway as he saw his new business associate at the corner table with a single pint of ale in front of him. Taking a deep breath, he marched towards him.

"Well?" His acquaintance spoke before he had the chance to sit down.

"I've delayed things until the end of the week."

"Did they suspect anything?"

Mr White shook his head. "Not a thing. They were ready to sign the papers and I took them completely by surprise. I think Mr Ball's keen to leave and so they should drop the price."

The man in the corner nodded. "You've done well. Go back next week but don't sign anything until you speak to me again."

CHAPTER TWENTY-THREE

Handsworth, Staffordshire

Mr Wetherby picked up his glass of port before reclining in his chair and stretching his legs under the dining table. He looked first to William Junior on his right and then to Mr Mountford sitting opposite, before he allowed himself to smile.

"You're looking pleased with yourself," Mr Mountford said as he put his own port on the table.

"I've had some good fortune this week and I wanted to share it with you. I was talking to Mr Smyth at the offices of the Artisans Dwelling Company and he told me a number of the enclosures in Lapworth are going to be auctioned."

"Lapworth?" William Junior said. "What do you want to buy some land down there for? It's miles away."

Mr Wetherby put his port down on the table and stood up. "Have you got no brains? Who do you think owns most of the land at the moment?"

William Junior stared at his father blankly.

"Come on, use some common sense. The land is owned by the aristocracy. Haven't you ever realised how they make their money? Do you think they work sixteen hours a day, six days a week only to earn enough money to survive? Of course they don't. They own half the country and let it out to farmers who work the land and pay them a handsome rent for the privilege."

"So you're hoping to become part of the landed gentry?" Mr Mountford laughed. "Not a day too soon if you want my opinion. You'll make an excellent country squire."

"I thought so too," Mr Wetherby said. "I've had an excellent year this year and I want to invest the money wisely."

"Will they let people like us buy land?" William Junior asked.

"What do you mean, people like us?" Mr Wetherby glared at his son. "People like us are the future of this country and don't you forget it. I'm going to Lapworth tomorrow to see what's available. Would either of you care to join me?"

Mr Mountford let out a sigh. "I wish I could, but Mondays are always busy and I'll be needed at the factory."

"William Junior, what about you? I'm sure you can leave Mr Abbott in charge, he practically runs the place at the moment anyway."

William Junior's brow furrowed before he answered. "Yes, why not. What time are you leaving?"

"I expect it will take a couple of hours to get there and so we should aim to leave by eight o'clock. That'll give us time to explore the area before we need to leave."

At precisely eight o'clock the next morning Mr Wetherby was waiting in the carriage for William Junior. He arrived a minute later looking flustered.

"Sorry I'm late," he muttered as he climbed in beside his father.

"You need to sort yourself out." Mr Wetherby glanced at his pocket watch as the carriage started to move. "You're never going to be successful if you're always late."

"I was one minute late and it wasn't for anything important."

"I don't like your tone. This meeting is important and if you don't think it is, perhaps you'd better get out now."

William Junior glared at his father before he turned to face the window. "I'm sure the land will still be there when we arrive."

Mr Wetherby and William Junior left the rows of back-to-back houses in silence, not speaking until they approached the open fields planted with crops that were bringing life to the previously barren soil. Mr Wetherby studied the small farms that dotted the landscape.

"I'm hoping to buy plots with farmhouses. There's one over there. They're what make the money."

"How are you going to manage them?" William Junior said. "You won't have time to travel every week to collect the rents."

"I'll arrange for someone to do that for me; it's not difficult nowadays. I do wonder what they taught you at school, too much Latin and not enough common sense, I'd say."

"Nothing about farming, that's for sure."

By half past ten they had passed a number of

smallholdings but had seen no sign of the village church or shop.

"Are you sure the driver knows where he's going?" William Junior asked. "We've been on this road for hours."

"Don't exaggerate. The postmistress at Hockley Heath said it was about a mile down here and then the second turning on the right. So far we've only passed one road. Stop being so impatient."

~

Lapworth, Warwickshire.

The turning into Lapworth was more of a track than a road, with hedgerows brushing each side of the carriage.

"Are you sure this is right?" William Junior asked.

"The sign said Church Lane and so you have to assume there'll be a church down here somewhere."

After five hundred yards the walls of an ancient building reared up before them.

"My word," Mr Wetherby said. "Look at that, and in the middle of nowhere as well." The driver stopped and they climbed out to admire the church with its imposing stone walls and impressive spire.

Mr Wetherby went to the door and rattled the handle.

"It's locked. Where does everyone live around here?"

"We passed a few houses on Church Lane."

"They were rather grand. Come with me and we'll see if we can find anywhere else."

Within a couple of minutes, they'd found the rectory, a school hidden behind the church and a post office. They went into the post office.

"Good day." Mr Wetherby raised his hat to the postmistress. "I believe there's some land near here being auctioned off. Could you tell me where I might find it?"

The postmistress smiled. "That'll be the land towards Bushwood. You need to go past the church and when you reach the junction, bear left until you meet the Stratford Road. Most of the land being auctioned is to the left and ends when you reach Bushwood Lane. The best place to go is the Royal Oak Inn. You'll pass it if you go that way and I expect you'll find who you want in there."

"This place is full of surprises," Mr Wetherby said as they returned to the carriage. "First a magnificent church and now an inn. I hope we can find refreshment for ourselves and the horses."

Twenty minutes later, Mr Wetherby and

William Junior were sitting in front of a roaring fire, each with a pint of ale, waiting for a couple of pies.

"Not a bad place this." William Junior cast his eyes around the small room with a bar across one corner. "At least you know there's somewhere to come if you do buy the land. I hope the sales agent doesn't arrive in a hurry, I'd like to finish my food before he does."

"Is that all you think about? Don't forget we have to get home yet and it's taken us the best part of three hours to get here."

"It'll be quicker going back; it always is."

As they spoke, Mr Wetherby noticed a man come into the bar. He was dressed in a tweed jacket and trousers, not at all like the locals.

"I reckon that's him," Mr Wetherby said. "I'll go and introduce myself before anyone else does."

William-Junior nodded but stayed where he was.

"Good day to you, sir," Mr Wetherby said. "Might I be right in thinking you're the gentleman to talk to about the land for sale?"

"I would indeed, Mr Jacobs is the name. I was going to have something to eat before heading over to the fields."

"Please, come and join my son and I. We're not

familiar with the area and so we'd value any information."

Mr Wetherby ordered and paid for the agent's dinner and ale drink before he escorted him to the table.

"What can you tell us about the lots?" he asked.

"We have six in total," Mr Jacobs said. "As you would imagine some are better than others, mainly on account of how much clay they have in the soil."

"Do any of them include houses?"

"Lots five and six do, but they're only small farmhouses with tenant farmers in."

"I need to view them first, although I was hoping to find something with more substantial accommodation. Is there anything suitable?"

Mr Jacobs shook his head. "No, nothing at the moment, but it's only a matter of time before they auction off some of the large farmhouses in Bushwood. I'll show you if you're interested and keep you informed."

CHAPTER TWENTY-FOUR

Handsworth, Staffordshire

As they waited for Mr White, William paced the floor of the office while Mr Ball sorted some papers at his desk.

"Will you sit down, man," Mr Ball said. "How do you expect me to concentrate?"

William took the seat opposite him. "What if he doesn't want to join us? What will you do?"

"We need to make sure that doesn't happen. I need those documents signed and if we have to lower our price, so be it."

"We can't go much lower ..."

The sound of the door announced Mr White's arrival.

Mr Ball stood up to shake Mr White's hand and waited for him to take a seat. "Have you made a decision?"

Mr White lowered his gaze. "I have, but it may not be what you want to hear."

William's stomach dropped. "Go on."

"I'd like to have a trial period with the company, to see if it suits what I'm looking for." William's eyes flitted to Mr Ball.

"A trial was not what we had in mind," Mr Ball said. "We need someone to buy into the business immediately."

"We do indeed," William said. "Thank you for your visit, but we'll have to advertise again."

Mr White held up his hands. "Please, gentlemen, let me explain. I've spoken to a solicitor who's advised me to take out an Agreement as to Future Partnership. I'd buy into the business as if I were a partner, but after a specified period of time I could either withdraw, in which case I get my money back, or else we formalise the partnership."

"That would leave me no better off," William said. "I'd be unsure whether I had a partner or not and what would happen if you decided not to stay? I wouldn't have the money to pay you because I need to give it to Mr Ball."

"If I chose to leave, you take another partner to

pay me, in much the same way as you are doing now. Also, as I'd only be signing up for a trial period, I'd work for a nominal fee of one pound per week for the duration of the trial."

"How much would you propose to pay in?" Mr Ball asked. "We'd be looking for the full amount."

"Five to six hundred pounds."

William turned to Mr Ball who returned his glance before he glared at Mr White. "We're looking for one thousand two hundred pounds. We can't settle for five hundred."

Mr White stared down at his feet. "I'm not going to be able to manage that."

Mr Ball ran his finger under his collar and stretched his neck. "When you first came to see me, I was clear with you how much money we needed and you didn't raise any objections. Now you're acting as if you're hearing the figure for the first time."

"I'm afraid I underestimated the burden it would put on me."

"Well we can't accept such a low bid and so I'll wish you good day." William turned to leave the office.

"I could manage eight hundred pounds," Mr White said as he stepped across William.

"That's still not close to one thousand two hundred, is it?"

"One moment, Mr Jackson." Mr Ball was on his feet. "You're making this hard work for all of us, Mr White. I thought we'd made it clear that we can't go so low. Mr Jackson, would you be happy for us to reduce our asking price to eleven hundred pounds?"

William glared at Mr White. "I wouldn't be happy, but if it secures the deal, I'm prepared to accept it."

"Mr White?"

Mr White studied both men. "If you bring it down to one thousand, you have yourself a deal."

William hesitated, but Mr Ball held out his hand to Mr White. "I'll ask my solicitor to draw up a contract immediately."

Mr White smiled as he left the workshop. His associate would be pleased with him. All he needed to do now was walk into Nechells and tell him what he'd agreed. His confident stride faltered as he opened the tavern door to see a pair of steely eyes staring directly at him. Pausing for breath, he walked over to the table and perched on a nearby stool.

"Well?" the man seated opposite said.

"They won't go lower than one thousand pounds."

The man snarled and took a mouthful of ale. "Did you offer five hundred like I told you?"

"I did, but they were ready to throw me out. They're not happy with a thousand."

"But they agreed?

Mr White nodded. "They did, or at least Mr Ball did. Mr Jackson wasn't happy."

"Very well. Go ahead and get the agreement drawn up and let me know when they need the money."

As Saturday evening approached, all William wanted to do was go home and pour a stiff drink. He watched the men in the workshop tidy up their workspaces before he went into the office to put all the paperwork back in the safe.

"Goodnight, Mr Jackson." William glanced up to see the men filing past the office, one after the other, each smiling as they left.

"Goodnight," William replied before glancing

at the clock. Only half past four. He should be home well in time for tea. He put on his coat and picked up the keys from the desk, but as he reached for his hat he heard the outside door open. Putting his hat on the desk, he walked to the entrance hall.

"Mr Wetherby. What are you doing here at this hour?"

"I was passing and thought I hadn't seen you for a few weeks."

"I'm just on my way out."

"I won't keep you, I only came to ask after Mr Ball. I believe he may have found you a new partner."

"Yes, how did you know?"

"I saw him at the Conservative Association. Now he's moving down to Birmingham I expect I'll see more of him. So who is it? Anyone I know?"

William sighed. "A fellow called White. Does it ring any bells?"

Mr Wetherby shook his head.

William perched on the edge of his desk. "That's a shame. I hope I'm doing the right thing."

"What's the matter with him?"

"I can't put my finger on it but for some reason I have a bad feeling about him. He won't sign a full partnership agreement and wants an Agreement as to Future Partnership. If he decides he doesn't want to stay, it could land me in trouble further down the line."

"Why don't you call it off until you find the right person?"

"Mr Ball's keen to move and is insisting we sign the deal. Do you think I should stop him?"

Mr Wetherby shrugged. "How much is he putting in?"

"Not as much as we wanted. Only one thousand pounds."

Mr Wetherby raised his eyebrows. "Is that all? I gave you considerably more than that."

William's forehead creased. "It's only for a forty per cent share, not the full value of the business. Anyway, you look pleased with yourself, what have you been up to?"

A grin spread across Mr Wetherby's face. "I've bought some land and a couple of tenant farms near Bushwood."

William raised his eyebrows. "What on earth have you done that for?"

Mr Wetherby shook his head. "Am I the only one who can see the sense in it? I own the land and the farmers pay me to live there while they work it. It can only go up in value too. That's how the aristocracy have made their money for centuries."

William nodded. "I suppose they have. How much land did you buy?"

"I went to the auction earlier this week and bought two plots. Between them I've approximately two hundred acres of land and a couple of farms. That's nothing yet though. The auctioneer showed me some magnificent farmhouses in Bushwood itself. He expects to sell soon and I've got my eye on one of them for when the time comes."

William sighed. *If only I could ask Mr Wetherby to be a partner. Why did Harriet upset him so much?*

CHAPTER TWENTY-FIVE

William forced himself out of bed and threw some cold water onto his face. Despite the early warmth of the sun, he shivered and grabbed the towel before putting on his clothes and going downstairs. Lydia was in the kitchen preparing breakfast and as soon as she heard him she brought a pot of tea into the morning room, placing it on the table.

"Do you want one egg or two?" she asked.

William felt a familiar knot in his stomach and shook his head. "Not today. A cup of tea and slice of bread will be enough."

"You're not still worried about Mr White, are you?"

"How can I be anything but worried? By ten

o'clock this morning the deed will be done and I'll have myself a new partner ... or at least one in principle. Mr Ball was such a godsend and to lose him for no reason ..." He had never told Lydia the reason he left was because of her father. It was for the best if it stayed that way.

"Sometimes these things happen," she said. "I'm sure you'll see a different side to Mr White once the paperwork's signed."

As soon as he finished breakfast, William took the carriage to his solicitor's office. By the time he arrived Mr Ball was waiting for him although there was no sign of Mr White.

"I don't know why you're so worried," Mr Ball said. "It's me he owes the money to."

"I think I'm more worried about him turning up than I am about him staying away. Can't I persuade you to change your mind? We can have the dissolution reversed and you need have no fear of Mr Copeland troubling you again."

Mr Ball flashed a rare smile. "Thank you for your confidence in me, but no, it's too late. The brass foundry have been more than generous in the time they've given me to sort this out."

"Well, if you do the same for them as you did for our business, they were right to wait. When I lost Harriet, I thought I'd lose the business as well, but thanks to you, not only have I survived, the business has grown. I hope Mr White can keep it up."

Mr Ball nodded towards the window as Mr White hurried past. "He's here now. Let's get this done with."

William returned to the workshop alone and went into the office, closing the door behind him. Mr White had promised to be in first thing in the morning and he had no choice but to trust him. He flicked through the paperwork on the desk in front of him. Several order forms; a couple from new customers, and more invoices that needed sending out. Despite his problem with numbers, he could tell they were for sizable amounts and he smiled. Everything would be fine.

As he pushed himself up from the chair, there was a knock on the office door and Mr Wetherby showed himself in.

"You are here. I called earlier, but the foreman said you'd gone into Birmingham."

William sighed. "Yes, Mr Ball signed his share of the business over to Mr White this morning. There's no going back now."

"Splendid. You need to think of the future not the past. That's my motto."

William grunted. "Quite. What can I do for you?"

Mr Wetherby took a seat and indicated for William to do the same. "I've called about Charles."

William gave a heavy sigh. "What's he done now?"

"Nothing I'm aware of, but he called on me yesterday. Did he say anything to you?" When William shook his head, Mr Wetherby continued. "You may recall, when he was expelled from school, I promised him that if he returned and caused no more trouble, I'd fund his apprenticeship in the merchant navy. Well, he hasn't forgotten and still has his heart set on the idea. I've come to tell you that I plan on making an application for him."

"He was only fifteen last week, you can't let him go yet."

"As I remember, you were only fourteen when you started your apprenticeship."

"That was different." William spluttered as he spoke. "I didn't leave home and go to sea."

"Maybe not, but he's at the age all young boys learn their trade. You can't have him lagging behind. Besides, I'd have thought you'd be pleased he won't be coming back to live with you."

William sighed. "Perhaps you're right, but it feels like such a big step."

"He won't go straight away. I have to make an application and they may not accept him yet."

"Of course they'll have him. A healthy and willing young lad. They're dragging any unsuspecting drunk off the streets and press-ganging them into service. How long do you think it will take?"

"He's at school until December and so I'll ask for consideration after Christmas."

William nodded. "By the time he's been home for a few weeks, I'll probably be glad to see the back of him."

CHAPTER TWENTY-SIX

Charles lay in bed with his eyes open. The day he'd been waiting for since he'd been about ten years old was finally here. It was still dark, but he sensed it was getting close to morning. Was it too early to get up? As his patience wore thin, he climbed out of bed and pulled on his trousers. The winter hadn't been too cold, but he still hurried to button his shirt and jacket. He lit the candle on the table from the small length of the nightlight on the wall and set it down. *Have I got everything?* He held one of his bags close to the light, but it was still too dark to see. *Why won't they let me have a gas lamp?*

He was about to go downstairs when the

bedroom door swung open and a moment later William-Wetherby peered round it.

"You're up. I thought you may be making the most of your last night in a comfortable bed."

"The beds on the ship will be fine for me. I was too excited to sleep. What time is it?"

"Five past six," William-Wetherby said. "I need to go to work soon and so I thought I'd come and say cheerio."

"Are you having breakfast before you go?"

"If that's what you call a couple of slices of yesterday's bread and butter."

Charles laughed. "You've persuaded me; I'll come down with you."

Once downstairs William-Wetherby lifted a loaf of bread from the pantry and set it between them on the table in the morning room. "You'd better get used to eating meagre portions."

"Why does everyone think going to sea will be such a hardship? The only person we know who's been is Mr Wetherby's brother and he was perfectly happy."

William-Wetherby shrugged. "Why else do they struggle to find willing recruits? They must love you."

"Of course they'll love me." Charles grinned as

he bit into his bread. "What will you do when I'm gone? Will you stay here?"

William-Wetherby put down his bread and placed his hands on the table. "I'm not sure. I must say, in many ways I envy you getting away from here. I can't take much more of seeing Father and Lydia together. She promised she wanted to be with me. How could she have lied?"

Charles took another bite of bread. "Father has more money than you."

"Is she that cheap? Would she really marry a man twice her age for the money?" William-Wetherby shook his head. "I thought she was better than that."

"Why don't you go and stay with Sid and Mrs Storey in Birmingham again? I know she's Mr Wetherby's sister, but you'd be away from Father, you wouldn't have to get up at this ridiculous hour either."

William-Wetherby grimaced. "I don't know. You will write and tell us how to contact you, won't you? If I do decide to leave, I'll need to let you know."

"You're the first on my list. I want all the news from here too, I need to know what I'm missing."

"Are you still here?" Lydia said to William-

Wetherby as she walked into the morning room. "You'll be late."

Charles laughed as William-Wetherby rolled his eyes.

"I'm sure Mr Wetherby will understand on a day like today. Not that he'll know," William-Wetherby said.

"You're right. He's picking me up at eight o'clock to take me to the train station in Birmingham. You'll easily be in the office before he arrives."

"I will, but I still better go." William-Wetherby landed a soft punch on the shoulder of his brother. "You take care, I don't want to hear you've been washed overboard."

Charles laughed. "You won't get rid of me that easily. I'll be in touch."

With William-Wetherby gone, Charles went back to his bedroom, closely followed by Lydia.

"Now, what's in your bag?" Lydia asked. "Did you pack those extra trousers I left on your bed?"

"They wouldn't fit."

"Wouldn't fit?" Lydia studied the items on the floor. "What are you taking? And how many bags do you have? The letter confirming your apprenticeship said you'll only have a small locker on the ship and belongings should be packed into one small bag. You can't take three."

Charles flopped down onto the bed. "I'm not leaving anything behind that reminds me of Mother. What if you move house while I'm away and they go missing?"

"Don't talk silly, we won't be moving anywhere."

"I'm still not leaving them. Do I really need three pairs of trousers?"

Lydia put her hands on her hips and shook her head. "Has it occurred to you that you'll get wet on the ship? You'll be glad of dry clothes."

"Well, what do I leave?"

Lydia opened each bag and peered inside. "I'm sure you don't need to take games with you. These wooden blocks can stay ..."

"They were ..."

"I know, the first present your mother gave you, but what are you going to do with them on a ship? Let me have all these toys and I promise I'll keep them safe until you come home."

As Lydia left him, Charles fingered the small metal train now lying in the middle of the stack of building blocks. *Mother gave me this for Christmas years ago.* He smiled at the thought. *I think I behaved myself for the rest of the day after that.* Picking it up he felt the weight before he slid it into the top of his bag. *I can't leave here with nothing to remind me of her.*

Five minutes later, Charles walked down the stairs with one small bag in his hand. William was waiting in the hall with Eleanor, Margaret and Florence.

"So, son, this is it. You'll likely be a man by the time you're back. Five years is a long time."

"That's if I decide to come home. I may stay on."

"Don't do that." Florence clung to his arm. "We'll all miss you."

"I won't miss him making fun of me." Margaret pouted as she folded her arms across her chest.

"Well, you shouldn't be so serious," Florence said.

Eleanor interrupted. "Come on, you two. No arguing at a time like this. Give Charles a hug. He needs to go in a minute."

"Don't forget to write," Lydia said as Charles pulled away from his sisters and headed for the door. "And tell us which ship you're on and where you're sailing to. We'll try and have letters waiting for you in each port."

Charles shrugged Lydia off as she stroked her hand down the back of his head.

"Don't be like that, we'll miss you," Lydia said. "And be careful in London. Don't go wandering around the docks by yourself or you may find yourself on the wrong ship."

"I'll be fine, stop worrying. I've not lived here for years with being kept at school. Once I'm gone, you'll soon forget about me."

"There's something different about being so far away," William said. "If you ever dock in England while you're on your travels, try and make the effort to come and see us."

"I promise I'll have your room ready and waiting for you," Lydia said.

Charles glanced from one to the other. "I need to go, Mr Wetherby's here."

CHAPTER TWENTY-SEVEN

As William took his seat at the breakfast table, Lydia handed him his letters and joined him.

"You've got one from Charles," she said.

"About time too, he's been gone almost three months." William put a napkin on his lap and reached for the letter from his son. "William-Wetherby had one almost immediately. Let's see what he's got to say for himself."

William read in silence while Lydia put her elbows on the table and rested her chin on her hands. "He's been to America already and he sent this message from Cape Town in South Africa." William smiled. "He said to thank you for the extra trousers, it seems nothing ever dries when you're in the middle of the ocean." William glanced up but the smile fell from his face. "Are you feeling ill again?"

Lydia nodded. "It's not too bad, but enough to put me off my food."

"You don't eat enough as it is. Do you think it could be ...?" He nodded towards her midriff.

"A baby? Yes, I think so." *At least something good's come out of this marriage.*

William's heart sank. "I thought you were being careful?"

"Don't blame me. I thought you'd be pleased." Lydia glared at him.

"I am, I'm sorry, but I've a lot on my plate at the moment. I'll ask the doctor to call. Don't do too much while you feel like you do. I'm sure the maids can manage."

The following Wednesday, it was after seven o'clock before William-Wetherby joined William and Lydia for tea. He hurried into the back room and sat down.

"Sorry I'm late," he said as he helped himself to a slice of bread.

"Has Mr Wetherby been keeping you behind?" William asked.

"No, not exactly, but he is the reason I'm late. I was engrossed listening to a conversation he was having with someone in the workshop."

"I'm sure talking to one of the workmen can't be overly exciting."

William-Wetherby didn't miss the smile William gave to Lydia.

"He wasn't talking to a workman, they'd all gone before this man arrived. I've never seen him before. I was about to leave myself when I overheard them talking about Aunt Charlotte."

William put down the newspaper and gave his son his attention. "What about her?"

"Has it occurred to you that she's been married for almost two years, but is still without a child?"

"William-Wetherby!" Lydia stopped dishing out a plate of stew for him. "That's no conversation for the likes of you."

"I'm sorry, but Father asked what I knew. It appears it is a topic of conversation at Wetherby House. When did you last see Aunt Charlotte? Mr Wetherby says she's suffering from melancholy because she hasn't had a baby."

"What a personal thing to be talking to a stranger about," Lydia said. "Was it a doctor?"

William-Wetherby shook his head. "No, I don't

think so, but he was asking if the man knew of any doctors. They were talking about London."

William blew out a sigh. "I've not seen her for months, but you may be right. Your mother was often cross about how Charlotte had received such a good education, but all she wanted to do was be a mother. I imagine she'll be upset. She always gets everything she wants."

"It's as well we don't see much of her." Lydia put the plate of food down in front of William-Wetherby and rested her hand on her stomach.

William-Wetherby's brow furrowed before he stared at Lydia. "You're not?"

Lydia's face turned scarlet as she nodded. "I'm sorry."

"Sorry! Is that all you can say?" William-Wetherby threw his cutlery onto the table and stood up. "You and ... *him*. How could you?"

"What did you expect?" William said. "We're married."

"I didn't expect you to carry on like that. Especially not you." He spat his words out at Lydia.

"How dare you be so insolent?" William stepped towards his son, but William-Wetherby pushed him away.

"What do you expect? If you think I'm hanging

around while the two of you start a new family, you can forget it. I'm off."

William-Wetherby picked up the last piece of bread before he stormed from the room, slamming the door behind him. Ten minutes later he was in the hall with his belongings packed. With a final glance around the empty hallway, he tossed his keys onto the side table and pulled the front door closed behind him.

CHAPTER TWENTY-EIGHT

Mr Wetherby sat in the carriage and hoped the late hour meant the journey back to Handsworth would be quicker than usual. The fact it was still light outside was probably one of the reasons he had misjudged the time. It was turned eight o'clock by the time he arrived home but, as usual, Sarah-Ann had his tea on the table and his mail stacked in a pile beside it.

"I wasn't expecting you so late," she said.

"No, I'm sorry, but nothing runs smoothly unless I'm there. I despair of William Junior sometimes; he doesn't care about the business the way I do and the whole workshop in Handsworth is underproducing. If I didn't know better I'd question if he really was my son."

"You have to admit, he's never been cut out for that sort of work. He's much more inclined to tell other people what to do rather than do it himself."

"You're right, but God knows I've tried. Anyway, enough of him. What's this here?" He picked up an unusually large letter from the table, and slit open the top. "It's from the auctioneer in Lapworth. He says a farm in Bushwood is about to be auctioned. Not any old farm either." He flicked through several sheets of paper before he passed one to Sarah-Ann. "Bushwood Farm. I'll have to visit this one."

"What are you going to do with that? Surely you don't expect us to move." Sarah-Ann's eyes were wide.

"Of course not, but I've had a few problems with the farms in Lapworth and I need someone to supervise them. It could also be exactly what I need for William Junior."

"What does he know about farming?"

"Nothing, but he won't need to. I'd only need someone to watch over things for me; it's the sort of thing he'd enjoy, parading around looking important. He shouldn't be able to do too much damage."

~

Bushwood, Warwickshire.

The following week, Mr Wetherby and William Junior took the train to Bushwood railway station, where they were met by the auctioneer.

"Mr Wetherby." Mr Jacobs held out his hand to greet them. "How good to see you again. I thought this property would be of interest to you. Have you had a chance to go through the papers?"

"I have indeed."

"As I told you previously, it's one of the largest farms in the area. Only the Lady from Leeds Castle and the Lord of Lapworth Manor himself own larger properties. It's empty and so we can take our time."

The property was larger than Mr Wetherby had imagined. Each of the rooms was generously proportioned and in addition to the family accommodation, the attic contained a series of servants' rooms.

"What do you think?" Mr Wetherby asked William Junior as they waited in the drawing room for Mr Jacobs to join them. William Junior peered out of the window overlooking the ornamental garden at the rear of the property.

"Very nice. When I return to the house on Westminster Road it'll seem quite pathetic."

"I was having similar thoughts and I didn't think many properties could put Wetherby House in the shade. I'm wondering if I could live down here and commute to Handsworth."

"Every day? I wouldn't think so."

Mr Wetherby rubbed his beard. "No, you're right. The trains won't run early enough. I'd end up living in Birmingham all week and coming here on Sunday. Sarah-Ann wouldn't be pleased."

"So what will you do?"

"I'll have to find someone to live here and take care of things for me."

William Junior walked to the fireplace and rested his shoulder on the beamed lintel spanning the six-foot opening over the hearth. "It's a shame William left us, you could have moved him down here out of the way."

"It's more than a shame." Mr Wetherby marched into the dining room. "I could have bought a second house down here with the money I gave him."

"What do you want two houses for?"

Mr Wetherby gave a deep sigh. "I don't, it was a figure of speech. Where's Mr Jacobs got to? I need to talk to him about the price. I need to make sure nobody outbids me."

CHAPTER TWENTY-NINE

Handsworth, Staffordshire

The fact that it was midsummer, but was nevertheless dark outside, reminded William it was time he should be in bed but what was the point? He wouldn't sleep. Lydia had gone upstairs over an hour earlier and he was relieved to be able to sit in the back room on his own. He didn't want to trouble her with his concerns.

How had it come to this? He hadn't heard from Charles for the best part of three months; William-Wetherby had left home without telling him where he was and even Eleanor was mad with him. Harriet wouldn't have let this happen. He took his handkerchief from his pocket and wiped his eyes. He would never love Lydia as much as he had Harriet and he missed her so much. She would know how to handle Mr White, although if she were here, he wouldn't have needed to take the fool man on in the first place. How he wished he had never laid eyes on him. He should demand that Mr Ball come back and put everything right again. It was all his fault.

William stood up and poured another measure of whisky. No, it wasn't Mr Ball's fault. He had no one to blame but himself. He'd left Mr White in charge of the business but his trust had been abused. He needed to understand how much damage he'd done and how he could turn things around, but who could he ask? Not William-Wetherby. Even if he knew where to find him, he couldn't expect any help from him. Not Mr Diver either. Mary-Ann had told him only the other day that Mr Diver was so busy with his own business, they were all moving to Birmingham within the month. How could his sister leave at a time like this? William slumped back down in the chair. What about Mr Wetherby? He was always interested in the business, but wasn't that so he could check up on him? What would he say if things fell apart? He couldn't bear the thought of his pompous voice saying, "I told you so." He downed his whisky and stared at the clock. Ten past two. He needed to go to bed.

The following morning he crawled out of bed and left the house without so much as a word to Lydia. He needed to confront Mr White, but first he needed to check his facts. His partner wasn't in the workshop when he arrived and so once he'd started up the machines, William went into the office and put the account books on the desk. Taking great care, he opened them and stared down at the numbers. They seemed to taunt him as they sat in their columns and as his eyes moved across the rows jumbled in his mind. He put his fingers at the top of the incoming and outgoing columns and worked slowly down the page, but it was no use. The only things on the page that jumped out were subtraction signs and they became more regular as he worked through the book. Were they losing money? How had that happened? William shook his head. Why hadn't Mr White said anything?

It was past ten o'clock when Mr White wandered into the office.

"What time do you call this?" William said. "You've been getting later and later recently."

"I told you weeks ago, I don't want to be a partner in this business. Have you done anything about finding a new partner? I want my money back."

"You have to take some responsibility. If you remember, when Mr Ball decided to move on, he was the one who introduced you to the business. It's about time you started pulling your weight."

"I come in and do my job. It wasn't in my contract to find a new partner."

"But you are contracted to be here from seven in the morning until six in the evening, yet I doubt you've put those hours in since you arrived. You can't pick and choose which parts of the contract you stick to."

"I do more than my fair share ..."

"And as for you doing your job, I would have to question that. I've been looking through the books and at first glance it appears we are running at a loss. How has that happened?"

"Don't blame me. I've done my job. It's your workmanship. It's impossible to sell."

"That's utter nonsense and you know it. You have to take some responsibility for this. You're the one charged with bringing in new business and there's nothing wrong with the quality of the nuts or rivets. If you spotted a problem why didn't you tell me?"

"I didn't come here to argue with you." Mr White placed his case on the desk and reached inside. "I came to bring you this." He handed William a letter.

"What's this?"

"Our most recent agreement runs out in a couple of weeks and I've put it in writing that I want my money by the end of the month."

William took the envelope he was being given and tore it open. "You can't do that. We need another partner in place before you can have your money, and in the meantime, you still need to turn up for work."

"You've had more than enough time to find someone else and if you read the contract we signed, you'll be aware you need to give me my money back."

"Based on the figures I was looking at earlier, you're not having your full one thousand pounds. I was running a thriving business when you arrived, and now it's almost on its knees. You have to pick up your share of the loss in value."

"I'm not taking a penny less than I paid in. The Agreement of Future Partnership document specifically states I would receive exactly what I put in. It also states that a new partner should be found in a timely manner following my request to leave. My solicitor is of the opinion that three months is a perfectly reasonable time to wait."

Despite the warmth of the air, William shivered. "Get out, and don't bother coming back. I'll find another partner myself and you can wait for your money, whether you like it or not."

~

Birmingham, Warwickshire.

As Mr White walked into the snug of the now familiar tavern, he approached the table in the far corner and sat down.

"Do you have the money?" his contact asked.

Mr White curled the rim of his hat between his hands. "He can't pay yet. He hasn't found a new partner and he doesn't have that sort of cash in the business; you've seen to that. Can't you give him more time?"

"I don't think you understand, Mr White. I want one thousand pounds by the end of this month and if it doesn't come from Mr Jackson, I'll expect it from you. Have I made myself clear?"

Mr White jumped at the sound of knuckles cracking and stood up. "Yes, sir. I'll do what I can." He backed away from the table, but didn't turn away until he closed the door behind him.

CHAPTER THIRTY

Handsworth, Staffordshire

The sun glared through the kitchen window and spread into the morning room, but it failed to put a smile on William's face. He held the newspaper up as he scanned the page for the advertisement he had placed for a new partner. There it was, in the third column across about a third of the way down. Not a bad placement. It should attract some attention.

"Is there anything of interest?" Lydia asked as she set a pot of tea on the table.

"No, nothing for you to concern yourself with." He folded the paper and stared at the boiled eggs in front of him before glancing at Lydia. "Aren't you eating?"

"I'll have something later."

"No, I insist, have one of these. You're carrying our baby, you need to eat for two."

Lydia rested her hands on her swollen belly. "Perhaps I will. It's more real now I'm changing shape. I'm so fortunate you take care of me."

The following day, as William drank his tea in the same seat, Lydia collected the post and brought it in. Most were bills, but one was personal. William hurried to slice open the top of the envelope and smiled as he read the contents. Someone called Mr Garrett was interested in the business.

"You look pleased with yourself," Lydia said. "Is it good news?"

"I hope so, I need a new partner for the business and I think I may have found one."

"You didn't say. What happened to the other fellow?"

William grimaced. "You don't want to know, but hopefully this letter means I can give him his marching orders. I must reply immediately and invite him to the workshop."

. . .

A week later, William watched through the window of the office as Mr Garrett climbed down from his carriage. A tall, well-built man with a glorious beard, he was well dressed with a tailored coat and sturdy bowler hat. William smiled as he went to the door to meet him.

"Mr Garrett." William extended his hand. "Thank you for coming. Did you have a satisfactory journey?"

"It wasn't one of the best. Eight o'clock this morning I left Nuneaton and what's the time now? Midday."

"Well, you're here now, come on in. Let me pour you a drink."

"The business seems well established," Mr Garrett said once William had shown him the workshop. "Why do you need a partner?"

"My current partner needs to move away and I can't manage everything myself."

"You could hire someone without them becoming a partner."

William nodded. "Unfortunately, Mr White invested money in the company and he needs it back. I wouldn't get anything from an employee."

"How much are you looking for?" Mr Garrett asked.

"One thousand pounds."

William shuddered as Mr Garrett sucked air through his teeth. "As much as that? I couldn't hope to offer such a sum."

"But you've seen the books and the equipment. We had a positive balance sheet of over three thousand pounds last time the books were audited, including assets of course."

"It's tempting, I can't deny, but I don't have one thousand pounds. The most I could go to is eight hundred."

It was William's turn to suck the air through his teeth. "I can't go so low. You're going to have to let me think about this."

"Well, that's my best offer, it won't be going any higher. Another thing, I might as well tell you now. I'd be a silent partner. In return for the investment, I'd expect a dividend. You'd have to find a clerk to do the bookkeeping."

Once the workers left the workshop that evening, William locked the door behind them and focussed on the accounts spread out on the desk in front of him. He couldn't afford to lose another two hundred pounds, not now Mr White had ruined his balance sheet, but what else could he do? Eight hundred pounds was still a lot of money and he was running out of options.

He sat at the desk for over fifteen minutes

before he stood up. As much as he hated to admit it, he needed to speak to Mr Wetherby.

When he arrived at Wetherby House, he was relieved that Mr Wetherby showed him straight into the front room.

"I don't often see you here," Mr Wetherby said. "What can I do for you?"

Mr Wetherby sat down and stroked his beard as William explained the problem with Mr White.

"It's a dilemma you've got yourself into," Mr Wetherby said once he had finished. "Can't you persuade Mr White to change his mind?"

"I don't think so, but to be honest with you, I don't want him around any more. He's not all he seems and it wouldn't surprise me if he's a crook."

"Do you think he's been stealing from you?"

"I can't say for certain but the men have been working as hard as usual and the orders are still going out and yet the business is making a loss."

"How much do you have in the way of creditors' debts?" Mr Wetherby asked.

William shrugged. "I'm not sure, Mr White deals with that side of things. Several hundred pounds I would think."

"That could be an option. If you assign the book

debts to Mr White, then he gets his money when the creditors pay you."

William nodded in agreement but had no idea what Mr Wetherby was talking about. "Is that usual practice?"

"It is for people who have no other options."

"I'm not sure. I think I'd prefer to accept the offer from Mr Garrett and then at least I can give Mr White some real money. Once he's out of the way, I'll find a more competent bookkeeper and pay him back gradually."

"That'll work if you have time, but I didn't think you did. You said Mr White wants all his money immediately."

"That's what he says but if I give him some now I'm hoping he'll mellow. I'll write to Mr Garrett tomorrow and tell him he's got himself a deal."

CHAPTER THIRTY-ONE

Mr Wetherby walked into the dining room of Wetherby House and surveyed the scene. The table had been set for six and Sarah-Ann had used the best china, but he wasn't sure it was enough. After a moment's thought he disappeared to the kitchen. Where had he put that bottle of champagne? Since Charlotte's wedding he'd been saving it for a special occasion and this felt like it. He found it lying in the back of a cupboard and placed it in a bowl of cold water. The wine merchant in London insisted it should be served cold, but in this weather it was the best he could do.

Twenty minutes later a knock on the front door announced the arrival of William Junior and Olivia. Once their son Henry had been dispatched to the morning room, they joined Mr Wetherby in the front drawing room.

"Are you on your own?" William Junior asked.

"Sarah-Ann and Elizabeth went to change before dinner. They won't be long."

"What about Charlotte and Mr Mountford?" Olivia said.

"They'll be here shortly." Mr Wetherby glanced at his pocket watch. "I have a bottle of champagne chilling and I want everyone to be here before I open it."

William Junior's brow furrowed. "What's the occasion? You haven't mentioned anything to me."

"A spot of business I concluded earlier this week. I wanted to tell you all together."

Within five minutes, Charlotte and Mr Mountford arrived and Mr Wetherby fumbled with the cork in the top of the champagne. A pop signalled it had been released and champagne spilled onto the floor before Mr Wetherby could pour it into a glass.

"The warm weather's made it rather lively." Mr Wetherby handed out the glasses. "It really is better to drink it in the winter, but I didn't want to wait."

"You need an icehouse, Papa," Charlotte said. "All the well-to-do folks have one nowadays."

Mr Wetherby smiled at Sarah-Ann before he replied, "Maybe I'll get one then."

"What's the celebration?" Mr Mountford asked. "Don't tell me you're now a fully paid-up member of the landed gentry."

Mr Wetherby raised his glass in salute. "I am indeed."

William Junior glared at his father. "You bought somewhere without telling me?"

"I travelled down to Lapworth earlier this week and arranged to buy Bushwood Farm. I'll show you all the details later but it has a splendid entrance hall with elaborate staircase, a living room, dining room and drawing room downstairs. On the first floor we have six bedrooms, as well as two WCs and a bathroom."

"And the second floor has accommodation for the servants," William Junior added.

Mr Wetherby nodded. "All the rooms are fitted with gaslights and the servants have two kitchens with modern amenities and a back staircase to the cellar."

"It sounds impressive. What about the land? How much does it come with?" Mr Mountford asked.

"The property itself has stabling to the front and rear as well as fifty acres of pasture, but I also bought another plot of fifty acres to make me one of the biggest landowners in the area."

Mr Mountford raised his glass for the toast. "I look forward to seeing it. It sounds like Charlotte will have the use of an icehouse sooner than she thought."

"It puts Wetherby House to shame." William Junior clicked his heels together as he stood up straight. "I can't believe you went to the auction without me."

Mr Wetherby studied his feet before addressing his son, "I wanted to surprise you."

William Junior's brow furrowed. "Surprise me? Why?"

"I want you to run the farm for me and manage the land in Lapworth too. I need someone I can trust."

"Manage the farm?" William Junior glanced at Olivia as he processed his father's words. "I can't do that from here."

"No. I want you to leave Handsworth and move to Bushwood Farm. I wish I could do it myself, but I can't leave Birmingham."

"Live in the country?" William Junior said.

"I thought you'd enjoy it. Rubbing shoulders with the landed gentry."

"Well yes, of course I would, but ..."

"Can I ask about the neighbours, Mr Wetherby?" Olivia stepped forward and took William Junior's hand. "Will we be surrounded by nothing but labourers and their unruly families?"

"My dear, of course not," Mr Wetherby said. "The farm sits close to the manor house itself where I'm sure you'll receive a warm welcome. The tenant farms are well away from the house."

Olivia bit her lower lip. "How far is it from here? I should hate to lose contact with my friends."

"The train station is nearby and Lapworth has a marvellous church. I'm sure you'll find a new circle of friends in no time."

"What about the workshop ... and all the work that needs doing at the Conservative Association?" William Junior said.

"Don't worry, it's taken care of. You also don't have to worry about furnishing the house, hiring men or buying any farm machinery. I'll take care of everything. All you need to do is move in, manage each of the farms and accept us as house guests every Saturday and Sunday."

CHAPTER THIRTY-TWO

Birmingham, Warwickshire

With the last of the signatures blotted on the transfer forms, William accepted the cheque his solicitor handed him. Eight hundred pounds. It was the best he could do, but it wasn't enough to stop the sinking feeling in the pit of his stomach. With an audible sigh he extended his hand to Mr Garrett.

"Welcome to the business. I hope this will be the start of a long and prosperous relationship."

"I hope you're right. That's the sum total of my savings and I'd like a decent return. I'll expect financial updates every six months and the dividend paid annually. I'll obviously leave the running of the business to you, but if you have any major concerns, I expect to be told."

William nodded. "Of course, although hopefully that won't be necessary. I'd better be going. This needs to be paid into the bank before they close."

The walk to the bank was short, but by the time he arrived William's heart was pounding. *Who do I pay first? I'd rather it wasn't Mr White, but do I have a choice?* Pushing open the door, he counted his footsteps as he walked towards the row of clerks. *I need a bookkeeper but how will I find one when I can't pay them?*

As he waited for the clerk, he realised he only had one choice.

It was turned seven o'clock that evening when William arrived in Frankfort Street. He wasn't sure if this was where he'd find William-Wetherby, but whether he did or not, he felt sure Sid would know where he was.

Sid answered the door within seconds of him knocking, and before either of them could speak William saw William-Wetherby at the table with Mrs Storey, holding a hand of cards.

"Good evening, Sidney. May I come in?"

Sid ran his hand through his dishevelled ginger hair and turned to William-Wetherby. Detecting a nod, he held the door open to allow William inside.

"What do you want?" William-Wetherby remained seated as he placed his cards face down on the table.

"I need to talk to you, you haven't been home for a while."

"You should have thought of that before you decided to give me another brother or sister by the woman I was walking out with."

William studied his feet. "We've been through this. I'm sorry. What else can I say? I didn't mean to drive you away but Lydia's my wife and I hoped you'd understand."

"How do you understand something like that? After everything that's happened, why should I speak to you?"

William took a deep breath. "I want you to come and work for me."

William-Wetherby shook his head. "You are unbelievable. I already have a job, remember, with that other, good-for-nothing ..."

"That's enough. I'm not asking you to stop working for him. I just need someone to go over the books for me, and I want it to be you. It would have to be of an evening and I can't pay you much, but I need your help."

"Why? You've not needed me for years; you even discouraged me from working for you when Mother died. What's changed?"

"It's complicated." William ran his finger under his collar as Sid and Mrs Storey stared at him.

William held his son's gaze, his eyes pleading as the silence between them grew. Eventually William-Wetherby spoke. "Will tomorrow do? I'll come to the workshop after work."

"Yes, thank you. The workshop will be best. Lydia doesn't need to know what's going on."

~

Handsworth, Staffordshire.

It was turned six o'clock before William-Wetherby arrived at the office and William was waiting for him.

"So, what's this all about?" William-Wetherby's tone was brusque.

"The business is in trouble and I need help working through the accounts."

"What sort of trouble?"

William told his son about Mr White and his demand for one thousand pounds.

"If he's responsible for the decline of the business, he can't expect to take out the same amount of money as he put in," William-Wetherby said.

William rubbed his forehead with his fingers. "The way the contract was drawn up means he's entitled to at least the money he put in. The business had been doing well with Mr Ball and the thought of him losing us money didn't occur to me."

"Let me see the books," William-Wetherby said.

William set them before his son and gave him time to study them.

Several minutes later, William-Wetherby looked up. "I haven't worked this out properly, but I'd say you have about two hundred pounds of debt here as well as owing the money to Mr White. How's that happened? At the last audit you were over three thousand pounds in profit."

William shrugged. "I've no idea. I let Mr White do the accounts. We bought a number of properties, which would explain some of it. Everything would have been fine if Mr White had agreed to stay ... or if Mr Garrett had paid the full amount."

"If everything you say is true, you need to pay off these debts and give Mr White as much as you can. Hopefully it'll keep him happy until you can find the rest."

William nodded. "Mr Wetherby suggested using the book debts to help pay Mr White. What do you know about that?"

William-Wetherby shook his head. "Not much, I've never used them to pay a debt before. Do you think Mr White will accept it?"

"I've no idea, but he's been getting angrier over the last few weeks and I've been told he can become violent. He implied yesterday that if he doesn't have all his money within days, he'll take it out on Lydia."

William-Wetherby flinched. "What about the police?"

"They're not interested in threats. He's going to have to kill me before they'll do anything about it."

William-Wetherby rubbed his hands over his face. "What do you want me to do?"

CHAPTER THIRTY-THREE

Bushwood, Warwickshire

Mr Wetherby opened the front door of Bushwood Farm as the carriage carrying William Junior, Olivia and Henry drove towards him. He waved as it stopped and William Junior opened the door.

"Welcome to your new home." He rushed forward to help Henry from the carriage.

"Where are we?" Olivia turned in a full circle. "We've been driving past nothing but fields and trees for miles."

"You'll get used to it; now come inside and I'll show you your new home. I've had all the rooms redecorated and the new furniture arrived yesterday."

"Are the dogs for us?" Henry asked as he spotted two German shepherds chained in the yard alongside the house.

"I thought they'd give your mother a better sense of security." Mr Wetherby winked at Henry. "Would you like to walk them for me?"

"Henry'll be at school in a few weeks," William Junior said. "I'm sure I can manage the dogs."

"I'm sure you can," Mr Wetherby muttered. "Now, come inside. Cook's made afternoon tea and Charlotte and Mr Mountford will be here anytime now."

"I hope she can put a smile on her face," William Junior said. "Why didn't you let her and Mr Mountford live here? I'm sure she's jealous."

"Mr Mountford has his own business to run and Charlotte isn't jealous. You know she's having problems."

"Mr Mountford should be more concerned about his wife then."

Mr Wetherby took a deep breath. "It's not that easy. She's seen some of the best doctors in the country and they can find nothing wrong with her. You can't talk either. You may have produced a son, but he hasn't had any brothers or sisters in the last eight years."

William Junior glared at his father before he stormed into the house. "Olivia, come with me, I'll show you to our room."

An hour later, Mr Wetherby smiled as Charlotte and Mr Mountford descended the main staircase into the hall.

"How lovely you both look." Mr Wetherby took Charlotte's hand. "We don't dress formally for dinner nearly enough. Is that another new outfit? Purple suits you."

"It is. Another one fitted at the waist, suitable for those who are single or not destined to be mothers."

Mr Wetherby raised his eyes to Mr Mountford. "You've time yet, I'm sure of it, but before everyone joins us, come into the drawing room. I have a proposition for you."

Charlotte raised her eyebrows but said nothing as she took a seat on the couch next to her husband.

"I've been thinking," Mr Wetherby started. "There are far too many young women in this country carrying children who will never know their fathers. They're a drain on society and the children can have no future living with such a mother. They bring shame on all of us, but I wondered if we could offer hope to one of them."

Charlotte studied her father. "What do you mean?"

"If we found the right child, we could adopt it for you to bring up as your own."

"Completely out of the question." Mr Mountford leapt to his feet. "I won't bring up such a child in my house."

Mr Wetherby squared up to his son-in-law. "Mr Mountford, your wife wants nothing more than to be a mother but hasn't been able to produce a child of her own. For a few pounds we could give her what she wants. Would you deny her a child by another means?"

"Where would you find such a child?" Charlotte gazed expectantly at her father.

Mr Mountford interrupted before Mr Wetherby could reply. "You can't seriously think this is a good idea, Charlotte?"

Charlotte ignored her husband and stood up to hold her father's arm. "Please can we try? Do you have a child in mind?"

"No, not at the moment, I wanted to see how you felt about the idea first. I must say Mr

Mountford has disappointed me. I thought he'd want the best for you."

"Of course I want the best," Mr Mountford said. "I just don't believe having the illegitimate child of an immoral woman is the best option."

"Well, what else do you suggest? You've been married for over two years and there's no sign of a child."

"Please let us try." Charlotte turned to her husband, dabbing her eyes with a handkerchief. "You're not the one people whisper about. You can go to work and nobody thinks to mention it. Every time I'm invited to afternoon tea, I'm asked the same questions again and again. There are some acquaintances I can no longer bring myself to visit."

Mr Mountford approached Charlotte and put his arms around her. "I'm sorry, I'm being selfish. Perhaps we can think about it."

"Excellent," Mr Wetherby said. "I'll start making some enquiries when I'm back in Handsworth."

"I must insist on some conditions though." Mr Mountford released Charlotte and paced the room. "Firstly, the woman must have blonde hair and blue eyes, like Charlotte. If we have this child, it has to appear as if it belongs to us. Secondly, the child's father must have a respectable background, he should preferably be a member of the aristocracy. I don't want to raise an imbecile. And thirdly, its arrival must coincide with our move to Edgbaston. We hadn't expected to move yet, but if this child is so important we must change our plans. Our neighbours must have no grounds for suspecting the child isn't ours."

Mr Wetherby took a deep breath. "That's quite a list, but it should be achievable. I'll visit the guardians next week to find out if they have anyone suitable."

CHAPTER THIRTY-FOUR

Birmingham, Warwickshire

William-Wetherby perched on the edge of his seat, staring at the books in front of him. It was only two o'clock in the afternoon, but as much as he tried, he couldn't keep his eyes open. He was roused from his slumber by the sound of the office door slamming.

"What's going on here?" Mr Wetherby said. "Are all those invoices up to date?"

William-Wetherby jumped to his feet. "Yes, sir, I'm sorry. I was just ..."

"You were sleeping on the job, that's what you were doing. If I catch you doing it again, I'll dock your wages."

"I'm sorry, Mr Wetherby, but can I have a word?"

Mr Wetherby glanced at his pocket watch. "I'm in a hurry, can it wait?"

"It's Father. You know his business is struggling because his partner Mr White left and wanted his money back, well I was wondering, would you be able to …?"

"Don't come asking me for money. I've given him my advice, but it's up to him now. He wanted his own business and so he has to accept the consequences. I told him that at the time."

"He'd only need a loan, he'd pay you back."

Mr Wetherby stopped and faced William-Wetherby. "My dear boy, I've seen his books and he won't be paying anyone back anytime soon. Besides, I don't have that sort of money lying around doing nothing. He's made this mess himself and he's going to have to sort it out himself. Now, I have to go. I want all those invoices logged in before you go tonight, do you understand?"

William-Wetherby watched the door close and slammed his pen into the inkwell. Mr Wetherby could do his own bookkeeping. Of course he had that sort of money. Who did he think he was fooling? His father had paid his debts and given Mr White six hundred of the pounds he owed him. He only needed four hundred pounds. Mr Wetherby could have paid the one thousand if he'd wanted to.

William-Wetherby flicked through the books in front of him. Mr Wetherby had well over a thousand pounds in his cheque account and what was more, he was involved with the Artisans Dwelling Company and was a shareholder in a hotel group and a bank, all of which were prospering. Heaven knows how much money he actually had. He gave Charlotte all the money she wanted, despite the fact Mr Mountford had more than enough for the two of them; and now he'd gone and bought William Junior a grand house in the country. Why was he treating his father so badly? Well, enough was enough. If Charlotte could have what she wanted, so could his father. Mr Wetherby just needn't know about it.

For several days William-Wetherby planned how he was going to take four hundred pounds from Mr Wetherby's account. It wouldn't be hard; he simply needed to cover his tracks. His father had started to put charges onto some of his properties, and was due to sign over the book debt next Thursday. He needed the money by then. As he sat with the accounts in front of him, William-Wetherby wiped the palms of his hands on his trousers before picking up his pen. It was now or never. With his pen shaking he held it over the expenses column, but a second later he threw the pen across the desk as if the shaft had burned his fingers.

"Mr Wetherby. I wasn't expecting you today."

"I'm not staying, but I need to draw some money out of the business. Have you seen the book of cheques?"

A cold shiver ran through William-Wetherby's body. "You're drawing money out? You never do that."

"Not usually, no, but I'm buying some livestock for the farm and I need cash. Do you have the ledgers? I want to check the balance."

William-Wetherby hesitated before he pushed the open book towards Mr Wetherby.

"Yes, that should do it," Mr Wetherby said after checking the latest entries. "It won't leave much but I'm expecting some money to be paid in anytime now; have you seen the cheques?"

William-Wetherby stared absently at his desk before Mr Wetherby spotted them under a pile of invoices. "There they are. Right, that's all I need, I'll see you next week. It's likely to be Wednesday before I'm back as I need to sort some matters out with Mr Mountford once I'm finished at the farm."

Once the door closed, William-Wetherby leaned back in his chair and sighed. How had that happened? Mr Wetherby hadn't used the book of cheques for over a year; all he ever did was sign the ones William-Wetherby filled out for him. Well, that was it. There were no more cheques in the office and by the time Mr Wetherby was finished, probably no money in the account either. What would they do now?

CHAPTER THIRTY-FIVE

William sat outside his solicitor's office, his arms hanging by his sides as he stared out of the window. He had been here the previous afternoon to assign the book debt to Mr White, but it hadn't solved anything. Mr White may have gone, but at what cost to his business?

At the appointed time the secretary asked him into the office where Mr Rodney, his solicitor, was waiting for him.

"Please, Mr Jackson, take a seat." Mr Rodney gestured to a round table in the corner of the office surrounded by four chairs.

"Now, as you're aware, yesterday we assigned the book debt to Mr White, which means that in terms of your day-to-day income, you're starting from scratch. You'll need to earn enough money to service the debts of your other creditors as well as pay your usual outgoings. I know you're aware of that, but I need to take you through the accounts so you fully understand your situation." Mr Rodney produced the ledgers from a cabinet next to his desk.

"The last audited figures you have are for the year ending thirty-first of December 1887." Mr Rodney turned to the appropriate page. "At that time things were looking healthy. You had liabilities of four thousand, eight hundred and seventy pounds, four shillings and eight pence but assets of five thousand seven hundred and thirty-two pounds, sixteen shillings and five pence. In addition, you had properties valued at two thousand, two hundred and fifty pounds, giving you a net worth of over three thousand pounds. In the last six months of the year, however, you made a loss of two hundred and four pounds, twelve shillings and five pence. This I believe coincided with the time Mr White joined you."

"Yes, that's right. When Mr Ball left we had a thriving business."

"Quite. The problem is that when you look at the unofficial figures for this year, the business has continued to lose money to the point where your assets are no longer greater than your liabilities. You also now have charges on the properties and I fear that with the transfer of the book debt, you're going to show a significant shortfall this year."

A wave of nausea passed over William and he moved to the window for some air. Mr Rodney hadn't told him anything he didn't know, but hearing it here, in the cold light of day, made it sound so much worse.

"I can still make the business work," William said once the nausea passed. "We have orders on the books we're working through and many of them are repeat orders."

"But can you afford to pay the men? You won't receive any payments until you issue new invoices."

"I have a little money. I could pay them for a few weeks yet."

"But what happens when that runs out? If you end up being forced into bankruptcy by your creditors, the business will be in a worse position than it is now. If that happens, you're likely to be dealt with harshly."

"So, what do you suggest?"

Mr Rodney closed the book in front of him. "As much as it pains me to say it, I have to advise you to file for bankruptcy yourself on the grounds of having a bad partner and hope the official receiver is lenient with you."

"But the business is still viable, I'm sure it must be worth something. Can't I try and find a buyer for it as a going concern? That way the creditors should receive their payments in full."

"That would be a sensible thing to do in any case, but you won't sell it in the next few weeks and so my recommendation would still be to file a petition for bankruptcy."

William turned to the window. The sun was shining brightly outside and he watched the pedestrians walking on the pavement beneath him. What would Harriet make of him? Most likely she'd be angry, and who could blame her? He was angry with himself. His thoughts turned to Lydia and their unborn child. How would he support them? In fact, how could he continue to pay for Margaret to go to school? And then there was Mr Garrett. As if reading his mind Mr Rodney joined him at the window.

"As he's so new to the company, Mr Garrett will be treated as one of the creditors. If you file now, while the business is viable, the chances are they'll get most of their money back and you'll be let off lightly. You'd protect yourself from further claims and may salvage something from the business. If you delay and the debts start to mount up, you'll be publicly condemned for being reckless."

"I don't have much choice, do I?"

"I'm so sorry, Mr Jackson, really I am."

William struggled to breathe as he staggered down the steps from his solicitor's office. Bankruptcy. Was that the only option open to him? He was a respectable businessman and homeowner; there must be another way. He leaned on the side of the building to catch his breath, but his head was swimming. If Harriet could see him now, she'd never forgive him for giving up so easily.

Staying close to the wall for support, William staggered round the corner and was grateful to find his carriage waiting for him. He needed to get back to the workshop.

Once in the office, he found a half-empty bottle of whisky in the cupboard and poured himself a glass. He didn't usually touch the stuff during the day, but this was an exception. How did he sort this mess out? *Maybe Mr Garrett has more money than he's admitted. I need to write to him anyway, so I could ask him for help. What about the house? If I sold it I should make some money ... but that will take time*

... and I don't have time. That leaves Mr Wetherby. Dare I ask him? William felt his heart racing and put a hand to his chest. *I can't, he'll be furious with me.*

William drained the whisky from the bottom of the glass and stood up to pour another. Before he reached the cupboard, William-Wetherby walked in.

"What are you doing?" William-Wetherby took the glass from his father and held it to his nose. "Whisky at one o'clock in the afternoon?"

William shrugged and sat down again. "It's been a difficult day. What are you doing here? Why aren't you at work?"

"I wanted to find out how you got on and Mr Wetherby's in such a good mood he said I could take as long as I needed to visit you."

William's brow furrowed. "Why's he so happy?"

"He's had an invitation to join the Home Secretary for dinner when he visits Birmingham at the end of the month."

"Is that it?"

"As far as I know, but it's all he can talk about. You'd think he was the only one who'd been invited, not one of about fifty. Anyway, enough of him, why the whisky?"

William-Wetherby's eyes grew wider as William told him of Mr Rodney's suggestion.

"Did you file a petition?"

"Not yet. Mr Rodney suggested I take a couple of days to think it over and go back on Monday morning."

"Will you file?"

William shrugged. "I don't see any other way out."

"Why don't you ask Mr Wetherby?"

"I was thinking the same thing when you arrived. I don't know, he's so distant nowadays, I'm not sure I want to approach him again."

"But this is different. The business is your livelihood. He can't want you to go bankrupt. If nothing else think of the damage it might do to his reputation, he's still your stepfather, after all."

William sat up straighter in his chair. "You're right. I hadn't thought of it like that. He won't want to be associated with a bankrupt."

"Come to Frankfort Street with me now and ask him. Thanks to the Home Secretary, you might be in luck."

CHAPTER THIRTY-SIX

As the carriage made its way along Summer Lane, William's heart rate quickened and he wiped his hands on his trousers. Why had he let William-Wetherby talk him into coming?

"Don't look so scared," William-Wetherby said. "He's your stepfather. Why would he want to see you go bankrupt?"

A hot flush coursed through William's body as he remembered the scene in Wetherby House when Harriet had demanded the money from the business.

"What's the matter?" William-Wetherby said. "You look as if you've seen a ghost."

William gave an involuntary shiver. "I can't do this."

"Of course you can. I'll make myself scarce so you can talk to him alone."

As the carriage came to a halt in Frankfort Street, William stepped out and took a deep breath. He needed to calm down.

Mr Wetherby was in the office when he arrived. "William. What an unexpected surprise. What brings you here?"

William rested his hands on the back of a chair and took another deep breath. "I've come to ask a favour."

The smile slipped from Mr Wetherby's face. "What sort of favour?"

"Since Mr White left the business, I've been struggling and I wondered if you'd lend me five hundred pounds, until I'm back on my feet."

The lines on Mr Wetherby's face hardened. "You've got a nerve. Not five years ago I was blackmailed by that wife of yours into giving you over five thousand pounds, and now you come here telling me that not only have you wasted the lot, but you expect me to give you more?"

"The only reason she did what she did was because you refused to give me what was rightfully mine."

"None of it was rightfully yours. I built that business up myself, but despite that I gave you what you asked for. I could have doubled my money if it wasn't for you."

"I had a thriving business before Mr White came along. Now he's gone, I can do it again as long as I'm given a chance."

"Well, you're not getting another penny from me. I've seen your type before. You take my money and think you are doing well, but a few months or years down the line, you're back again with another hard-luck story. If I keep bailing you out, it'll never end."

"So you'd rather I was declared bankrupt?"

Mr Wetherby stopped and stared at William. "Bankrupt?"

"That's what it'll come to, if you won't help. What will the Home Secretary say about that when you meet him?"

"Don't bring the Home Secretary into this. You will not tarnish my name with your incompetence."

"It was Mr White who ruined me ..."

"I don't care who it was. If you're so close to being declared bankrupt, the last place I should put my money is in your business. In all probability, I'd never see it again."

William straightened up and walked towards Mr Wetherby. "Listen to yourself. Mother will be turning in her grave. You help William Junior and

Charlotte with the most trivial matters, but you won't help me when my whole livelihood's threatened."

"Your mother would have stopped you getting into this mess in the first place. I've told you countless times before, you only have yourself to blame for letting that wife of yours become involved."

"It's nothing to do with her, except for the fact that if she was still alive none of this would have happened. If you'd gone to help her rather than watching her drown, she'd still be with us today ..."

Mr Wetherby's face grew scarlet. "Get out of here now. I don't want to lay eyes on you again and if I hear you repeating those words outside this office you'll have more than a bankruptcy to worry about. I'll sue you for slander." Mr Wetherby marched to the door and held it open. "You can find some other fool to bail you out."

William followed and stopped inches from Mr Wetherby. "Don't worry, you won't see me again, but let me remind you of one thing. You can't frighten a man who's got nothing left to lose."

CHAPTER THIRTY-SEVEN

Handsworth, Staffordshire

It was late by the time William arrived home and despite several pints of ale and a couple of whiskies his heart still pounded as the scene with Mr Wetherby raced through his mind. He tiptoed into the back room hoping Lydia was in bed, but stopped by the door when he saw her sitting by the fire with William-Wetherby.

William-Wetherby jumped up as soon as he saw him. "He said no?"

William nodded and took a seat opposite his wife.

"That man is unbelievable and with all the

thousands he has in the bank. Do you know what he's planning to do for Charlotte? He's only ..." William-Wetherby stopped and stared at Lydia. "No, not now. I'm going to bed. I'll speak to you tomorrow."

William watched William-Wetherby leave the room before he put his head back and closed his eyes.

Lydia glared at him from her seat by the fire. "Don't think you can just walk in here and go to sleep when you come home at this hour of the night, smelling of ale. What was William-Wetherby talking about? He started a conversation partway through and ended it as abruptly. What's going on?"

William pushed himself up from his chair. "I'll tell you tomorrow. Goodnight."

The following morning Lydia was waiting in the morning room when William arrived downstairs. She banged a cup of tea down in front of him and stood by the table, her arms folded above her heavily swollen belly.

"What's going on?"

"Can't I have my breakfast in peace?"

"No, you can't. I've not slept a wink wondering what's going on. You can tell me now."

William sighed. "Sit down."

Lydia did as she was told.

"I had a problem with my business partner earlier in the year and I'm going to have to file for bankruptcy. I have a meeting with my solicitor later."

"Bankruptcy!" Lydia pushed herself back up from the table. "You can't do that. What about me and the baby?"

"You'll be in the same situation as me. I'm not doing this for the fun of it. If I had another option I'd take it."

Lydia put her hands on her hips. "Why has every man I've ever known let me down? If it hadn't been for my father I never would have married you."

"You married me because of your father?"

Lydia gave William a withering stare. "It wasn't for your youthful good looks was it? He told me if I accepted your proposal I'd be leaving poverty behind. You had your own business, this house, the children all went to private school. That was what I wanted for my children ... but you lied to me."

"I lied? I never said anything about money. For your information everything was running smoothly until I met your father. He was the reason Mr Ball left." William stood up and ran his hand across his head. "My God, what a mistake I've made."

"What a mistake you've made? I ruined my relationship with William-Wetherby because of you, and for what? At least William-Wetherby still has a job and won't be labelled a bankrupt for the rest of his life."

"You and William-Wetherby? He hasn't come of age yet. Besides, I won't be labelled a bankrupt for the rest of my life, I'll be discharged by this time next year, but you won't need to worry about that. If I'm such a bad husband you can pack your bags and leave. See how you manage without me. Living in the workhouse won't enhance your reputation."

"I've friends in London I can stay with whenever I want."

William pushed past her and walked to the door. "Well, good luck to you, I hope your friends have enough money to make you happy."

Birmingham, Warwickshire.

As he strode up Summer Lane, William-Wetherby's nostrils flared and his teeth were clenched so tightly that his jaw hurt. He barged into the office and slammed the door behind him, thankful Mr Wetherby was nowhere to be seen. Sitting down at his desk, he took a deep breath. He needed to calm down if he wanted to speak with him.

It was several hours later that Mr Wetherby arrived and he peered over William-Wetherby's shoulder.

"Are they new invoices? Didn't I see you doing them yesterday?"

William-Wetherby glared at him before he took a deep breath to control the pitch of his voice. "No, you didn't. Can I have a word with you?"

Mr Wetherby took a step away and nodded.

William-Wetherby continued slowly. "I overheard one of your conversations at the end of last week ... about Aunt Charlotte."

"What about her?"

"I didn't hear much, but it sounded as if you want to find a baby for her."

Mr Wetherby went to his own desk. "That was a private conversation, you had no right to be listening."

"I didn't do it on purpose, but it may be fortunate that I did. I may have a solution for you."

Mr Wetherby turned back. "Go on."

"I'm not sure if you've heard, but Lydia's expecting a baby in the next few weeks. Given Father's problems, I imagine they'd let you have the baby ... for the right price."

Mr Wetherby's posture stiffened. "Has your father put you up to this?"

"No, he's no idea. I've spoken to no one about it."

"Charlotte's not ready for a baby yet. Mr Mountford has to find a new house first."

"She only lives round the corner from Father. If they're not ready, perhaps Lydia could nurse it and Aunt Charlotte could come and visit."

Mr Wetherby's eyes were like slits. "How much do they want?"

"I'd say one hundred pounds would be fair."

"One hundred pounds! I could get one from the workhouse for ten."

"And accept an illegitimate child into your family? I don't believe you. At least this way you know its background and that it's from a legitimate marriage."

"I told your father yesterday, I am not giving him any more money to waste in that business."

"It needn't go to the business. It would give him a bit of money once the bankruptcy is filed ... and it would help Aunt Charlotte. Why can't you see it for the straightforward transaction it is?"

"Because there's more to it than that, now get back to work. I don't want to hear any more about it."

CHAPTER THIRTY-EIGHT

Handsworth, Staffordshire

It was turned six o'clock when William-Wetherby arrived home to find Eleanor standing at the front door.

"What's the matter?" he shouted as he approached the driveway.

Eleanor rushed to meet him. "Have you seen Father?"

"Not since last night. Why?"

"We need the doctor. Lydia's baby's coming." Eleanor's voice was breathless.

The colour drained from William-Wetherby's face. "It can't be. Not yet."

"Well, it is. She's in a lot of pain and we need

the doctor. Will you go for him?"

William-Wetherby hesitated. "What about a midwife?"

"She's here already but we need a doctor. What's up with you?"

"I don't think Father can afford a doctor. Not at the moment."

Eleanor stared at her brother. "What are you talking about? Of course he can afford a doctor."

William-Wetherby kicked at some loose stones on the driveway and when he didn't respond, Eleanor continued. "What's going on? You've been acting strangely for the last couple of days."

"It's nothing for you to worry about."

Eleanor shook his arm. "Look at me when I'm talking to you. I've every right to know. Tell me."

William-Wetherby sighed and glanced up to see his sister's blue-grey eyes questioning him. "He's having trouble with the business."

"What sort of trouble?" She fixed William-Wetherby with such a stare he had to turn away.

"I'm not sure how much you know, but a few months ago his partner left the business and demanded immediate payment of the money he'd invested. Father didn't have it but the partner wouldn't wait. He managed to find a new partner but things didn't work out and so he's had to file for bankruptcy."

"Bankruptcy?" Eleanor's face paled. "There must be some mistake. Why didn't he ask for help?"

"He did. I've been trying to help him for the last couple of months, but in the end there wasn't much anyone could do." Eleanor walked to the front doorstep and sat down as her brother continued. "The solicitor advised him to file the petition himself, so they'll treat him more leniently."

Eleanor's eyes were moist as she looked up to her brother. "Lenient? They don't know the meaning of the word. I need to find myself a job."

"You ... take a job? What will you do?"

"Don't sound so surprised. I've been thinking for a while I'd like to be a governess and so as soon as Father comes home and the baby's born, I'm going to make some enquiries. I could earn a reasonable wage and because most of the jobs involve living with the family you don't have many living expenses. I'll send home as much money as I can."

"You can't do that." William-Wetherby knelt by the side of his sister.

"I can and I will. Now, will you go and fetch the doctor? We might not be able to pay him today, but we will pay him."

It was almost eleven o'clock at night before William arrived home and he prayed Lydia wasn't up waiting for him. He wasn't sure if he preferred her to be in bed or in London, but he knew he didn't want to see her. Opening the front door carefully, he prepared to creep down the hall, but stopped in his tracks when William-Wetherby and Eleanor appeared from the back room. He looked from one to the other, before Eleanor answered the question that was evidently on his face.

"You have another son," she said.

The lines on William's forehead deepened. "Already? There was no sign of it this morning."

"He came quickly; he was born a few minutes past eight this evening."

William rubbed his hand across his face. "I suppose I'd better go and see them."

"I'd leave them if I were you," Eleanor said. "The baby was crying for a long time earlier and Lydia may have only recently got to sleep. You won't be popular if you wake her up at this hour smelling of ale."

William walked into the back room and flopped into a chair. "I'm not popular at the moment anyway, but maybe you're right. I'll blame you if I'm accused of showing no interest."

"Everything's going to be all right." She made her way to the door. "I'm going to bed now. I'll speak to you in the morning."

Once they were alone William stood up and poured himself a whisky. "It's done," he said to William-Wetherby. "I'm going to be a bankrupt. It's not sunk in yet, but it makes me so angry to think of Mr White and the trouble he's caused. After everything I've worked for."

"I'm surprised you could still walk home, you smell like you've had a fair few pints. Do you know when you have to go to court?"

"Not yet, they'll write to me in the next few days." William took a seat at the table. "Life has a strange way of carrying on. You can file for your own bankruptcy but become a father on the same day."

William-Wetherby sat beside him. "I've been thinking about that. I bet you'd rather have some money than a new baby, wouldn't you?"

"Of course I would. Why?"

"You remember I told you Mr Wetherby wanted a doctor for Aunt Charlotte because she hadn't had a child?"

William nodded.

"I found out last week he's now looking for a baby to adopt for her ... and he's willing to pay."

William's eyebrows shot up. "How do you know?"

"I overheard him. I'm not sure who he was talking to, but it was someone who knew what he was up to."

"How much will he pay?"

"I'm not sure. I spoke to him this afternoon and asked for one hundred pounds. He said it was too much but ..."

"You've spoken to Mr Wetherby?"

"I thought you'd want the money so I didn't think you'd mind. I'll speak to Aunt Charlotte next. If Mr Wetherby won't pay, perhaps Mr Mountford can find the money."

"You can't go straight to Charlotte."

"Why not? Mr Wetherby's not going to tell her and you're desperate."

William closed his eyes, resting his head in his hands as the room started to spin. *What a mess.*

The following morning, William knocked on the bedroom door and hovered in the doorway until Lydia looked up and glared at him.

"H-How are you?" he asked. "He took me by surprise. I didn't think he was due yet."

"He wasn't." Lydia spat her words at him before turning to stroke the face of her baby. "That's why he's so small. The doctor thinks it was the argument yesterday morning that brought it on."

"You told the doctor about our personal business?"

"What else could I do? I needed something to calm my nerves."

William nodded and edged forward to peer into the crib. "Have you chosen a name for him?"

"Arthur."

"Arthur ... for any particular reason?"

"It was my mother's father's name."

"Oh." William nodded.

Lydia turned to face him. "How are we going to manage? Just look at him. He's so helpless and you've gone and made yourself bankrupt. What sort of a life will he have?"

William took a deep breath. "There might be a way, but I need to speak to Charlotte."

Lines formed on Lydia's face. "Charlotte? What's it got to do with her?"

"I'm hoping she, or at least Mr Mountford, might give us some money. It won't be enough to stop the bankruptcy but it might give us something to live on afterwards." William hesitated. "It will involve giving her something in return though."

"What? We haven't got anything to give them."

"We have the one thing Charlotte wants, but can't have." Lydia followed William's gaze as he glanced at Arthur.

"No ... not my baby! Please, William. She can have anything, but not him. Don't do this to me."

"I'm not certain whether they'll pay us yet, but the facts of the matter are that if we keep him, we'll have no money and may end up in the workhouse. Alternatively, they give us enough to live on until I can find another job and Arthur would be brought up with every privilege you can think of. He'll want for nothing if he lives with them ... I could even ask about you being his nanny. Frankly I think it's selfish not to let him go."

Lydia stared at William. "But he's my baby, look at him, he's perfect, we can't ..."

"I'm sorry ... I don't think we have any choice."

As William left the room he caught sight of Lydia throwing herself onto the bed and burying her sobs in the pillow. He pulled the door closed behind him and leaned against the wall, tears running down his cheeks. *How many more lives will I destroy before this is over?*

CHAPTER THIRTY-NINE

It was turned six o'clock in the evening when William knocked on the door in St Peters Road. The maid answered and showed him into the back room where Charlotte sat knitting.

"My, that takes me back," he said as he entered. "For a moment I thought you were Mother."

Charlotte smiled. "Wouldn't it be lovely if it was. What can I do for you? You don't call here very often."

William glanced at the expensive ornaments covering the sideboard. "Are you alone or is Mr Mountford home? I was hoping to speak to both of you."

"He'll be here shortly, he must have been delayed. Have a seat and tell me what it's about."

William hesitated. "I'm not sure where to start. It's a bit delicate."

"I won't bite." Charlotte smiled at him.

"No, of course not ... I've been led to believe you and Mr Mountford are looking to take in a child."

Charlotte pursed her lips together, and when she said nothing, William continued.

"I'm not sure if you heard, but Lydia had her baby earlier this week, a little boy. With the situation I'm in at the moment we wondered if you and Mr Mountford would like to raise him as your own ... for a small fee?"

Charlotte's face softened. "Do you mean that? What about Lydia? She can't want to give up her baby."

William studied the floor. "Unfortunately she doesn't have a choice, and we agreed that we'd like you to have him ... if you want him."

"Oh William, of course I do. Can I come and see him?"

"Of course you can."

Charlotte clutched her brother's hand. "I can't tell you how happy you've made me. Thank you so much."

"I'm happy to help and Lydia will be able to watch him grow up even if it is from a distance. All

I need to do is discuss the fee with Mr Mountford."

"How much do you need? You could have as much as you wanted if it was up to me."

William smiled. "That's very generous, but perhaps we'd better speak to Mr Mountford first."

"He's here now." Charlotte stood up. "I think Papa's with him."

William's stomach lurched as he jumped from his seat. Moments later the two men entered the room.

"What are you doing here?" Mr Wetherby glared at William as soon as he saw him.

"I came to see Charlotte and Mr Mountford."

"Papa." Charlotte spoke with a broad smile on her face. "He came with wonderful news. Lydia's had her baby and they've said we can have him to bring up as our own."

Mr Wetherby stepped forward until his face was no more than two inches away from William's. "You had no right coming here and raising her hopes. Your child is not coming to this house and that's the end of it."

William's heart skipped a beat, but he raised his shoulders and stared back at Mr Wetherby. "I don't believe it's your decision to make. I offered Arthur to Charlotte and Mr Mountford."

"If I'm paying, I'll have a say in which child we have."

"And you'd rather they have an illegitimate child from the workhouse than let her have a child from a respectable background?"

"Papa, William, stop it." Charlotte put her hands between the two of them but neither moved. "What's going on? I've never seen you like this before."

"I will not give this man any more of my money, whether it's for a child or anything else. There are plenty of other respectable children in need of homes."

"I want this one. I was going to go with William to see him."

William spoke through gritted teeth. "And if Mr Mountford's prepared to pay for him it's got nothing to do with you."

All eyes turned to Mr Mountford before Charlotte took his hand.

"Please, darling, can we have him?" she said.

"Well ... naturally, I could pay for him, but ... well, it was meant to be a gift from your father and I don't want to tread on his toes."

"You'll be doing more than treading on my toes if you give him a penny."

"Papa, what a terrible thing to say. William, how much do you want?"

"Well, he's a fit and healthy baby and his mother and I are respectable members of the community ..."

"Respectable? Who are you trying to fool?" Mr Wetherby took a step towards William. "You're a bankrupt and your wife's the daughter of a traveller. William-Wetherby's already asked for a hundred pounds. I told him, and now I'm telling you, you're not having it. Now get out of here."

"You knew about it?" Charlotte's voice squeaked as she spoke. "Why didn't you tell me?"

"Because I knew you'd be upset. You can have any child in Birmingham or Handsworth ... but not that one."

"What about my feelings? Don't you care?"

Mr Wetherby's face was crimson. "Of course I care. If you remember it was my idea to find a child in the first place. I just didn't want to upset you by telling you about this one, when I could never allow it into the house."

"It would be my child in my house, you have no right to make such an important decision on my behalf."

"We can work something out ..." Mr Mountford stepped forward and put his arms around

Charlotte, but Mr Wetherby glared at him before he grabbed William by the arm and pushed him towards the door.

"Get out of this house now. If I see you round here again, I'll have you locked up for breaking and entering."

CHAPTER FORTY

Birmingham, Warwickshire

From his seat in his carriage, William watched Mr Rodney as he waited for him outside the county court. He was a small, round man with a cheerful-looking face, even when he was being serious. Today, for the initial bankruptcy hearing, he wore his court robes and gave a courteous nod to William as he climbed down from the carriage.

As they entered the courtroom William paused. The walls were clad in a dark mahogany wood that matched the rows of benches facing the official receiver's chair, which was elevated on a podium of more dark panelling.

"We need to be in the front row." Mr Rodney

pointed to the empty row of seats in front of the benches where the creditors were gathering.

William glanced at the faces staring at him before he spotted several men with pencils and notepads. "Are they from the newspaper?"

"I would say so," Mr Rodney said. "There mustn't be much else going on today."

At half past ten, the official receiver entered the room and took his seat. He opened the proceedings by introducing the case and giving a step-by-step summary of the history of the business.

"That brings us to September of this year," he continued. "Mr Jackson voluntarily filed for bankruptcy after which time a new balance sheet was drawn up. The business currently has liabilities of four thousand, seven hundred and sixty-nine pounds, four shillings and tuppence, with assets of one thousand five hundred and ninety-six pounds, eleven shillings and five pence. In addition, the company owns six properties that are let to tenants.

"From everything that's been put forward, it would appear that the demise of the company began with the departure of Mr Ball and the introduction of Mr White as a temporary partner. The fact that Mr Jackson was unable to prevent Mr White leaving without taking any reduction in his investment seems to have played its part. Mr

Jackson, will you now take the stand and hold the Bible in your right hand."

William did as he was asked and repeated the oath that was read to him by an official. Once he had finished the receiver addressed him.

"Do you agree that this summary is an accurate reflection of why we are here today?"

"Yes, sir, I do. All the problems stem from Mr White."

"And do you believe this court should declare you bankrupt?"

"No, sir, I do not."

"Explain yourself, please," the receiver said.

"As you pointed out, the business is not without money and it owns a number of properties. They've been valued at two thousand, two hundred and fifty pounds and bring in a modest income. I believe that in its current state it would be feasible to sell the business as a going concern. If we took that course of action, I believe all the creditors would be paid in full."

"If you believe that, why did you file for bankruptcy rather than trying to sell the business?"

"Mr White refused to wait for his money and I ran out of time. My solicitor advised that voluntary bankruptcy was the best course of action."

"And did your solicitor also advise you to

transfer the book debts to Mr White as a way of payment to stop him harassing you?"

"It had been suggested to me by another party and Mr Rodney agreed."

"And since you filed for bankruptcy and relinquished your book debt, have you found a buyer for the business?"

"Not yet, sir, but there are several interested parties."

The receiver studied the notes in front of him. "The trading account for the last six months of 1887 showed a loss of two hundred and four pounds, twelve shillings and five pence; it appears that you've lost significantly more this year. As you've now assigned all the book debt to Mr White, I wonder why anyone would find the business attractive. In fact, Mr Jackson, I put it to this meeting that the assignment of the book debt, made on the thirtieth of August, may have been a fraudulent act."

William glanced towards Mr Rodney who remained in his seat as the receiver continued.

"It occurred when you were aware the business was in difficulty and yet you prioritised Mr White above all other creditors." The receiver paused and eyed the rows of creditors seated behind Mr Rodney. "Mr Parish, do you have anything to say?"

"I do indeed, sir." Mr Parish stood up. "As representative of the creditors I'd like to thank you for pointing this out as we'd not been made aware of it. I'd like it recorded that we are appalled that such a transfer has taken place and we shall contend it was a fraudulent act."

Mr Rodney jumped to his feet. "May I point out that Mr Jackson has been unfortunate in all of this. He had a partner he thought he could trust, but who ultimately let him down. He entered into the agreement with Mr White under the impression he'd become a partner, but Mr White was a disaster for the business and at short notice demanded his money back. The book debt was assigned before there was any talk of bankruptcy. It was weeks later before I deemed that the business had become unsustainable and the most honest course of action was to submit the petition before things got worse. There was nothing fraudulent about the actions of either Mr Jackson or myself.

"Can I also point out that Mr Jackson has sunk a considerable sum of money into the properties, all of which could be sold if necessary. It should also be noted that the business showed a substantial dividend last year."

"That, I'm afraid, Mr Rodney, is no substitute for payment, and it in no way excuses the preferential treatment given to Mr White," the receiver said. "Mr Parish. Do you or your fellow creditors have any further comments?"

The creditors spoke in hushed whispers as they huddled together before Mr Parish turned to the bench. "Speaking on behalf of the creditors, given what we've heard about the book debt, we're no longer confident Mr Jackson can save the company and so we unanimously agree that the business should be placed with a trustee."

William broke into a cold sweat and stared at the creditors. "You can't ... you know me ... I'll make sure you're paid."

"You've had your chance to speak, Mr Jackson." The receiver turned to the creditors. "Are you all in agreement?" When he saw each man nod his head, he continued. "I think it's clear that Mr Jackson has failed to keep this company solvent and is in no position to restore it. I'll therefore bring the session to a close by declaring that under The Bankruptcy Act of 1883, Mr Jackson, trading as the firm Ball and Jackson of the Northern Rivet Works is abridged to be bankrupt by this county court. With immediate effect, Mr Fisher will become trustee and he and his team of inspectors will take over the management of the company, with the aim of recovering as much money as possible for the creditors. Mr Jackson will appear before the county court for public examination on Wednesday the tenth of October."

William sank back in his chair and watched the receiver collect up his papers. How had that happened? He had been so confident he'd be given time. *Damn that book debt.*

CHAPTER FORTY-ONE

Handsworth, Staffordshire

Once back at the workshop, William closed the front door behind him and walked into the office to collect his personal property before the bailiffs arrived. As he stepped towards his desk, he flinched at the sight of William-Wetherby waiting for him.

"How did you get on?" he asked.

William shrugged. "I was declared bankrupt. Mr White's contribution was almost ignored and there was no consideration for all the work I've put in ... or the fact that I might have a buyer."

"Did Mr White turn up at the hearing?"

William forced out a laugh. "He wouldn't dare,

although it would have been interesting. The creditors are furious because I shouldn't have written the book debt over to him. I should never have listened to Mr Wetherby. It was the one thing that finished me off."

"So what happens now?"

William sighed. "The receiver appointed a trustee who'll take over the running of the business and try and find a buyer. He'll appoint inspectors to see if there's anything they can sell to pay the debts. Fortunately, I think the house is safe for now."

"How will you sell the business if they take everything out of it?"

William shrugged. "It won't be my problem. My main concern is keeping hold of the house. If I can't make the repayments to the bank I'll end up losing that as well."

William-Wetherby's face paled. "Where will we live?"

"We'll be all right for the next few months. There's enough stuff of value that we can sell to pay the mortgage until I can find some work."

"What will you do?"

"I've no idea but until all the formalities are over, I can't do anything. Thank the Lord Eleanor found that job in Sutton Coldfield and that Margaret's school bills are paid for the next couple of months. At least they're away from all this. I don't know what I'll do about Lydia and Florence though. Why didn't Lydia clear off to London when she said she would?"

"Perhaps it's because she gave birth to your son."

William shrugged. "Well it isn't because she wants me, that's for sure."

The two men sat in silence until William changed the subject. "I expected Mr Wetherby to be in court but he wasn't. What's he up to?"

William-Wetherby gave a wry smile. "He's got his dinner tonight with the Home Secretary. It's at the Conservative Association, and several other Members of Parliament will be there as well. He's taken charge as usual and so needed to organise everything."

"Typical. I shouldn't have expected him to think about me when he's got more important things to do. It's strange how life goes on as if nothing's happened. Lydia had the baby on the day I filed the petition, and Mr Wetherby's fraternising with the Home Secretary on the day I'm declared bankrupt."

"Not everyone's forgotten about you. I know we haven't seen eye to eye lately, but I'll be here for you. So will Eleanor and the girls. Don't forget that," William-Wetherby said.

"Thank you, you're probably the only ones who will be. I've not seen your Aunt Mary-Ann or Mr Diver since they moved to Birmingham. Three months they've been gone."

"You can write to them, I'm sure they'll help if they can. What will you do in the meantime?"

William shrugged. "Go home and see what sort of reception I get, I suppose. Don't worry about me. I'll be fine once I'm over the shock and I've told Mr Watkins what I've done with his business."

William hadn't finished breakfast the next morning when two bailiffs arrived. Having dismissed the maids the previous evening, Lydia let them in and followed them into the morning room.

"We're here to check whether you have anything in the house belonging to the business."

William put his napkin on the table and stood up. "Shouldn't you be starting with the workshop? This is my personal property."

"We'll be heading over there as soon as you hand us all the keys and we've checked you haven't taken anything from the workshop that no longer belongs to you."

William glared at the men before he went to the dresser in the hall and took out a selection of keys. "You'll find everything here. The only things I brought from the workshop were my own personal property."

"What about the horses and carriage?" The inspector nodded to the stabling through the window.

William's face paled. "They're mine. I need to sell them to keep a roof over my head."

The inspector peered at the sheet of paper he was holding. "This inventory indicates they were bought with money from the business. That makes them part of the settlement. How many other items do you have that weren't bought with your own money?"

"None. Why would I buy furniture with money from the business?"

"I was thinking about cash. Would you normally keep it in the office or would you have it here?"

William glanced at Lydia. Had she seen him with the cash box last night? "I have it upstairs. I'll fetch it for you."

William made his way down the hall but stopped when he realised the inspectors were following him.

"We need to make sure we recover all the money from the business," one of them said. "It will all be checked against the balance sheet, but it will make life easier if everything's present and correct."

William nodded. "Walk this way."

William paused by the bedroom door as the bailiffs peered into every drawer and cupboard in the room. Once they were finished, they moved onto the next room. William clenched his fists as he watched them.

"Are you going to go into every room like this?"

"Only doing our job. You've no need to stay, we'll leave things as we find them."

William watched as they stuffed everything back into the cupboards before he walked away. He couldn't stand by and watch them defile everything he owned.

With his heart pounding, he put on his hat and coat and walked to Mr Watkins's house. He paused to catch his breath before knocking on the front door. A minute later a woman William presumed to be a housekeeper answered the door and invited him in.

Mr Watkins sat in the corner of a small living room reading the newspaper. The room was sparsely furnished with a single upholstered chair, a settee and a small dining table with two chairs.

Unlike his house in Grosvenor Road, which he had shared with his wife, there were no ornaments. Mr Watkins coughed and William thought how frail he looked.

"Good morning, uncle." William took a seat on the end of the settee closest to the old man. "I'm sorry it's been so long since I've called."

"This is you in the paper, isn't it?" Mr Watkins said without greeting. "You've gone bankrupt."

"I didn't realise it was in the paper. Can I see?" William's hands shook as he read the four-inch column. Everything was included. "Yes, that's me."

"Has it all gone?"

William folded the paper and handed it back. "The business is still running and we're hoping to find a buyer for it."

"That business was my life. What happened?"

"It was pretty much as they said in the paper. I was investing in property, but then I got a bad partner who wanted his money back."

For the first time Mr Watkins looked him in the eye. "Why did you have a partner in the first place? I didn't need a partner."

"Times have changed. We were busy and after Harriet died, I couldn't manage."

"Harriet. Is this all her doing? I told you she'd be trouble."

William shook his head. "No, you can't blame her. She encouraged me to run my own business and while she was alive, she did all the office work for me. She was good at it too. You'd have been proud of her if you'd seen what she did."

"I'm not sure about that, but you knew how to get the best out of her. I certainly didn't."

They sat in silence for a minute before Mr Watkins spoke again. "Do you have any money?"

"I doubt it. The bailiffs were at the house when I left. Goodness knows what I'll return to."

"Will you lose the house?"

William shrugged. "I don't know. I should be all right for now, but if I can't make the repayments to the bank, they'll take it from me. At least I have things to sell, and William-Wetherby is still working. Eleanor has a job as a governess too."

"You can't take money from a woman."

William hung his head. "I wish I didn't have to, but desperate times call for desperate measures."

"Have you still got that new wife of yours?"

"I have, her name's Lydia. She's recently given me another son."

Mr Watkins shook his head. "That's all you need. Here, take this." He reached down into a jar by the side of his chair. "Don't tell anyone about it. You have more need of it than me."

"Five pounds! Mr Watkins, I can't possibly."

"Take it, please. I believe you when you say you've been dealt a bad hand. I expect Mr Wetherby will be a lot more generous, but I want to help as best I can."

"Mr Watkins you have no idea how much this means to me. Mr Wetherby won't help. He thinks I've got what I deserve."

"I'm sorry to hear it, but you'll always be welcome here; only don't leave it so long next time."

CHAPTER FORTY-TWO

By the time William returned home, it was still only two o'clock and Lydia was in the back room with Arthur on her lap. He saw tears streaming down her face.

"I'm sorry, Lydia, I never meant for this to happen."

"Arthur's not been himself for the last few days. It's as if he can sense something's wrong. This is the quietest he's been all day. I thought of calling the doctor, but I didn't know if we could afford it." She continued to sob as she clung to Arthur.

William gazed down at the tiny bundle in her arms. "If I could make any of this right I would. I'll understand if you don't want to stay."

"Where would I go?" Lydia's voice squeaked. "I

didn't save enough money to go anywhere and with Arthur crying so much nobody will have us at the moment."

"Stay here then ... at least until Arthur's better."

Lydia nodded. "Thank you, I know I don't deserve it after what I said."

William sat down on the floor beside her. "I'm sure we've both said things we shouldn't. I'd like nothing more than for you and Arthur to stay here, if we can make it work."

Lydia's eyes brightened. "You mean if I stay with you we can keep Arthur?"

William took hold of the child's tiny hand. "I mean I want you with me and I'd like to keep him ... but I'm not sure we can."

"Will you try?"

William studied Lydia's tear-stained face. "Yes, I'll try."

William was in the back room when William-Wetherby came home from work. Florence was home from school and knelt by the fireside rocking Arthur in his cradle.

"Did the inspectors leave the house intact?" William-Wetherby asked William.

"For the most part, but they took the horses and

carriage. I'd planned on selling them to pay the mortgage, but now I'm going to have to sell some furniture instead."

"But we need everything we have." William-Wetherby glanced around the room. "There has to be another way. And can't someone shut that child up?"

"Don't think we haven't tried. I don't like it any more than you do," William said.

"Where's Lydia? Why isn't she feeding him?"

"She's preparing tea for us. Arthur won't take anything from her and I can't waste money on the doctor."

"So what are we supposed to do? I can't sleep with that noise going on."

"I'm looking after him." Florence smiled down at the baby as she held his hand. "He'll be better soon."

William gave his daughter a feeble smile before turning to William-Wetherby. "Why don't you go to Frankfort Street? I'm sure Mrs Storey will have you until we sort him out."

William-Wetherby nodded, and William watched his son leave before following him into the hall.

"Don't go yet; have tea first. I'm not trying to get

rid of you, but we're all unhappy tonight and you may be better off away from here."

"But how could you let this happen? I can't believe you've done everything you can to get Mr Wetherby to change his mind. He could have helped at any stage leading up to this so why won't he ... and why is he refusing to let Aunt Charlotte adopt Arthur?"

"He wants to punish me for leaving the business and effectively wasting the money he gave me; that's all he's bothered about."

"Hasn't he seen you suffer enough? You need to go back and appeal to his better nature ... if he has one."

"There's no point."

"There's every point. What have you got to lose? I'm only going to Frankfort Street for tonight, but I'll be back tomorrow. You need to go and talk to him before I'm back."

Once William-Wetherby had gone William walked into his own bedroom. Absently, he wandered to the cupboard between the chimneybreast and the wall to close the door. The inspectors must have rifled through everything. As he did he noticed a shape in the back corner. He reached in to find the small train he had played with as a boy. The red wheels and yellow funnel had all but lost their paint, but it was his and he clutched it to his chest.

His grandmother had packed up this little train for him when they had first moved to Birmingham and he had tried to remember her every time he played with it. It was such a long time ago but then he'd mislaid it only for his mother to give it back to him one Christmas. Harriet must have packed it up and brought it here. His mother, grandmother and wife; without doubt the three most important people in his life. He went to the window and rested his head on the glass. Was he going to let Mr Wetherby get away with ruining everything? He could almost hear Harriet telling him to go and talk to him. She wouldn't let this happen without putting up a fight. He looked down at the train again. For Harriet and for his mother, he had to face Mr Wetherby one more time.

CHAPTER FORTY-THREE

Birmingham, Warwickshire

The following day, the September sun was still warm as William walked into Birmingham. He was in no hurry to see Mr Wetherby and only arrived as the men were leaving for the day. William-Wetherby looked up when he opened the door.

"I thought you'd have gone by now," William said. "Is he here?"

"Yes, I am." A cold voice spoke from behind him. "William-Wetherby, out."

William spun around to find Mr Wetherby standing behind him. William-Wetherby scurried for his hat before he headed out the door, which was firmly closed behind him.

"What do you think you're doing here?" Mr Wetherby said. "Do you think I want to be seen associating with a bankrupt?"

"It didn't worry you last week."

"I didn't think you'd have the nerve to show up here. You're a disgrace to the family. A number of your creditors are personal friends of mine, how do you think that makes me look?"

William glared at his stepfather. "I'm sorry if I've been an embarrassment to you, but you could have prevented this whole thing."

"This mess is of your own making, as I've told you often enough. What were you thinking of assigning the book debts to Mr White when they should have gone to the creditors?"

"But it was your idea. I'd never heard of it, but you said it was usual practice."

"I didn't realise you had so many other creditors; your solicitor should have advised you on that."

"You saw the books, you knew as well as anyone else."

"I didn't expect you to leave yourself with no working capital."

"You've always told me the best place for my money was in property."

"Only if you had enough of it to spare, I didn't tell you to invest it all. Didn't you listen?"

"Yes, of course I did, but you encouraged everything I did to the point where the money ran out. I only needed one thousand pounds and the whole bankruptcy would have been prevented. It might be a lot to me, but it's probably no more than you give Charlotte to spend on dresses in a year."

"What I do with my money is none of your concern."

William walked to the window. "You've never forgiven me for leaving the business and you couldn't stand by and watch me make a success of things."

Mr Wetherby's eyes narrowed as he glared at his stepson. "I would hardly say that getting rid of Mr Ball was making a success of things."

"I had no choice, I wanted him to stay."

"Not as much as you wanted to get your hands on the traveller's daughter. I know all about it."

"That was completely separate."

"Not when Mr Ball had told you he wouldn't deal with that particular traveller."

"You seem to know an awful lot about things.

Did you interrogate Mr White as much as you did Mr Ball?"

Mr Wetherby glanced at his pocket watch. "I've never met Mr White, now get out, we've finished this conversation."

"Oh no, we haven't. There's the small matter of Arthur. Your daughter desperately wants a baby and I have one; couldn't you give me fifty pounds for him? Do you want me to suffer so much that you'd deprive your precious daughter of the one thing she wants?"

"If I gave you any money now it'd go straight to the creditors."

"No it wouldn't. My personal money is still my own."

"Nonsense. If anyone sees you walking around with money, they'll assume it came from me."

"Have you no sympathy? I'm not going to go on a spending spree; I only need help to pay the mortgage and buy some food and coal. Is that too much to ask?"

Mr Wetherby's steely eyes didn't falter. "I can't do that and you know it. I can't be seen aiding and abetting a criminal."

William stopped and stared at the man he had admired for so long. "What has happened to you? You're not the man who married my mother; he wouldn't stand by and watch me struggle like this. I genuinely thought you cared for me, but now I can see how wrong I was. Well, you can tell Charlotte the offer of having Arthur is off. I refuse to give him away for nothing.

"Get out of here ... now. And you can tell William-Wetherby not to bother coming back as well. I've had enough of the pair of you. You see me as a never-ending pot of money that you're entitled to whenever you want. Well, let me tell you, you're entitled to nothing; you've had enough money off me to last a lifetime and I'll make sure you don't see another penny."

"So you'd see us starve before you'd do anything to help?"

"The guardians won't let you starve. I suggest you pay them a visit."

William grabbed Mr Wetherby by the collar of his jacket. "How can you pretend to be a respectable and God-fearing man when you don't give a damn about anyone but yourself? I hope you rot in hell."

William pushed him against the wall and stormed from the workshop. With his heart racing and his eyes fixed on the road, he didn't notice where he was going until twenty minutes later he found himself near the Town Hall. As he approached the building he stopped to take in the details of the Roman columns with their sloping roof, before he noticed the steps across the front. He remembered his mother sitting there over forty years earlier, trying to sell the clothes she had made so they had enough money to eat. In his mind he saw himself and Mary-Ann playing in the square and remembered how excited he'd been by Mr Wetherby, the nice man who would give him and Mary-Ann a penny and who took them to the fair. Would his mother have married him had he not encouraged her? He walked over to the steps and sat down as tears rolled down his cheeks. He had worshipped Mr Wetherby, so much so that he'd named his first-born son after him. How had it gone so wrong?

He remained on the steps for over half an hour, oblivious to everything around him, until a police constable moved him on. It was the final straw. He reached into his pocket and felt for the money Mr Watkins had given him. One drink wouldn't do him any harm.

Once he left the office, William-Wetherby hurried

down the street to Mrs Storey's house, hoping Sid was at home.

"I thought you'd patched things up with Mr Jackson," Sid said when he arrived.

"I have, but he's called at the workshop to see Mr Wetherby. I wanted to wait here until he'd finished."

"Well, sit yourself down and have some tea with us," Mrs Storey said.

William-Wetherby stayed for longer than he had planned and when he returned to the workshop the place was in darkness. Presuming his father had returned to Handsworth he went back to the Storeys' house, hoping to spend the night. Several hours later, as they finished their card game, there was a knock on the door.

"Who's this at this hour of the night?" Mrs Storey said. "Probably some shameless drunk I shouldn't wonder."

Sid opened the door as William leaned forward and fell into the living room.

"Father, what's happened?" William-Wetherby jumped up to help William to his feet. "Sid, help me. I can't lift him."

Once inside, William fell into a chair but said nothing.

"Father, what happened? Who gave you the

money to get yourself into such a state? Was it Mr Wetherby?"

William shook his head.

"Well, somebody did. Who was it?"

William's face stayed blank.

"You must remember. Do you have any left?"

William put his hand in his pocket and pulled out some notes.

"He's got four pounds here, and a ten-bob note. Where on earth did he get it from? You don't think he stole it, do you?"

"He wouldn't steal. He may be going through a hard time, but he's still a gentleman," Mrs Storey said. "He must have got it from Mr Wetherby."

William-Wetherby stared at his father. "If he's like this now, what will he be like after the public hearing?"

"I'm sure Mrs Jackson will take care of him," Mrs Storey said.

"Lydia?" William-Wetherby shook his head. *She won't support him, especially not with Arthur as he is.* "He needs more than Lydia; he needs a miracle."

CHAPTER FORTY-FOUR

William's stomach somersaulted as he spotted William-Wetherby waiting for him outside Birmingham County Court. He knew he was trying to help, but he shouldn't have to witness this.

"How are you feeling?" his son asked as William approached. "Did you manage to sleep last night?"

"Do I look as if I did? Arthur won't be quiet for more than a few minutes at a time and at this moment I feel like a condemned man about to go to the gallows."

"I'm sure it won't be that bad." William-Wetherby patted him on the arm.

"You're not the one who'll be standing in court

with everyone you've ever known listening to how you ruined a thriving business."

Three hours later, William stood in the dock, clutching the rail before him. He'd been standing for so long he feared he would collapse if he let go. He lowered his face towards the floor and closed his eyes. How tightly did he have to squeeze them to block all of this out? The receiver had spent the last two hours going through every transaction, and every mistake, he had made since Mr Ball had left the company over a year earlier. To be ridiculed by one man in the privacy of an office would have been bad enough, but this. This was beyond anything anyone should be expected to bear. He would never forget the judgement on the faces of his previous employees and creditors, his neighbours, friends and acquaintances as they squashed into the public gallery. He'd even spotted a couple of brethren from the Lodge. He had listened to the gasps and sniggers as the receiver had detailed his business to the point where all he wanted to do was curl up and hide. How would he ever be able to face them again?

Once the ordeal was over, William-Wetherby helped him down from the dock.

"I need to sit down," William said. "Find me somewhere private. I can't bear anyone watching me."

William-Wetherby escorted him to a chair at the side of the room. "It's over now. In a few days' time everyone will have forgotten and moved on to some other poor soul."

William shook his head. "No they won't. I've got to come back again, and did you see the people who were here? Everyone I've ever known."

"They were here to support you."

"They were here to ridicule me. Couldn't you see it in their eyes? They're not going to forget this; nobody will. How will I show my face in public again? It's bad enough facing you. No son should ever have to watch his father go through such an ordeal."

"I don't think any less of you." William-Wetherby put his hand on his father's shoulder. "I know what happened and it wasn't your fault. Let's take you home and you can stay indoors for a few days until you're ready to face the world again."

William pushed down on the base of the chair to ease himself up, but stopped before he was upright when a man wearing a dark overcoat approached him.

"Mr Jackson," the man said.

William straightened himself up. "Mr Black. I didn't expect to see you today."

Mr Black's face remained stern. "We saw the notice in the newspaper and the Grand Master asked me to give him a report of the proceedings."

William glanced at his son. "I've never told you before, but I joined the Freemasons a couple of years ago, after your mother died. This is Mr Black from the Lodge."

William-Wetherby extended his hand to the stranger.

"I'm sorry I've brought disgrace on the Lodge," William said.

"Fortunately, because the society values discretion, I don't believe any harm's been done. If I understood the proceedings correctly, you weren't solely responsible for the fate of the company. I'll make sure the Grand Master knows. In the meantime, I wanted to tell you that if you need any help, the brethren will be there for you. All you need to do is ask."

William gave the man a weak smile. "Thank you, I appreciate that. There are not many willing to help."

As he arrived home, William heard Lydia trying to

soothe Arthur's cries in the back room and went straight upstairs and sat on the bed. William-Wetherby followed him and offered him a small bottle of whisky from his pocket.

"Here, drink this," he said. "You look like you could do with it."

"Is this what it's come to, drinking from a bottle?" William said. "Are you having some?"

"No, you can finish it. I need to find myself a job if you remember. Someone has to earn some money ... I mean I need a job. I'm sorry, I didn't mean it to come out like that. I'm going to ask Mrs Storey if I can move in with her as well. You don't need an extra mouth to feed at the moment and it'll make life easier if I find a job in Birmingham. I'll see you later."

Once he was alone, William emptied the rest of the bottle. He wasn't sure if he was relieved or frustrated that it was so small, but at least the decision to drink himself into a stupor had been taken from him. Once it was empty, he tossed it across the floor and lay on the bed, staring at the ceiling. What did he have to live for now? With few exceptions, everything and everyone he had ever cared for was gone: his mother, his wife, his business, and his relationship with Mr Wetherby. Four of his children had left home and he was stuck with a wife who didn't want to be with him. He could still picture the receiver going through his accounts and see the reactions from the people who were crowded into the courtroom. Did he have a friend left in the world?

As the light faded, he drifted off to sleep. The sound of crying brought clarity to the image in his mind and he shouted out as everyone in the public gallery stood up to jeer at him. His eyes sprang open and he sat bolt upright expecting to face his tormentors, but the nightlight had burned out and he saw nothing in the pitch black. He gasped for breath as he listened to the crying coming from the other room. With his heart racing, he lay back on the bed and shivered. Whether it was due to the perspiration soaking through his shirt, or fear, he had no idea, but he couldn't close his eyes again. Not if the demons were going to dominate his dreams.

As the daylight increased, William moved to the chair and dozed by the window. He wasn't sure how long he had been there when Lydia knocked on the bedroom door and let herself in. He glanced up and noticed the red rims around her eyes as her hair hung limply around her face.

"You need to go and fetch the doctor. I can't take much more of this. Arthur's had me up half the night and he needs something to settle him. I know we're short of money, but this is urgent, especially if Charlotte's going to visit him."

William turned his gaze away from her. "She's not having him."

"She's not? Why?"

"Ask Mr Wetherby."

"Don't be ridiculous, I can't ask him. Tell me what happened." As she spoke, Arthur's cry's filtered into the room. "All right, tell me later, but you have to go and fetch the doctor."

William shook his head. "That would mean going outside."

"Of course it would." Lydia stood with her hands on her hips.

"I can't."

"What do you mean, you can't? Of course you can, you put on your hat and coat and walk out the front door."

William remained silent as he broke into a cold sweat.

"William, what's the matter? Are you all right? Talk to me."

His breath came in gasps. "I can't go out. They're waiting for me."

"Who are?"

"Everyone. The neighbours, people I used to

think of as friends, those who used to work for me. They'll be outside ready to point their fingers and laugh at me."

"Of course they won't." Lydia walked over to the window. "Look, nobody there."

"They'll be waiting round the corner or looking out of their windows ready to pounce."

"Don't be ridiculous. People have better things to do than wait for you to go into the street. What's the matter with you? If it makes it easier, I'll come with you."

William's eyes were wide as he pleaded with her. "Didn't you hear me? I'm not going out. Not now, not ever. If you want something for Arthur, you'll have to go yourself."

CHAPTER FORTY-FIVE

William-Wetherby leaned back in his chair as he finished his second cup of tea. With no job to rush off to he reached for the newspaper but put it back on the table when Mrs Storey handed him a letter.

William-Wetherby took it from her and frowned. It was Lydia's writing. He took it from the envelope and scanned it.

"I'll have to change my plans for today. Father won't leave the house. He thinks people are waiting in the street to ridicule him."

"That doesn't sound normal," Mrs Storey said. "What will you do?"

William-Wetherby shrugged. "I've no idea. I remember when Mother thought Mr Wetherby wanted to send her to prison, you couldn't reason with her. That was when she ended up going back into the asylum. I hope he's not having a funny turn like she did."

"I wonder if he should talk to someone his own age?"

William-Wetherby thought for several seconds. "He hasn't seen much of Aunt Mary-Ann since they moved to Birmingham and I think he misses her. Perhaps I'll pay her a call."

It was eleven o'clock by the time William-Wetherby arrived at the Divers' house. Mary-Ann was alone and showed him into the back room.

"What brings you here at this hour of the day? Shouldn't you be at work?"

"I take it you haven't heard? Father and Mr Wetherby fell out over the bankruptcy and I ended up losing my job."

"Good grief." Mary-Ann put two cups and saucers on the table and took her seat. "You'd better tell me what I've been missing."

William-Wetherby scratched his head. "Where do I start? You've missed so much."

Mary-Ann shook her head. "I wish we hadn't had to move away but it was unavoidable. How did your father's hearing go? Mr Diver deliberately stayed away so your father wouldn't be embarrassed. Was it as bad as it sounded in the newspaper?"

"Mr Diver was one of the few who did stay away, along with Mr Wetherby. It was terrible to see him humiliated in front of so many people. People who used to respect him."

"I should have written to him."

"I'm not sure it would have helped, but I've come to ask if you'll pay him a visit. He seems to think everyone's waiting outside the house to humiliate him again. I'm hoping that seeing a few friendly faces might help."

"Hasn't it helped having a new baby in the house?"

William-Wetherby snorted. "You won't know the saga about Lydia either. It turns out she only married Father for his money, and now he's a bankrupt she doesn't want to know him. On top of that, Arthur's not well and spends half his life screaming. It's a terrible place to be at the moment."

"I'm glad you called, I'd have visited sooner if I'd known." Mary-Ann glanced at the clock on the mantelpiece. "Mr Diver will be home shortly. Why don't you stay for dinner and I'll ask him if one of his men can run us to Handsworth this afternoon."

Handsworth, Staffordshire.

Sarah-Ann stood by the front door of Havelock Road and took a deep breath. She wasn't sure if she was doing the right thing but she'd read about the bankruptcy in the newspaper and Mr Wetherby refused to talk to her about it. It took a minute for the door to be opened and she was shocked by the appearance of the girl before her. She was of average height but was the thinnest woman she had ever seen. Her dress was at least a size too big for her and her fair hair was crudely taken up into a knot on the top of her head.

"Can I help you?" Lydia said.

"I'm here to visit my nephew, Mr Jackson. Is he in?"

Lydia stared at her, her eyes almost vacant, before she invited Sarah-Ann in. "He's not receiving visitors. I can take a message."

Sarah-Ann noted everything was still intact in the hall. "Would Mrs Jackson be in? We haven't met and I'd like a word with her."

Lydia showed Sarah-Ann into the back room and gestured for her to sit down. "I'm Mrs Jackson ... Lydia. What can I do for you?"

"You?" Sarah-Ann's eyes were wide.

"Don't tell me, I don't look old enough. You're

right, I'm not old enough to have to deal with this." Tears formed in Lydia's eyes but she brushed them away.

"I don't know what to say. Have you been eating? You're so thin ... and tired."

"Eating's the last thing I've got to worry about. I've a child who's sick, a husband who thinks the world is out to get him, and no money in the cupboard. Eating isn't an option."

Sarah-Ann glanced around the room. "Where is the child? Can I see him?"

"Not at the moment. He's upstairs and I've just got him to sleep after nursing him for the last three hours. I need to sleep myself while he does."

"Have you had the doctor to him?"

Lydia shook her head. "Until we sell some furniture, we have no money and William won't do anything."

"You can't leave him feeling sorry for himself. You have to be firm with him."

Lydia studied the well-dressed woman standing in front of her. "You don't understand, he's living in a different world. He's imagining that everyone he's ever known is waiting for him in the street ready to ridicule him. It's as if he can see them. I'm scared." Lydia collapsed onto the settee, her sobs evident. Sarah-Ann put her arm around her shoulders.

"Don't cry. I'll ask Mr Wetherby to help."

Lydia jumped from her seat and glared at Sarah-Ann. "Mr Wetherby? Are you his wife? Don't you know that he's the cause of all this. He's the one who wouldn't help William and the one William's having the most nightmares about."

Sarah-Ann's face paled. "He told me William didn't want his help."

"He's a liar." Lydia wiped her cheeks with the back of her hand. "William begged him to give us some money so Charlotte could have Arthur, but he refused."

Sarah-Ann put a hand on her chest as her face flushed. "That explains so much. I've never seen Charlotte so angry with him before. What's he up to? He may be my husband but William is my brother's son. Tell me what you need. I'll make sure the doctor visits both of them, and if you have any more trouble, you must tell me. Write to me at Wetherby House. He doesn't read my letters."

As Lydia sat back down the front door opened and William-Wetherby came in with Mary-Ann.

"Aunt Sarah-Ann." William-Wetherby stopped in his tracks. "What are you doing here? You're not with Mr Wetherby, are you?"

Sarah-Ann let out a deep sigh. "No, I'm not and I can only apologise for him. He's been in such a bad mood these last few weeks, I've not been able to talk to him. I'd no idea he wouldn't help."

"It wasn't that he didn't offer, he actively refused to help despite the fact Father begged him," William-Wetherby said. "I don't know whether the two of them will ever be able to talk to each other again after what's been said."

"Can I see William?" Sarah-Ann said. "I need to tell him we're not all like that."

"I'm here for the same reason," Mary-Ann said. "Shall we see him together?"

CHAPTER FORTY-SIX

Lydia led the way upstairs and knocked on the bedroom door before she went in. William slouched in a chair by the bed with the curtains closed.

"William, can we come in? You have visitors."

William jumped to his feet. "No, send them away. I don't want to see anyone."

"It's your sister and aunt." Lydia took hold of his hands. "They won't hurt you. They want to help."

"My aunt? Which one? Not the one who married the devil himself?"

Mary-Ann walked towards him. "William, please don't say that. Aunt Sarah-Ann wants to help."

"How can she help when she's married to *him*?" William spat the last word out.

"William, that's enough," Sarah-Ann said. "Mr Wetherby's been generous over the years. There must have been a misunderstanding."

William glared at her as he pulled his hands from Lydia. "There was no misunderstanding, he knew exactly what he was doing. He wanted me ruined and ridiculed in front of my friends and colleagues. Well, they can wait outside for as long as they like, I'm not going out."

"William, there is no one outside," Lydia glanced at those around her. "I've told you before."

"You can't see them, they're hiding. Of course they won't come out for you."

"She's telling the truth," William-Wetherby said. "I came down Havelock Road and saw no one."

William moved to the wall, his eyes darting from one to the other. "Why should I believe you? How do I know you're not trying to trick me?"

"Because we're telling the truth," Sarah-Ann said. "Mr Wetherby doesn't know I'm here and I'm not going to tell him. I have my own money and I'm going to ask the doctor to call and visit you and Arthur. We all want you well again."

As if on cue, the silence in the room was

disturbed by the sound of Arthur crying in the other bedroom. "That's not a normal cry," Sarah-Ann said. "Let me see him."

~

Mary-Ann watched her aunt leave the room with Lydia before she stepped towards William and took his hand.

"Look at me," she said. "This isn't like you."

William gazed at his sister through narrowed eyes. "Who sent you? Was it Mr Diver?"

"No, of course it wasn't."

"I went for her," William-Wetherby said. "We're worried about you. You had a difficult time in the courtroom, but it's over now. We want to help."

William slumped into the chair. "Nobody can help me any more, I'm finished."

"That's enough; of course you're not finished," Mary-Ann said. "What would Harriet say if she saw you like this?"

"It's all her fault. If she hadn't left me ..."

Mary-Ann rolled her eyes. "She didn't do it on purpose. She loved you and you still have her five children to take care of, not to mention Arthur. You can't give up on them. They all need you, I need you."

"William-Wetherby and Eleanor don't need me. I'm nothing more than a drain on them at the moment and Charles isn't here."

"What about the other three? You need to find yourself a new job."

"What can I do? Nobody will employ me and I can't start another business until I'm discharged from the bankruptcy. I've still got to endure the final hearing as well. I can't do it."

William leaned forward, his elbows resting on his knees, as Lydia and Sarah-Ann came back into the room.

"Have you seen that child?" Sarah-Ann said to William. "You should be ashamed of yourself not getting the doctor to him. He's nothing but skin and bone. I'm going to fetch him now and I'll take Florence back to Wetherby House with me when she comes home from school. She can't possibly stay here when you can't even take care of yourself. I'll tell Mr Wetherby she's staying with us for the foreseeable future and Margaret can join us when she finishes school for Christmas."

As Sarah-Ann left the room, William-Wetherby perched on the edge of the bed.

"I'll speak to her." Mary-Ann looked between

the two men.

"What's the point? She's right," William said. "I can't take care of my own daughters while I'm like this. It'll be better for both of them if they have nothing to do with me."

~

Lydia had only just dropped off to sleep the following morning when a hammering on the door brought her back to reality. She fumbled her way down the stairs and opened the door to the doctor. With one look at her, he took off his hat and stepped into the hall.

"If you're the only member of the family who's healthy I shudder to think what else awaits me."

"I'm sorry, Doctor. Arthur's had me awake for most of the night and I'd only just dropped off to sleep. He was sleeping himself, but it sounds as if the noise has disturbed him again."

"You'd better take me to him."

Once in the bedroom, the doctor studied the tiny figure in the cradle. Setting his bag on the floor, he picked Arthur up and laid him on the bed.

"This child's starving," he said to Lydia. "Has he been taking milk?"

"I don't know." Lydia's voice was barely a

whisper. "He seems to suckle, but I've no idea how much he takes before the crying starts again. Anything he does take comes straight out the other end. I don't know what to do." She sat on the bed and held Arthur's tiny hand.

"For a start, I'll give him some laudanum. He's too small for it really but I would say this is an emergency. It should slow his bowel movements and help him sleep. It should help you too. Now let me see you."

Lydia put Arthur back in his cradle before the doctor began his examination.

"When did you last eat?" he asked.

"I had a piece of bread and butter last night."

"And before that, when did you last have a hot meal?"

Lydia stared out of the window, her face concentrating. "Last Sunday, William-Wetherby brought a small piece of bacon."

"My dear, you can't hope to feed a small child when you're not eating yourself."

"What can I do?" Lydia's eyes filled with tears. "My husband's a bankrupt and until he sells some of the furniture I can't buy anything."

The doctor shook his head. "Let me see him."

Lydia knocked on William's bedroom door before she pushed it open for the doctor and let him go in. William was in his now familiar position by the window, with the curtains drawn, but didn't move when they went in.

"Good morning, Mr Jackson," the doctor said.

"William, the doctor's here," Lydia said when William failed to answer.

"Can you tell me what's been happening?" the doctor asked Lydia. "I read in the newspaper about the bankruptcy."

Once Lydia had explained, the doctor approached William and raised a hand in front of his eyes. William flinched before he stared at the doctor.

"I would say he's severely traumatised." The doctor took hold of William's wrist to feel his pulse. "His heart's racing. Has he been sleeping?"

Lydia shrugged. "I never see him in bed, he barely moves from this chair. Can you help him? I can't manage with him being like this."

"I think the three of you need to sleep. I'm going to give you some laudanum for Mr Jackson as well as Arthur and I want you to sleep while you can as well. Do you have anyone who can help you?"

Lydia thought of William-Wetherby. Would he help her after everything that had happened? She nodded. "I think so."

CHAPTER FORTY-SEVEN

Lydia walked down the stairs into the hallway but felt no pity for the now empty space where the dresser had once stood. Neither did she have regrets over selling the sideboard from the back room. They hadn't got as much money for them as she'd hoped, but feeling the crown coins in her pocket, more than made up for them. The dining table and chairs, and settee and armchairs from the front room were going tomorrow. William-Wetherby had been busy.

She smiled to herself in the mirror as she put on her hat and coat. It was amazing what three full nights' sleep could do. She had even managed to eat breakfast and tea for two of those days. Still, with winter approaching, the money wouldn't last long.

Knowing Arthur would sleep for the rest of the morning, she opened the front door and stepped outside. She had things to do.

The advertisement in the newspaper said that being a tobacconist's assistant came with a decent rate of pay. Her father had smoked a pipe and she had often filled it for him. That must qualify her for the job. She made her way to Birmingham on foot and soon found the shop on Summer Lane. After a moment's hesitation she went in.

"Have you come about the job?" the woman behind the counter asked.

"I have, is it obvious?"

"We don't see many women in here. Men prefer to buy their own tobacco. Would that trouble you?"

Lydia stifled a laugh. "Not at all. I'm a married woman with a couple of stepsons; I'm used to men."

"Can you leave them on their own?"

"Neither lives with us, only my young son."

The woman raised an eyebrow at her. "What will you do with him? You can't bring him here."

"Why not? He sleeps most of the time."

"Maybe now he does, but they grow up. You said you were married, why do you need a job?"

Lydia's eyes welled with tears. "My husband's

ill and can't work at the moment. Please help me, I've nowhere else to go and we need the money."

The woman studied her. "I'll tell you what. I've a friend who lives on Birchfield Road; she takes babies in. I'll give you her details and if she'll take yours, you can have the job. Tell her Mrs Firth sent you."

Lydia took the piece of paper from Mrs Firth and went outside. This Mrs Cousins didn't live far from them in Handsworth. If she could take Arthur for a couple of months that should give them enough time to sort themselves out and she could have him back in the New Year. As she stared at the address, a knot formed in her stomach. She didn't want to leave her baby. Sensing tears in her eyes, she blinked them away and took a deep breath. She was doing this for Arthur and two months would pass in no time. She had to do it.

When Lydia knocked on the door in Birchfield Road a woman in her mid-fifties, wearing an apron and carrying a scrubbing brush, answered.

"Mrs Cousins?" Lydia said. "Mrs Firth from the tobacconist's on Summer Lane sent me. She said you take in children."

"I do indeed, come on in." Mrs Cousins ushered her into a small living room surrounded by cribs. "Are you expecting?"

"No, I have a baby, Arthur, he's two months old, but my husband can't work and I need to take a job."

"You've come to the right place, my dear; I have a space for a baby at the moment. If you want me to take care of him I'll need a lump sum of ten shillings up front."

Lydia's eyes were wide. "Ten shillings ... in advance?"

"That's cheap, there are others who want a lot more."

"But I don't have ten shillings ... not to spare." Lydia felt tears forming but did nothing to stop them. "Can I pay some of the money in advance and give you the rest once I start work?"

"I'm sorry, dear, I need payment in advance. Come back to me when you have the money."

Lydia hesitated as tears rolled down her cheeks. "I'll find it, I promise ... although it may take a few weeks. Please say you'll take him. We're desperate."

CHAPTER FORTY-EIGHT

William stood in the hall of Havelock Road staring at his hat and coat. All he had to do was put them on and walk out of the front door, but he couldn't move. Despite having a dose of laudanum with breakfast, his heart was racing and he held on to the wall to stop himself swaying. He was about to go back into the living room, when William-Wetherby arrived.

"Are you ready?" he asked.

"I can't do it." William's breath was fast and shallow.

"Of course you can. No one is going to say anything that hasn't been said before and not many people are likely to turn up."

"But what if they do?"

"They won't. Now come on or we're going to be late. Let me help you with your coat."

As they left, William picked up the walking cane propped up by the front door.

"You won't need that, I've got enough money for the omnibus," William-Wetherby said. *I need to make this as easy as possible.*

Thirty minutes later, as they approached the court, William stopped and gazed up at the building.

"Come on, you're doing well," William-Wetherby said. "Remember, this is the end of it and it won't be as bad as last time. It should only be you and the trustees."

"Look at me," William said. "My hands are shaking."

"Take a few deep breaths. I'll be there for you."

The courtroom was almost empty when they arrived and William let his shoulders relax. There were no neighbours or ex-employees, and thankfully it didn't appear as if the press would turn up either. They took a seat on the front row and within a minute, Mr Rodney joined them.

"What can we expect today, sir?" William-Wetherby asked.

"It won't be much. The trustees will summarise the amount of money they expect to raise from the sale of equipment and other effects, before discussing what to do about the shortfall."

The hearing was over within half an hour but William felt physically sick as he left the building. The auditors had determined that some of the cash belonging to the business was in fact missing and he was ordered to repay ten pounds.

"Where am I going to find that sort of money?" William said to his son. "You've already sold most items of any value and I bet you didn't get much for them."

"I didn't."

"It may be that you need to put the house up for sale," Mr Rodney said.

William shook his head. "They're still building houses in the area. How can I sell mine at a profit, when the builders are still offering them at a discount?"

"You still need to try," William-Wetherby said. "You won't sell it if you don't advertise. You need to think about getting a job too. Mr Diver has said you can work for him."

"Making cardboard boxes won't give me the money I need."

"Stop making excuses. If you don't want to work for Mr Diver I'm sure there'll be something for you, but not if that's your attitude. What about the man who came to see you from the Freemasons? Mr Black. He said they'd help, but I'm guessing you haven't been to a meeting since."

"How can I face them again after this?"

"You walk into the Lodge with your head held high and find out if anyone knows of any jobs where they work. You have to start helping yourself. Lydia and I can't do it all."

By the time William arrived home Lydia was in the kitchen with a pot of broth bubbling on the stove. She smiled when she saw him. "How did it go?"

William took a seat in the morning room. "I think we're going to have to make that broth stretch, they need more money from me."

"More?" Lydia's eyes were wide. "They can't."

"They've realised ten pounds was missing from the cash register and want it returned. I'm not sure what else we can sell."

"If you take ten pounds, we'll have nothing left. What will I give to Mrs Cousins?"

William stared at Lydia. "Who's Mrs Cousins?"

"She's going to take Arthur in for a few weeks. I've taken a job in Birmingham."

"A job?" William was on his feet. "You can't work."

"At this rate, if I don't, we're going to end up in the workhouse and I've no intention of letting that happen."

"But it should be me who provides for us."

"Yes it should, but I've seen no sign of that happening. We can't sit here until the bank call to take the house off you."

"But who's this Mrs Cousins? Where did you find her?"

"I was introduced to her because she takes in babies for women who need to work. She seems nice enough."

"Lydia, what are you doing?"

Lydia's eyes were like slits. "I'm trying to salvage some sort of respectability. At least I'm doing something positive. I've managed to save two shillings from the money William-Wetherby and Eleanor gave us last week, and I found a couple of silver candlesticks in the cupboard that should fetch a reasonable price. I'll try and sell them this week."

"You can't sell them, they were Harriet's ... a present from her aunt and uncle."

Lydia shrugged. "Well they're no use to her now, are they? Do you think she'd rather you starve?"

William sat down and sighed. "You shouldn't have to do this. Where will you be working?"

"In a tobacconist's shop on Summer Lane."

"It will cost you half your wages to travel there and back every day."

Lydia stared at the top of William's head. "There's a small flat above the shop. Mrs Firth, the owner, said I can use it free of charge."

William jerked his head up to look at her. "What about me? I can't stay here on my own."

"For the time being you'll have to. I'll visit Arthur when I can and call here too. Why don't you leave this house? It's not a home any more and it's only going to get colder. How are you going to pay for coal?"

William slumped in his chair. "If I leave here my old life will be gone. How can I do that?" He pushed himself up and walked into the hall, stopping at the bottom of the stairs to catch his breath. By the time he reached the bedroom, stars floated in front of his eyes, and he threw himself onto the bed before he collapsed. Did this mean Harriet had finally gone?

CHAPTER FORTY-NINE

Lydia wiped the tears from her eyes as she gazed down at Arthur. This tiny baby had been part of her life for eleven weeks, but those weeks coincided exactly with the time his father had been bankrupt. She glanced at the small selection of knitted cardigans, breeches and hats waiting to be put into a paper bag. That was the sum total of all he owned. He should have had a good life. The man she married had been wealthy, owned his own house, his own business, horses and a carriage. His older children all had gone to private school. Her son should have had that, but instead he was going to Mrs Cousins so she could work.

"Come on, Arthur." She bent down to pick him up. "Time to say bye-bye to Papa."

William was in the kitchen when she found him. "We're going," she said.

He stroked his son's head. "It won't be for long. We'll come and get you soon, I promise. If there's one thing that will make me well enough to find a job, it's the thought of bringing you home again." He gave Lydia a feeble smile. "Please tell Mrs Cousins to take care of him, won't you?"

Lydia walked to Birchfield Road with Arthur clutched to her chest. He was still painfully thin and only the laudanum stopped him from crying, but he was hers and she didn't want to do this.

Mrs Cousins saw her arrive and opened the front door before she reached it. "Come in, dear," she said. "I presume this is Arthur." Mrs Cousins took him and laid him in the empty basket waiting for him.

"He's had some laudanum this morning to settle his stomach." Lydia pulled a near empty bottle from the bag. "There's a little left if you need it."

"Don't worry, dear, I've plenty here. The foster mother's best friend." Mrs Cousins patted the pocket of her apron. "You won't find an unhappy child here. Do you have the money?"

"I do ... well, some of it." Lydia reached into her pocket. "I can give you five shillings now, and I'll pay the rest in December. I've worked out I'll be able to save over a shilling a week and so I'll be back on the sixteenth of December with the rest."

"That's not the way I work, I can't take him if you don't pay upfront."

"Please, Mrs Cousins, we're desperate. If I could pay you now I would, but I need to work to earn the rest of the money."

Mrs Cousins stared at her. "Very well, I'll make this an exception, but if you're not here by the sixteenth, I'll have to move him on."

"No, please, you can't do that. I'll be here, I promise. Please take care of him. One day I want to take him home."

Mrs Cousins patted her on the shoulder. "Of course you do, dear. Trust me, I'll do what's best for him."

Fighting the tears that threatened to overwhelm her, Lydia walked to the basket where Arthur now slept. "Goodbye, Arthur. I love you."

CHAPTER FIFTY

Bushwood, Warwickshire

Mr Wetherby surveyed the table that was set for breakfast. A bowl of freshly boiled eggs sat in the centre surrounded by a selection of home-made jams, butter and sweet buns. A newly baked loaf of bread was waiting to be sliced.

"That bread smells good," he said to Sarah-Ann as he took his seat at the head of the table.

"So it should, Cook's only just taken it from the oven. You might want to leave it a few minutes before you slice it. Take a couple of eggs first while they're still soft; they're the first batch from the new hens."

Mr Wetherby helped himself before he cut a

thick slice of bread and spread it generously with butter. He ate in silence while Sarah-Ann poured some tea.

"Will we spend Christmas here this year?" Sarah-Ann said from the seat opposite him.

"I would think so. We have everything we need and plenty of room for everyone. I imagine William Junior and Olivia will be expecting us. We can have a marvellous tree in the bay window of the front room."

"I presume Elizabeth's invited ... and Margaret and Florence?"

"Of course, they're part of the family now. Why do you ask?"

Sarah-Ann hesitated. "I wondered if you might consider inviting William and Mary-Ann."

Mr Wetherby threw his napkin on the table. "Why would we do that? There'd be another ten of them if they all came, and they're not bringing that baby here. I'm not having Christmas ruined."

"I feel guilty about what's happened to William this year. We should have helped him."

"Well you can stop feeling sorry for him, he brought it on himself."

"Why are you so harsh? Surely people can be forgiven for making mistakes."

"His mistake cost me a lot of money. I'll never

forgive that wife of his, and he did nothing to stop her."

"I don't think in his wildest dreams he'd have imagined being bankrupt."

"When you go into business you have to be prepared for everything."

Sarah-Ann put down her tea and stared at her husband. "Is this solely about money or is there more to it than that?"

Mr Wetherby checked his pocket watch and rose to his feet. "He left me and took a sizable chunk of my business with him. He wanted nothing to do with me, thinking his fool of a wife could help him more than I could. Have you any idea how much that hurt? I was like a father to that boy and he threw it in my face. He's never shown any sign of regret or apologised for anything he's done and then he expects me to bail him out; well, I'm sorry, he made his bed and he can lie in it. I want nothing more to do with him. Now, come on or we'll be late for church."

Handsworth, Staffordshire.

William sat alone by the stove in the kitchen of

Havelock Road, reading the newspaper. It wasn't today's paper, just one William-Wetherby had found and delivered to him, but at least he was warm and the stove meant he only needed a candle to read by. As he turned the page, he was disturbed by a knock on the front door. *Who's this at this time of night?* Cursing the fact he had to go into the hall and let out some heat he pulled a blanket tightly around his shoulders and walked to the front door. His trustee, Mr Fisher, was waiting for him.

"What can I do for you?" William asked, as he invited him in.

"Good evening, Mr Jackson. You have a little more colour in your face than last time I saw you."

"I've been better, but then again I've been worse. What can I do for you?"

"Nothing at all. I've called to tell you someone's interested in buying the business."

A smile lit up William's face. "That's marvellous news. Who is it?"

"I can't tell you at the moment, we're still in negotiations, but I thought you'd appreciate knowing. As soon as I have any more news, I'll let you know."

"Thank you, I appreciate it. When do you think that'll be?"

Mr Fisher shrugged. "I can't say for sure, but I'd estimate a few weeks."

"Will that be the end of things once it's sold? I can put all this behind me?"

"Yes, now you've paid the ten pounds owing, we'll be able to wrap everything up with the sale. I'll be in touch when I have more news. Good evening to you."

CHAPTER FIFTY-ONE

Birmingham, Warwickshire

It took William almost an hour to walk to Mr Watkins's house on Tower Road and the further he travelled from Handsworth the more he relaxed. Nobody knew him around these parts and at least Mr Watkins would be pleased the business was being sold as a going concern.

The house was a small terraced property set in the middle of a row of six. He knocked on the door but when he received no answer he knocked again and tried the door handle. The door opened as he pushed it and he stepped into the small living room to find the table was still set for breakfast. It was almost eleven o'clock. Mrs Twainley, Mr Watkins's housekeeper, must have gone out.

The stairs were situated in the back left-hand corner of the room and William walked to them before shouting up for Mr Watkins. When he got no reply, he returned to the room but hesitated when he heard a noise coming from upstairs. Taking the stairs as fast as he could, he hurried into the bedroom and found Mr Watkins lying face down on the floor.

"Mr Watkins, whatever happened? How long have you been like this?"

Mr Watkins lifted his head, but couldn't speak.

"Don't worry, there's no need to talk," William said. "You've hit the side of your head on something, relax and let me help you onto the bed." William tried to lift Mr Watkins but almost fell himself when the old man collapsed beneath him. He tried again until, on the third attempt, he bundled Mr Watkins onto the bed.

Gasping for breath, William perched on the side of the mattress and stared at his late wife's uncle.

"I'd say you need a doctor." William wiped the blood from the side of Mr Watkins's head with a face cloth. "Let me get you some water before I go and fetch him." Still panting, William ran downstairs but when he returned to the bedroom and gave Mr Watkins the cup, he was unable to hold it.

As William moved to help him, voices appeared in the living room. Within a minute Mrs Twainley appeared at the top of the stairs accompanied by a man William presumed to be a doctor.

"Mr Jackson," she said, quite startled. "What are you doing here?"

"I called on a social visit but when I arrived I found Mr Watkins lying on the floor."

"I couldn't move him," Mrs Twainley said. "I found him here this morning when he didn't come down for breakfast, but he was a dead weight. Thank goodness you managed to haul him onto the bed."

The doctor moved over to the patient and started an examination. It wasn't long before he spoke. "I'm afraid it's as I feared from your description, Mrs Twainley. He's suffered an attack of apoplexy. He's lost the use of his right arm and leg and he won't be able to speak properly or see much out of his right eye. Other than the cut on his head, he doesn't seem to have hurt himself as a result of the fall, but he may have concussion."

"Apoplexy, what caused that?" Mrs Twainley asked.

"It can be a difficult thing to determine," the doctor said. "As far as I'm aware, he didn't eat or drink to excess and he didn't smoke tobacco, so he must have had some excitement that caused the pressure of his blood to rise."

"Excitement?" William said. "He's in his seventies. What sort of excitement do you mean?"

"It could be all manner of things but you're right, given his age most of the physical things are unlikely. Was he worried about anything?"

William shook his head but stopped when he saw Mr Watkins. Although dazed, he was trying to follow the conversation.

"Have you been worried about me and the business?"

Mr Watkins said nothing but turned his head away.

"He has." William faced the doctor. "Oh God, this is all my fault. What can we do to help him?"

"First of all we need to make him comfortable," the doctor said.

"We have to do more than that, we need to help him walk and talk again."

"Mrs Twainley, will you be able to care for him?" the doctor asked, ignoring William.

Mrs Twainley crossed her arms across her

ample bosom. "I'd say that's above and beyond the call of duty for a housekeeper."

The doctor nodded. "Very well, if you can't, we'll have to move him into hospital. I need to remove some blood from his system to reduce the pressure, but even then he's unlikely to regain the use of his right side. Unfortunately he'll spend the rest of his days in bed."

"We can't send him to the hospital for the rest of his life." William's face was white. "Mrs Twainley would you consider staying on if we hire a nurse to perform the caring duties. If Mr Watkins has any money set aside I'm sure he'd want to use it to stay out of hospital."

Within a few hours a nurse arrived and the doctor gave Mr Watkins a sleeping draught before he took a substantial amount of blood. Once it was over, William sat down by the bed.

"Please don't worry, Mr Watkins. We have a buyer for the business, that's what I came to tell you. It'll be sold as a going concern. Everything's going to be fine." William didn't take his eyes off Mr Watkins, and when it was clear he was unlikely to wake again that night, he went downstairs.

"I must be going, Mrs Twainley," he said when he reached the bottom of the stairs. "If there's anything I can do to help, please let me know."

"Thank you, dear, but I don't think I need anything. Mr Watkins's nephew often calls on a Thursday afternoon and so I'll ask him if I need anything."

"He has a nephew?" William's brow furrowed.

"One of his late brother's sons, another Mr Watkins. He had a lot of them over the years but there are not so many of them left now."

"He must be one of my late wife's brothers," William said. "Funny I never met any of them."

"He's only recently started calling, when one of his older brothers died. I'm sure if he needs anything, he'll write to you."

William picked up his hat. "I'll call again at the beginning of next week. Good evening, Mrs Twainley."

CHAPTER FIFTY-TWO

Handsworth, Staffordshire

Although it was almost half past eight in the morning, the kitchen of Havelock Road was still cold and dark. William walked in with a candle and set it down near the sink before staring at the pile of dishes. *When's Lydia coming home? I need her here.* With a sigh, he reached into the cupboard but his shoulders slumped as he squeezed the remains of the two-day-old bread. It was as hard as rock and there was only so much a thinly spread layer of butter could revive. Setting some water to boil over the stove, he wandered to the front door to pick up the post and spotted an envelope with writing he didn't recognise. He tore it open and read the letter from Mrs Twainley.

Dear Mr Jackson

I am writing to tell you that Mr Watkins died in his sleep last evening. The doctor believes he had a second bout of apoplexy. Mr James Watkins is taking care of the funeral arrangements and will inform you of the date in due course.

Yours sincerely
Mrs Twainley

William inspected the envelope. The letter had been posted yesterday meaning Mr Watkins must have died the day before. He flopped into his chair by the stove and put his head in his hands. It was his fault; he'd killed Mr Watkins. Until the bankruptcy, the old man had been perfectly healthy. Now, barely three months later he was dead. Was there no end to it?

With his breakfast forgotten and heart thumping William went back upstairs. He couldn't take much more. How many others would be affected by his stupidity? Drinking the remainder of the laudanum from the bottle he lay on the bed, reliving the events since the summer. It would have been better if he'd died with Harriet ... or instead of her. She wouldn't have made such a mess of things.

As the cold of the bedroom forced him back downstairs he crouched in front of the stove rubbing his hands together. Lydia was right. What was he doing alone in this house? His wife had left him, his children had either gone voluntarily or been taken from him, and he spoke to nobody. No one needed him.

Arthur needs you. A small voice spoke in the back of his head. *You promised you'd bring him home.* William sat up straight; it was right. He needed to get Arthur back; he wouldn't have any more casualties from this sorry state of affairs. *And if Arthur comes home, Lydia may come back too.*

Finally, not caring what the neighbours thought, William put on his hat and coat and left Handsworth in the direction of Summer Lane. It took him over an hour and a half, but when he arrived it didn't take him long to find the tobacconist's. Lydia's brow furrowed when he walked in, but with a number of customers William had no option but to join the back of the queue.

When he reached the front, Lydia glanced at the four men who had come into the shop after him.

"You'll have to be quick," she whispered. "What are you doing here?"

"I had a letter this morning telling me Mr Watkins died the day before yesterday. It was all my fault and I needed someone to talk to."

"Who's Mr Watkins?"

"He was my late wife's uncle, the one who brought her up as his daughter and who gave me his business. I visited him earlier this week and found him collapsed on the floor. The stress of the bankruptcy killed him."

"You don't know that, he may have been ill before then."

"But this won't have helped. He died of apoplexy, which the doctor said could have been brought on by worry. When I asked him if he'd been worried about me, he refused to answer."

"Don't be silly, you weren't even close. I've known you for over two years and you've never mentioned him."

"We haven't been of late, but we used to be. I trained under him when I was doing my apprenticeship and Harriet and I lived with him when we were first married."

"That was years ago ..."

"Oi," a voice shouted from the back of the

queue. "Stop all the talking and let the rest of us get served. If I'm not in work on time you'll have my death on your hands as well."

William's cheeks flushed and Lydia squeezed his hands. "Don't worry, come back at six o'clock and we can go upstairs."

"Do you make offers like that to all your customers or only the old ones?" a second man shouted.

"You can count me in." Laughter reverberated around the shop.

"That's enough." Lydia's voice cut through the noise. "He's my husband, and if I have any more comments like that I'll turn you all out."

William stared at the men in the queue. How dare they speak to his wife like that? He felt blood rising to his cheeks. Why didn't he say something? She shouldn't have to deal with things like this on her own. As the words stuck in his throat, he cast his eyes to the floor before glancing up at Lydia. "I'll see you later."

At six o'clock, William waited in the entrance of the shop as Lydia came to the door to lock up. As soon as she saw him, she beckoned him in.

"Thank you," he said as she closed the door behind him. "It's freezing out there."

"Have you eaten?" Lydia asked. When William shook his head, she continued. "Let me fetch my hat and coat and we'll go and find something. The street vendors won't be far away and we can have some hot soup and bread."

It was another fifteen minutes before William had the soup in his hands and he wrapped them around the side of the cup before savouring the warmth from each sip. Once they got back to Summer Lane they went up to the small room Lydia now called home and he made up the fire.

"Are you putting the fire on at home?" Lydia asked as she watched him with the coals.

"I keep the stove on when I'm in, but I can't justify spending the money on any of the other rooms."

"You must be cold."

"The weather's been kind so far this winter, it's only this last few days it's gone cold. I wear plenty of clothes."

Lydia stared into the fire, her eyes moist.

"What's the matter?" William asked. "Is it work?"

Lydia shook her head. "I know I've not been the wife you wanted, but I want to cry over what's happened to you. You shouldn't be so desperate you can't put the fire on to keep warm. Look at you, you're about half the size you used to be and that belt won't fasten any tighter. I saw William-Wetherby earlier in the week and he told me he had a new job. Has he sent you any money?"

"He won't have been paid yet but I'm not desperate. I have a slate with the shop and coal merchant. They've told me I can pay them back when William-Wetherby and Eleanor send some money but I don't want to build it up too much."

Lydia glanced at William as tears rolled down her cheeks. "Do you think we can bring Arthur home soon? I miss him so much and I'm frightened that if we don't, Mrs Cousins will move him on and I won't see him again."

"Of course we'll see him again. I'm determined to find another job and as soon as I do, we can go and collect him."

"Do you mean that? Where will we live? We can't stay in Havelock Road ... not as it is and if I'm not working, we can't stay here."

William shrugged. "I don't know, we'll sort something out. Give me until after Christmas and I'll find a job. If I can find something in Birmingham the rent will be cheaper and if I can't sell Havelock Road perhaps I'll rent it out like Mr

Diver does. That way we may be able to save a bit of money." William took Lydia's hand and kissed it. "Despite everything, I've missed you while you've been away. Can we start afresh, just the three of us?"

CHAPTER FIFTY-THREE

William jumped from his chair by the stove and rushed to the front door as he heard it open. Lydia was home.

"Come in," he said as he took her coat. "You're early."

"I had to be. I had enough money to buy a small piece of mutton, but I need to start it cooking. I'm visiting Mrs Cousins this afternoon too, to give her the five shillings I owe her."

"Do you have five shillings?"

Lydia nodded. "I've been saving ever since I started work."

William paused. "How long will that last? I know I promised to find a job, but what if I can't? Will she keep him a little longer?"

"We haven't discussed it but I expect she will for another shilling a week."

"Can you afford that out of your wages?"

Lydia put down the meat she was preparing and faced him. "I don't want to afford it, I want him back. I'd like to tell her he's coming home in January. Can you have a job by then?"

William took a deep breath and noticed his hands weren't trembling as much as they had been five or six weeks ago. "Yes, I'm going to do it. I promised Arthur I would, despite the fact the thought of it terrifies me."

"You've no need to be scared. Do you have any laudanum?"

William nodded. "I've enough for another couple of days."

"That's not enough. With the money I save next week I'll buy you some more. If it means you getting a job, it'll be worth it."

William sank down into his chair. "I'm sorry, Lydia, you don't deserve this."

"Stop feeling sorry for yourself. In the New Year you're moving out of this house. It holds too many memories. Once you're back in Birmingham, we'll start again. I'm going to tell Mrs Cousins we'll have Arthur back in the New Year and in the meantime I'm going to find you a job. Is that understood?"

William stared up at Lydia, his mouth open. "I suppose so. I want Arthur home too."

It was only a five-minute walk to Mrs Cousins's house and Lydia went alone. The woman was expecting her and had all the children asleep when she arrived.

"Mrs Jackson, come in. Do you have the money?"

"I do," Lydia said once the door was closed, "but I want to see Arthur first, is he here?" Lydia studied the row of four baskets lined up against the wall, but didn't recognise her son.

"Here he is." Mrs Cousins pointed to the third basket along. "He's no trouble. He sleeps most of the time."

"He hasn't put any weight on. What are you feeding him?"

"He has cow's milk in the morning and he's started to take some cornflour mixed with water."

"But his face looks so old. I don't remember him being like that."

Mrs Cousins tilted her head to study him. "I

don't think so, he's just growing up. Now if that's everything I'll take the five shillings."

"Actually, no, there's one other thing," Lydia said. "My husband will have a job by January and I'd like to take Arthur home when he does."

"You want him back?" Mrs Cousins raised an eyebrow. "I didn't think you meant it."

"Of course I meant it. Why wouldn't I?"

Mrs Cousins shrugged. "Many of the women who leave their babies here never come back. I had you down for one of them."

"Why?"

Mrs Cousins shrugged. "Just a feeling, anyway, his tummy problems have cleared up and so I'll feed him up before January."

Lydia leaned across and stroked Arthur on the cheek. "Thank you. I don't know yet when I'll be back, but I'll give you one shilling for each week he's here. Please take care of him."

CHAPTER FIFTY-FOUR

William leaned against the stove, his grip tightening as he read the letter in his hands. It concerned Mr Watkins's funeral, but it was telling him to stay away. Mr James Watkins had decided he was now an embarrassment to the family and wasn't welcome. William screwed the letter into a ball and threw it on the floor. Who did this fellow think he was? If he had any idea where he lived he'd pay him a visit and set the record straight. He reached for the bottle of laudanum as William-Wetherby let himself in.

"What's the matter with you?" William-Wetherby said.

"I'm not even fit to attend a funeral any more." William drank a mouthful from the bottle.

"Apparently your mother's younger brother is perfect and has decided I'm not."

William-Wetherby took the bottle from his father before he picked up the letter from the floor. "Is that what this is about?"

William nodded. "I bet he's only been calling on Mr Watkins to get some money from him."

"You don't know that."

"I know his type. They turn up years after everyone else, in perfect time to collect all the money when their wealthy relative leaves this world."

"Did Mr Watkins leave a will?" William-Wetherby asked.

"I've no idea, but I imagine he did."

William-Wetherby smiled. "He might have left you something."

William snorted. "After what I did to his business, I doubt it."

The following day the postman handed William an official-looking envelope. Suspecting what it was, he tore it open.

Dear Mr Jackson

I am writing to inform you that following negotiations with potential purchasers for the business lately carried out at the Northern Rivet Works by Messrs Ball and Jackson, we were made an offer on the 14th inst. by Messrs Thomas Haddon and Co. of Villa Street, Hockley. They plan to continue the business at the current address as manufacturers of brass and iron shoe rivets, gimp pins and oval wire nails under the name of The Rivet and Wire Nail Company.

The proposed purchase price is seven hundred and fifty pounds and this, along with proceeds from the sale of the machinery and residential properties, means we can now turn our attention to paying the debts from the aforementioned Northern Rivet Works. We believe there will remain a residual debt although until all the works involved in administering the estate are complete, we cannot say how much. Your liabilities will of course be covered under the bankruptcy agreement. As a result we have accepted the offer and expect to complete the transaction in the next couple of weeks.

We will contact you again once the sale is finalised.

Yours sincerely

. . .

G Fisher
Trustee

"They've accepted seven hundred and fifty pounds!" William spoke to himself. "It was worth more than that." He'd told them they shouldn't accept anything less than one thousand pounds. He started to screw the letter into a ball before he stopped. The debt was their responsibility, not his. *Why should I worry? It's only the creditors who'll lose out. It serves them right for forcing me into the bankruptcy in the first place.*

William turned back to the letter. Tom Haddon; he was from the Lodge. He hadn't realised he was in the same line of business, but this must be his way of helping. William smiled. *Good for him, he's got himself a good deal.*

CHAPTER FIFTY-FIVE

William lay in bed listening to Lydia as she went downstairs. It was lovely to have her home, even if it was only for a couple of days over Christmas. He glanced at the clock on the mantelpiece, seven o'clock. It was time he was out of bed.

An hour later, William stood in the hall and watched as Lydia tied the ribbons of her bonnet under her chin. It was a hat she had bought before their troubles, and he had always liked it.

"Are you going to be all right?" Lydia asked as she pulled her heavy cloak over her shoulders.

"I think so. I couldn't spend Christmas Day here but going to the Divers' should make it bearable."

"You don't mind going outside any more?"

"I've had no choice. Being here on my own has forced me to go out, whether I wanted to or not. Besides, I need to be able to find a job next week."

Lydia smiled. "I'm so looking forward to getting Arthur back. I hope everything will work out in the end."

As William and Lydia arrived outside the church in Small Heath, Mr Diver and Mary-Ann were waiting for them.

"Merry Christmas," they said in unison as they stepped down from the carriage.

"Thank you for sending the carriage," William said.

"And for inviting us." Lydia clung to William's arm.

"It's the least we could do," Mary-Ann replied. "After everything you've gone through this year." She gestured to the church. "Shall we go in? It's cold out here."

Mary-Ann, Mr Diver and their daughters took their usual seats halfway down the right side of the church. William and Lydia went to the first available pew behind them. As he sat down, William scanned the faces of those around him. He didn't want to see anyone he knew. With the service about to start he glanced to his right and froze. Mr

White was seated no more than ten feet away. *What's he doing here?* As far as he knew, the man didn't live in these parts.

"What's the matter?" Lydia said.

William nodded. "It's him. Mr White. The man's who's caused all the trouble."

Lydia stared over at him. "I don't think he's seen you. Sit quietly and we'll leave as soon as we can."

William nodded and squeezed Lydia's hand. "I can't face him. Not after everything ..."

The sounding of the church organ cut off his words and he fumbled for his hymn book as the choir took to their feet. *Please God; give me strength.*

The service was mercifully short and as soon as the vicar walked down the aisle, William reached for Lydia's hand. "Let's get out of here."

"Shall we wait for Mr and Mrs Diver?"

"No." William looked to Mary-Ann but let his hand drop from Lydia's when he saw Mr White greeting Mr Diver. "I don't believe it. Come on, we need to go."

William and Lydia waited around the corner from the church door while William caught his breath.

"What was all that about?" Lydia asked.

William shook his head. "I've no idea."

"Shall I go and find your sister and tell her where we are?"

"Not until he's gone."

Lydia peered around the corner of the building. "He's leaving now. I'll go and fetch them."

"What are you doing here?" Mary-Ann said when she rounded the corner after Lydia.

William's voice was breathless. "What was Mr Diver doing talking to that man?"

Mr Diver's brow furrowed. "You mean the tall, thin man with a pencil moustache?"

"Yes, him. Have you any idea who he is?" William said.

Mr Diver shrugged. "I bumped into him several months ago when he was in a tavern with Mr Wetherby. I don't recall his name."

William lurched towards the wall as if he'd been hit. "You saw him with Mr Wetherby? Are you sure?"

"Only briefly. He was barely in the tavern long enough to be introduced to me. He gave Mr Wetherby an envelope, which didn't seem to please him, and he left soon after."

William paused to catch his breath. "That was Mr White. Mr Wetherby told me he didn't know him. What were they doing together?"

Mr Diver stared at William before he glanced

at Mary-Ann. "I've no idea. I-I don't know what to say."

"Tell William-Wetherby, he'll know what to do. There is no reason why those two should have been in a tavern together. No reason whatsoever."

CHAPTER FIFTY-SIX

Bushwood, Warwickshire

Mr Wetherby stepped down from his carriage as it stopped outside Lapworth church and waved to the vicar. After assisting Sarah-Ann he left Mr Mountford, Charlotte and Elizabeth while he walked towards the vicar.

"Good morning and Merry Christmas, Vicar." Mr Wetherby extended his hand to accept the limp handshake of the vicar. "What a beautiful morning to celebrate the birth of Our Lord."

"Whatever the weather, Mr Wetherby, Christmas morning is always a marvellous occasion, and what a delight to see you've brought the whole family."

Mr Wetherby turned to see William Junior and Olivia helping Henry, Margaret and Florence down from the second carriage. "Naturally. We're all staying at Bushwood Farm for a few days. You must call in for a sherry when you have time, we'd be delighted to get to know you better ... and your lady wife of course."

"That's most kind, I'll try my best. How long are you staying?"

"Until this coming Sunday. I want to feel part of Lapworth and Bushwood. There isn't enough time when I'm only here for one day a week."

The vicar smiled. "I'm sure you'll be warmly welcomed in both villages. I presume you're coming to the box-giving service tomorrow. Most of the landowners generally attend to give their boxes to the farmers and labourers. There'll be a tea afterwards for those contributing. It's not often everyone gets together and so it's an excellent opportunity to meet everyone."

"It sounds splendid. I'm keen to make sure the workers are rewarded. Does His Lordship attend the service?"

The vicar shook his head. "Unfortunately not. He often sends his apologies and a deputy, although I haven't had any from him this year and so you may be fortunate. Have you met him yet?"

"No." A scowl crossed Mr Wetherby's face. "I've called at the manor several times, but he's never at home. I'll be sure to keep an eye out for him tomorrow."

~

Birmingham, Warwickshire.

As William and Lydia arrived home with the Divers, the maid had some mulled wine waiting for them.

"Come and sit by the fire, and I'll pour you a drink." Mary-Ann ushered everyone into the front room.

William settled back and let the warmth of the fire wash over him. How long was it since he had stretched out in front of a fire rather than huddling before it? The maid disturbed him and he accepted the mulled wine as he idly watched his sister walk to the Christmas tree.

"While we wait for dinner, let me give these out." She took a present from the base of the tree and was about to pass it to Lydia before William stopped her.

"You can't give us presents."

Mary-Ann put a hand on her hip. "Of course I

can. Despite everything that's happened it's still Christmas. We don't expect anything in return."

William glared at his sister as he sank further into the chair. *Another humiliation.*

"Gloves," Lydia said. "Exactly what I needed."

She slipped them on as she watched Mr Diver open a fine-looking snuffbox before his daughters each unwrapped a home-made jumper.

"Will you give this to William?" Mary-Ann passed Mr Diver a small package, which he in turn offered to William.

"I'm sorry it couldn't be more, but I hope this helps," Mr Diver said.

William fingered the present nervously before he pulled on the string holding it together. Inside he found a pair of gloves, but there was something else. He felt the hard disks in his hand before he tipped them out of one of the gloves. Five gold sovereigns.

William stared at the coins in his hand. "I can't accept this."

"You can and you will," Mary-Ann said. "We couldn't help you when you needed us, but we want you to make a fresh start. You can keep the money here in case it causes any problems with the trustee."

William glanced at Lydia and saw tears in her eyes.

"Does that mean we can have Arthur back?"

William nodded. "It does. Some of it will have to go to pay the tab with the shop and the coalman but we'll be able to collect Arthur sooner than we planned and pay the mortgage for a little longer."

Lydia wiped her eyes. "Thank you both so much. As soon as we've finished dinner I'll write and tell Mrs Firth at the tobacconists that I won't be back."

After a dinner of roast goose with roasted vegetables followed by a large helping of plum pudding, William dozed by the fire. It was almost four o'clock before he woke to find the room had changed. He rubbed the sleep from his eyes.

"What's going on?"

"We've brought some more chairs in," Mary-Ann said. "We're having guests for tea."

"Who?"

Mary-Ann smiled. "Don't worry, nobody you don't want to see. They'll be here soon."

William eyed his sister. "As long as it's not Mr Wetherby."

Mary-Ann stared at him. "Don't be ridiculous, why would I want him here? Give me some credit for common sense."

William nodded and took a deep breath. "Of course, I'm sorry."

With the velvet curtains pulled across the window, William didn't see anyone walking up the drive, but at half past four there was a knock on the door. Seconds later the voices of his son and daughter filtered into the room.

"Happy Christmas, Father," Eleanor said as she joined them. "You didn't think we'd let a Christmas go by without seeing you, did you?"

William stood up and put his hand on his daughter's shoulder. "I thought you had to work?"

"Only until dinner time, but once the children went for their nap, I was allowed to leave."

"And I wanted to escort her here." William-Wetherby shook his father's hand.

"I don't know what to say. Thank you all so much. I've been worried about today for weeks, but you've made me so happy. Next year I want Margaret, Florence and Arthur to be with us as well."

"That's the spirit," Mr Diver said. "Mary-Ann and I have been talking as well and we want you to stay with us for a few weeks. At least until Twelfth Night."

Lydia shot William a glance. "But we must go for Arthur."

"And you will. As soon as you're ready I'll take you to Handsworth and we can bring him here."

Lydia put her hands to her face and rubbed her fingers over her eyes. "Thank you, when can we go?"

Mr Diver turned to William. "Saturday would be best for me."

William nodded. "That suits me."

"That's not all though," Mr Diver said. "I'd like you to come and work for me ... at least until you find something more suitable. Mary-Ann will have Arthur if Lydia can't stop work straight away."

William stepped forward and shook Mr Diver's hand. "Thank you so much, you've no idea what this means to me."

Mary-Ann smiled. "We're not going to let you struggle any more."

CHAPTER FIFTY-SEVEN

Bushwood, Warwickshire

The box-giving service wasn't due to start until half past ten but Mr Wetherby breakfasted early to allow time to inspect the boxes he would hand out. He needed a dozen in total for the families of those who worked at Bushwood Farm and in Lapworth.

"Where are the eggs we were going to put in?" he shouted to the maid as she came into the kitchen. "We said six in each, but there are only four."

The maid fidgeted with her fingers. "The hens haven't laid enough. I've been to check again, but this is it."

"Not enough? There were plenty last night. What happened to them?"

"We cooked twenty for breakfast."

"Twenty! What were you thinking? You and Cook will have to go without and put five in the other boxes. The men have been looking forward to this ..."

The maid's cheeks glowed red. "Yes, sir, I'm sorry, sir. Everyone in the family asked for eggs this morning ..."

"Enough of that and hurry up." He glanced at his pocket watch. "We need to get these to the carriage. We're going to be late."

"Why are you rushing?" Sarah-Ann asked as she came into the kitchen. "We have plenty of time. It's not ten o'clock yet."

"We need them all in church before people start arriving. You can come with me now and the others can follow. I haven't time to wait for them."

The church service that preceded the box-giving lasted for over an hour and a half and as the vicar continued his sermon, the rustling from the pews grew louder. Eventually, the vicar paused and called for the boxes to be given. It took over half an hour to bless the gifts and hand them to their recipients before the workers left for their own homes.

"Lovely service, Vicar," Mr Wetherby said as he and William Junior followed the last of the farmhands to the back of the church. "You attracted more people than I expected."

"Yes, we usually have most of the village here on Boxing Day. The workers are always eager to receive their gifts. Unusually as well, the Lord of the Manor himself is here." The vicar nodded in the direction of an older man with magnificent bushy sideburns, wearing a country tweed suit.

Mr Wetherby glanced in the direction the vicar indicated. "Would you be able to introduce us?"

The vicar pulled at his clerical collar. "He's a busy man. Today might not be convenient."

Mr Wetherby's lips thinned. "Could we try?"

Mr Wetherby ignored the vicar's glare and waited for him to walk towards His Lordship. He gave a slight cough before interrupting.

"Your Lordship, may I introduce Mr Wetherby and his son, Mr Wetherby Junior?" The vicar made a small bow. "Mr Wetherby's the new owner of Bushwood Farm and keen to make your acquaintance."

Mr Wetherby waited while the Lord of the Manor ran his eyes over him. "So you're new to the area, Mr Wetherby? What line of business are you in?"

"Manufacturing." Mr Wetherby puffed out his chest. "I have a workshop in Birmingham employing twenty men as well as numerous women and boys. I'm also involved in a number of other projects including the redevelopment of the housing in Birmingham and running the Conservative Association."

His Lordship raised an eyebrow. "That must keep you busy."

"It does, sir, and it was this latter point I was hoping to have a word with you about. Do you have a Conservative Association in Lapworth?"

His Lordship waved a dismissive hand in the air. "No, no. We don't need one around here. None of the local men would vote for anyone but the Conservatives and any Liberal supporters don't have the vote."

Mr Wetherby nodded. "I suspected that may be the case, but from my experiences in Birmingham I worry that as more of the workers become entitled to vote, things will change. We need to be ready for it. If we set up a Conservative Association that welcomes all villagers, we'll have them in the fold should the unthinkable happen."

"I was talking to Lord Salisbury after he became Prime Minister," His Lordship said. "He assured me that voting rights would not be extended while he had breath in his body."

"Fine sentiments, I'm sure, and I have a great deal of respect for the Prime Minister, having met him myself on several occasions, but Birmingham has shown us how successful the Liberals can be. If they're elected again they're likely to allow the vote for the working classes. They're their natural supporters and we need to be prepared."

His Lordship turned to walk away. "Men who don't have the vote won't be interested in attending a Conservative Association."

Mr Wetherby stepped to one side to stop the man from leaving. "I'm sure we could find ways to persuade them. If we offered free food or drinks for example, not many of them would refuse, and once they were there ... well, that would be for us to take advantage of."

"Would you run this yourself?"

"Good grief, no, I've too much on my plate and I'm not here during the week. My son is, though." He acknowledged William Junior. "I'd like to propose that he sets things up in the first instance, under my supervision of course, and then you and I could attend the meetings to do what's necessary. We'd only need a small allowance to provide food for each event."

His Lordship took a step backwards. "From me?"

"As Lord of the Manor, it would be helpful if you were seen to be supporting the first few meetings. Once we have regular attendees, they'd pay a small fee to be members, which would make it self-financing."

"I'm not a charity, I'll have to think about it. Now, if you'll excuse me, I must circulate."

Mr Wetherby watched His Lordship join another group before he addressed William Junior. "Is everyone here as stupid as him? He doesn't have any idea of what's happening in the real world."

"You should try living down here," William Junior said. "They think we're still living in the eighteenth century."

Mr Wetherby glanced around him. "I'd no idea, everyone seems so pleasant."

"They're pleasant enough, but it's different when you come on Saturday, compared with the rest of the week. Olivia and I wondered if we could have a small place in Handsworth as well as here. That way I could help you out, but be here when you arrive on Saturday."

Mr Wetherby nodded. "I've been thinking about that. The house next to Charlotte in St Peters

Road is up for sale. If I buy it, you could split your time between the two properties."

William Junior smiled. "That sounds splendid. Olivia will be pleased."

CHAPTER FIFTY-EIGHT

Handsworth, Staffordshire

William smiled at Lydia as they sat opposite each other in Mr Diver's carriage. She'd had her hat and coat on since long before Mr Diver had arrived home from work and the sparkle in her eyes told him how excited she was to be back in Handsworth.

"It's been too long since I held Arthur." She pulled her arms across her chest as she spoke. "Do you think he'll remember me?"

William smiled at her. "I'm sure he will. You were inseparable before you started work."

"I'm so nervous, I want it to be right this time. I hope his tummy's better."

"Mrs Cousins told you it was and so I'm sure he'll be fine."

"We're here now," Mr Diver said as they turned into Birchfield Road. The carriage stopped directly outside Mrs Cousins's house and William helped Lydia down the steps before they went to the front door. William knocked several times but when no one answered Lydia went to the window.

"It looks like she's out." A frown creased her forehead.

"That's strange. You said she cared for four babies, she couldn't possibly have taken them all with her."

Lydia turned back to the window. "You're right, but why isn't she answering? Perhaps she's gone out for a few minutes. The cribs are against the back wall and I can't tell if the babies are in them."

"I tell you what," William said. "We wanted to call at Havelock Road while we were here so why don't we go now and come back. She can't have gone far."

They reached Havelock Road within five minutes and Mr Diver steered the carriage to the back of the house. He went into the stables to get water for the horses while William and Lydia went to the front of the house. William was about to open the door when he saw a letter jammed between the door and the door frame. It was addressed to Lydia and had the word PRIVATE written in large letters across the top.

"What's this?" William passed the letter to his wife.

Lydia stared at it. "Who's writing to me?"

William noticed her hands trembling as she opened it and read the text. A moment later she started to sway. "Is everything all right? What does the letter say?" Lydia raised her tear-filled eyes to his but before she could say anything she fell in a dead faint, banging her head on the hard ground.

"Lydia, what is it?" William dropped to his knees, but there was no response. "Mr Diver, come quickly."

Within seconds Mr Diver arrived at the front of the house and the two of them bent down beside Lydia.

"What happened?" Mr Diver said.

"I've no idea. There was a letter, but as she read it she started to sway and the next minute she was on the ground. We need to get her inside, it's too cold out here."

"What did the letter say?" Mr Diver said as they carried her into the house.

"She didn't tell me. I'll read it once we've got her upstairs."

Once Lydia was on the bed, William raised her eyelids, but there was no reaction.

"Do you have any smelling salts?" Mr Diver asked.

"I doubt it. Do you think we'll need the doctor?"

"Why don't you read the letter and see what it says. If she's not recovered in a few minutes, I'll run and fetch him."

William turned on the spot as he searched for the letter. "It must have fallen as we carried her in, I'll go and find it. You stay here."

William hurried down the stairs and out the front door. He eventually spotted it blowing down the drive. "Come back here," he said as he caught hold of it. *Let's see what we have here.*

Mrs Jackson

I'm writing to tell you that Arthur died on Monday (24th Dec). The doctor certified it and I registered the death on Thursday before we buried him in Perry Barr. There was no hint of suspicion.

Yours sincerely

Mrs Cousins

. . .

William felt the blood drain from his face and stumbled back to the house where he propped himself up against the wall. Was there to be no end to it? Not only had the bankruptcy dishonoured the family, it had now led to the death of his son. If he hadn't been so wrapped up in his own problems Lydia wouldn't have needed to work and leave Arthur with this stranger. He glanced at the letter again, "*...no hint of suspicion...*" Was this what Lydia had planned all along?

Without another thought he screwed the letter into a ball and threw it across the garden before he staggered down the drive. He didn't know where he was going, but he hoped to find a tavern before he got there.

Mr Diver stayed with Lydia for a couple of minutes until he went downstairs looking for William. With no sign of him, he was about to go back into the house when the doctor arrived.

"Good afternoon, Mr Diver," the doctor said. "I've not seen you in these parts for a while, are you here with Mr Jackson?"

Mr Diver's forehead creased. "Haven't you

come here with Mr Jackson? I thought he'd gone to fetch you."

"No, I was passing and thought I'd call and see how Mrs Jackson was."

"How did you know there was anything the matter with her? She only banged her head about ten minutes ago. When I left her she was still out cold. Can you have a look at her?"

The two men hurried upstairs and found Lydia trying to open her eyes.

"It's all right, Lydia," Mr Diver said. "You've had a bang to your head but the doctor's here."

"I suspect she has a concussion," the doctor said after brief examination. "Other than that I don't think she's done any damage. We need to sit her up and keep her awake for as long as possible. I'll leave you some smelling salts in case you think she's drifting. I presume this is a result of the news about Arthur?"

Mr Diver stared at the doctor. "What news? We've just come over from Small Heath and I'm sure they hadn't had any news about him. They were coming to collect him."

The doctor glanced at Lydia. "Shall we step outside for a moment?" Once outside he pulled the door closed before he continued. "The child died on Christmas Eve. I thought Mrs Cousins would have told you. I signed the death certificate and he was buried on Thursday."

Mr Diver put his hand to his head. "Great Scott! That'll finish them off. How did he die?"

"Putting it bluntly, he starved to death. He was literally nothing but skin and bone when I saw him; his skin was hanging off him. I couldn't be sure whether it was accidental or deliberate. It's not the first time Mrs Cousins has been responsible for a child who's died, but the fact they were coming to collect him reassures me it was the former."

"Isn't she registered with the authorities?"

"She is, but they can't find anything to charge her with. Mrs Jackson's milk was poor quality when she was feeding Arthur and the fact he had diarrhoea would have made the problem worse. In the absence of any evidence we have to assume Mrs Cousins didn't appreciate the situation and she too failed to feed him properly. The poor fellow didn't stand a chance."

"Poor William," Mr Diver said. "There was a letter ... he went looking for it and I imagine he read it and took off. He can't take much more."

When the doctor and Mr Diver went back into the bedroom it was clear Lydia's memory had returned and she lay curled up on the bed, her body shaking as she sobbed.

"What do I do with her, Doctor? I'm going to have to find William, but I can't leave her here."

"I'll give her some laudanum. It can't be much because of the concussion, but it will at least calm her down. Give her half an hour to compose herself and then you'd better go."

CHAPTER FIFTY-NINE

Half an hour later, Mr Diver helped Lydia down the stairs and out into the carriage. The laudanum had calmed her down and she was more asleep than awake, but at least she was quiet and the sobbing had subsided. By the time they were both seated, dusk was falling and the waning moon struggled to be seen through the clouds.

"Where on earth would he have gone?" Mr Diver said to himself. He gazed up and down the road before he turned right and headed towards Birchfield Road. *Would he have gone to confront Mrs Cousins?* Making the short distance to her house, Mr Diver knocked on the front door, but as before there was no answer. *She must be keeping a low profile.*

Mr Diver scratched his head. A few times since the bankruptcy he had heard tales of William being seen in local taverns. In fact, he'd been told of an incident where he was so drunk he'd had to stay in Frankfort Street for the night. There were more taverns in the direction of Birmingham; was that the way to go?

Over the next half an hour, Mr Diver called in at half a dozen inns and taverns, but with no success. *He must have gone the other way.* He studied the clouds as he went back outside. The moon was trying its best to shine through them but the light it released was pale and muted. There was no time to waste. Driving to the junction of Birchfield and Wellington Roads, he continued towards Perry Barr and stopped at the first two taverns but there was no sign of William.

As he climbed back into the carriage, he glanced at Lydia. She cut a pathetic figure as she huddled in a corner of the carriage; her eyes red from crying. He needed to take her home. One more inn and he'd call it a night.

As he continued up the road he noticed a tavern set back with some water troughs outside. He pulled up and attended to the horses before he went inside.

"I'm looking for someone and wondered if you

might have seen him," he asked the landlord. "He's in his late forties, about five foot ten inches tall with white hair and a white beard. He'd have been quite disturbed, maybe even crying?"

The man shook his head. "No, I've not seen him, but I've been in the cellar. Ask the barman."

Mr Diver approached a man pulling beer from a cask and asked him the same question.

"He was here all right. Left no more than half an hour ago I would say. I remember him because he ordered two pints of beer and drank them both before I found out he had no money. I doubt I'll ever get it off him, the cheating swine."

Mr Diver closed his eyes and took a deep breath. "Here, let me pay for them. He's not feeling himself at the moment. Did he say where he was going?"

"He didn't have a chance the way I chased him out, but looking at him it wouldn't surprise me if he'd gone and thrown himself into the canal. Not that he'd get any sympathy from me."

"The canal, of course. I hadn't thought of that. How do I get to Tower Hill from here?"

"Turn left and then left again across the fields. You'll struggle to find the footpath in this light."

Mr Diver gave the barman another shilling for his trouble and hurried out of the pub. It was only a short distance to the canal, but the clouds weren't ready to reveal any more light. Nevertheless, he had to find William tonight. If he left it until daybreak it might be too late ... if it wasn't already.

Mr Diver found Lydia where he had left her sobbing in the corner of the carriage, but he had to be firm.

"Lydia, I don't have time to explain, but you need to come with me ... do you hear?" Lydia turned to him, but stayed where she was. "Please, Lydia, I know you're upset, but this is urgent." He grabbed hold of her hand and pulled her from the carriage. "We need to walk to Tower Hill, I can't take the horses in case they injure themselves and I can't leave you by yourself. You must come with me."

Mr Diver started walking as fast as he dared, pulling Lydia behind him.

"Why do we have to go to Tower Hill? I don't want to, I want to go home."

Mr Diver glared at her. "Let me assure you there is no place I'd rather be right now, but we have to find William and I think he might be at Tower Hill."

"Why would he be there?"

"Who knows? Now be quiet and concentrate

on where we're walking. I don't want you spraining an ankle on top of everything else."

Within minutes, Mr Diver had found the footpath leading to the canal. He stooped down to study the direction of the track and through a mixture of memory and feeling the ground with his feet, they edged their way forward. Before long he heard the sound of the water lapping against the bank. He gazed up at the clouds, hoping they would part, and a minute later a small shaft of light appeared.

He stopped and turned to Lydia. "Remember, we're looking for William; can you see him?" Lydia said nothing for a few seconds, but then pointed.

"What's that over there? It looks like a rock, but it could be a person."

Mr Diver nodded and put his finger to his lips. "We must be quiet. I don't want to startle him." They crept towards the shape and as they got closer they saw it move.

"That's him," Mr Diver whispered.

The two of them continued to creep towards him, but as they did the light of the moon disappeared and a second later they heard a splash. When the moon reappeared, William had gone.

CHAPTER SIXTY

As soon as he heard the splash, Mr Diver let go of Lydia and ran towards the spot he had last seen William. For a moment he saw nothing but then a pair of flailing arms appeared from out of the water, followed by William's head.

"William, what are you doing?" he shouted. "Kick your legs to stay afloat, I'll find something to bring you in." Even as he said it, Mr Diver knew it was a stupid thing to say. How would he see anything in this darkness? He could barely make out Lydia who was standing where he had left her.

"Lydia, come here and help me. I'm going in after him."

Lydia stayed where she was. "I can't go in."

Mr Diver watched William disappear under

the water again. "I'm not asking you to, but you need to steady me, now come here."

Mr Diver bent down to take off his shoes while Lydia joined him. "I want you to stay as close to the edge of the water as you can and be ready to help me out with him. Are you listening?"

Lydia nodded and did as she was told while Mr Diver climbed into the water. As he stepped out, his knees buckled as a rock slipped from under his feet almost dragging him under the water. He reached for William, who was close but not close enough. For a moment William disappeared again, but resurfaced seconds later.

"William, go down again and push yourself towards me," Mr Diver shouted. "It's not as deep as you think."

At first William didn't respond and Mr Diver shouted again until William sank once more. Mr Diver thrashed the top of the water with his outstretched arms causing it to lap into his mouth. "Come back, damn you. I'm not going home to tell Mary-Ann she's lost her brother." He was about to step further into the canal when he felt William's fingers brush against his hand. A second later William's face surfaced before him. Without thinking, Mr Diver grabbed hold of him and the two of them teetered back and forth, before Mr

Diver found his footing and pulled William towards him.

"Pull me back," Mr Diver shouted to Lydia as he reached out for her with his free hand. Lydia leaned over the water and stretched her arm out to catch hold of him. Once they were at the bank, Mr Diver grabbed William by his jacket and heaved him out of the water before he pulled himself out. Lydia rolled him onto his front and pummelled his back as William coughed the water out of his lungs.

"What the hell are you playing at?" Mr Diver shouted as he knelt on the bank beside him. "You could have killed us both."

"You weren't meant to be here."

"So you'd have been happy for Lydia to be a widow, would you? Not only a widow to a bankrupt, but to someone who committed suicide as well. Don't you remember how you felt when they found Harriet in the canal and there was speculation it might have been suicide. It was a terrible time. Did you want to put Lydia through that on top of everything else?"

William's tears were indistinguishable from the water coating him. "I can't take any more. Everyone I care about's been taken from me. I wanted to end it with Harriet."

"Harriet isn't here, we buried her at St Mary's.

If you'd succeeded in killing yourself, we wouldn't have been able to bury you with her."

"Her spirit's not at St Mary's," William wailed. "She hated that church. She's here, can't you sense her?"

"No I can't, now come on, we have to go. We're both soaked to the skin and it's freezing cold. We can't possibly travel to Small Heath like this. We'll go back to the tavern you called at earlier and hope they have a couple of rooms for us."

William stared at Mr Diver, his eyes wide. "I can't go there."

"Yes you can. I paid for your beer and you can go and apologise to the barman and thank him for saving your life."

As they went into the tavern, Mr Diver and William found a large fireplace in one of the empty rooms and stood before it shivering. Lydia was not far behind them.

"You found him then?" the barman said as he saw them. "Was I right about him being by the canal?"

Mr Diver nodded.

"I'm glad, but I'm not sure I should serve him after the way he behaved last time."

"The drinks are on me this time, and I'll pay in advance," Mr Diver said. "We'd also like a couple of rooms for the night and some stabling for the horses."

The barman studied the three waifs standing in front of him and nodded. "Sit yourselves down." He nodded at a table close to the fire. "I'll find you some blankets to dry yourselves and some broth as well. You look like you could do with it."

The following day, with his clothes dry and some breakfast inside him, Mr Diver arranged for the carriage to be brought to the front of the tavern. He went up to the bedroom William and Lydia had shared and knocked on the door.

"Are you two coming? Mary-Ann'll be wondering where we are."

William came to the door. "We're not coming with you. Now we don't have Arthur we might as well go home. We're not much company."

"All the more reason for you to come. You've no money for food or coal and after last night I can't trust you not to try something similar again. I'm not taking no for an answer. Besides, you can tell Mary-Ann why we've been away all night. You're not leaving it to me."

Ten minutes later, Mr Diver watched as William and Lydia picked at some bread and butter. "Come on, you need to eat more than that."

"You've not just lost your only son," Lydia snapped. "You've no idea what we're going through."

William stared at Mr Diver who stood up and left the room. Lydia watched, her eyes wide.

William studied his hands as he addressed Lydia. "Many years ago, before Mr Diver and Mary-Ann had the girls, they had a son, Charles-Jackson. He was their pride and joy. When he was about two months old Mary-Ann found him dead in his cradle one morning. It nearly broke her ... and Mr Diver. If anyone knows what we're going through it's them. Please don't say anything like that to Mary-Ann."

CHAPTER SIXTY-ONE

Birmingham, Warwickshire

As soon as the carriage pulled up the drive at the Divers' house, Mary-Ann rushed outside to meet them.

"Where've you been? I've been worried sick about you."

Mr Diver glanced at her as he walked past. "Ask William."

William was still helping Lydia from the carriage when Mary-Ann approached him.

"What have you been doing? I was expecting you back at five o'clock yesterday afternoon and you arrive here at nine o'clock this morning as if nothing's happened. Where's Arthur?"

William ushered Lydia through the front door.

"Don't walk past me," Mary-Ann said. "Tell me what happened."

When William refused to speak, Lydia paused to wipe her eyes. "Arthur's dead and William tried to kill himself. If you'll excuse me I'm going to lie down."

Mary-Ann stared after her sister-in-law before she went into the back room and perched on the edge of her chair. *Arthur's dead and William tried to kill himself? What on earth happened?* She glanced at the half-finished cup of tea on the side table and pushed it away. She needed something stronger than that. With trembling hands she retrieved the bottle of sherry from the sideboard and poured herself a glass. How could Arthur be dead? They were bringing him home. Unbidden tears leaked from her eyes and rolled down her cheeks as the image of her own baby appeared in her mind. *Why is life so unfair?*

She emptied her glass and was about to pour another when a knock at the door stopped her. A moment later the maid let William-Wetherby in.

"It's nippy out." He rubbed his hands together before blowing on them. "Is Father here?"

Mary-Ann wiped her eyes. "You'd better take a seat."

"What's the matter?" His brow creased as Mary-Ann shut the door behind him.

She told him the little she knew about the previous evening and watched the colour drain from his face.

"He tried to kill himself? How?"

"I can't say. Nobody'll talk to me."

William-Wetherby sank back in the chair. "This is going to set them back months."

"I know." Mary-Ann sat down. "If your father's not able to work next week, Mr Diver won't be able to wait for him. He needed a new supervisor before Christmas but held off appointing one until he'd spoken to William. I get the impression they're not on the best of terms either at the moment."

William-Wetherby put his hand to his head. "Oh God, what a mess. What do we do?"

Mary-Ann shook her head. "I don't know." They sat in silence until Mary-Ann looked up at her nephew. "Why did you want to see him, anyway?"

William-Wetherby stared at his aunt before he remembered. "Mr Watkins's will. It was in the paper that it'll be read in Birmingham next week. I wondered if he wanted to go."

"I doubt it. Even before all this I don't think

he'd have wanted to see your mother's brother. The one who told him to stay away from the funeral."

"I suppose you're right but I hoped he might have been left some money."

"You could go," Mary-Ann said.

William-Wetherby shuffled in his seat. "I don't want to go on my own, I've never been to one before. Will you come with me?"

"Me? I hardly knew him."

"That doesn't matter."

Mary-Ann cocked her head to one side. "I don't suppose it does. I'll come if you want me to, I don't have anything else planned."

William-Wetherby and Mary-Ann arrived at the solicitor's office to find about a dozen people in the waiting room, all with the same purpose. William-Wetherby didn't recognise any of them, but judging by their ages he guessed that most had been friends of Mr Watkins. At the appointed time, they were shown into a meeting room, where a solicitor was waiting for them.

"Sit here at the back," William-Wetherby said. "I'm sure they're all wondering who we are."

Mary-Ann took her seat before the solicitor started.

"We are here today to hear the Last Will and Testament of Mr Andrew Watkins of Clifton Road, Birmingham." The solicitor peered over the paper in his hand as if checking he had everyone's attention. "Probate has now been granted for an estate worth one thousand eight hundred and sixty-seven pounds, five shillings and sixpence."

William-Wetherby gasped causing the solicitor to pause and stare at him before he continued. After announcing the executors, he moved on to the main body of the document.

"My four freehold houses situated on Tower Road, Aston will go to Mr Akers upon payment of one hundred pounds to my estate. I also bequeath to Mr Akers the oil paintings of myself and my wife."

William-Wetherby studied the faces in the room to determine which one might be Mr Akers and why he might want oil paintings of Mr and Mrs Watkins. When he saw a man near the front smiling, he nudged Mary-Ann and pointed him out.

As executor, Mr Akers was also left with a number of bequests and actions and it was a further ten minutes before the solicitor moved on to the part of the reading most of the room were interested in.

"To each of the children of my late brother, William ..." The solicitor paused and glanced around the room. "I leave one hundred pounds. In addition, to each of the children of his daughter Mary I leave twenty pounds. I also leave twenty pounds to Mary's husband Mr George."

William-Wetherby's forehead creased. "His brother William? Wasn't he my mother's father?" Mary-Ann was about to answer but was interrupted by the solicitor.

"To the five children of my late niece Harriet Jackson, also a daughter of my late brother William, I leave one hundred pounds to be divided between them."

"That's us!" William-Wetherby spun around in his chair to face Mary-Ann. "He left us something. What about Father though?"

"Let's listen, shall we?" Mary-Ann said.

The solicitor paused and glanced at William-Wetherby until he had his attention.

William-Wetherby tried to listen to the rest of the reading, but he couldn't concentrate. What would he do with one hundred pounds? How much would he have to give to his brother and sisters? Not much he hoped. His attention was drawn back to the reading, when the solicitor neared the end.

"I direct my executors to pay the residue of the funds to such charitable institutions in Birmingham, using their sole discretion, as they see fit for the relief of human nature."

William-Wetherby turned to Mary-Ann. "Charity? He hasn't left anything to Father. He needs the money more than the charities do and any payment to him would qualify as a relief of human nature."

"I don't think he'd qualify as a charity though," Mary-Ann said.

"But what happens to Mother's money? She was obviously a daughter of William Watkins and so her share should pass to her next of kin."

Mary-Ann shrugged. "Why don't you go and ask? The solicitor said that if anyone had any questions he'd be happy to answer them."

William-Wetherby hurried to join the queue that was forming but within a couple of minutes the solicitor addressed the room again.

"Ladies and gentlemen, can I have your attention, please. I've been asked several times to clarify the meaning of the will with regards to the children of William Watkins who have already passed away. I was with Mr Watkins when he drafted this will and I can say with certainty that he wrote it to mean that only the living children of his brother would receive any money. Once his nieces or nephews died, their share was to go into the estate."

"So Mother's money will go to charity?" William-Wetherby's voice carried across the room. "My father is struggling to live and the money goes to charity? All I can say is that if there's a God in this world, he surely hates him."

CHAPTER SIXTY-TWO

William-Wetherby travelled back to Small Heath in a carriage with his aunt. He stared out of the window into the fog that had settled since they'd been in the solicitor's office.

"This weather just about sums everything up. I bet it freezes tonight." He let out a deep sigh. "Has Father spoken of returning to Handsworth lately? He can't afford to keep the place warm with the weather like this."

"Not to me, but who knows what he's thinking. He and Lydia sit in silence most evenings and are in bed before nine o'clock. Will you come in and speak to him when we're back at the house?"

William-Wetherby hesitated. "I suppose so,

although I've arranged to go for a game of dominoes with Sid tonight. One of us has to keep going."

Mary-Ann put her hand on his knee. "I know it's not easy for you. You shouldn't have to deal with this at your age. If you stay for half an hour, I'll ask Mr Diver to take you back to Frankfort Street."

When they arrived at the house, William and Lydia were sitting on either side of the fire in the back room. Although William glanced up, neither of them spoke.

"Aren't you going to say good evening?" William-Wetherby said. "I hoped you'd be pleased to see me."

William rubbed his hand across his face. "I won't because it's not a good evening, like it's never a good morning or a good day. The only part of the day worthy of the phrase is at night when I can have a large dose of laudanum and drift off to sleep."

"I'm sorry I came." William-Wetherby turned to leave. "You know where to contact me when you're ready."

He marched into the hall, pulling the door behind him more severely than he'd planned. The noise brought his aunt from the morning room.

"What's the matter?" she asked.

"I don't know how you put up with them. I want to grab him by the shoulders and shake him."

"If you'd lost a child, you might find it in your heart to be a little more sympathetic, although I do agree with you. I don't remember Mr Diver being this bad ..."

"I suppose he hadn't had a bankruptcy to contend with as well."

"You're right, they've had a difficult time, but they still need to buck their ideas up. Have you spoken to him about getting a job?"

William-Wetherby shook his head. "What do I say? Mr Diver said he can't work for him in his current condition and I feel guilty kicking him when he's down."

"Why don't you stay and talk to Mr Diver? He'll be home soon and may have some ideas."

William-Wetherby went into the morning room and accepted the cup of tea Mary-Ann pushed in his direction.

"Do you hear much from Eleanor?" Mary-Ann asked.

"I get a letter from her most weeks. She asked about visiting Father, but I told her not to bother. I think she's better off not seeing him like this. She seems happy enough where she is."

"That sounds like Mr Diver now." Mary-Ann walked into the hall. "Come and join us in the morning room when you're ready. William-Wetherby's here."

Mr Diver rested his hand on the coat stand as he struggled to breathe.

"Are you all right?" Mary-Ann rushed forward to take his arm. "Come and sit down."

Perspiration dripped from Mr Diver's forehead as he stumbled into the morning room. Mary-Ann helped him off with his coat as William-Wetherby jumped from his chair.

"Do you want me to fetch a doctor?"

Mary-Ann stared at her husband. "I think you'd better ... and quickly."

By the time William-Wetherby arrived with the doctor, Mary-Ann had helped Mr Diver upstairs and into bed. They left the two men alone and went down to the morning room.

"Was he all right this morning?" William-Wetherby asked.

"He had a cold, but nothing he was worried about. I hope it's nothing serious."

They sat in silence until the doctor came downstairs and joined them.

"I would say he has influenza," the doctor said. "There's a lot of it about and he said he spent time in the canal shortly after Christmas. That won't have helped."

Tears formed in Mary-Ann's eyes. "Influenza! He will be all right, won't he?"

"It's difficult to say. He needs to stay in bed and be kept warm at all times. I'd suggest you make some soup and feed it to him regularly, even if he complains he's too hot or he's not hungry. He needs the fluids and the energy to be able to fight it off."

"How long will it take to clear?" William-Wetherby asked.

"We'll hope to see signs of improvement within a couple of weeks. He's an otherwise healthy, well-nourished young man but I'll call in each day to check on him."

The following week, William-Wetherby took a deep breath as he knocked on the door of his aunt and uncle's house. He hadn't heard anything about Mr Diver's condition and prayed he was making a recovery. Mary-Ann was in the back room when he was shown in and William-Wetherby noted the rings around her eyes

"How is he?"

"The doctor was here earlier and thinks his breathing is getting easier. He's still exhausted, but at least I can have a conversation with him."

William-Wetherby breathed out a sigh of relief. "Thank the Lord for that. Can I see him?"

Mary-Ann stood up and went to the door. "You can, I'll take you up. As it happens he asked if you would pop in when you called. He wants to speak to you."

William-Wetherby's brow creased. *Why would Mr Diver want to speak to me?*

Mr Diver smiled when he walked in. "Thank you for calling." His voice was breathless as he spoke. "I wanted to see you about something your father told me on Christmas morning. With everything that's happened since, I haven't had a chance to say anything."

William-Wetherby took a seat, his brow furrowed. "What did he say?"

"Not much, to tell you the truth, but he asked me to tell you ... I worried that I wouldn't have a chance." Mr Diver paused for breath. "It was when we were at church on Christmas morning, a man I'd met briefly came to shake my hand and wish me season's greetings. I'd only met him because I'd seen him in a tavern with Mr Wetherby a few months earlier, but he remembered me. The interesting thing is that your father knew him. It was Mr White."

William-Wetherby's eyes bulged. "Mr White of

all the trouble? And you'd seen him with Mr Wetherby? Mr Wetherby told Father he didn't know him."

"That's what your father said."

"Did they look like they were acquainted?"

Mr Diver coughed to clear his throat. "I've been thinking about that and I'd say their acquaintance was more of a business transaction than a friendship. They didn't have a drink together, but Mr White gave Mr Wetherby an envelope. He only opened it enough to glance inside, but he wasn't happy with it. Mr White left almost immediately."

William-Wetherby stood up and paced the room. "When was this? Do you remember?"

Mr Diver shook his head. "Now you're asking. I've been thinking about it while I've been lying here and I'd say probably during August. I think the girls were home from school."

"When you mentioned it to me, you said the man looked frightened of Mr Wetherby," Mary-Ann said.

Mr Diver nodded. "He did, it was most peculiar. The other strange thing was they were in Nechells, over at the other side of Birmingham." Mr Diver leaned forward as a series of coughs racked his body. It was several minutes before he continued. "I was over there delivering boxes, but why Mr Wetherby was there I've no idea. It wasn't the sort of place you'd expect to find him."

"That's around the time Father needed money to save the business. What were they up to?"

"I've no idea, but when we realised who Mr White was your father told me to tell you."

William-Wetherby leaned back in his chair, voicing the thoughts racing through his mind. "Could all this be down to Mr Wetherby? It wouldn't surprise me, especially after the way he was with Aunt Charlotte having Arthur. Was he really responsible for the bankruptcy and indirectly for Arthur's death?"

Mr Diver took a sharp intake of breath that produced a further fit of coughing. "You can't go around making accusations like that."

"But if he is, he shouldn't be allowed to get away with it."

"I don't disagree with you, but Mr Wetherby's a powerful man and it's not in your interests to upset him."

"We need to prove it ... and report him to the police."

Mr Diver's already pale face lost all colour. "Listen to me, don't go and do anything stupid. If we're going to do anything, the evidence has to be solid."

CHAPTER SIXTY-THREE

William stood at the bottom of Summer Lane studying the scene before him. The rows of shops and houses on either side were familiar but he didn't remember it being so long. He had to walk to the top and he was already exhausted after walking from the town centre. It was clear that he and Lydia had outstayed their welcome at the Divers' house and they needed to go home. That meant he needed to find a job.

He started to walk up the road but stopped at the window of every shop to check whether they had any job vacancies. His hopes were raised when he found several establishments offering work, but as soon as he spoke to the manager they all wanted to know about his past. As soon as they knew he was a bankrupt, the answer was always the same.

By the time he reached Frankfort Street he was tired and cold and needed to sit down.

"Mr Jackson, what a pleasant surprise, come in," Mrs Storey said. "It's a long time since we saw you here."

"I'm sorry, but I don't like calling any more in case I bump into Mr Wetherby. Today I was beyond caring and knew I could rely on you to make me a cup of tea."

"Of course you can, and you don't need to worry about my brother. One of his collie dogs from Handsworth has gone missing and he's got everyone walking the streets looking for it. He's even offering a reward for it. Our younger brother Edward's been staying with me, but he's gone to Handsworth to help with the search."

"I'm sorry about the dog, but I hope they don't find it in a hurry," William said. "It's a relief having him out of the way."

By the time Mrs Storey made the tea, Sid had arrived home with William-Wetherby.

"What are you doing here?" William-Wetherby asked his father. "Is Mr Diver all right?"

William smiled. "Fortunately, he went into work for a few hours yesterday and he was there again when I left. His chest is still wheezing, but the fever's gone and his energy's returned."

"What a relief, I'll call on him in the next few days, but that doesn't answer my question. "What are you doing here? The last time I saw you, you weren't speaking to anyone."

"Your Aunt Mary-Ann's had enough of me and I need to find a job."

"I'm sure she's not had enough of you, but it's for your own good. You can't spend the rest of your life sitting around moping."

"What sort of work do you want?" Sid asked.

William shrugged. "The way things are looking at the moment, I'll take anything."

"Have you spoken to Mr Black from the Lodge?" William-Wetherby said.

"I can't, not yet. Let me find something first and then I'll feel better about facing them."

Sid looked from father to son and shrugged. "The Barrel on Lower Tower Street is looking for someone to pull ale. What about that?"

"I would if they'd have me, but every time someone finds out about the bankruptcy, they're not interested."

Sid rolled his eyes. "Well, don't tell them. Say you had an accident at work and can't use the machines again or something similar."

"I can't lie. What if they find out?"

"Once you've been there a few weeks and they trust you, they won't care. Listen, why don't we go now and I'll put in a word for you. They know me well enough."

Leaving Mrs Storey behind, William walked to Lower Tower Street with William-Wetherby and Sid.

"All you'd need to do is stand in the corner pulling ale, deliver it to the tables and collect up the empties. You can do that, can't you?"

William glanced at his son before looking back at Sid. "Do I have to take the money?"

"Yes, but it's easy enough. A penny a mug. You only need to count to ten. Men usually pass out once they've had that many." Sid laughed.

William felt himself relax. "I think I can manage that."

"Here, Bob," Sid shouted to the barman. "Come and meet your new barman. Mr Jackson. Solid worker he is, and able to start immediately. What do you say?"

Bob looked William up and down. "Have you done this work before?"

William shook his head, but Sid interrupted before he could answer.

"He's a highly qualified man. Had a slight

mishap in his last job and so can't do detailed work any more. That's right, isn't it, Mr Jackson?"

William nodded. "Y-Yes, exactly."

"And you can start tomorrow you say?"

"Yes, whenever you need me."

Bob nodded. "You're on, be here for ten o'clock. It'll all come crashing down on your head, Sidney Storey, if anything goes wrong."

"Which it won't," Sid said. "He'll be the best worker you've ever had. Now, can we have three mugs of your best ale to celebrate?"

William took a handkerchief from his pocket and wiped his forehead. "Did you have to make me sound so accomplished? I've never done anything like this in my life."

"You should see the types he usually takes on. I can assure you, you'll be fine."

As soon as the drinks arrived, William took a mouthful before he sat upright slamming his tankard on the table.

"What's up, the ale's not that bad, is it?" Sid asked.

William stared at him. "Mr Wetherby."

"Where?" Sid turned around.

"No, not now, but does he ever come in? We're not far from Frankfort Street."

"He used to, but not any more. He prefers more high-class establishments nowadays."

"Does he know the landlord though?"

"Yes of course he does, why?"

William watched Bob move between the tables. "Don't tell Mr Wetherby I'm working here. One word from him and I'll lose the job before I start."

"He wouldn't do that."

William and William-Wetherby spoke together. "Oh yes he would."

Several hours later, when William arrived back at the Divers' house, he put down a stack of letters he had picked up from Handsworth and accepted the cup of tea Mary-Ann gave him.

"Did you find yourself a job?" she asked.

"I did, or rather young Sid Storey did. In one of the inns on Lower Tower Street."

"An inn?" Lydia and Mary-Ann said together.

"Once you're a bankrupt, you can't be choosy. It'll be fine until I'm ready to move on."

Lydia's shoulders slumped. "You're not going to earn much though."

"Maybe not, but I've been thinking. If I rent out the house in Handsworth I'll be able to pay the mortgage and have enough money left to pay for somewhere to live around Summer Lane."

"That's what Mr Diver does," Mary-Ann said. "The money we get from the house in Handsworth more than pays for this one."

William stared at her. "I wish you'd told me sooner."

Mary-Ann put her hand on his arm. "You were in no fit state to move any earlier, this is a real sign that you're getting better."

William smiled. "I am. I'm going into work tomorrow and I actually feel happy about it. I'll put an advertisement in the newspaper on my way." William reached for the letters he had left on the table. "I visited Handsworth while I was out. It looks like I've got more bills."

"Let's hope we can rent Havelock Road out quickly then." Lydia eyed the pile of letters.

"They can all wait, I'll pay them when I'm ready." He worked his way through the pile until he reached a large embossed envelope. "It's from the bank," he said as he took the letter from the envelope.

As he read, his stomach lurched and he let his head rest on the back on the chair.

"What's the matter?" Lydia took the letter from him. "In light of the bankruptcy and owing to the fact the mortgage has not been paid for the last three weeks, the bank is calling in the loan ..." She looked up. "Can they do that? It's your house."

William took a deep breath. "It's my house that happens to be mostly owned by the bank."

"But we've just discussed how we can pay the mortgage. They'll get their money."

"Can we help?" Mary-Ann said. "How much do you owe?"

William shook his head and turned to face Lydia. "Did you read the last line?"

Lydia glanced back at the letter. "This decision is final and not open to negotiation. They're just going to take your house, without even having the decency to talk to you about it."

William closed his eyes and took a deep breath. "Because I haven't been paying, they'll take the house, sell it to get their money and give me what's left. Most likely I'll end up with nothing."

Lydia stood up. "That's it. I'm going to Summer Lane with you tomorrow to see if I can have my old job back. If we both live and work in the same area, we'll be able to afford a room in someone else's house. I'm not going to sit around and do nothing any longer."

CHAPTER SIXTY-FOUR

As soon as Mrs Storey opened the front door to him, William-Wetherby dived into the house on Frankfort Street.

"You're early tonight," she said.

"With the weather being so foul I ran most of the way home. I need to buy myself an umbrella."

"Spring will be here soon enough, and not before time. It's been a hard winter in more ways than one."

William-Wetherby sat down. "It has. At least Father and Lydia are settled again. She was fortunate to get her old job and the flat back. It's a bit of a squeeze for the two of them, but at least they can heat it cheaply and they can get to work easily enough. Sid and I will nip into the inn and see Father tonight."

Within an hour, William-Wetherby was sitting in the inn watching his father collect up the empty beer mugs. He sighed. This time last year he'd been a proud man running his own business. Now he was reduced to this. Damn Mr White. Damn Mr Wetherby. Did they really know each other? How could he prove Mr Wetherby had anything to do with the bankruptcy?

"A penny for them," Sid said.

William-Wetherby glanced at him. "What?"

"You're deep in thought. What's worrying you?"

"Nothing. I was watching Father."

"I'd say he's taken to it well." Sid smiled. "Looks like he's been doing it for years."

William-Wetherby shook his head. "My mother would be horrified if she could see him now. We have to find him a better job than this. He must be able to do something else."

William groaned and rolled over in bed as Lydia shook him from his sleep.

"Don't roll over," she said. "You have to get up, you need to be at the inn by eight o'clock."

"What time is it now?"

"Gone seven. I've put a couple of eggs on the table for you. Hurry up before they go cold."

William sighed as his wife left the room. What possessed him to agree to being in work so early? What was so important about Birmingham being granted city status? It was doing all right as a town …

"William, come on, you'll be late," Lydia shouted. "I have to go and open the shop and I'm not leaving you in bed."

William dragged his legs over the edge of the bed and sat up before reaching for his trousers. He was about ready when Lydia came back into the room.

"I told you not to take any laudanum last night. It's time you were off it."

William shuffled past her and sat down at the small table. "I wouldn't have slept a wink if I hadn't taken it and I'm going to need all the energy I can find today."

With two boiled eggs and a cup of tea inside him, William walked up Summer Lane to the inn. At least it was only a small place, two back-to-back houses that had been knocked together, but Bob had ordered extra ale for the day. Goodness knows where they were going to put it.

By ten o'clock, the room had been rearranged to give them more space and William pulled a tankard of ale from the cask to sample it. He needed this; his head was spinning and they hadn't even started yet. He had barely finished when banging on the front door disturbed his peace. Half past ten. The first of the regulars were here.

As three o'clock approached, William wondered if most of the men of Birmingham were in their upstairs rooms. He'd lost count of the number of times he'd been up and down the stairs but despite the continuing demand for ale, he needed a rest. His head was spinning and with breakfast now forgotten he poured himself a mug of stout. The thick, almost black ale, should at least line his stomach. He was about to take an unofficial break in the back room when William-Wetherby and Sid found him.

"Has it been like this all day?" Sid said.

William nodded and went to pour them both a drink.

"You're looking pale," William-Wetherby said as he sat down.

"I'm exhausted." William flopped onto the

empty stool between them. "I've been rushed off my feet. I've never known it so busy."

"It's like this in the rest of town too." Sid took a gulp of ale.

"You mean in the rest of the city." William-Wetherby smiled. "I've never known people so excited about anything before. What time are you here until?"

"Until everyone leaves. Thankfully the moon's still new and so they shouldn't be late."

Sid laughed. "Many of them don't have far to go and so I wouldn't be too sure. It's not like being in Handsworth."

"Well, on that cheery note I'd better do some work." William stood up, but as he did stars danced before his eyes and he grabbed for the table to steady himself. William-Wetherby jumped up and helped him back to his seat.

"Are you all right?"

"I think so, I just went dizzy."

"You're sweating too and it's not hot in here."

William moved to stand up again. "I need some air. Help me to the door for a minute and I'll be fine." William-Wetherby held his father's arm and pushed a way through the crowd. They had almost reached the door when Bob saw them.

"Where are you going?" he asked.

William's breath was laboured. "I need some air."

"I don't pay you to stand outside, there are two tables upstairs with empty mugs. I'll go and take the order and you better be back to pull the beer and deliver it."

With the wind howling around outside, William was soon back inside.

"Are you sure you'll be all right?" William-Wetherby asked him. "Sid and I can't stay long."

"I'll be fine, I feel better for the air. You go when you're ready and I'll see you tomorrow."

When William-Wetherby and Sid arrived in Frankfort Street, Mr Wetherby was by the fire talking to Mrs Storey.

"Well, well, I wondered if I'd see you," he said to William-Wetherby. "Are you still looking after that father of yours? You should have committed him to Winson Green the state he was in."

"Is it any wonder he was in a state? When you lose your home and business and the one person who could prevent it refuses to do anything to help."

Mr Wetherby glanced at his pocket watch. "He's moved somewhere near here, hasn't he?"

William-Wetherby glared at his namesake. "What does it matter to you?"

"How are Margaret and Florence getting on with you?" Mrs Storey asked.

"They seem happy enough. I don't see much of them, Sarah-Ann takes care of them."

"Father would like them to come to Birmingham," William-Wetherby said. "We haven't seen them for months. Could they come here?"

"I would say that the less they see of your father the better. I don't want them having a setback."

"Do you have to be so vindictive? Haven't you made him suffer enough?"

"I haven't made him suffer at all, it was entirely of his own making. I think you'll find I'm doing the children a favour." Mr Wetherby turned to his sister. "I must be going. I have to say I'm disappointed about the quality of the guests you entertain here. Can you do something about it before I come again?"

Mrs Storey put her hands on her hips. "Throw William-Wetherby out onto the streets, you mean? No I can't. It's about time you put your quarrels behind you and remember you're family. What have you done with that parcel you wanted delivering?"

"I put it in the corner near the window. Please take the utmost care with it."

As Mr Wetherby closed the front door William-Wetherby sat down and put his head in his hands.

"Will there never be an end to it?"

"Maybe one day, but it'll take time," Mrs Storey said. "Let me make you a cup of tea. Oh, before I do, Sidney, you need to deliver that parcel to the accountant before you go to the workshop in the morning. They're the books for the business and they need to be there by the end of the week. Mr Wetherby's travelling to London tomorrow and can't take them."

"Do I have to?" Sid replied. "The accountant is in the opposite direction to the workshop."

"Don't be so lazy, it'll only take you five minutes longer."

"And the rest ..."

"I'll do it," William-Wetherby said. "If he still uses the same accountant he used to, I go that way to the foundry."

CHAPTER SIXTY-FIVE

William-Wetherby breathed a sigh of relief when he saw the first rays of sunlight shining through the bedroom curtains. He doubted he'd slept a wink last night, but his time hadn't been wasted. Jumping out of bed, he was pleased to be downstairs before Mrs Storey. He grabbed his hat and coat but as he reached for Mr Wetherby's books, she appeared.

"You're an early bird this morning, couldn't you sleep?"

"Yes, I slept well enough, but I want to be in time for the accountant." He patted the parcel under his arm.

Mrs Storey reached for the kettle. "You'll arrive

long before him at this rate. Sit down and let me make you a cup of tea. Have you eaten anything?"

"No, thank you, I need to go. I'll grab a pie or something on my way."

Mrs Storey put her hands on her hips. "That won't do you any good. Will you be home for tea tonight?"

"I will, but I may be a bit late. I need to call and see how Father is. He had a bit of a turn yesterday."

"A turn?"

William-Wetherby's face flushed as he reached for the door. "I'm sorry I can't stay. Sid was with me, he can fill you in."

The light remained dull as William-Wetherby walked down Summer Lane towards the town centre. He glanced up at the sky; it wasn't going to get light anytime soon. The streets were still quiet when he reached the Town Hall and he found a sheltered spot to sit, out of the way of prying eyes. He needed to see these accounts. Taking the books from their wrapping he found August 1888 and saw his own familiar writing staring up at him. He found the entry confirming Mr Wetherby had taken money out to buy some livestock for the farm. There were several invoices from familiar suppliers, but that was it. William-Wetherby scratched his head. Nothing. Not a hint. Why was he surprised?

Mr Wetherby wouldn't leave the evidence for everyone to see.

As his shoulders slumped, he leaned back against the wall and flicked through the rest of the book. Nothing he hadn't seen a hundred times before. He plonked it down onto the floor beside him, but as he did, an envelope became visible from between the blank pages at the back of the book.

His heartbeat quickened as he opened the envelope and found a loose page from another set of accounts. He scanned the information but it made no sense. It started on the twentieth of August and appeared perfectly normal. There were transactions in and out to local suppliers, many of whom he was familiar with. *Why would he hide a page like this?* William-Wetherby turned the paper over in his hand. There must be thirty or forty transactions here; they must have some significance. *What do I do?* He gazed out over the square in front of the Town Hall. Mrs Storey had said the books only needed to be with the accountant by the end of the week. Nobody would miss them if he kept them for a day. He just needed to find somewhere safe for an hour where he could copy them out.

Once he'd finished work, William-Wetherby

walked up the driveway of his aunt and uncle's house and knocked on the door. If there was anyone in the world he trusted, it was them. The maid let him in and showed him into the back room.

Mary-Ann looked up from her sewing. "This is a nice surprise. What brings you here?"

William-Wetherby flushed. "Do you think I could use a table for about an hour to do some bookkeeping?"

Mary-Ann's brow furrowed. "Why would you want to do that here? What are you up to?"

"Please can I do it first and explain later when Mr Diver gets home?"

Mary-Ann nodded. "Very well but you'd better have a good reason."

William-Wetherby was in the morning room when Mr Diver arrived home. He came in to see him, closing the door behind him.

"This is most unusual. What are you doing?"

William-Wetherby put down his pen. "I'm trying to find out what Mr Wetherby's up to."

Mr Diver raised an eyebrow. "What do you mean?"

"I've got the books here for Mr Wetherby's business, and I want to find out if any money was transferred between him and Mr White in August or September."

Mr Diver's eyes bulged. "Where did you get them from?"

"He wanted someone to take them to the accountant and I offered."

"Are you sure? That doesn't sound like Mr Wetherby."

"All right, he asked Sid to take them, but he didn't want to do it and so I offered."

"If he finds out ..."

"I know, my life won't be worth living, but he won't find out. Not yet. I'll deliver them to the accountant tomorrow and he'll be none the wiser."

"What do you hope to find? He wouldn't be daft enough to write everything down."

"Then why would he have a page of someone else's accounts hidden in his books? Something doesn't add up."

Mr Diver picked up the piece of paper and scanned it. "You won't be able to prove anything with this."

"Maybe not, but there are a lot of entries for the time we're interested in and I'm going to go through them one by one. Then I'm going to pay Mr White a visit."

CHAPTER SIXTY-SIX

As he sat in the inn watching William serve the customers closest to him, William-Wetherby glanced at the clock again. Nearly eight o'clock.

"You're here late tonight," William said. "Is Mr Wetherby at Mrs Storey's again?"

William-Wetherby sighed. "It looks like it. Sid wouldn't leave me here this long if he wasn't."

"Do you think he's doing it on purpose?" William said. "You know, to try and get rid of you?"

William-Wetherby feigned a laugh. "Do you think he's doing it for any other reason? He hasn't spent so many evenings with Mrs Storey in all the time she's been in Birmingham."

As William moved into the front room, his son once again took the copy of the loose page from his pocket. He had spent hours poring over it, but still it made no sense. *What am I missing?*

"What's that you're looking at?" Sid beckoned William for a drink before he sat down beside William-Wetherby.

"Nothing, just a bit of work." He folded the paper up and put it back in his jacket. "Where've you been? Has Mr Wetherby been at the house all this time?"

"He has. His brother's leaving tomorrow and he wanted to speak to him before he went. I don't think Mother will be sorry to see him go."

"Me neither, if it means me spending half my life in here."

"You're late tonight, Sidney." William put a mug of ale on the table for him.

"Mr Wetherby's up to his games again." Sid took a gulp of his ale. "You're looking pleased with yourself though, Mr Jackson, what have you been up to?"

William smiled. "Nothing I shouldn't have been, but I'm feeling much better than I have been. Things are working out well here and Lydia and I are thinking about moving to a house rather than staying in that room."

"Where will you go?"

"We might not be going anywhere yet, it was

only talk, but we'll stay near Summer Lane. A lot of people look down on us for living here, but everyone's in the same boat and no one judges you, not like in Handsworth. I'm surprised how happy we are, given the circumstances. It's just a matter of money; we don't want to overstretch ourselves again."

"If you and Lydia found a house," Sid said, "William-Wetherby could live with you and help towards the rent. Not that we want him to leave, but it is Mr Wetherby's house and if he's going to cause trouble it might sort out both your problems."

William gazed at Sid. "How long have you been thinking about that?"

Sid shrugged. "I haven't, it seems obvious."

William turned to his son. "It could work, I suppose. We'd have to check the money side of things, but what do you say, William-Wetherby? Could you bear to live with me and Lydia?"

William-Wetherby glared at Sid before he looked down at his ale. *Could I live with Lydia knowing she's with Father?* "Let me think about it. I suppose it couldn't be any worse than not being allowed home at night."

As soon as William-Wetherby finished work the

following Saturday, he set off for Ladywood, a part of the city he wasn't familiar with. He had a vague memory of Mr White's address from his time working for the business, but he had no idea where he was going. There were a lot more houses in the area than he expected and after stopping to ask several people, he reached an address that sounded familiar. He stood on the street corner and stared at the house opposite. It was one of the smarter terraced properties in the area with a bay window on the ground floor that was dressed with heavy curtains.

He marched towards the house and stared at the front door. He should have thought of this, but what did he say? Taking a deep breath he knocked purposefully on the door but flinched when a maid opened it immediately.

"Is Mr White in, please?" William-Wetherby asked.

"Who shall I say is calling?"

"I've come on an errand from Mr Wetherby, I believe he knows him."

The maid nodded and closed the door in his face. William-Wetherby glanced up and down the street. It didn't strike him as the place where people had maids. *If he has so much money, why does he live here?*

A minute later, the maid returned. "Mr White said he knows nobody by the name of Wetherby. You must be at the wrong house."

"No, this is definitely the right house," William-Wetherby said. "Number forty-one. Perhaps he's forgotten. Can you go and ask again? He worked for him about six or eight months ago, I believe. Mention the name Mr Jackson. That might jog his memory."

This time the maid was away for longer and when she returned she opened the door only enough to poke her face through.

"Mr White does remember dealing with Mr Jackson, but he doesn't know a Mr Wetherby and asked if you'd kindly leave the premises."

"They were seen together ..." William-Wetherby said.

"You'd better leave." The maid stepped back to close the door. "Mr White doesn't want to be disturbed."

William-Wetherby glared at her. "I'll speak to Mr Wetherby about this, he doesn't usually make mistakes."

CHAPTER SIXTY-SEVEN

The door shut in William-Wetherby's face and he turned to leave. Why would Mr White deny knowing Mr Wetherby when they had been seen together? His pace was slow as he debated what to do next. He needed to speak to Mr Diver; he was the one who had seen the two of them together.

Mr Diver was sitting in front of the fire waiting for his tea when William-Wetherby arrived. The maid ushered him into the back room and closed the door behind him.

Mr Diver put down the newspaper. "What are you doing here?" Mr Diver didn't stand up and William-Wetherby noted that his uncle's breathing was still laboured.

"I've been to see Mr White."

"What in God's name did you do that for? What did you say to him?"

William-Wetherby's shoulders slumped as he took the seat opposite his uncle. "I didn't say anything. The maid wouldn't let me in but said Mr White didn't know any Mr Wetherby."

Mr Diver's forehead creased in thought. "Perhaps your father made a mistake and the man who greeted me at Christmas wasn't Mr White?"

William-Wetherby shook his head. "He won't ever forget Mr White. Don't forget he worked with him for the best part of a year before he caused the trouble."

"So what are you thinking?"

William-Wetherby looked his uncle in the eye. "I think he's lying. Which tavern were they in when you saw them?"

"It was in Nechells. I thought it was strange at the time because it's not a part of Birmingham you'd expect Mr Wetherby to visit."

"That makes it more suspicious. Can you remember the name?"

"The Dog and Partridge. It's one of the taverns on the main road."

William-Wetherby cocked his head. "When

you were introduced, did you mention Mr Wetherby's name? Perhaps Mr White genuinely doesn't know a Mr Wetherby."

"Because he used another name, you mean?"

"Exactly." William-Wetherby was on his feet. "If you're going to conduct business like that you don't use your real name; he wouldn't want anyone to find out what he was up to. That would explain why they met all the way out there. I bet Mr Wetherby was furious when he saw you."

"Now you come to mention it, it was me who approached him. He kept his head down until I stood next to him."

"I think this calls for a trip to the Dog and Partridge to see if anyone remembers them. Someone may have overheard what they were talking about."

"You're clutching at straws now," Mr Diver said. "It was over six months ago. Even if anyone did notice, I'm sure they won't remember anything."

William-Wetherby stared at his uncle. "You may be right, but if we don't try we'll never learn the truth. Will you come with me?"

"Now?"

"Of course, now. The place should be full at this time on a Saturday." William-Wetherby noticed Mr Diver's reluctance. "All right, if you won't come with me, I'll go on my own."

It took almost an hour for William-Wetherby to walk to Nechells, but he found the Dog and Partridge as Mr Diver had described. He marched into the bar and asked for the manager.

"Aren't you having a drink?" the barman said.

"I will if the manager comes to speak to me. Can you find him first?"

William-Wetherby leaned against the wall studying the men as they relaxed at the end of their working week. He hoped the manager was available; he desperately wanted a mug of ale.

"What can I do for you?" A burly man with an unkempt beard approached.

William-Wetherby stood up straight. "First, can I have some of your fine ale, then can we go somewhere to talk?"

With his ale in his hand, William-Wetherby followed the manager into a private room and put his mug down on the table. "I'm interested in someone who might have been here in August last year."

The landlord turned to walk away. "Be off with

you. Have you seen how busy we are? I couldn't tell you everyone who's in now, let alone six months ago."

"Please don't go." William-Wetherby caught hold of the man's arm. "It wasn't a usual customer. I believe he used to arrive around late morning, shortly after you opened and would sit in the snug. He'd arrive in a carriage and would have been impeccably dressed."

The manager squinted at William-Wetherby, the lines on his forehead prominent. "I remember him. He came in a few times. He wore an expensive hat and coat, which was completely out of place. I remember him asking the barman for water for the horses too."

"Do you remember anything else? Was he on his own?"

"He was always the first to arrive, but a second gentleman would join him. The second fellow always appeared scared and never stayed long enough to buy a drink. That doesn't happen often either."

"Did you overhear any of their conversations?"

The manager shook his head. "No, but the last time they were here, it looked like the toff was threatening the other man. The fellow cleared off pretty quickly, I can tell you. I didn't see them again."

William-Wetherby thanked the manager and took a penny from his pocket. "Take a drink for yourself." He finished his ale and set off on the long walk home.

CHAPTER SIXTY-EIGHT

William-Wetherby opened the front door to his new home and went in. He shivered and rubbed his hands together as he studied the selection of chairs that had come with the property. Choosing the one with the most padding he sat down and pulled his coat tightly around him. What did he do now? Since he had been to Nechells, he had proof Mr White and Mr Wetherby knew each other, but what did he do with the information? Meeting someone in an inn wasn't a crime, but why would they go to such pains to hide the fact if it was nothing more than a simple business relationship?

His thoughts were interrupted by Lydia opening the front door. She shivered as she walked in.

"It feels colder in here than it does outside," she said. "Why didn't you light the fire?"

William-Wetherby glanced at the empty grate and shrugged. "I wasn't sure if I should use the coal, besides, I've never done it before. Isn't that your job?"

Lydia bustled past him and knelt before the fire. "Of course you can use the coal, we have three wages coming in. Come here and kneel next to me and I'll teach you how to do it. I'm not doing all the chores when I've done a full day's work."

William-Wetherby pushed himself up and joined her by the fire.

"Here, take these and clean out the grate before we add new coal." Lydia passed him the brush and pan, accidentally touching his hand as she did. They both froze and William-Wetherby searched her face before their eyes locked. Her skin was fair and her blue-grey eyes had regained the sparkle they had lost. He leaned forward and tucked a stray piece of hair behind her ear. "Don't." Lydia averted her eyes and reached for the coal.

William-Wetherby swallowed hard. "Have you any idea how difficult it is living here when I know you and Father are together in the next bedroom."

Lydia played with the coal in her hands. "We've

been through this. As much as we might want to change what's happened, we can't."

William-Wetherby placed his hand on hers. "Father's at work every evening ... he'd never know."

Lydia glanced up, her eyes glistening. "I'd know and I can't live a lie. Hasn't he suffered enough without the two people he trusts most deceiving him?"

A shiver ran down William-Wetherby's spine. "I'm sorry. I didn't think you cared for him."

"Maybe I didn't marry him because I loved him, but that doesn't mean I don't care. He's a gentle, sweet man who doesn't deserve what's happened. I'm not going to do anything more to upset him. It would ruin everything."

William-Wetherby stroked the back of his finger down her cheek before he pushed himself to his feet. "You're right, I'm sorry. I'll see you later, I'm going to the pub."

The following morning, knocking on the front door woke William-Wetherby from a deep sleep. He heard Lydia answer it before the sound of talking caused him to roll over and open his eyes. Who made social calls before seven o'clock in the morning?

By the time he arrived downstairs, Lydia had set the table for breakfast and a letter rested on his side plate.

"What's this?" William-Wetherby picked it up.

"It was hand-delivered about quarter of an hour ago. The man said he was from the solicitor's office sorting out Mr Watkins's estate."

William-Wetherby tore at the envelope and pulled out a letter written on headed paper. "It's about the money we've been left." As he read, the smile disappeared from his face. "They want all five of us to go to the solicitor's office. How are we supposed to do that? The five of us haven't been together for over a year and Charles isn't in the country. Is this some sort of trick? 'We have some money for you, but you have to work out how to get it.'"

"You'll have to go and talk to them."

"I don't know when. They don't open until after I'm due in work and they're closed again by the time I come home. I'll have to slip out in the middle of the day and hope I'm not missed."

By midday, William-Wetherby sat in the wood-panelled office across the desk from a solicitor who appeared to take great delight in outlining the conditions for releasing Mr Watkins's money.

"So you're telling me that unless the five of us come here together, the only option is to get signed agreements from my brother and each of my sisters so you can give me a cheque on their behalf?"

The solicitor nodded. "We have to be sure you only receive your share of the money and the others are aware you'll be handling it on their behalf."

"But my brother's at sea. I'm not sure where he is at the moment and even if I find out, it'll be months before he gets a letter to me."

"Are your sisters able to sign?"

William-Wetherby shrugged. "One of them will be but the youngest two are only fifteen and twelve. Unfortunately, they're living with Mr Wetherby at the moment and I haven't seen them for months."

"I'm sure I could have a word with Mr Wetherby ..."

"No!" William-Wetherby stood up and ran his hand across his head. "No, I'm sorry, but please don't involve Mr Wetherby."

The solicitor stared at William-Wetherby as he clasped his hands together on his desk. "I was going to suggest we ask Mr Wetherby to act as a guarantor to make sure the money is distributed fairly. With the family being separated that might be the most viable option."

"I'm not involving Mr Wetherby. Let me find someone else, I'd rather not have the money at all than let him become involved."

As soon as he'd finished work, William-Wetherby walked to the Divers' house and arrived as they were starting their tea.

"Come and join us," Mary-Ann said. "I prepared more than I needed."

William-Wetherby smiled as he sat down.

"What brings you here?" Mr Diver asked. "Are things working out all right living with your father and Lydia?"

"As well as can be expected." William-Wetherby pictured Lydia arriving home from work alone. "I don't see much of Father with him being at the inn, and I tend to go out with Sid in the evenings." *It's the only way.*

"You look like you have something on your mind though," Mary-Ann said.

"It's Mr Watkins's solicitor. They're ready to pay the money from his estate but unless all five of us go into the office, or we give them written permission from everyone to handle the money on their behalf, they won't release it."

"Are you looking for a guarantor to handle it for you?" Mr Diver asked.

William-Wetherby nodded. "The solicitor suggested Mr Wetherby, but I absolutely forbid it. Would you do it? You'd need to put the money in a bank account and make sure we each receive our share."

Mr Diver nodded. "If I open an account for you with one of the friendly societies, you could deposit the money until you need it. We'd have to set it up so that you'd need my permission to take any out."

"What about the girls?" William-Wetherby said. "We can't visit Margaret and Florence at the moment."

"Let me speak to Aunt Sarah-Ann," Mary-Ann said. "There's no reason why you can't see them, even if Mr Wetherby won't let them see your father."

William-Wetherby smiled. "I'm sure they'd like that, even if they only come for the day. I just wish we could contact Charles as well. I do miss him."

CHAPTER SIXTY-NINE

William sat at the living room table, his breakfast set out before him. Lydia and William-Wetherby had both left for work and he smiled as he tucked in to the first of two boiled eggs.

As he was breaking into his second egg, he was interrupted by a knock at the door. William glared at it and a moment later it opened and the postman popped his head around the door.

"You are in." He waved a letter at him. "You've got an interesting one here."

Once he was alone again, William studied the envelope before tossing it to the far end of the table. He returned to his egg, but a knot had formed in his stomach and he pushed his breakfast away. *Why won't these people leave me alone?* With another glance at the letter he stood up from the table and went for his coat.

When he returned home that evening Lydia was waiting for him. She had the letter in her hand.

"You have a letter from the trustees," she said.

William's shoulders slumped. "I'm not opening it now. I've had a busy day and all I want to do is go to sleep."

Lydia put her hands on her hips. "You need to know what they want."

"It can wait."

"I'd say it's waited long enough. Why won't you open it?"

William went to the stairs. "We've moved on from that, Lydia. We have a new life now, we have enough money to eat and pay the rent. I don't want to be reminded of ... all that trouble."

"I'm going to open it for you."

"Do what you like, I'm going to bed. I've felt dizzy all day thanks to that letter."

Lydia opened it and read it to herself before she spoke. "There's nothing to worry about. It says the date has passed for creditors to put in a claim and they've worked out the dividend payments. Nine shillings and eight pence to the pound. That's good, isn't it?"

William was halfway up the stairs. "It's more than most creditors get, but that doesn't help us. We won't see a penny of it."

"Maybe not, but it shows you weren't as reckless as some have made you out to be."

"The damage is done. When will the payments be made?"

"It'll be posted in the paper in the next couple of weeks and the payments will start on the twenty-fifth of July."

William stopped where he was and closed his eyes. "Not the papers again. Are they determined to ruin my reputation every time I try to make something of myself?"

The following morning, a noise outside the window roused William from his sleep and a glance at the clock told him he had overslept. He rolled onto his back and counted to ten. It felt like he had only just gone to sleep and yet he had to go back to the inn again in less than half an hour. Dragging himself from the bed he threw some water over his face before he dressed and went downstairs, helping himself to a slice of bread as he went out.

His breath was laboured by the time he arrived, and he hurried to prepare the casks before the first customers arrived.

"What time do you call this?" Bob said when he saw him.

"I'm sorry, I didn't sleep last night and ..."

"I don't want excuses, I want you here at ten o'clock on the dot, whether you've slept or not. Now, the tables in the top room need cleaning and take a jug of ale up for Mr Potts when he arrives."

William watched Bob disappear into the cellar and closed his eyes to stop the room swaying. He should have had more breakfast. When the dizziness subsided, he pulled a jug of ale and set it on a tray with a tankard. Mr Potts would be here any minute. He climbed the stairs but as he reached the top his vision blurred and black spots appeared before his eyes. He grabbed for the handrail but before he could steady himself he tumbled backwards, spilling the beer as he went. His descent came to an abrupt and painful stop when he hit the bottom step. The noise brought Bob rushing to the bottom of the stairs where William lay in a heap.

"What's going on here?" Bob said. "Is that a full jug of ale you've wasted?"

William's eyes flickered open. "I'm sorry, I don't

know what happened. One minute I was at the top of the stairs …"

"Well, you can clean this mess up. The beer'll be coming out of your wages."

Bob's stocky frame blurred in and out of focus, and as William moved to stand up he fell back onto the stairs. "My ankle … I think it's broken."

"That's all I need. Mr Potts is here. Move out of the way, I'll deal with you later. I need to clean this mess up."

William was sitting up in bed when he heard William-Wetherby arrive home, seconds before he rushed up the stairs to the bedroom.

William-Wetherby stared at his father. "What happened?"

"Those stairs at work are too much for me. I'm too old for all this."

"Nonsense. Mr Wetherby must be twenty years older than you and he still runs around all over the place."

"I'd be fit and healthy if I had his money."

"Have you seen the doctor?"

William rolled his eyes. "We might be able to eat nowadays, but I don't have money for the doctor as well."

"That's nonsense, I'm going for him now, whether you like it or not."

Half an hour later, the doctor bandaged William's ankle.

"At least it's not broken, you should be able to walk on it in a couple of weeks." The doctor took out his stethoscope and listened to William's chest. "I'm more concerned about your heart. Have you noticed it beating faster than usual?"

William shrugged. "I suppose it does, but I've grown so used to it, I don't take much notice any more."

The doctor put his stethoscope in his bag. "Are you worried about anything at the moment?"

Only that my reputation's about to be destroyed again. "No."

"Are you sure?" When William refused to answer, the doctor continued. "I want you to rest completely for the next two weeks, which means I don't want you to leave this bed. If I find out you've been up, I'll have to admit you to hospital so they can watch over you."

William's head jerked up as he glared at the doctor. "That means I'll lose my job."

"Mr Jackson, I'm going to be blunt with you. Your heart's struggling to pump blood around your body. That's why you keep going light-headed and it may be the case that you either lose your job or you lose your life. You need to take time to rest and I'm ordering you not to leave this bed for at least a fortnight, irrespective of how your ankle feels. I'll reassess you in two weeks, but if you're still having irregular heartbeats, you'll have to stay there. Have I made myself clear?"

William nodded. The doctor had made himself perfectly clear.

CHAPTER SEVENTY

Three weeks later, William ventured down the stairs for the first time since his accident. He walked out into the court at the back of the house and lifted his face to the summer sun while he waited for Lydia and William-Wetherby to arrive home. He allowed himself to smile. Perhaps there was a God after all. The announcement of the creditors' payment had been in the papers while he was housebound and had barely caused a ripple amongst those he knew. Not only that, his heart was now functioning without him noticing every beat. His only concern was that he no longer had a job.

William-Wetherby joined him shortly after he'd gone outside and sat beside him on the bench.

"The postman gave me these." William-Wetherby held a selection of letters in his hand.

William took the first envelope that was addressed to him. "At least it's not official." William took the letter from the envelope and turned it over. "It's from Aunt Sarah-Ann." William scanned the letter and sighed. "Uncle Richard died last week. Poor fellow. The funeral's on Friday and she wants me to go."

William-Wetherby paused. "That's a shame, especially as you hadn't seen him for so long. Did he die in the asylum?"

William shrugged. "I presume so. Nobody told me he'd come out. Another one of Mr Wetherby's casualties."

William-Wetherby turned to his father. "You do realise he'll be at the funeral."

William leaned back against the wall. "He's my uncle. I should be able to pay my respects without that fool intimidating me. He's no right to be there the way they argued with each other."

William-Wetherby followed his father's example and leaned against the wall. "Why did they dislike each other so much?"

William shrugged. "I never found out, but I suspect it was to do with your grandmother. She was always friendly with Uncle Richard and I suspect Mr Wetherby was jealous."

"In that case I would say Grandmother would want you to go."

William took a deep breath. "I don't know if I can; my heart's racing at the thought of it."

William-Wetherby studied the other envelopes in his hand.

"What else do you have?" William said.

"I don't know, but there are two the same, one each. I'll open mine."

"What is it?" William leaned over to read it.

"A wedding invitation from Aunt Sarah-Ann and Mr Wetherby. Aunt Elizabeth's getting married in September. This invite's for me and Eleanor, I expect this one's for you."

William eyed his envelope before opening it to read:

Mr and Mrs W Wetherby
request the pleasure of the company of
Mr and Mrs W Jackson
at the wedding of
Miss Elizabeth Flemming
to
Reverend Jacob Bloor

on Thursday, the 19th September, 1889 at 10 o'clock
in St Mary's Church, Handsworth

"I can't go to a wedding," William said. "Not in Handsworth and not with everyone there."

"Take a deep breath," William-Wetherby said. "It could be their way of making amends."

"After everything he's done to me, do you think a wedding invitation's going to put everything right? No, Aunt Sarah-Ann's invited us. It wouldn't surprise me if he doesn't know about it. Will you go?"

William-Wetherby shrugged. "I'll ask Eleanor what she thinks, but there's something else to consider. Margaret and Florence will be there."

William closed his eyes and sighed. "How can I not go and see my own daughters when I haven't seen them for almost a year? Your mother would never forgive me. God, I'm such a failure."

"Stop that now. You're not a failure. Look at everything you've been through. Most people would've given up long ago, but you haven't and you should be proud of yourself. There's only one person who thinks you're a failure, but he thinks that of most people. I'll tell you what, why don't we go to the funeral and see how you feel?"

"We?"

"Of course, *we*. I'm not going to let you go on your own."

William nodded. "You're right, I shouldn't be hiding myself away, not any more. The bankruptcy's over and I want to pay my last respects to the uncle I would have known better had it not been for Mr Wetherby."

CHAPTER SEVENTY-ONE

As Mr Diver's carriage came to a halt outside the church, the coachman held the door while Mr Diver and Mary-Ann climbed down. William and William-Wetherby followed them and William stood behind his son to shield himself from the people milling around the entrance to the church.

As they went inside, the church was already half-full and they moved to the far right-hand aisle. William saw several cousins with their families in the congregation.

As the clock on the tower struck eleven, the coffin was carried into church. Mrs Richard and her children walked several paces behind it, followed by Aunt Sarah-Ann and Mr Wetherby, Aunt

Martha and their youngest sister Aunt Adelaide. The hairs on the back of William's neck stood on end as he saw the deadpan expression on Mr Wetherby's face. *Does the man have no emotions?*

As the service ended, the mourners followed the coffin out of the churchyard and walked the short distance to the burial site where the open grave waited for them. William followed some distance behind and waited for Mr Wetherby to position himself before he chose a spot that wasn't directly in his line of sight. William-Wetherby and Mr Diver stood on either side of him, their legs spread and hands crossed before them, as if acting as guards.

William struggled to breathe as he kept his eyes fixed on the coffin. At least his uncle had received a respectable send-off, although how many would be at the wake, he couldn't say. One thing was certain; he wouldn't be there.

As soon as it was acceptable to leave, Mr Diver led the way back to the church to find Mary-Ann standing with Aunt Sarah-Ann.

"Thank you for coming, William," his aunt said. "It can't have been easy."

William shook his head. "I wanted to pay my respects." He glanced over his shoulder. "We need to be leaving though."

Sarah-Ann smiled. "Don't look so worried. Mr Wetherby isn't on his way back yet, but don't you think it's time the two of you made up?"

William opened and closed his mouth several times but words failed him.

"I think it might take more than a funeral," William-Wetherby said.

Sarah-Ann nodded. "You will come to the wedding, won't you?"

William put his hand on William-Wetherby's shoulder and took a deep breath. "Can I let you know?"

"Yes, of course, but we'd like you to come. Margaret and Florence insisted I ask you as well. They're going to be bridesmaids and I've ordered dresses for them from London. I know it's not easy, but we need to rebuild the family, and something like this may help."

"They're going to be bridesmaids?" William took another deep breath. "How can I say no? Tell them I'll be there."

CHAPTER SEVENTY-TWO

As far as William-Wetherby was concerned, the second of August, 1889 was just another day. He left home at quarter to eight in the morning and was in work before eight o'clock. He spent the day doing the bookkeeping at the brass foundry and after work he went straight home. When he arrived, William was in the yard waiting for Lydia to come home.

"Happy birthday," William said. "You're earlier than I expected,"

William-Wetherby sat on the bench next to his father. "I'm always home at this time."

"But you're not twenty-one every day. I thought you'd go for a drink on the way home at least."

"I didn't tell anyone at work, I didn't want to waste my money."

William turned to face him. "You can't let today pass unnoticed; you should go out later. I remember Mother making me a special tea when I reached twenty-one before Mr Wetherby took me for a drink. It's hard to believe now."

"I hadn't planned on it, but I suppose I could. Why don't we go now, before Lydia comes home, and leave her a note?"

Five minutes later as they turned into Summer Lane they saw Sid walking towards them. Once they told him where they were going, he forgot his plans to go home and joined them.

"Have you tried getting your old job back, Mr Jackson?" he asked as they walked.

"What's the point? Bob won't want to see me again."

"That's a shame, I used to enjoy calling in after work. Do any other places down here need staff?"

"Not that I know of," William-Wetherby said. "The only place is the Saracen's Head, but they want a new landlord, not just a barman."

"That'd be better and it's almost on your doorstep. What do you think, Mr Jackson? You used to run your own business and so I'm sure you could run a beerhouse."

William feigned a laugh. "It doesn't matter what I think, I'm sure the terms of the bankruptcy wouldn't let me."

"While we're so close, why don't we go in anyway?" Sid said.

Five minutes later the three of them arrived at the Saracen's Head. It was a beerhouse William hadn't been in before and he admired the long mahogany bar that ran one length of the room before it rounded the corner and disappeared into the snug on the other side of the wall. The wooden tables and chairs filling the long, narrow room were full of men on their way home from work.

"I suppose the drinks are on me." William-Wetherby walked to the bar as William and Sid found a table. "Three tankards of your best ale, and one for yourself," he said to the barman when he got his attention. "Are you always this busy?"

"At this time of night we are, but we'll be closing down soon if we don't find another landlord."

"Has anyone else shown an interest?"

"Not yet. The brewery wants a manager to run the place but they want three months' rent in advance, which is putting everyone off."

William-Wetherby sucked the air through his teeth. "How much is that?"

The barman looked him up and down. "Why? Are you thinking of taking over?"

"No, but I know someone who might be interested. How much are we talking?"

"About twelve or thirteen pounds."

William-Wetherby nodded. "Who do I speak to if I'm interested?"

"You'll need to go to the brewery; they're the ones dealing with it."

William-Wetherby found Sid and William in the corner of the room and he plonked the drinks on the table in front of them.

"Happy Birthday," William said, raising his tankard. "May you have many years ahead of you."

Sid followed suit before he put his ale on the table. "Did you find anything out from the barman? I noticed you talking to him."

"He said the brewery are looking for a manager." He turned to his father. "You could do that, it's not like it would be your business."

William shuddered. "It's a busy place, I'd need staff and everything."

"They'd come with the beerhouse surely, you wouldn't have to hire them, not to start with. Besides, you've worked in a bar before. You mark my words, there's money to be made here; I think we should make some enquiries."

By the time each of them had bought a round of drinks, the idea of taking over the beerhouse was being discussed more seriously.

"Lydia could pull some pints, I'm sure the locals would like that." Sid winked at William-Wetherby.

"That's my wife you're talking about, Sidney Storey, not some woman of disrepute, and she'll do no such thing. Besides, she's happy enough at the tobacconist's and we could do with a separate income."

"I've heard that before," William-Wetherby said. "You never want anyone from the family working for you."

"I think you should go to the brewery tomorrow and speak to them," Sid said. "They may be pleased to have someone who's interested."

It was almost nine o'clock that evening when William-Wetherby and William returned home and Lydia stood with her hands on her hips as they let themselves in.

"Where've you been? Just look at the state of you and I'd bought something special for tea with it being William-Wetherby's birthday."

William-Wetherby's smile dropped. "I'm sorry, it was my fault. I didn't think we'd be so long but we met Sid." He moved to put his arm around her but she pulled away. "We have some good news though. There's a position available for a manager at the Saracen's Head. Father's going to apply."

"Now I know you've been drinking too much. He's not going to get a job like that with his record. You need to start being realistic."

William-Wetherby's shoulders stiffened. "I am being realistic. They only want a manager for a beerhouse, not someone to take full control of a public house. Anyway, we're going to the brewery tomorrow after I finish work."

Lydia raised an eyebrow before she glanced at William. "I'd wait and see how you feel tomorrow. Now, do you want some of this tea before it's completely ruined?"

CHAPTER SEVENTY-THREE

At four o'clock the following afternoon, William paced outside the gates of the brewery while he waited for his son. He sniffed the faint smell of hops in the air, thankful there had been no brewing that day. As he paused, William-Wetherby walked up behind him.

"Are you all set?"

"Are you sure we should be doing this?" William's body sagged. "My heart's pounding at the thought of going in."

"Stop worrying." William-Wetherby took his father by the arm and turned him towards the building. "Do you want to stay as you are for the rest of your life or do you want to rebuild what we once had?"

William sighed and followed William-Wetherby inside. It took several minutes to find someone who could help and they were shown into an office and asked to wait.

"What do I say?" William's voice squeaked as he spoke.

"Leave the talking to me, I'll give a good account of you."

"We can't lie." William's eyes were wide.

"I won't be lying, now sit down. Someone's coming."

As William took his seat, a portly man with a magnificent moustache walked into the room. He extended his hand to William-Wetherby as he introduced himself as Mr Briggs.

"Pleased to meet you, Mr Briggs; I'm Mr Jackson." William reached across the desk and as they shook hands their eyes momentarily locked. *He's a Freemason.*

"We're here about the Saracen's Head on Summer Lane." William-Wetherby spoke as his father retook his seat. "I understand you're looking for a manager."

"We are, but you're not old enough. We want someone over thirty and with experience."

"No, it's not for me, it's for my father. He has

experience from The Barrel, further up Summer Lane."

Mr Briggs's forehead creased. "I don't remember you at The Barrel. Were you managing it?"

William coughed to clear his throat. "No, sir. I was the barman, but I sprained my ankle and the landlord had to replace me."

"Before that, he ran his own business." William-Wetherby said. "Unfortunately a bad partner let him down and they had to close."

Mr Briggs studied William before he turned to William-Wetherby. "Could you step outside while I speak to Mr Jackson in private?"

Lines appeared on William-Wetherby's forehead as he looked to his father.

"We won't be long," William said. "I'll come and find you as soon as we're finished."

Once they were alone, Mr Briggs studied William. "I've not seen you at the Lodge before, which one do you attend?"

"New Street."

Mr Briggs smiled. "That explains it; I'm at Severn Street. That's not to say I can't help. How long have you been a member?"

William's face flushed. *Perhaps I should have paid this year's fees.* "Almost four years."

"And you've experience working behind a bar as well as running a business?"

William nodded.

"Splendid. We'd normally require references and three months' rent in advance, but I think we can make an exception. I'll pull the paperwork together and if you come back this time next week with four pounds, which is equivalent to one month's rent in advance, we can get everything signed."

William felt a bead of perspiration running down his back. "Thank you, sir. I'll see you this time next week."

As soon as William left the office, William-Wetherby rushed towards him.

"What was that all about? Why did I have to leave?"

William ushered his son out of the building before he spoke.

"You've got me into a right mess. I need to find four pounds by next week."

William-Wetherby's brow furrowed. "Four? I thought they wanted three months' rent; that sounds like it's only one month's. What happened?"

"I can't talk about it, other than to say the place is mine if I can find four pounds. I couldn't bring myself to tell him I didn't have that much money."

"You knew they wanted three months' rent in advance."

William hesitated. "Maybe I did, but I thought they'd want to see references and then tell me to be on my way."

William-Wetherby stopped. "So you're telling me that Mr Briggs will let you have the place for one month's rent and no references?" He stared at his father until a smile spread across his face. "He's a Freemason, isn't he?"

William glanced around. "Keep your voice down. Let's just say he's letting me have the place on very favourable terms ... if I can find a spare four pounds."

"Stop worrying, I can find the money for you. You go home and I'll sort it out."

As was becoming habit, William-Wetherby arrived at the Divers' house as they were sitting down for tea. He joined them and once they were finished, he went into the front room and told Mr Diver about the Saracen's Head.

"It could be the making of him but he needs to pay a month's rent in advance. It's four pounds, which he obviously hasn't got, and so I wondered if we could use some of Mr Watkins's money to pay it for him. It's a busy place and I'm sure he'd be able to repay us in the first few months. If the girls agree, can you withdraw the money?"

"Didn't they ask to see any references?"

William-Wetherby shook his head. "No, the man at the brewery seemed to know him and said that one month's rent was enough."

Mr Diver shrugged. "Lucky him. It would appear that his fortune's changing. For four pounds, I'd say you just need a letter from Eleanor. He should be able to pay it back before anyone knows it's missing."

CHAPTER SEVENTY-FOUR

Bushwood, Warwickshire

Sarah-Ann put her hands to her head as she gazed at the boxes and tissue paper spread out all over the living room. The seven dresses of deep plum satin with their high necks and long, lace-edged sleeves, looked delightful as they adorned the chairs surrounding her.

"Elizabeth darling," she called into the drawing room. "Come and see the bridesmaids' dresses. They're perfect."

Elizabeth smiled as she joined her mother. "They're wonderful."

"When's Cousin Hannah bringing the girls to

try their dresses on?" Sarah-Ann asked. "She's changed her mind so many times, I've lost track."

"I've invited her and the children to dinner on Sunday ... with Mr Goodwood of course. It was the only time they could make."

Sarah-Ann's eyes flicked to her daughter. "Have you told Cook?"

Elizabeth smiled and patted her mother's hand. "Stop worrying, of course I have. I've also told her Aunt Martha and Cousin Catherine will be visiting on Saturday. I'm so glad you and Aunt Martha are speaking to each other again, it wouldn't be the same not having Catherine here."

Sarah-Ann returned her daughter's smile. "I'm only anxious because I want it to be perfect. After the secrecy of my marriage to Mr Wetherby, I want to tell the world about yours."

Elizabeth turned around to admire the dresses. "Shall we fetch Margaret and Florence in here to try them on? I don't think I can wait until Saturday."

Five minutes later, Elizabeth escorted Margaret and Florence into the living room.

"Have you two washed your hands?" Sarah-Ann said.

"They have," Elizabeth said. "I supervised them myself."

"Which one's mine?" Florence picked a dress up from the settee.

"Not that one. Put it down this minute. You're not playing dressing-up now."

"This one's yours." Elizabeth held up the dress for Florence. "Would you like me to help you put it on?"

Florence nodded as she took off her dress. Margaret watched and waited for Sarah-Ann to give her permission to try hers on.

With Florence dressed, Elizabeth stepped back and smiled. "You look lovely."

Florence did a pirouette before swishing the skirt around her legs.

"Will you stop that," Sarah-Ann said as she fastened Margaret's dress. "You'll have it ruined before we get to church."

"But it's so pretty." Florence looked down at herself. "Will Father be at the wedding to see us?"

"He hopes to be, but he's been so busy lately he's not sure he'll be able to make it."

Florence's shoulders drooped. "I wish he wasn't always doing other things, we never see him. I miss him."

"And I'm sure he misses you too, but after what happened he needs to work." Sarah-Ann smoothed the material that Florence had ruffled.

"What's he busy doing?" Margaret asked. "He doesn't even come to school to see how I'm getting on. I want to live with him again."

Sarah-Ann glared at Margaret. "You can't possibly want to live in Summer Lane rather than here or at Wetherby House. You should be grateful for what you have, now I don't want to hear any more about it."

"What's all the noise?" A smile spread across Charlotte's face as she stood in the doorway and admired the girls. "Don't you look lovely."

"Charlotte dear, I'm glad you're here. Would you mind trying your dress on as well? I'd like to inspect as many as possible before the others come on Saturday. This one's yours."

Charlotte ambled across the room to collect her dress but stopped to run her fingers over the dresses for Sarah-Ann's great-nieces. "The little ones are going to look divine, don't you think?"

"You all are." Sarah-Ann smiled before turning to Elizabeth. "Darling, can you go with Charlotte and once you're finished, see if you can find Henry. He's probably outside with William Junior."

An hour later, with the dresses locked away in one

of the spare bedrooms, Sarah-Ann joined Mr Wetherby in the back lounge.

"We're going to have to do something about Margaret and Florence. They've been asking for William again. Telling them he's busy isn't going to work for much longer. Can you please stop this pursuit of him and at least let them visit him?"

Mr Wetherby glared at her. "Those children are better off without him, besides, if I start making concessions he'll think all is forgiven and before you know it he'll be back here wanting more money from me."

"You don't have to go soft on him, but don't be so hard. If he comes to the wedding, ignore him or at least don't do anything to cause an argument."

Mr Wetherby grunted. "I'll see, but if I sense any hint of him wanting more money, there'll be trouble."

CHAPTER SEVENTY-FIVE

Birmingham, Warwickshire

It was still a pleasant evening when William Wetherby left work and he relaxed as he strolled up Summer Lane. He hadn't gone far when a To Let board on the Saracen's Head caught his eye. *What's that doing there?* His father was going into the brewery tomorrow to pay the rent. He walked towards the public house, but as he got closer he saw that the board belonged to the property next door, a tobacconist's shop. *How have I missed that?* Granted, he didn't smoke and it was in a small space that had probably once been an alleyway, but he was amazed it was there at all, let alone available to let.

William-Wetherby glanced at the shop on the other side before he walked to the tobacconist's and opened the door.

"What'd you want?" An elderly man appeared from a room behind the counter.

"The shop," William-Wetherby said. "It's available to let and I know someone who might be interested. Can you tell me who owns it and what the rent is?"

"The brewery own it, but I don't know about the rent. I pay six pounds a year, but they want to put it up, that's why I'm off. Since the one further up the road opened there aren't enough customers to make it pay."

William-Wetherby inspected the tiny space lined on three sides by glass cabinets containing pipes and tobacco. "Can I see the living accommodation?"

The man screwed his eyes up to study him "I've told you we have no customers but you're still interested?"

William-Wetherby shrugged. "I might as well take a look while I'm here."

As he left the shop, William-Wetherby almost collided with Sid.

"Why have you just come out of a tobacconist's?" Sid asked.

"I saw it was available and thought it would be ideal for Lydia."

"She's happy enough at the other one, isn't she?"

"Maybe, but with Father working next door, I thought it would make life easier and I'm sure they'd make their money back."

William-Wetherby walked up Summer Lane with Sid and when he arrived home his father was sitting by the fireplace reading the newspaper.

"Is Lydia not home yet?" he asked.

"She won't be long, but you're late. Did you bump into Sid again?"

"I did, but that's not why I'm late. Have you ever noticed a tobacconist's next door to the Saracen's Head? I hadn't, but there is one and it's available to rent."

William paused to think. "I can't picture it, but haven't we got enough to deal with taking on a beerhouse?"

"I think it would be perfect for Lydia."

"What would be perfect for me?" Lydia said as she came in.

"The tobacconist's at the bottom of Summer Lane. I presume you know about it, but did you know it's up for rent?"

Lydia shook her head. "It's a dreadful place. I don't think I've ever seen any customers in there."

"That's because it's an awful place, but I bet half your customers walk past that shop to reach yours. If you smartened it up, I reckon you could do well there."

"She shouldn't be working at all, let alone running her own business," William said.

Lydia put her hands on her hips. "I'm perfectly capable of running my own business, but I'm not sure it's a viable proposition."

"I've been thinking about it and I reckon it would be worth it," William-Wetherby said. "If the three of us live above the Saracen's Head, we could let out the rooms over the shop, which would help with the rent."

"Are they big enough?" Lydia asked. "The shop's tiny."

"There are two rooms, which together aren't much smaller than the flat you used to live in."

Lydia studied the room and let her gaze rest on the empty table. "I'll think about it on one condition. I'm sick and tired of coming home at night to make tea for everyone. The least you could do is put some cheese and bread on the table and have some water boiling."

"William-Wetherby's been working all day,"

William said.

"In case you haven't noticed, so have I. If I'm going to have my own business I can't do everything myself."

"Father will be working too," William-Wetherby said. "In fact, I don't suppose we'll see much of him of an evening unless we go and drink in the bar."

"I'm not having Lydia drinking in a bar, besides, we haven't got the place yet."

"We'll have it by tomorrow," William-Wetherby said. "If we ask about the tobacconist's while we're at the brewery, I reckon they'll bite your hand off. What do you say? Are you both going to start again and have your own businesses?"

William watched Lydia as she nodded and let out a deep sigh. "I suppose we could." *There's no point trying to stop her working.*

"The only downside is the wedding," Lydia said after a moment, "If we're both working, we won't be able to go."

William-Wetherby's smile dropped. "You have to. Eleanor's joining us and we'll see Margaret and Florence. You can't disappoint them."

"We'll find a way," William said. "Come hell or high water I'm going to see my daughters and that's a promise."

CHAPTER SEVENTY-SIX

Handsworth, Staffordshire

As Mr Diver's carriage pulled up outside St Mary's church, William peered through the window, subconsciously wiping the palms of his hands on his trousers. He took a deep breath and turned to William-Wetherby and Eleanor who sat with him.

"Stop worrying," William-Wetherby said. "People are here to see Aunt Elizabeth, not you."

"Only because they don't expect me to show my face around here again."

"Don't be silly." Eleanor edged towards the door as the coachman held it open. "Come on, follow me out and you'll be fine. Aunt Mary-Ann and Mr Diver are waiting for us."

William peered through the window as Eleanor alighted. "Is Mr Wetherby here yet?"

"I would hope not. He's giving Aunt Elizabeth away and so we're late if he is."

Exhaling an audible sigh of relief, William followed Eleanor towards his sister.

"Don't look so scared," Mary-Ann said. "Margaret and Florence will be here soon. Do you want to wait for them?"

William nodded and looked up to the sky. "At least they've got a nice day for it. I haven't told them I can't stay for the wedding breakfast and so I need to speak to them before they go into church."

"What time do you need to be back at the Saracen's Head?"

"I can't leave here any later than midday. The barman can only manage on his own for so long."

Ten minutes later, two carriages arrived carrying the bridesmaids and pageboy. Charlotte, Catherine, Margaret and Florence climbed from the first and the younger girls raced over to William.

"You came." Florence threw her arms around him. "I was so worried you wouldn't be here."

"I wouldn't have missed seeing you for anything." William stepped back and admired his daughters. They'd grown so much. "Look at you both; you look splendid. Mother would be so proud."

"Why are you so busy all the time?" Margaret said as she nestled up to his arm.

"I've not been busy, who told you that?"

"Aunt Sarah-Ann. She said you wanted to see us, but you were too busy."

William paused before he spoke. "She shouldn't have told you that. I'm never too busy for you."

"So why haven't you been to visit us?"

"I ... I – It's not easy with you being at Wetherby House."

"There's plenty of room," Florence said.

"Father runs a tavern now, so he can't get away," William-Wetherby said. "You need to come and visit us. I live with him and Lydia and there's a spare bedroom especially for you."

"Not only that," William said. "I want you to come and live with us as soon as we settle in."

Florence bounced on the spot. "Can we be like a proper family again? I don't like not seeing you."

"I don't like it either, but things will change, I promise." William put his hands on the shoulders of his daughters.

"Father, we need to go," William-Wetherby said a second later.

William lifted his head to find Mr Wetherby approaching them.

"Good morning, William." He looked William up and down. "I wasn't sure whether to expect you; I believe you're not coming back to the house."

"No ... I have to go back to work."

"You're not coming back ...?" Florence said. "But you must."

"Your father works in a beerhouse now and so he can't leave it for too long. Isn't that right?" Mr Wetherby couldn't hide his contempt. "I must come and pay you a visit, find out what all the fuss is about."

William scowled at his stepfather before lowering his head to talk to Florence. "I'll see you again soon and I'll be watching you walk into church."

"Promise?"

William was about to respond when a hand appeared on Florence's shoulder. He looked up to see his cousin Hannah beside him.

"Can I take these two girls from you? We'll be going into church soon." She nodded towards Elizabeth and Charlotte standing by the church gate. "Don't they look lovely? The white of Elizabeth's gown looks splendid against the plum of our dresses."

William nodded. He supposed it did, but what had he expected? It was always going to be *splendid*. He watched his daughters as Hannah led them away. "We'll be together again soon. I promise."

As the service progressed, William found himself staring at the second hand of his pocket watch. The groom may well be a man of the cloth, but had it been necessary to have four hymns, two readings, prayers and a sermon that he had thought at one point was never going to end? It was five to twelve and he needed to leave. As the pounding in his chest increased, the bride and groom rose from their kneeling positions and left to sign the register with their adult attendants.

As soon as they disappeared, he crept down the side aisle to where Margaret and Florence waited. He sat down next to Margaret. "I have to go now, but I wanted to say goodbye."

Margaret's bottom lip jutted out. "Do you have to? I've so much to tell you about school."

"And I have," Florence said.

"I'll tell you what, I'll write to Aunt Sarah-Ann and ask her to bring you to my new house. That way we can talk to each other without all these other people disturbing us. Would you like that?"

Both heads bounced up and down.

"Will Lydia be there?" Florence asked.

"She will," William said. "She works in a shop now, that's why she couldn't be here today."

Creases formed in Florence's forehead. "Who takes care of Arthur if Lydia's at work?"

William stared at her, his eyes wide. "We ... we don't have him any more. He was very ill and didn't pull through."

"Poor Arthur." Tears welled up in Florence's eyes.

William reached for his daughter's hand. "I'm sorry to have to tell you today; I thought you knew."

"They don't tell us anything," Margaret said. "Sometimes I think they wish we weren't there."

"Perhaps that means you should live with me again," William said. "William-Wetherby and Eleanor are going to Wetherby House after the service. Why don't you tell them everything and they'll tell me."

"Please write to Aunt Sarah-Ann soon," Florence said. "We don't want to stay with Mr Wetherby any longer."

As William left the church, he wiped the back of his hand across his eyes. He'd asked William-Wetherby to speak to Aunt Sarah-Ann about the girls visiting, but more than ever he knew he had to get them back permanently.

CHAPTER SEVENTY-SEVEN

With the marriage ceremony over, William-Wetherby and Eleanor strolled back to Wetherby House and waited outside for the wedding party.

"Are they driving around the whole of Handsworth before getting here?" William-Wetherby said after they had waited for over five minutes.

"I think so. The direct journey to the house was too short and Mr Wetherby wanted to make sure everyone knew how grand the procession was."

William-Wetherby rolled his eyes. "Isn't that typical? I wish they'd hurry up." He stared down the street, but with no sign of them, he stepped back and perched on the garden wall. "Have you had any news from Charles?"

"I had a letter a few weeks ago." Eleanor reached into her bag and handed it to William-Wetherby. "He was in Australia when he posted it, so goodness knows where he is now."

"Did he get the letter about the bankruptcy?"

Eleanor nodded. "He picked it up in Cape Town. I can't say he took it well."

"He's the lucky one, being away from all this. There are times I wish I was with him."

Eleanor stared at her brother, her eyes wide. "Please don't say that. Father needs you. We all do."

William-Wetherby smiled. "Don't worry, the feeling never lasts. I do wish Charles was here though. I've found out things about Mr Wetherby but I don't know what to do about them. I've spoken to Mr Diver but he's frightened of me causing trouble. Charles wouldn't be so worried."

"What sort of things?"

William-Wetherby sighed. *Do I tell her?*

"Stop keeping things to yourself," Eleanor said. "I've as much right to know as you."

William-Wetherby nodded. "All right, but promise you won't tell anyone. I think Mr Wetherby was responsible for the bankruptcy, although I haven't got enough evidence to prove it."

Eleanor stared at her brother. "What? Why? How? What makes you say that?"

William-Wetherby told Eleanor all he knew.

"Have you been to see Mr White since you confirmed he met Mr Wetherby?" Eleanor said.

"I tried but he still won't speak to me. The maid said he didn't know Mr Wetherby and threatened to call the police if I didn't stop harassing him."

Eleanor shrugged her shoulders. "You might be as well leaving it alone. The damage has been done, and even if you prove Mr Wetherby was behind it, what good would it do other than bring back all the memories? I'm sure Father would prefer to forget everything and move on."

William-Wetherby stood up. "But Mr Wetherby can't keep getting away with it. How many other lives has he ruined that we don't know about? He needs locking up."

"I don't disagree, but what can you do? For the first time in over a year, Father's like his old self, can't you let him be?"

William-Wetherby stared into the distance and after a few seconds he realised the carriages were approaching. He pointed them out to Eleanor. "Here they come. He's had his money's worth out of them."

Elizabeth and Reverend Bloor were the first to

arrive but they waited in the carriage for the rest of the entourage to arrive before they entered the house through a guard of honour.

"Wasn't that wonderful?" Sarah-Ann said as she saw William-Wetherby and Eleanor. "I'm so relieved Margaret and Florence didn't disgrace us."

"Why would they ...?" William-Wetherby said, but he was interrupted by Mr Wetherby.

"A family gathering, how nice." His eyes were like slits as he smiled at them. "Such a shame your father couldn't stay. I was hoping to have a word with him."

"I thought you'd said enough," William-Wetherby said.

"Well, as your aunt pointed out, we are family. Perhaps I'll visit him at work. Which beerhouse does he manage?"

William-Wetherby hesitated. "I'm surprised you don't know. The Saracen's Head."

"I wanted to be sure. It's not the sort of place I'd normally visit."

"No, I hear you prefer quieter places. The Saracen's Head's very popular and Father's always busy. He never has a minute."

Mr Wetherby turned to Sarah-Ann. "Perhaps we should invite him to the farm instead. In fact, why don't you all come? I'll see if we can arrange it."

"Why would he invite us to the farm?" William-Wetherby said to Eleanor as soon as they were alone again. "And why was he being so pleasant? Perhaps Mr White's tipped him off and he thinks we're onto him. He may be trying to find out what we know."

"Will you stop it?" Eleanor said. "Can't a man be pleasant without a reason?"

"Not when that man is Mr Wetherby and he was responsible for your mother's death and ruining your father's business."

Eleanor rolled her eyes at him. "Leave it be. I'm going to find Margaret and Florence, and I don't want to hear any more of this nonsense."

CHAPTER SEVENTY-EIGHT

Birmingham, Warwickshire

As soon as he finished work, William-Wetherby went to the bar of the Saracen's Head to wait for Sid. As usual his father was too busy to talk and so he sorted through the rubbish in his pockets. In one pocket, he found a couple of old omnibus tickets, a receipt for a bag of nails and several sweet wrappers. In the other was the piece of paper containing the names he had copied from Mr Wetherby's accounts book, along with a newspaper clipping reporting that Mr Wetherby, Aunt Sarah-Ann and William Junior had together contributed two hundred pounds to the church for hospital Sunday. He hadn't looked at either since

Eleanor had told him to stop causing trouble, but seeing the newspaper article still made his blood boil. He studied the list of names again and was about to put it back in his pocket when Sid arrived.

"You're late," William-Wetherby said. "Has Mr Wetherby got you doing overtime?"

"No, I forgot to bring my money out and had to go home."

William-Wetherby was about to collect up the rubbish from the table when his father joined them.

"There you go," he said as he put two mugs down in front of them.

"My, that's good service, Mr Jackson," Sid said. "I'll have to come here more often."

"Come here any more often and you might as well move in," William said with a laugh.

"Now there's an idea. Do you still have that spare room?"

"We do, but Margaret and Florence are coming over for a few days when they finish school for Christmas and so you'll have to wait." William spotted the piece of paper in William-Wetherby's hand. "What have you got there?"

"Nothing much, only a list of names I copied from Mr Wetherby a while ago. I was having a clear-out."

William took the paper from his son. "Let me

see that." As he read, the colour drained from his face and he grabbed for the nearest stool. "Where did you copy this from?"

William-Wetherby flushed and glanced at Sid. "Sid, can you go and tell Mr Foster he'll have to take over for a while ... and can you give him a hand? I need to talk to Father."

Sid reluctantly pushed himself up from the table. "Why do I always miss the interesting bits?"

Once he had gone William asked the same question again. "Where did you copy this from?"

William-Wetherby shuffled in his seat. "From a piece of paper I found in Mr Wetherby's books."

William stared at his son, his eyes boring into him.

"I got it earlier this year," William-Wetherby said. "The list was on a page that had been taken from another book and hidden in the back of his accounts."

"Have you any idea what this is?"

William-Wetherby shook his head. "No, but I'm guessing you do."

William glanced at the list again. "It's a list of all the people who owed me money, and the amount they owed me. Nobody had these details except for me, my solicitor, the trustees and Mr White."

William-Wetherby's eyes shot up to meet his father's. "The book debt? We've got him then. He can't deny being involved with the bankruptcy with this."

"What do you mean?" William put his hand to his chest. "Are you saying Mr Wetherby was involved with the bankruptcy?"

"Not only was he involved. I believe he was directly responsible." As he spoke William-Wetherby saw the colour drain from his father's face. "Are you all right? I know it's a bit of a shock, but ..."

"A shock? It's more than that. Why didn't you tell me sooner?"

"I didn't know what it was and when I mentioned it to Eleanor she told me to stop causing trouble."

"Eleanor knows about this? You'd better tell me what you told her."

William-Wetherby glanced around the bar. "Not here. Let me help you upstairs first."

Once they were settled in the living room, William-Wetherby explained about the piece of paper.

"But that doesn't make sense," William said. "The book debt had to be paid to Mr White, and even if he could arrange it, why would Mr

Wetherby incriminate himself by having the payments made directly into his own bank account? What else was in the accounts?"

"Nothing; that was it. What do you think we should do?"

"I don't know." William picked up the list of names, his hands trembling. "If we confront him with this he'd accuse us of stealing private documents and still deny any wrongdoing."

"What about approaching the businesses on the list to find out who they made the payments to?"

William sighed. "There are over thirty names on this list, and they won't talk if it means upsetting Mr Wetherby."

"Are any of them in the Freemasons? They may be more likely to help."

William shook his head. "I can't go to them. I had a letter last week telling me I'd been excluded because I hadn't paid my fees for the year."

William-Wetherby groaned as he threw his head back. "Why didn't you ask for the money? If anyone could help it's them."

"After everything that's happened, I couldn't go back. The shame would have killed me. I just can't believe Mr Wetherby would do such a thing. Did he hate me so much?" William paused for breath and put his hand to his chest.

"Are you all right?"

William shook his head. "I need to lie down, my heart feels as if it's about to explode. We'll speak again tomorrow."

William-Wetherby helped him to his feet, but as soon as he stood upright William fell to the floor, perspiration covering his face.

"Take deep breaths," William-Wetherby said as he crouched over him. "Stay awake; I'll go and find Sid."

Within a minute Sid and William-Wetherby got William up and helped him to the bedroom. They were surprised to find Lydia in there.

"What's going on?" Lydia asked as she pulled back the bedcovers for William to climb into bed.

"It's his heart. He's had a shock and needs to rest," William-Wetherby said. "I didn't see you come in, have you finished for the day?"

"I should hope so. It's seven o'clock and I've been up since six this morning."

William-Wetherby glanced at the clock. "So it is. Can you stay with him while I fetch the doctor?"

By the time the doctor arrived, William's face was grey as he fought for every breath.

"We need to get him to hospital," the doctor said without examining him. "His heart's been struggling for months and it may be about to fail completely."

"How will we get him there?" William-Wetherby asked. "He can't walk in this state."

"Someone came into the bar in a wheelchair," Sid said. "If they're still there I'll borrow it from them."

William-Wetherby nodded as he turned back to his father. *Eleanor was right. I should never have told him.*

CHAPTER SEVENTY-NINE

William arrived in hospital struggling for every breath. He was immediately put into a bed and William-Wetherby and Lydia stayed in the corridor while a hospital doctor attended him on the ward.

Half an hour later, the doctor found them. "He needs close supervision. His heart isn't beating as it should and we need to force it back into a normal rhythm. First and foremost, he needs complete bed rest to stabilise his condition."

"He will recover, won't he?" William-Wetherby asked.

"It's difficult to say, but the truth is he won't be able to do the things he used to."

"But what about the business? He's not been at the Saracen's Head for long. That's his livelihood."

The doctor shook his head. "I've spoken to the personal doctor who brought him in. Apparently he told Mr Jackson several months ago that if he didn't rest, his body would rest for him. I'd say he didn't heed the warnings. I'll tell you what the other doctor told him. If he wants to stay alive, he's not going to be able to work. It's as simple as that."

William-Wetherby and Lydia walked the short distance home in silence, the dull, cold evening mirroring their feelings.

"What I don't understand is what brought it on?" Lydia said as they approached the Saracen's Head. "He was quite content when I arrived home, not more than twenty minutes earlier."

William-Wetherby kicked a loose stone from under his foot. "I wouldn't ask him, it may trigger another attack." *But I'm going to get that damn swine if it's the last thing I do.*

The following evening, with William-Wetherby and Lydia gone, William lay propped up on pillows staring at the wall opposite. What had he done to deserve this?

The beerhouse was his last chance of salvaging some respectability and starting a new life, but instead he was likely to lose his home and income once again. Not only that, Margaret and Florence were due to visit on Sunday, but there was no point them coming. The doctors were unlikely to let them visit him in here.

How had he missed all the signs that Mr Wetherby was behind the bankruptcy? The book debt was the most obvious. Throughout the whole period only two people ever mentioned it, Mr Wetherby and Mr White. He must have known that paying Mr White ahead of the other creditors would cause trouble. It all made sense now.

Closing his eyes he focussed on his breathing. He needed to keep it steady, but how could he when the only image in his head was of Margaret and Florence in their bridesmaid dresses with tears in their eyes because he wasn't going back to Wetherby House? They would be so upset to learn their visit had to be cancelled. He grabbed at the bedclothes as the tightness in his chest increased and perspiration gathered on his forehead. *What a useless father I've been.*

As he struggled for breath, he heard footsteps approaching.

"William, are you all right?" Mary-Ann rushed

to the side of the bed and grabbed his hand. "Call a doctor," she said to Mr Diver.

As Mr Diver hurried away, Mary-Ann pulled up a chair. "Take deep breaths, the doctor will be here in a minute, you need to stay calm."

"I'm going to have to ask you to leave," the doctor said when he joined them. "He's incredibly anxious at the moment and stress or excitement of any sort will weaken his heart further. Having visitors is too much for him."

"He was like this when we arrived," Mr Diver said. "I'd suggest that lying on his own is giving him too much time to think. He needs to talk. Can we come back once you've seen to him?"

The doctor glared at Mr Diver through narrowed eyes. "He needs some medication. I've tried him with a low dose of digitalis extract, but it appears not to be enough. Please wait outside and I'll call you."

By the time Mary-Ann and Mr Diver returned, William's breathing had steadied.

"What happened?" Mary-Ann said. "You've been looking like your old self recently."

"Have you spoken to William-Wetherby?"

"He came to tell us you were in here, but that was all he said," Mary-Ann said.

William closed his eyes. "I haven't got the

energy to tell you, but go and ask him. Tell him I said you could know. I wish I'd never found out, but now I have, I can't forget."

Mary-Ann's brow creased. "What are you talking about?"

"Leave it." Mr Diver touched her on the arm. "I have an idea what this is about and I don't think it should be William to tell us. He needs to rest."

"I should be seeing Margaret and Florence this Sunday and I'm not going to be able to do that either. They can't see me like this."

"I'll visit Aunt Sarah-Ann and explain what's happened," Mary-Ann said. "As soon as you're well enough, they can come over."

William nodded. "In a few weeks, perhaps after Christmas. It'll give me something to live for."

Four weeks later, William stood on the steps of the hospital and took a deep breath.

"It's marvellous to be out in the fresh air again," he said.

"Well, let's take it slowly." William-Wetherby took his father's arm. "It's a new year now, so let's have a new beginning and put everything behind us."

"I'll be fine once I'm back at work."

"That's out of the question. If I'd have known four months ago how ill you were, I'd never have suggested you take the place on."

"So what will we do? I haven't earned enough money yet to repay the three months' rent."

"We'll manage. Sid and I have been working there while you've been in hospital and Lydia helps when she can."

William looked at his son. "She didn't tell me. She's too busy with her own shop, she'll be exhausted."

"She's doing fine and I don't suppose she wanted to worry you. Sid's there even when he doesn't need to be and he keeps an eye on her."

William frowned. "Not too close an eye I hope."

CHAPTER EIGHTY

Mr Wetherby pulled the key from the door of the workshop and put it in his pocket before striding across the court on his way to Frankfort Street. He hadn't gone far when he stopped and looked around. It was too dark to see more than a couple of feet ahead but he peered into the blackness listening for the sound that had stopped him.

"Who's there?" His voice echoed around the court.

When he received no reply, he continued his walk, but he hadn't gone much further when a voice called out from the shadows of the alleyway.

"Stop where you are. I've some information for

you, but it would be better if we weren't seen together."

"Mr White? Is that you?"

"Shut up, you fool. Do you want everyone to know I'm here?"

"Why are you here? I told you I didn't want to see you again."

"I thought you'd be interested to know I had a visit from Mr Jackson's son last week."

"William-Wetherby? Why on earth ...?"

"I said shut up." Mr White spoke through clenched teeth. "It wasn't the first time he's called, in fact it was the third, but this time was the most troubling. They've worked out you were responsible for Mr Jackson's business problems."

"I most certainly was not. William had no one to blame but himself and that damn wife of his."

Mr White sucked air through his teeth. "That's not how they see it."

"You denied it of course?"

"I've told them I don't know you ... but they don't believe me. We were seen in the Dog and Partridge and they believe that proves you were up to something."

"They've no proof of anything." Mr Wetherby spun around and glared at Mr White. "You need to get rid of him."

"That's why I'm here. The money you gave me was only for the initial job. It didn't cover the cost of being harassed years later."

"Because we were seen in a tavern together? You'll have to do better than that."

"Oh, I can do much better than that, but not before I have more money."

"How much do you want?" Mr Wetherby spat his words out.

"Another one hundred should do for now."

"One hundred pounds!" Mr Wetherby's voice rang in the air.

"Keep your voice down," Mr White said.

"But one hundred pounds is extortion. I won't be blackmailed."

Mr White stepped out of the darkness and shrugged. "The information might be worth a lot more to the Jacksons if their suspicions are confirmed."

"Stay where you are." Mr Wetherby pushed Mr White back into the shadows and glanced around the court. "I don't have that amount in cash."

"Oh, I think you do. I'll be here tomorrow at the same time and if the money isn't here I'll be calling into the Saracen's Head for a drink on my way home."

~

William smiled as he handed a mug of ale to one of his customers and sat back. He couldn't do much, but at least sitting here, pulling the occasional pint and talking to his customers, made him feel as if he'd been given another chance. He was never alone and he watched William-Wetherby and Sid as they cleared the tables. It would be impossible without them.

He was about to help himself to a small mug of ale when he spotted Aunt Sarah-Ann being let in.

"This is a surprise." William eased himself from his seat and walked towards her. "What brings you here at this late hour?"

"I wanted to see how you are. I heard you had a terrible turn before Christmas but I couldn't get here any sooner. With all the preparations and spending time in Bushwood I haven't had a minute. I have to confess, you look a lot better than I'd expected."

William smiled. "Yes, I'm fine. The doctor gave me some pills and they've worked wonders."

"That's good, we don't want anything happening to you. It also ties in with the other reason I called. Do you remember before you were ill, Margaret and Florence were due to visit? Well, they're asking again when they can come and I thought Easter would be ideal. Can you manage them for a few days?"

William's smile spread across his face. "Yes, I'd like that. I felt so guilty about letting them down when I was in hospital. Tell them they can come anytime, as long as they let me know when." A frown suddenly settled on William's face. "Does Mr Wetherby know about this? I'm surprised he let you come on your own."

Sarah-Ann smiled as she turned to leave. "Yes, it was his idea. I think he might be coming to his senses at last."

Mr Wetherby returned his pocket watch to the front of his waistcoat as he squinted through the window of the workshop. He had told the coachman to bring Sarah-Ann here as soon as she'd seen William, but she was taking longer than expected. As soon as he saw her walking across the court he went out to meet her.

"Have you seen William?" he asked. "How was he?"

Sarah-Ann studied her husband. "Why are you so concerned all of a sudden?"

"How was he? What did he say?"

Sarah-Ann continued walking into the workshop. "I have and he was fine. The doctor's put him on some pills and he's working again."

"How did he respond when you told him Margaret and Florence could visit?"

"He was delighted; you could see it in his eyes."

"Did he mention me at all?"

Sarah-Ann studied Mr Wetherby. "Why would he mention you? Of course he didn't. No, I tell a lie, he did, but only to ask if you knew about Margaret and Florence's visit. He was relieved you knew about the arrangements."

"And that was it?"

"Yes, that was it. What's wrong?"

"Nothing's wrong," Mr Wetherby snapped. "I'm interested in how he is. Was there anything strange about him?"

"No, other than he was in better health than I expected. Is that all you wanted me for? You could have asked me to call tomorrow instead of dragging me out at this hour of the night."

"I might be in late tomorrow. Another meeting, you know ..."

Sarah-Ann's eyes narrowed as she stared at her husband. "What are you up to? I hope it's nothing to do with William. By all accounts, you've already done more than enough."

CHAPTER EIGHTY-ONE

Mr Wetherby felt the envelope in his breast pocket and took a deep breath. He should have Mr White arrested for blackmail, but the man knew too much and he couldn't risk any awkward questions. He paused for a moment longer before he stepped outside and took his keys from his pocket.

"I was beginning to think you weren't coming." Mr White spoke from behind him. "I hope you've kept the matter between the two of us and we're not expecting any visitors."

"There'll be no visitors, but I don't believe William-Wetherby knows about our arrangement. I think you're bluffing."

"Why don't you call my bluff and find out?"

Mr Wetherby thrust his face into Mr White's. "Prove to me what he knows."

"I told you yesterday. He came to tell me we'd been seen at the Dog and Partridge. The landlord remembered you because you insist on travelling in that conspicuous carriage."

"That doesn't prove anything."

"I know and I put him off twice, but he called again last week with some new information, something extremely damaging for a man of your reputation."

"What's he got?"

"When I sent you the record of the payments for the book debts, it seems your clerk was foolish enough to keep it with your accounts. It would appear William-Wetherby has got hold of the list, and outside of the trustees and solicitors, nobody knew of that list except Mr Jackson and me. If it became known you'd received those payments ..."

Mr Wetherby felt the blood drain from his face and he held up his hand. "Where did they get that information from?"

"I've no idea, but it wasn't from me. Now, are you going to pay me that one hundred pounds or do I have to stop off for a drink on my way home?"

. . .

As soon as Mr White left, Mr Wetherby stormed into the workshop, slamming the door behind him. How had William-Wetherby managed to see the accounts? Surely he wouldn't have broken in. There'd been no sign of a break-in. Did he have inside help? Perhaps William-Wetherby had put one of the workers up to it? Mr Wetherby grabbed the remains of a bottle of whisky from the cupboard and took a gulp. He was going to find out what had gone on, and when he did ... when he did ... somebody's life wasn't going to be worth living.

He paced the office until the bottle was empty. Throwing it into the bin, he was about to go back to the cupboard for another one, when he stopped. Sidney! He was always at the Saracen's Head nowadays, and by all accounts he spent most of his spare time with William-Wetherby. He must have let the scoundrel into the office while it was empty; he had access to the keys. That had to be it; there could be no other explanation. He would fire Sidney first thing in the morning. But what did he do about William-Wetherby? The boy was a liability. He needed him out of the way, but the question was, who else knew? Had he told William? From what Sarah-Ann had said, he suspected not, but it would only be a matter of time.

He needed to silence William-Wetherby before anyone else became involved.

CHAPTER EIGHTY-TWO

William-Wetherby rolled over and pulled the covers over his head to keep out the sound of banging. *Who's knocking on the door at this hour of the night?* A second later, he sat bolt upright. It was light outside. *What time is it?* He jumped out of bed and pulled on his trousers before he hurried downstairs. As he rushed into the bar, he saw Sid talking to his father.

"What are you doing here at this time of the day?" he asked.

"I've been sacked."

William-Wetherby stopped in his tracks. "Sacked? By Mr Wetherby? He's your uncle. Why's he done that?"

Sid shrugged. "He said I knew full well what I'd done and that I should be ashamed of myself."

William-Wetherby tasted bile rising to his mouth. "Did he say anything else?"

"Never mind what Mr Wetherby said," William interrupted. "What have you been doing? You're late for work."

"Not as late as I thought I was." William-Wetherby turned to Sid as he opened the front door. "You're sure he didn't say anything else?"

"Not with words, but I've never seen him so angry in my life."

As he left the inn, William-Wetherby knew he should hurry but he was already late for work. What difference would another hour make? He changed his route and headed for Mr Diver's manufactory. It wasn't much further.

When he arrived, Mr Diver was sitting at a large oak desk alongside several clerks working at considerably smaller positions. He glanced up as William-Wetherby walked in before he gave a sideways glance to the clerks.

"What are you doing here?" He stood up and ushered William-Wetherby back outside. "What's happened?"

"There's been a development and I'm ashamed to say it was probably my fault."

"Go on."

"When Father told me that the piece of paper I'd found contained the names and details of his creditors, I went back to see Mr White."

Mr Diver's face paled. "Did you speak to him?"

William-Wetherby nodded. "I said to the maid that I wasn't leaving until I had. I told him he'd been seen with Mr Wetherby and we'd found details of Father's creditors in Mr Wetherby's records. He denied it, of course, and threatened to call the police if I didn't leave him alone."

"But ..."

"But I told him I'd be happy if he did, so they could go through all the paperwork and convict them both of extortion."

Mr Diver flinched. "So why are you telling me now?"

"Because Sid arrived at the Saracen's Head this morning after he'd been sacked. My guess is Mr White told Mr Wetherby of my visit and he's assumed it was Sid who helped me."

Mr Diver puffed out his cheeks and blew the air through his lips.

"Mr Wetherby's as guilty as hell, isn't he?" William-Wetherby continued. "But what do we do about it?"

. . .

The first person William-Wetherby saw when he arrived home that night was Sid. He was behind the bar pulling a mug of ale with a huge grin on his face.

"You look pleased with yourself," William-Wetherby said.

"It's not often you lose your job and get offered a new one on the same day. Mr Jackson said I can work here full-time. I'm going to use the spare room here as well until your sisters come to stay. I'd rather not bump into Mr Wetherby at the moment."

William-Wetherby breathed a sigh of relief. "I'm sure that will suit both of you. I must admit I feel guilty about you losing your job."

Sid stopped where he was. "Why? What did it have to do with you?"

William-Wetherby walked around the bar towards the stairs. "I'll tell you later. Have some ale waiting for me once you lock up."

It was turned eleven o'clock when William-Wetherby sat in the corner of the bar watching Sid throw out the last of the customers.

"So what's all this about?" Sid asked as he put two mugs of ale on the table.

William-Wetherby took a long gulp of his drink before he set down his tankard. "I think I was the one who got you into trouble with Mr Wetherby."

Incomprehension crossed Sid's face. "How? When? You haven't seen him for months."

"Do you remember last year, when he left his books for you to deliver to the accountant, but I took them instead?"

Sid nodded.

"Well, I didn't take them straight away. I wanted to see if there was anything in them about the bankruptcy. I found some information I was interested in and kept hold of them for a couple of days."

Sid sat up straight. "Did he find out?"

William-Wetherby shook his head. "Not immediately, but when I couldn't make any sense of the payments I copied them onto a piece of paper. That was the piece of paper Father saw before he went into hospital. He told me the names were all the creditors who owed him money and that nobody but him, Mr White and the legal people knew the full list."

"So how did Mr Wetherby have it?"

William-Wetherby took another mouthful of ale. "Isn't it obvious? Mr White must have given it to him."

Sid's eyes widened. "Are you sure?"

"I am after this morning. I visited Mr White last week. He denied everything, but when I mentioned the list, you could tell he was scared. I don't think it's any coincidence that less than a week later Mr Wetherby sacks you."

"But what's it got to do with me?"

"My guess is that Mr Wetherby knows we have the list and has jumped to the conclusion that you gave it to me ... or at least helped me get it."

Sid said nothing as he shook his head.

"I'm sorry," William-Wetherby said. "I didn't mean for you to become involved, just like I didn't mean to make Father ill. The problem is, now I know, I can't let Mr Wetherby get away with it. I'm going to go and see him."

Sid's head shot up. "You can't do that, not in the mood he's in at the moment. He'll kill you."

"I have to do something and Mr Diver's going to come with me. If we could only get back the money he stole from Father it would be a start."

CHAPTER EIGHTY-THREE

William sat on the stairs, his head in his hands. Why had he listened in to a conversation that wasn't intended for him? He moved to push himself up but as he did he swayed and grabbed hold of the handrail to stop himself falling. He needed to get back to his room before anyone knew he was there. Eventually he made it to the top of the stairs, but once he reached the bedroom he collapsed onto the bed, sweat covering his face.

Lydia was in bed when he arrived.

"What's brought this on?" she asked. "Have you taken your medicine?"

"I haven't had any all day," William lied. "Can you fetch it for me? I've left it in the other room."

"It's fortunate we have the money for this," Lydia said as she came back into the room. "It's going down too quickly. We'll have to buy some more."

The following day, William stayed in bed. The mere thought of getting up was enough to tire him out and he lay against the pillows panting for breath.

"What are you doing in here?" Sid asked when he popped his head around the bedroom door. "You were fine yesterday."

"I'll be fine later. I didn't sleep well and need to doze for a bit longer."

William closed his eyes and what seemed like moments later he opened them to see Sid showing the doctor into the bedroom.

"He's been like this for the last three days, but he's showing no sign of recovery," Sid told the doctor. "Can I leave you with him? I need to open up."

The doctor nodded and closed the door as Sid left.

"Have you been working again?" The doctor pulled a stethoscope from his bag.

William shook his head. "All I do is sit by the

bar, it's my mind that does this to me. If anything upsets me, it's as if I can't breathe."

"I'd say you've been standing up too much as well. Your feet and ankles shouldn't be swollen to such an extent. We need to get you back into hospital to make sure you have complete bed rest. I'm going to restrict visitors too, to give you a chance to recover."

The wheezing in William's chest caused him to cough. "I need to see my wife and children, surely that won't hurt. Sidney too."

"Let's wait a few days and I'll see."

Once he was in hospital, William studied his surroundings. He was in a bed on the same ward as he had been five weeks earlier, with many of the same patients. It was a ward of twenty metal-framed beds, and the winter sun shone bleakly on the stark white walls. He didn't want to be here. If he could just switch off his mind and stop upsetting himself, he'd be fine. It was the only thing he needed to focus on if he wanted to be home to see Margaret and Florence.

The following morning when the doctor visited, William sat propped against a bank of pillows, staring at the wall opposite.

"How are you today, Mr Jackson?"

"I'm bored. Do I have to sit here on my own day after day?"

"Until your breathing stabilises and we remove some of the fluid from your body, I'm afraid you do. It might help if you think of happier times. Putting a smile on your face often helps."

William stared up at the doctor. The man had no idea. He had lost everything in his life that he'd valued and thinking about them was more likely to upset him than cheer him up.

"Would it be possible to have a pen and paper?" he asked as the doctor was about to leave. "Last time my wife was in hospital, writing things down helped her recover. I'd like to see if it will do the same for me."

With his pen and paper resting on a thin piece of board, William looked around him. Harriet had noted down things happening on the ward and dotted her comments amongst them, but here, nothing was happening. Everyone was in the same boat, lying in bed staring straight ahead. They weren't even allowed to talk to each other in case they exerted too much energy.

That wasn't all Harriet had written about though, was it? She had written down what she had seen between Mr Wetherby and Mr Flemming when Mr Flemming had died as a result of Mr Wetherby knocking him to the ground and beating him mercilessly about the head. Once Mr Wetherby had given them the money for the business, he'd insisted she burn the notebook, but that hadn't erased William's memory. The memory Mr Wetherby had tried to distort. Perhaps it was time for him to write down all the things he remembered about Mr Wetherby. The good and the bad.

Several days later, William sank back into the pillows gasping for air. He couldn't write any more today, not after reliving Harriet's death, but it had been worth it. It was all clear now. Mr Wetherby had deliberately watched her drown ... because she had dared to demand from him what was rightfully theirs. How could he do that? Put money before a human life? Did the man have no conscience? In all probability that was what the bankruptcy was about too. Mr Wetherby couldn't bear to part with so much money and hired Mr White to siphon it from the business for him ... not caring about the consequences. William would write about that tomorrow ... if he had the energy.

• • •

A week later, with his memories hidden under his pillows, the tension ebbed from his muscles. It was done. William-Wetherby could do as he pleased with the letter now. It may not stand up in court, but it would put the fear of God into Mr Wetherby and if it made him suffer, it would be worth it.

He must have drifted off to sleep because when he opened his eyes the doctor was leaning over him, lines etched across his forehead.

William tried to talk but felt as if he was drowning. The doctor held his hand up to stop him.

"I'm going to lift the restriction on the visitors, for the next couple of days," he said. "No more than one at a time. I'll write and tell your son."

William smiled. The doctor must be pleased with him. That was a start.

When he woke the following afternoon, Sid was in the chair beside the bed.

"Good afternoon, Mr Jackson. I hope you don't mind me being the first visitor. We only got the letter this morning and William-Wetherby and Lydia are both working. They said to tell you they'd be in later."

William smiled. "It ... it will be nice ..." A cough interrupted him. "... to see them."

"Have you had your medication?" Sid glanced up and down the ward. "Let me find a nurse."

"No." William reached under his pillow. "Take this ... give it to William-Wetherby. He'll know what to do."

"You've been busy. Have you written a story?"

William's eyes were moist as he looked at Sid. "Please give it to him ... promise me?"

CHAPTER EIGHTY-FOUR

Sid studied the pages in his hand before he glanced up at William. His eyes were shut. Should he wait in case he woke up or leave and let William-Wetherby speak to him later? He saw the matron by the door but other than that, he was the only visitor. Perhaps he should wait.

Returning to the pages, he unfolded them and smiled as he started to read. It was a tribute to Mr Wetherby. Mr Jackson must have been reminiscing. There were notes about how Mr Wetherby had married Mr Jackson's mother and taken care of him and his sister. Descriptions of the treats and outings he had given them. Mr Jackson said he'd respected Mr Wetherby, so much so that he'd named his first son after him. Gradually as the pages went on, the comments became less complimentary. It spoke of Mr Wetherby as a bully, of someone who liked controlling everything, and everyone. Sid nodded as he recognised some familiar traits, but stopped when he read about Mr Flemming. Sid hadn't known the man, but he'd heard of him and knew he was Aunt Sarah-Ann's first husband. Mr Jackson must have been hallucinating. His uncle wouldn't kill anyone. He paused for breath but his eyes grew wider when he read of Mr Wetherby's relationship with Aunt Sarah-Ann, Mrs Flemming as she was. That couldn't be true.

Sid kept turning the pages until he read about the death of Mr Jackson's wife. His uncle was a God-fearing man who would do anything to help anyone. He wouldn't stand by and watch somebody drown, even if they had been responsible for taking some of his money. Sid shook his head and glanced up at William.

"Mr Jackson, what are you trying to do? My uncle may have wronged you in the business, but I can't believe he did all these things."

William's breathing was shallow and when he failed to answer, Sid went back to the notes. Details of the bankruptcy were all listed in greater detail than William-Wetherby had told him. *Does William-Wetherby know all this?* He'd never mentioned anything about Mr Wetherby refusing to let Charlotte have Arthur. Was that why it was so important to get this message to him?

Once he'd finished, Sid lifted his head again. "I can't do this, Mr Jackson. Whatever his faults, Mr Wetherby's my uncle. If news of this came out it would send him to the gallows. I can't be responsible for that."

Sid paused to see if he got a response, but when he didn't he folded the papers up and stuffed them in his pocket. They couldn't be left lying around. He was so engrossed in his thoughts he didn't hear the footsteps behind him and he leapt from his chair when a nurse tapped him on his shoulder.

"What is it?" he said.

"You've been with Mr Jackson quite long enough. I'm going to have to ask you to leave."

"Yes ... right, he's asleep now so I'll be off. I'll call again tomorrow, Mr Jackson." Sid stood up and touched William on the shoulder before turning to leave.

As he reached the end of the ward the nurse called him. "One moment, please. I'm going to have to ask you to stay until I find a doctor."

Sid frowned. "I don't need a doctor."

The nurse didn't reply, but hurried off down the ward. She returned a minute later with a doctor hurrying after her. The doctor moved to William's side and listened to his heart before reaching for his wrist. Once he had finished, he looked up at Sid.

"Mr Jackson has left us."

"Left us?" Sid's eyes were wide as he stared at William. "He can't have, I was only talking to him a few minutes ago ... you must be mistaken."

"I'm sorry, there's no mistake. Are you his next of kin?"

"No, he's my friend's father."

"Is your friend his next of kin?"

Sid nodded. "His name's William-Wetherby Jackson. He's visiting tonight."

"The body will have been moved by then. Can you tell him to ask for me when he gets here? We'll have to go through the formalities."

"Formalities? He won't be up to that. I can register the death if that's all you need."

"I'll still need to speak to his son, but yes, that would help."

As the doctor disappeared down the ward, Sid sat down again. Mr Jackson couldn't be dead. How had he not noticed? He'd been right next to him for goodness' sake. As the nurse covered William's face, Sid wanted to reach out and touch his hand, to feel some life in it, but he couldn't bring himself to do it. What if it was cold?

He thought about William-Wetherby. He already blamed himself for his father being in hospital, how would he deal with this? And what about Lydia?

As Sid left the hospital he lingered at the top of the steps and scratched his head. What did he do now? William-Wetherby wouldn't be home for another couple of hours, but he couldn't go back to the Saracen's Head and carry on as if nothing had happened. He gazed at the clock on the front of the hospital. Three o'clock. Enough time to walk up to Frankfort Street.

"I wasn't expecting you," Mrs Storey said when she saw her son. "I thought you'd be at the beerhouse."

Sid said nothing but sat down by the fire, struggling to find the right words.

"Are you sickening for something?" his mother continued. "You look terribly pale. I've made some soup here if you want it. I was going to save some for you anyway."

Sid shook his head. "Come and sit down, I've something to tell you."

"Don't be so dramatic, you'd think someone had died judging by your expression."

When Sid's face didn't change, Mrs Storey took hold of the chair and took a deep breath.

"Mr Jackson died, Mother. While I was with him. I had to leave all my details with the hospital in case there's an inquest. Nobody else knows yet and I don't know what to do."

"May God rest his soul." Mrs Storey made a sign of the cross before she sat down. "After everything that poor man's been through I hope this brings him peace."

"Do I open up the beerhouse tonight or keep it closed?"

Mrs Storey's eyes darted to her son. "You can't open up tonight, what are you thinking? Have you been in and closed the curtains and stopped the clocks?"

Sid shook his head. "I've done nothing. I didn't know what to do. William-Wetherby can't find out about it by seeing the curtains closed."

"But it has to be done. Have you no respect?"

"Of course I have, but he's not at home, he's still in hospital. I thought it could wait."

Mrs Storey stood up and handed Sid his hat. "You'd better go. You have to show you're in mourning. It will also let the customers know why you are closed."

. . .

Sid sat in the bar with a tankard of ale in front of him. The curtains were closed and the door locked. He had wanted to go next door and tell Lydia but he couldn't bring himself to do it. Better to wait for everyone to come home. As six o'clock approached, hammering on the front door roused him from his trance.

"What's going on? Why's the place closed ... and the curtains drawn? Don't tell me ..." William-Wetherby stared at his friend.

Sid nodded. "I'm sorry. I didn't know what else to do. He passed while I was with him at the hospital ... He was peaceful at the end."

William-Wetherby pulled himself some ale and sat down. "Dead. It was all my fault. I should never have pursued Mr Wetherby."

"I think Mr Jackson had enough to be angry with Mr Wetherby about, besides this latest spat."

William-Wetherby looked up. "What do you mean?"

Sid stood up and pulled himself another drink.

"Sid, what aren't you telling me?"

Sid wiped his eyes with the back of his hand before he put his hand in his pocket and dropped William's letter onto the table. "I wasn't going to give it to you at first, but I've had a chance to reread it. Mr Wetherby would be furious if he saw it, but after some deliberation I don't think they'd stand up in court."

"Did Father give you this?"

Sid nodded. "He must have written it while he was in hospital. No wonder his heart failed him if he's put himself through all that again."

William-Wetherby flicked through the pages. "I need to read this properly. Does it say anything we didn't know?"

"I'm not sure what you know, but I would say there are things that would seriously ruin Mr Wetherby's reputation if they were true. If they're not true, he'll sue you for every penny you have left."

"Why didn't he tell me this sooner? We could have used it."

"The man was exhausted," Sid said. "Perhaps in the end he just lost the will to fight."

"He may have, but I haven't." William-Wetherby stood up. "If there's anything I can use against Mr Wetherby, then by God I'm going to use it. He is going to pay for destroying my family."

CHAPTER EIGHTY-FIVE

Handsworth, Staffordshire

William-Wetherby took a deep breath as the hearse carrying his father's body pulled up outside the house on St Peters Road. He'd travelled on the front with the driver and as they arrived, a group of men he'd seen at the side of the road jumped to attention. As the horses came to a standstill the glass panelling surrounding the coffin was opened and the men carried the coffin into the front room of William Junior's house, laid it on the table and removed the lid. As the housekeeper saw them out, William-Wetherby moved to the side of the coffin.

"I'm sorry," he whispered. "I'm not going to let

him get away with this. I've no idea what I'll do, but I won't rest until I've done something."

"What's that you're saying?" Sarah-Ann walked into the room and stood at the foot of the coffin.

"Nothing important, but thank you for letting us use the house. Father didn't have any final wishes, but he always wanted to be buried with Mother. We couldn't have done it without you."

"It's the least I could do. William Junior's never here these days and so we might as well use it."

"Well, thank you."

She nodded at William. "I can only apologise for the way Mr Wetherby treated him, but I was powerless to stop him."

"There are many people who've said that."

Sarah-Ann wiped a tear from her eye. "It's not right that I went to the burial of his father so many years ago and now him. I remember holding him soon after he was born. Such a lovely baby, but look at him now. He's lost so much weight, and with his white hair he looks much older than his forty-nine years. Life hasn't been fair to the male members of my family."

"Was he like my grandfather? He never spoke of him."

Sarah-Ann gazed at her nephew. "He wouldn't have, he didn't know him. He was only a baby when my brother died. Your brother Charles reminds me much more of your grandfather than your father did. He wouldn't have taken Mr Wetherby's nonsense. Has anyone written to Charles?"

William-Wetherby nodded. "Eleanor has, but he won't find out for months yet. It's a shame the timing's worked out as it has. He's due to dock in England some time this year, although whether he'd be able to come here, I'm not sure."

Sarah-Ann remained silent as William-Wetherby took hold of his father's hand. "So much has changed since he left."

"Come on. Let's go into the other room." Sarah-Ann linked her arm through William-Wetherby's. "I'll find you some whisky."

William-Wetherby took a seat by the fire while his aunt found a bottle and a couple of glasses.

"Is Eleanor coming tomorrow?" Sarah-Ann said as they sat together by the fire. "I haven't seen her for such a long time."

"She is. Mr Diver and Aunt Mary-Ann are bringing her. Lydia will be with them too."

"A funeral's no place for a young girl."

William-Wetherby stared into his glass and gave a weak smile. "You try stopping her. She's too much like Mother."

"I only wish Florence was. Will you come to Wetherby House with me? She needs to see you."

William-Wetherby looked up. "She's taken it badly?" When his aunt nodded, he continued. "Will you bring her here? I don't want to see Mr Wetherby if I don't have to."

"You don't need to worry, he won't be home for hours yet. Finish your drink and I'll tell the driver we're ready to go."

CHAPTER EIGHTY-SIX

From the front room of the house on St Peters Road, William-Wetherby stared through a crack in the curtains onto the street beyond. Staying alone in a strange house last night hadn't been wise and he hoped Mr Diver's carriage would be the next to appear. He studied the clock on the mantelpiece; still an hour and a half to go. It might be too early to expect them yet. He pulled a chair up to the window and sat down, but jumped straight back up when he saw Mr Wetherby helping Aunt Sarah-Ann from his carriage. His stomach lurched and he hurried to replace the chair.

William-Wetherby wondered if the

housekeeper had been waiting for them by the door as seconds later Sarah-Ann walked into the room.

"I knew we'd be the first here."

"We're supposed to be the first here," Mr Wetherby said. "We're hosting the event. We can't leave it all to a boy." Mr Wetherby flicked his hand in William-Wetherby's direction.

"Good morning, Mr Wetherby." William-Wetherby's heart pounded as he spoke. It wasn't helped by the glare Mr Wetherby shot in his direction.

"I'll deal with you later." Mr Wetherby breezed from the room with Sarah-Ann in his wake, leaving William-Wetherby to collapse onto the nearest chair. *Where is everyone? I can't do this on my own.*

It was another half an hour before the mourners began to arrive and William Junior and Mr Mountford had joined Mr Wetherby as he played the grieving host. William-Wetherby stayed where he was; he had no desire to stand with them. People would find him soon enough. He breathed a sigh of relief when he heard Mr Diver's voice. Moments later Eleanor and Lydia joined him.

"What are you doing in here on your own?" Eleanor said. "You should be in the hall with the others."

"And stand with him?"

Eleanor linked her arm in his. "Don't be like that, you should be pleased he's paying for the funeral. Have you seen the carriages outside? There are six of them."

"That's got nothing to do with us or Father. It's to keep his reputation intact. You haven't had to sit here for the last half hour while he's accepted everyone's condolences and spoken of Father as if he were his only son."

"Here." Lydia took two glasses of sherry from the maid and handed one to William-Wetherby. "Today was never going to be easy."

"He doesn't have to rub it in though, does he?" William-Wetherby wiped the back of his hand across his eyes.

"Come on, this isn't like you," Eleanor said.

"I'm sick to death of him. He's destroyed everything and everyone we've ever cared about and now has the nerve to stand there as chief mourner pretending he's grieving."

"Don't let him upset you," Lydia said. "Sid will be here soon. He usually takes your mind off things."

William-Wetherby gave a short laugh. "Just like him to be late though. Is that Aunt Martha arriving?"

Mr Wetherby's voice confirmed it was. "Mrs Chalmers. Thank you for coming."

"Mr Wetherby." Aunt Martha's tone was aloof. "Please don't think I've come on your account. I've come to pay my last respects to my nephew and to give his children my condolences."

"Very well," Mr Wetherby said. "You'll find them in the front living room. Shall I tell Sarah-Ann you're here? She's with Elizabeth and Charlotte."

"Please don't let me trouble you, I'm sure I can find them on my own."

"Your bitterness doesn't suit you after so long," Mr Wetherby said.

"After everything you've done to this family, what do you expect?"

William-Wetherby grinned as he listened to the conversation.

"I've done more for this family than you'll ever know," Mr Wetherby said. "My conscience is clear."

Martha's voice almost disappeared to a whisper. "You never had a conscience."

A shiver ran down William-Wetherby's spine and he smiled at his aunt as she flounced into the front room. *Why can't I speak to Mr Wetherby like that?*

With the coffin lid sealed, William-Wetherby reluctantly stood beside Mr Wetherby as the two of them led the mourners from the house. He hesitated as Mr Wetherby ushered him, Eleanor and Lydia into the first carriage before he joined them with Aunt Sarah-Ann. William-Wetherby tasted bile in the back of his throat. This was going to be the longest ten minutes of his life.

The service was short with only two hymns and although the vicar had known William, he said nothing other than read a brief acknowledgement of William's life that had been written by Mr Wetherby. There was no mention of any of his achievements or how much he would be missed.

As they followed the coffin from the church, William-Wetherby was numb. He glanced down the path towards the open grave sited in the lower level of the graveyard. Was it less than five years ago that he had taken the same path to bury his mother? The vicar had still not let them put up a headstone for her. Well, he couldn't stop them putting one up for his father and so he would have one stone engraved with the two names and position it between them. They might be gone, but he wouldn't let them be forgotten.

. . .

The journey back to the house was no less painful than it had been on the way to church and the five of them travelled in silence until the carriage pulled up outside the house.

"The housekeeper will have laid some food out for us," Sarah-Ann said to everyone. "Nothing fancy, just cold meats, cheese, pies, cakes, that sort of thing. It should be enough."

"Thank you," William-Wetherby said. "You've been very kind."

"More than she needed to be," Mr Wetherby said as he climbed past them and left the carriage.

William-Wetherby glanced at Eleanor before he too stepped out of the carriage and helped the ladies down.

"Ever the gentleman," a voice said from behind him. William-Wetherby spun round to see Sid grinning at him. "I hope you've been on your best behaviour."

William-Wetherby allowed himself to smile. "Am I glad you're here. What a dreadful ordeal this has been."

"You need a drink inside you. If I know Mr Wetherby, he'll have a bottle of port open. I'd say you could do with some."

"He won't share it with me."

Sid winked. "You leave it to me, he'll never know."

With a couple of glasses of port inside him, William-Wetherby stood with Sid and picked at the food on the table. "We need to be going soon. I don't want to be the last one here with him."

Sid glanced around the room. "You've got time yet. Have you spoken to Mr Diver since you got your father's writing?"

"I haven't had a chance. I had hoped to talk to him today, but he's been too busy escorting Aunt Mary-Ann. Today's probably not the time. I'll visit him next week and work out what we can do."

"In that case, give me your glass," Sid said. "I reckon we have time for one more before we go."

William-Wetherby smiled and watched his friend disappear into the kitchen. What would he do without him? He turned to the table to help himself to a pie but froze when he heard Mr Wetherby's voice behind him. His fear turned to terror when he noticed people moving away and the latch of the door clicked behind him.

"Don't you have the nerve to look me in the eye?" Mr Wetherby said.

William-Wetherby turned slowly to find Mr

Wetherby standing no more than six feet away. William Junior stood behind him guarding the door.

"Why would I want to make eye contact with a cheat and murderer?" William-Wetherby's voice sounded more confident than he felt.

Mr Wetherby's eyes became slits. "Because I'm nothing of the sort."

"Would you rather I call you a bully or embezzler? There are plenty of other labels I could attach to you; the trouble is you've committed so many crimes it's hard to choose which to be most appalled at. You ought to be ashamed of yourself."

Mr Wetherby stepped forward, holding William-Wetherby's gaze. "If I ever hear you repeat those or any similar words about me, I will make sure you never see the light of day again. I would sue you, but with nothing to your name, it would be a waste of time."

William-Wetherby took a deep breath. "If you take me anywhere near a court, I'll make sure the whole of Birmingham knows the sort of man you are."

"You do not have one shred of evidence against me and if it comes down to your word against mine, there will only be one winner."

"Try it if you like, then you'll find out what evidence I have."

Mr Wetherby grabbed him by the lapels of his jacket, but William-Wetherby took hold of his hands and pushed him away. "Are you going to do the same to me as you did to Mr Flemming?"

Mr Wetherby's eyes darted towards William Junior before they fixed William-Wetherby to the spot.

William-Wetherby didn't flinch. "Does your son know that you killed him? What about Aunt Sarah-Ann. Did she ever find out?"

"There was nothing to find out because it's all lies."

William-Wetherby felt his confidence rise. "If it was lies, why did you give Mother and Father the money they wanted when they threatened to expose you? That doesn't sound like the actions of an innocent man."

Mr Wetherby's face paled. "Who told you that? Your mother was a liar."

"Is that why you stood by and watched her drown? Because she knew something about you that you wanted kept hidden?"

"I wasn't there."

"You mean you weren't on the bridge by the canal, just like you didn't hit Mr Flemming; or you'd never met Mr White when he came looking for a partnership; or you forgot that both you and

Aunt Sarah-Ann were married when you started a liaison with her. There seems to be a pattern emerging. If you take things in isolation people might believe you, but when you put all the pieces together they show a different picture."

William-Wetherby glanced towards the door as the handle moved, but a second later William Junior turned the key in the lock and strode to the side of his father. Mr Wetherby gestured with his head and William Junior lunged at William-Wetherby, yanking his arm behind his back.

"You watch your mouth," William Junior said. "You've no idea how much Father's done for you over the years."

William-Wetherby's eyes bulged as Mr Wetherby stepped forward and leaned towards him until their noses were almost touching.

"Prison would be too good for you. If I hear another word, it won't only be your mother who ends her days in the canal."

William-Wetherby struggled as William Junior tightened his grip. "If you want me to keep quiet ..." He paused for breath. "... you'll repay the money you stole from Father's business. It will never bring Mother and Father back, but knowing how much it would hurt you would at least give us some pleasure."

Mr Wetherby glanced again at his son and William-Wetherby screamed as he felt his shoulder twist.

"You won't get a penny from me until I'm dead and buried but even that comes with conditions. I don't want to ever see you again and I don't want you near anyone who knows me."

"Almost everyone in Birmingham and Handsworth knows you."

"Exactly and if any of them catch a whiff of your slander, I'll make you so sorry you'll wish you'd never been born."

"You can't do that." William-Wetherby's voice squeaked as he spoke.

"I can do what I like, and if I want to ruin you, I will."

Using his free arm, William-Wetherby elbowed William Junior in the abdomen and broke free from his hold.

"You're not going to get away with this. I have written proof of everything you've ever done and by God I'll use it unless I get something from you."

William Junior straightened up as Mr Wetherby hesitated. "You've got nothing."

"Father had a lot of time to reminisce while he was in hospital and fortunately for me, he wrote it all down. If you don't ever want his memories to see the light of day, it'll cost you one hundred pounds."

Mr Wetherby rushed at him and pinned him to the wall. "Show me the document."

William-Wetherby gasped. "I wasn't stupid enough to bring it with me. I want the money in my hand first."

"You're not getting anything until I've seen it."

"If you don't believe me, ask Sid." William-Wetherby wriggled free and unlocked the door. He was nearly flattened as Sid fell through it, two drinks in his hands. "Sid, tell Mr Wetherby what Father gave you before he died."

Sid stared at William-Wetherby before he glanced up at his uncle. "Some writing ... about you."

"And you've read it?" Mr Wetherby's face coloured.

Sid nodded. "I didn't know what it was. I'm sorry ... it said some nice things too."

Mr Wetherby turned back to William-Wetherby. "For one hundred pounds, not only do I want those papers, I want you out of Birmingham and Handsworth ... permanently."

William-Wetherby stared at the man who had caused him so much pain. Would it be such a hardship to leave? Once Florence moved to the secondary school, he would be the only one left in the area. He paced the room, moving his head to keep Mr Wetherby in his sight. "You'll leave us the money from Father's business as a legacy?"

Mr Wetherby nodded. "You have my word."

William-Wetherby's eyes narrowed as he studied his grandfather. "How can I trust you after everything you've done? I want it in writing."

"If you think I'm giving you a hand-scribbled note passing half my business to you, you're very much mistaken. I need to speak to my solicitor and review the terms of my will before I make any decisions about the size of the legacy."

"But you'll confirm your intentions once you've done that?"

"I'll do what's right for the future of this family."

William-Wetherby took a deep breath. "All right, but there's one other condition. Sid had nothing to do with me taking the books. You have to give him his old job back."

Mr Wetherby studied his nephew. "Is that true?"

Sid's head bounced up and down before he shook it with equal vigour. "Yes, I swear. It was nothing to do with me."

Mr Wetherby nodded. "I don't suppose you'll

be working in the Saracen's Head any more. All right. This is what I'll do. On the day you leave Birmingham, Sid gets his job back."

William-Wetherby shook his head. "I don't think you understand. I'm not leaving Birmingham until I have my money. Once I have it in my possession I'll deliver the writing to Sid. He'll hand you the papers in exchange for his old home and job."

"I'm not handing over ..."

"They're my terms ... and I expect confirmation of the legacy in due course." A smile reappeared on William-Wetherby's face. "If you don't like them I'll keep hold of the papers and do with them as I see fit."

CHAPTER EIGHTY-SEVEN

Birmingham, Warwickshire

William-Wetherby stood outside the Saracen's Head and glanced up at the red bricks that formed its structure. To the outside world, they gave no indication of the events they'd played host to over the last six months. He sighed and returned his attention to the front door as Lydia joined him.

"Are you sure you'll be all right on your own?" he asked her.

She nodded. "I'll be fine. The flat above the shop's big enough for me and I was never much company of an evening after I'd spent all day at work."

"You're a strong woman, Lydia. I hope one day you can put this behind you and find happiness."

"I could say the same to you. Have you decided where you're going?"

"Liverpool. I spoke to Eleanor after the funeral and she said Charles is due in next month. I'm going to try and find him. Once I've done that, I've no idea where I'll go."

"You won't go to sea?"

William-Wetherby smiled. "No. I'm used to sitting at a desk, not climbing masts. I'll find something. Liverpool's a busy port and I'm sure they'll have room for one more clerk."

Lydia nodded towards Summer Lane. "Here's Sid, late as usual."

"What do you mean, I'm bang on time!" Sid grinned. "William-Wetherby's still here, isn't he?"

"Only just, I've got a train to catch. You two will take care of each other, won't you?"

"Aren't you forgetting something?" Sid said.

William-Wetherby's brow creased.

"The papers, you fool. I need them to get my job back."

"And there was me thinking you'd forgotten." William-Wetherby winked at Lydia as he reached into his pocket.

"Did he give you your money?" Sid asked.

"He did. I called at Wetherby House to tell Margaret and Florence what's happening. Mr Wetherby wasn't in of course, and the girls were terribly upset I was leaving, but we'll keep in touch. Eleanor'll see to that."

"So that's it." Sid held his hand out to William-Wetherby. "Take care and write and tell me where you end up."

William-Wetherby shook his hand and turned to Lydia. At first he offered her his hand, but when she held his gaze he leaned forward and kissed her cheek. "How different things might have been. Take care, Lydia."

With a final glance at both of them he picked up his small bag and set off towards the train station. Only as he rounded the corner into Snow Hill did he reach into the breast pocket of his jacket. The papers that would act as his insurance policy were still safely there.

~

Thank you for reading *Only One Winner*.
I hope you enjoyed it.
If you did, I'd be delighted if you'd share your thoughts and leave a review on Amazon

~

I'd love to keep in touch with you!
I send out regular newsletters with details of new releases and information relating to The *Ambition & Destiny* Series.

By signing up for the newsletter you'll also get a FREE digital copy of *Condemned by Fate*, a short story prequel to the series.

To get your copy and keep in touch, visit:
www.vlmcbeath.com

THE FINAL INSTALLMENT...

Different World

After a bitter family breakdown William-Wetherby seeks a new life. But being rid of Mr Wetherby isn't as easy as it seems.

Setting off in search of his brother, William-Wetherby goes to Liverpool. Since they were last together his world has changed and he needs a friend.

When he rents a room, he refuses to tell his landlady or her daughter Bella, about his past. But their curiosity is piqued ... and Bella needs to know.

As their friendship develops, Bella hopes he'll settle down, but a final surprise from Mr Wetherby reignites old grievances ... and William-Wetherby is ready for a fight.

To order your copy visit:
mybook.to/DWAMZ

ALSO BY VL MCBEATH

The *Ambition & Destiny* Series

The full series:

Short Story Prequel: *Condemned by Fate*

Part 1: *Hooks & Eyes*

Part 2: *Less Than Equals*

Part 3: *When Time Runs Out*

Part 4: *Only One Winner*

Part 5: *Different World*

***Eliza Thomson Investigates*:**

A historical cozy murder mysteries series:

A Deadly Tonic (A Novella)

Murder in Moreton

Death of an Honourable Gent

Dying for a Garden Party

A Christmas Murder (A Novella)

For further details visit: **www.vlmcbeath.com**

AUTHORS NOTE AND ACKNOWLEDGEMENTS

With hindsight, I would say that the story contained in this book was the reason I wrote The *Ambition & Destiny* Series. Whereas the earlier books were works of fiction based on a factual skeleton, *Only One Winner* is predominantly fact embellished with fictional subplots.

The bulk of the story regarding the bankruptcy, going as far back as Harriet's untimely death and William's decision to partner with Mr Ball, was based on a four-inch column in a local Birmingham newspaper. As you can imagine, it was written in a dry, factual tone, and gave no hint of the human element involved.

Initially I underestimated the consequences of the bankruptcy, not appreciating quite how traumatic it must have been. There was one thing more than anything else that brought it home to me, however. Arthur's death certificate and the word *marasmus*.

Despite my medical background, it wasn't a word I'd come across before, but a quick online search told me it is an old-fashioned word for a form of severe malnutrition. It is most common in children, and a child with marasmus is severely underweight to the point where they may be little more than skin and bones (imagine the images we see of starving children in Africa). Even today many will die if there is inadequate treatment.

The timing and nature of Arthur's birth and death, and the fact that a previously unknown woman registered his death, brought home the severity of the situation. It also opened my eyes to some of the childcare arrangements women had to rely on if they needed to work. Whether Mrs Cousins was indeed a childminder, I don't know, but it certainly seemed to fit the story.

On top of all this, the tragedy was compounded by the knowledge that Mr Wetherby was so wealthy. The storyline about him becoming a major landowner and buying Bushwood Farm (not the real name) was also true and must have been an additional source of frustration for William. The burning question I have is why didn't Mr Wetherby help William out? I'll never know the answer to this, but something must have gone terribly wrong with their relationship for such a rift to develop.

I was originally going to end the series at this point, but there are a couple more twists to the story as William-Wetherby sets off for his new life in Liverpool. I decided they needed including and so Part 5, *Different World*, came into being.

Once again I have family and friends to thank for being supportive of my work and for reading and providing comments as I strive to provide the best story I can. As always, thanks go to my husband Stuart who continues his role as unofficial proofreader, and friends Rachel and Marie for their feedback and comments. I also need to thank Wendy and Susan for their professional editing services. They have helped me make these books what they are and I couldn't have done it without them. Finally, I would like to thank my mum, dad and brother-in-law Dave for their continuing support.

Finally, thank you for reading and I hope you'll join me for the last leg of the journey.

ABOUT THE AUTHOR

Val started researching her family tree back in 2008. At that time, she had no idea what she would find or where it would lead. By 2010, Val had discovered a story so compelling she was inspired to turn it into a novel. Initially writing for herself, the story grew beyond anything she ever imagined.

Prior to writing, Val trained as a scientist and has worked in the pharmaceutical industry for many years. In 2012, she set up her own consultancy business, and currently splits her time between business and writing.

Born and raised in Liverpool (UK), Val now lives in Cheshire with her husband, youngest daughter and a cat. In addition to family history, her interests include rock music and Liverpool Football Club.

For further information about The *Ambition & Destiny* Series, Victorian History or Val's experiences as she wrote the book, visit her website at: vlmcbeath.com

FOLLOW ME

at:

Website:
https://valmcbeath.com

Facebook:
https://www.facebook.com/VLMcBeath

Amazon:
https://www.amazon.com/VL-McBeath/e/B01N2TJWEX/

BookBub:
https://www.bookbub.com/authors/vl-mcbeath

Made in the USA
Middletown, DE
14 September 2020